Award-winning author **Amanda Bouchet** grew up in New England and studied French at undergraduate and graduate levels, first at Bowdoin College and then at Bowling Green State University. Amanda moved to Paris in 2001 and has been there ever since. She met her husband while studying abroad, and the family now includes two bilingual children who will soon be correcting her French. *A Promise of Fire* won several Romance Writers of America chapter contests, including the Orange Rose Contest and the Paranormal Category of the prestigious Golden Pen.

Visit Amanda Bouchet online:

www.amandabouchet.com
www.facebook.com/AmandaBouchetAuthor
www.twitter.com/AuthorABouchet

'Absolutely fabulous. Amanda Bouchet is now on my auto-buy list! I highly recommend her books to my readers and to anyone looking for a great blend of fantasy and romance' C. L. Wilson, *New York Times* bestselling author

'You will fall in love with these delicious characters' Darynda Jones, *New York Times* bestselling author

'Griffin and Cat are beautifully matched—together, her magic and his might make for a sparkling read' Sarah MacLean, *New York Times* bestselling author, for *The Washington Post*

'In a class of its own. Give this to your *Game of Thrones* fans. They will love the political plays, the dragons, and the adventure. Bouchet is a debut author to watch' *Booklist, starred review*

'Action-packed, emotionally charged and skillfully plotted' *Kirkus, starred review*

'I can say, without a doubt, that *A Promise of Fire* is going on my keeper shelf. I cannot remember the last time I wanted to both savor and devour a book' *Smart Bitches, Trashy Books*

'One of the best books I've read in year ... This is something quite new' *Night Owl Reviews*, 5 Stars, Top Pick!

'Utter catnip. This one's a winner!' *Fresh Fiction*, Fresh Pick!

By Amanda Bouchet

Kingmaker Chronicles

A Promise of Fire

Breath of Fire

BREATH
of
FIRE

AMANDA
BOUCHET

piatkus

PIATKUS

First published in the US in 2017 by Sourcebooks, Inc.
First published in Great Britain in 2017 by Piatkus

1 3 5 7 9 10 8 6 4 2

Copyright © 2017 by Amanda Bouchet

A CIP catalogue record for this book
is available from the British Library.

ISBN 978-0-349-41256-6

Printed and bound in Great Britain by
Clays Ltd, St Ives plc

Papers used by Piatkus are from well-managed forests
and other responsible sources.

MIX
Paper from
responsible sources
FSC® C104740

Piatkus
An imprint of
Little, Brown Book Group
Carmelite House
50 Victoria Embankment
London EC4Y 0DZ

An Hachette UK Company
www.hachette.co.uk

www.littlebrown.co.uk

For my husband, without whom no meals would have been cooked for the last two years.

CHAPTER 1

WAKING UP FROM A DEEP, HEALING SLEEP REMINDS ME OF rushing toward the surface of a lake, brightness beckoning from above and bubbles fizzing all around me.

Consciousness threads through me in a delicate weave. It's afternoon. The air smells of bright sun, hot stone, and endless days of summer drought. Insects chirp, their droning song a parched melody, the heat so thick I could cut it with a knife. I don't question the time of day, just *which* day, and I'm guessing it's not the same day I fell asleep. And almost died. Again.

Under the sheet, I brush my fingers over the tender skin on my stomach, finding the raised bump of a fresh scar there. Just one more mark to join the others, inside and out.

I look toward Griffin's side of the bed, not surprised to find it empty and the sheets cold. He has things to do, a realm to run.

I sigh, which is absurd. I never sighed until I met Griffin.

The indent of his head still creases the pillow, and I slide my hand into the hollow, thinking about how far we've come since he abducted me for my Kingmaker Magic and I fought him at every turn.

But Griffin got more than he bargained for with me, and I still can't bring myself to tell him the worst.

Harbinger of the end. Destroyer of realms.

I squeeze my eyes shut, craving the blissful avoidance of heavy sleep again. But I'm not tired anymore, and half-truths and glaring omissions fester in my belly, cold blocks of dread sitting right there under the heat of my new scar. Who I am. The dreadful prophecy. I wasn't even truthful about Daphne's lurking and threats, and hiding things from Griffin is exactly what landed me in this bed, injured and aching. Griffin's former lover knew what she was doing when she hid in the shadows and threw a knife into my gut. What she didn't know was that I would pull it out and throw it back.

The door opens, and I turn my head, my heart thudding at the sight of Griffin. Tall, broad, muscular but sleek, he stalks into the room like a predator, his gait balanced and sure, his glittering, gray eyes focused entirely on me. Inky hair, a hawkish nose, that stubborn jaw, and thick, black stubble make him look hard and intimidating. With his sword strapped on and his dark brows lowered, he's a warlord on the prowl.

I shiver. I couldn't want him more.

A lightning storm sizzles to life in my magic-charged veins. I look at Griffin, feel him near, and I can ignore all the terrifying things that make me want to crawl inside of myself and disappear. He stops next to the bed, and my blood simmers with heat and need. I wonder what he'll do to me. What I'll do to him.

I reach for him, but Griffin crosses his arms and stares down at me from above.

My hand hangs awkwardly in the air, and my heart hovers along with it. An awful tightness clamps around my throat, turning my voice to gravel. "I can still feel you inside me."

His stony expression doesn't change, but his iron gaze dips to my bare breasts. When his eyes flick back up, they're like frosted granite. "Have you enjoyed making a fool out of me?"

The bottom of my stomach drops out with sickening force. I pull the sheet up to cover myself, clutching it hard to keep my hands from trembling. It doesn't work. Adrenaline roars through me, making me shake.

"What do you mean?" My eyes are wide, my words reedy. Guilty. It's a good thing I'm not a gambler if this is my game face. But I've never had so much to lose.

Griffin reaches out and rips the sheet from my hands and right off the bed. He holds on to it. "I think you know. Or are there too many lies to choose from?"

I sit up, shame and anxiety splashing red-hot color all over my naked skin. At the realm dinner, Griffin vowed to uncover my secrets. I didn't think he'd do it this fast. "I haven't lied to you."

His lip curls in disgust. "And there's another one. How easily they slide from your tongue."

The usual steadiness in his eyes is gone. A storm boils in them instead. Anger and violence roll in on dark clouds. Something devastated and terrible in the way he watches me makes the tiny hairs on the back of my neck stand up.

Warily, I reach for the sheet, but his knuckles whiten on the linen. Instead of getting into a tug-of-war I'll lose, I twist, ignoring the sharp twinge in my middle, and then grab a pillow to shield myself. My unbound hair slides over my shoulders, covering me somewhat from Griffin's livid stare.

"I may have left out a few details," I admit, turning back around. *Really important details.* "But what I told you was the truth."

His eyes flare with a promise of punishment he's never directed at me before. "Is that so...*Lukia.*"

I grip the pillow hard, something breaking inside me. Griffin remembers everything I tell him. As his Magoi advisor—his expert on all things magic, royals, realms, creatures, and Gods—I once told him Beta Fisa's name is Lukia. The missing heir to the Fisan throne. The Lost Princess.

Her name isn't Lukia, and somehow Griffin knows that now. He knows it's me.

A dull numbness starts to cut me off from the nausea churning in my empty stomach, and I realize I've gone light-headed.

"You're good and just and fair," I say hoarsely. Looking at him is like seeing a mirage. Here one moment, and everything I could possibly want. Gone in the blink of an eye.

Harshly, he asks, "And what are you?"

The question opens a barely scabbed-over wound, and the answer hurts. I'm a murderer. Fratricide? All in a day's work. Twice. Serving up innocent people to an evil queen, knowing it was their doom? Been there. Done that. Abandoning Fisa, *Fisans*, to the whims of a vicious sociopath because I was too scared to stick around? Yeah, that's me, too.

Bile stings my throat. I swallow, and it tastes like the bitter end. "A liar, a killer, and a coward."

Intense stillness overtakes Griffin, giving the impression of calm. It makes me shudder on the inside. Before I even see him move, he whips the pillow from my grasp and flings it across the room. It knocks over a vase, and the painted jar shatters, leaving broken pieces on the floor.

I shatter, too, the person I was just becoming fragmenting into shards like the broken vase. That woman only had a tenuous, tentative grip on my heart and mind to begin with. Now, my new, stupidly hopeful expectations float around me in a vortex of shame.

"What are you doing?" I whisper, heat searing the backs of my eyes.

"You don't share what's on the inside," he grates out.

Griffin stares at me, but there's no desire in his eyes. Only raging disappointment, and I've never felt so exposed and vulnerable in my entire life. I don't just feel stripped. I feel stripped raw.

"So you'll look your fill at the outside?" I ask.

His nostrils flare. After a charged breath, he tosses the sheet back to me. "Cover yourself."

My throat closes up. Those two words hurt me more than I ever imagined they could. Like a ringing body slap, they sting from head to toe.

"Catalia Fisa." Griffin chews up and spits out the name I never told him in full. I'll never be "just Cat" again. I'm not even Cat of Fisa. I don't just come from my realm. I *am* my realm. "Body and soul, *Your Highness*. Inside and out. I want both. Or neither."

My heart goes into painful overdrive, twisting and hammering against my ribs. "Neither?"

His flat stare says, *You heard me.* He doesn't open his mouth.

"But Griffin—"

"Don't." He turns like a caged animal and prowls the length of the room. His voice the low rumble of a breaking storm, he growls, "Don't you dare lie to me again."

Pressing my lips together, I wrap the sheet around myself, knot it, and then stand. Physically, I'm at a huge disadvantage compared to Griffin, and lying down only makes it worse. Standing isn't much better. My legs are weak. My chest feels hollow. "How did you find out?"

"That you're Beta Fisa? The absent link in the Fisan line? The runaway princess?" He barks a harsh laugh I don't like at all and then cuts me a sidelong glance from under slashing brows. "That your bloodthirsty mother is one of the few people that can keep me from fixing this Gods damned place and making it better? That you're the oldest living spawn of the scourge of Thalyria!"

I flinch. That last part isn't a question, even rhetorical. It's a condemnation. A slur. Griffin whips another savage look in my direction, his strong hands balling into fists. My eyes track those big, powerful hands. I used to wonder if he would use them to hurt me. Maybe I should never have stopped.

I shrug, a hot-cold knot tightening in my chest. "That's one way of putting it."

Griffin's stare turns blistering. Then his bellow rattles the windows, and what's left of his usual iron self-control deserts him faster than I can blink. He picks up a chair and hurls it across the room. It cracks against the wall with a menacing thud, one leg snapping off completely. A bowl follows, a basin, and then a pitcher filled with water. I watch in dumbstruck anguish as things splinter, shatter. His face is terrifying to look at. Every inch of his body is coiled taut in anger. He picks up another heavy chair and pounds it into kindling. When there's nothing left to destroy, he overturns the table with a vile curse and then kicks the underside so hard the wood cracks. The solid piece of furniture screeches across the floor, and I wince.

He swings back to me, looming large and dark and breathing hard. "Flippancy." His eyes rake over me. "Why am I not surprised?"

Something wilts inside of me under the searing heat of Griffin's wrath, seeing in the towering man before me the warlord I know is capable of explosive violence. Despite all the times I've provoked him, he's never once looked at me this way before—like he could hurt me.

Usually I laugh, or at least pretend to, in the path of

danger or in the face of unmitigated rage. Not this time. I manage to lift my chin, though. "The truth is out. I don't know what you want me to say. You got me?"

"You got me?" he thunders, stalking forward. "*You got me!*"

I clamp my mouth shut and hold my ground. I'm indefensible. I'm a lot of things, but a hypocrite isn't one of them.

My silence always irks him. This time, it drives him into a full-blown fury. Griffin unsheathes his sword, not even a shred of his rational, reasonable, steady self remaining. When he reaches for me, my blood runs cold, but all he does is manually—and none too gently—remove me from my spot next to the bed. Once I'm out of the way, he hauls back with a two-handed grip and swings down with a furious shout. His blade sinks into the mattress, and I gasp. He heaves his sword back up and then brings it down again. And again. Each hit harder and more savage than the last. In a mighty cyclone of destruction, he slashes, spears, cracks, slices, and breaks *everything*. In mere minutes, he reduces what was once our huge bed into a heap of mangled feathers, fabrics, and splintered wood.

A hot ache crawls up the back of my throat. My eyes sting, and I tuck my lips between my teeth, biting down to keep my tears in check. My mouth still trembles. He demolished the bed, the one thing in this room with any meaning to *us*.

Cats don't cry. I will not *cry.*

Griffin turns to me, his chest heaving and his eyes feral. I almost can't hold his stare. "Helen, *your cousin*, had her baby."

I blink. My emotions are tumbling like a wild tide, deafening me with their rip and roar, and it takes a moment to latch on to the change in topic. "Here?"

He nods, the movement terse like his words. "She heard you were attacked, for some reason thought she'd be blamed for it, and panicked. It must have triggered labor. Her whole family ended up staying here while the rest of the realm dinner guests left."

"Her family?" Alarm hits me like a fist in the face. *I have to run!*

"Her husband's family."

Oh. Right. "Who is her husband?" I never took the time to find out. Helen and I barely talked at the realm dinner when we accidentally crossed paths. I was too focused on getting her away from Griffin before she gave away my secrets, or I did something unforgivable, like force her to back off with Compulsion Magic.

"Oreste," he answers.

"Oreste? Agatone and Urania's son?" I remember him being preoccupied and waiting for someone to join him at the realm dinner. Helen, I guess.

A scathing smile twists Griffin's lips. "Not jealous, I hope?"

I scoff. "That's not funny, you know." And he obviously knows a lot.

"Oreste and I had an interesting conversation while my mother, Egeria, and Jocasta were tending to Helen behind closed doors. Nerves made him prattle incessantly throughout the entire ordeal, and guess what I learned?" Griffin spears his sword into the upturned table, leaving both the blade and the heavy hilt vibrating from the force of his thrust.

"Helen wasn't his original choice of brides. He and his parents set their sights much higher, aiming for a Fisan princess and thinking their old lineage, strong magic, and deep coffers could buy them the best there was to have, even if she was little more than a child at the time. But

Alpha Fisa must have had other plans for her daughter. She wouldn't give her up. In fact, Andromeda was so enraged by their presumptuous offer that she sent their messenger back in the form of a bloody stump." Griffin levels accusing eyes on me. "Know anything about that?"

I don't answer. I can hardly breathe.

"Oreste, it turns out, is very satisfied now, after all these years of waiting for the ideal wife. Apparently, he's thrilled he didn't 'get saddled with that hellion Catalia. She was wild, hostile, and unpredictable, too much like her mother, and now she's Beta Fisa and bloody gone, leaving her family in a right mess.'" Griffin's eyes blaze, burning straight to the bottom of my polluted soul. "Sound like anyone you know, *Talia*?"

I nod, sickened, unable to force a single word past the awful lump in my throat.

"He described you perfectly. Not physically, but all the rest." Griffin scrapes his hand through his hair, gives the overlong strands a vicious pull, and then kicks the table again. The central board buckles this time, splintering. "I've been so bloody thick about this! About *you*." He laughs, and the broken sound makes me flinch. "It had to slap me in the face for me to see it. I just... I never thought you could be part of that...despicable family."

His words carve a hole in my chest. *Despicable. I am despicable.*

I start to shake again. A day ago, Griffin was vowing we'd live together, or die trying. Now, he can't even look at me.

Foreboding, accusing, he asks, "What's it like being the Lost Princess? The woman everyone is looking for?"

"They're not looking for me. They're hunting me."

"You do a fine job of hunting back."

I feel myself pale. Griffin saw me kill my own brother. He knows our connection now. Otis deserved it, and it was us or him, but I still did it. I'm *that* person. I'm everything Griffin despises.

"I didn't tell you for a reason. This is it." I hate the way my voice falters, but I can't help it. Every breath seems to stick in my throat.

"This is what, *Talia*?"

"Don't call me that."

"It's your name."

"My name is Cat. I'm Cat." I don't want to be Talia. I don't want to be Beta Fisa. I don't want to be the girl her brother tortured, or the girl who got her sister killed. I don't want to be Andromeda's daughter, and the person who saw that Sintan messenger get his arms chopped off and then his legs. His blood splattered me, and I stood there, watching.

Griffin's eyes are like stones. "I don't even know you."

He believes that. My Kingmaker Magic tells me as much. Any lie would feel like a bonfire inside of me, but this is the marble-cold truth. "I'm the same person I was yesterday. And the day before. Nothing's changed."

He lunges for me, grabbing my shoulders and ramming me back against the wall. His fingers dig into my skin, and the impact drives most of the air from my lungs. I struggle to breathe as the knotted sheet slips low.

Granite eyes bore into mine. "Nothing's changed?"

I force down a tight breath, shaking my head. "Not if you don't want it to."

"I think you have no idea what I want. Or who I am." He leans close, but there's nothing lover-like in the near embrace. It's sheer menace. "What's the one thing I value above all else?"

I swallow, my throat almost too dry for words.

Yesterday, I might have said me. Today… "Loyalty," I answer, my stomach cramping hard. And loyalty means telling the truth.

"So you do listen?" His grip tightens painfully. "Not just talk?"

I gasp. "Griffin! You're hurting me."

He glances at his hands and then releases some of the pressure on my upper arms. "*This* is the reason you didn't tell me who you really are? Getting caught?"

"Getting caught?" A surprised, slightly unhinged laugh flies from me. "I didn't tell you for much more selfish reasons than that."

He frowns. Heavy lines bracket his mouth, and starkness wars with the dangerous gleam in his eyes. "Then you were just waiting. Biding your time. You never wanted to be here. You always wanted to leave us."

By us, he means him. And he's wrong. "I didn't tell you because I couldn't bear for you to see me the way I see myself!"

He stares down at me, his expression still hard but also unnervingly blank. "What?"

"I'm not right for you."

"*What?*" he snarls, shaking me. The back of my head thuds against the wall, and he stops.

"I don't belong here! It was only a matter of time before you figured that out."

"What are you saying?" Griffin demands. "That you're too high and mighty? Too good for me?"

What? No! "I'm saying I'm not fit to lick the dust from your boots!"

Anger flashes in his eyes. For a horrifying heartbeat, I think he's going to hurt me. I'm strong, and I'm fast. Griffin is stronger and faster, and he's immune to harmful magic, so even the terrifying amount of Dragon's Breath I have stored up can't stop him. When we killed Sybaris, I absorbed everything I could of the She-Dragon's deadly Fire Magic. It's mine now. Despite that, the frightening truth is, if Griffin wants to punish me, he can.

His breathing turns erratic. The wild look in his eyes scares me as he pushes me flat against the wall, his hard body caging me there. His grip is biting.

"Ow! Griffin! Let go!"

His nostrils flare. Some of the fury clears from his expression, and he steps back, dropping me so fast I stagger. The sheet starts to unwind from around me, and I grab it, yanking it back into place. Griffin retreats, one foot behind the other. Slowly. Watching me.

"Let you go." He takes another step back and then looks around the room like he's never seen it before. He keeps backing away from me, backing toward the door. His big hands clench and unclench by slow degrees, pulling inward toward his sides. His eyes sweep the rage-battered room again before skating back to me.

"Griffin?"

His gaze hits mine with the force of a thunderclap. He looks...*appalled*. "I-I won't do this. I can't...be with you."

My lips part in shock. Tears flood my eyes. He can't mean that. What happened to our vows? What about his promise to never give up on me?

My heart plummets, the crash painful, wrenching, and fast. I know what happened—*me*.

Before I can think of anything to say, any way to keep him with me—now and forever—Griffin jerks his sword from the cracked wood of the table and then storms from the room, leaving.

Leaving me.

CHAPTER 2

I CAN'T BE WITH YOU.

I slide down the wall, a deep, painful ache spreading through me and settling fast and hard into every corner of my body, inhabiting my blood and bones. Tears distort my view of the ruined bed. I squeeze my eyes shut, blocking the sight. Trying to block the tears. But they keep coming, hot drops tracking down the sides of my face. A sob scrapes its way up my burning throat. Hot and clawing, it rises, making the whole room quake.

I slap my hands down, my eyes popping open as I brace myself against the rumbling floor. I swallow everything in a panic—my heartache, this magic, and my terrifying potential for destruction. The glacial shard in my necklace pulses with magic, and I force a powerful flood of cold through me, shocking my body, numbing my pain, and calming the storm. The room settles.

Shaken, guarded, I breathe shallowly, my lungs too tight and my pulse hammering like a drum. The Gods only know if I could have brought the whole castle down with the force of my emotions. Trying to stay numb, I gather the wrinkled sheet around me. It smells like Griffin, and me, and my heart shatters all over again, nearly toppling my fragile control.

Balling the material in my fists, I press down hard, feeling the sting of my own nails. It wasn't supposed to be this way. Griffin asked me to take a chance. On him. On trust. On love. I did, and look where it got me. That my misery is my own damn fault doesn't escape me. It just makes it worse.

Pressure clogs my throat. I think only a raw, primal scream might clear it, but I don't let it out. I'm too afraid of what I could unleash.

The numbness I forced upon myself wavers dangerously as I take in the devastation of the room, the destruction an accusation, the wreckage the ruins of what I almost had.

The stone around me groans with a low vibration, and I scrape my fingers over my scalp, dragging my loose hair back and burying my face in my knees. Rocking, I try to hold myself together.

Griffin and I exchanged a vow. But he's Hoi Polloi and not bound by promises like Magoi are. The magic in my blood makes verbal pledges permanent and unbreakable, physically binding *for the rest of my life* unless Griffin releases me.

I curl in on myself. He won't release me. He'll never release me. Griffin needs the Kingmaker, even if he doesn't want Cat.

A terrible weight settles in my chest. I'm magically tied to Griffin, but he's not tied to me. I'll be forced to be here with him, without being *with* him. I'll have to watch him move on.

Deep breath in. Long breath out.

Who cares if I cry?

The room rattles again, and I draw in a sharp breath. Apparently, unleashing more tears isn't an option. My options are horrifyingly limited, in fact.

Standing, I scrub my face with my hands to wipe it dry and then unwrap the sheet from around my body, leaving it on the floor. Moving mechanically, I dress and strap on my knives and sword before gathering my other belongings and dumping them into the center of the sheet, clearing Griffin's room of anything and everything that's mine.

There's not much, and I stare at the pile with gritty, burning eyes, not nearly as numb as I need to be. My inhale catches. I press the heels of my palms to my eyes, hard, forcing the insistent, rising heat back down. This was supposed to be my home. More fool me for actually believing that.

Trying to not shake the castle again with power I have no idea how to control, I tie the corners of the sheet together to create a makeshift sack. I heft it over my shoulder and don't look back. I never look back. But the frosted wall just barely caging my emotions is still fragile, and no matter how hard I try to shore it up, my necklace helping me, pain still hammers at my heart, unrelenting and bold.

A focused thought separates a familiar thread of magic from the rest of the power surging inside of me. I turn invisible, and by extension, everything attached to me turns invisible, too—clothing, weapons, my improvised bag. My worn boots are silent as I move through the shadowed back corridors of Castle Sinta, avoiding any occupied rooms. No one would see me—but I don't want to see them.

I walk across the Athena courtyard, trying not to feel or look at or think about anything. I can't cry again. I can't afford that. No one here can. The magic inside me is still crashing like a storm. My grief right now is so deep, so raw, so raging and powerful that I have no idea what would happen if I let it out. Nothing good. I think I shortened my name to Cat for a reason—as in *Cataclysm*.

My patently unwise vow to stay with Griffin makes it physically impossible for me to walk away from him, leaving me only one place to go. After what feels like a long march through hostile territory, I swing open a nondescript door and stare at the small, dim room in the barracks I used to occupy. A narrow bed. One small chest. A rough-hewn table that's seen better days. A chair.

Home, I guess.

Compared to the opulence of the castle, it's as unappealing as it could possibly be.

I light the lone lamp in the windowless room and then push the door closed behind me, letting go of my invisibility. Aching and brittle, I unpack my sheet and put my clothes and weapons away, the methodic chore helping to calm the violence of the sorrow inside me. That done, I know of only one escape—apart from death—from this kind of constant, overwhelming pain.

I undress and then slip on one of my new nightgowns, squeezing my eyes shut again as thoughts of how I'd wanted to wear the flimsy garment for Griffin flood my mind. His storm-gray eyes would have burned with passion. Strong, battle-roughened hands would have reached for me. His breath would have quickened, and I would have melted at his first touch.

My heart jolts painfully, and I open my eyes back up to stare at my cold, small bed. None of that happened. We only had a few nights together in that way before...*this*.

Turning to the table, I blow out the lamp, my breath shuddering dangerously, and then crawl under the blanket in the utter darkness. Beneath me, I'm not surprised to find a bare mattress with no sheet covering the coarse surface. I vacated this room. No one thought I was coming back—least of all me.

Fighting tears, I lie there for hours, trying to find sleep and doing my best to think about nothing. Because nothing is all I have.

I wake up to the door crashing open and the sudden blaze of a torch brightening my barren room. Sitting up, I push hair out of my face and squint against the light. Has someone come to arrest me? Am I to have the dungeon instead of the barracks? That wouldn't surprise me. I *am* the enemy.

Flames whoosh as someone whips the torch from side to side, illuminating first the room and then...*Griffin?* He comes into focus in front of other large, dark figures. As my vision adjusts to the light, I gasp.

What happened to him? His eyes are wild, his face haggard. His features aren't just drawn, they're *ravaged*.

Passing off the torch, Griffin leaps forward and yanks me into his arms. Our bodies connect, and a spasm wrenches my chest. It feels so perfect, so right, when he holds me like this. Surrounding me, squeezing me until I almost can't breathe, he rains kisses all across my face. His thick stubble scratches—my nose, my cheek—and I want more of the light scraping. The subtle sting proves he's here. That this is real.

Griffin's low, raw voice rips through me like a dull knife. "Thank the Gods and all of Olympus." He shudders. "I thought you'd left me."

My pulse roars, deafening. "I don't understand. *You* left *me*."

"No. *No*." His heavy breath pounds against my neck. "*Never* leave you."

"But...did I dream that entire fight?" Is that even possible? *Good Gods! Maybe I am insane!*

Griffin just shakes his head, his warmth and his sunshine-and-citrus scent enfolding me in what feels like the best dream I've ever had. I glance over his shoulder at the other men. Kato and Flynn block the doorway. Carver hovers behind them, all of them scruffy-jawed and tired-eyed. They look like they haven't slept in a while. Flynn nods to me and then slips the torch into the sconce on the otherwise bare wall. They back out, shutting the door behind them.

I curl my fingers into Griffin's tunic. My hands are trapped between us against his solid chest, and his heart-beat thuds fast and hard against my knuckles. I ache to hold him. I'm terrified to let myself. I'm not sure I could survive losing him twice.

"I couldn't find you," he rasps, his face still buried against my neck. "All yesterday. All night. All day again. It's past midnight."

"I slept *that* long?" Healing requires extended periods of sleep, and my stomach was still sore the last time I woke up...*a day and a half ago?* It doesn't hurt anymore. But I doubt that's why I slept so deeply. I've always been good at denial. I didn't know I'm such an expert that I can crawl into an abandoned room and put myself into a coma.

"All your things were gone, like you never even existed. I searched the castle. The woods. The city. The circus."

Anxiety spikes inside of me. "Oh Gods. Selena." My sort of adoptive mother threatened Griffin with a variety of fates worse than death if he ever let anything happen to me. "What did she do?"

He grunts, respect mixed with a certain amount of wari-ness in the sound. "She just about eviscerated me with her eyes alone. She looked at me, and I swear to the Gods, I felt my gut heating up and twisting around."

I have no trouble believing that, which makes Selena one of the scariest people I know. The owner of the trav-eling circus where I took refuge for nearly eight years, Selena is overprotective of me almost to a fault and not particularly keen on Griffin—or my choosing to stay with him. In all fairness, he did snatch me out from under her nose, an abduction I wasn't exactly on board with for a long time, either—to say the least.

Without letting go of me, Griffin sits on the edge of the bed and pulls me onto his lap. "I thought..." He clears his throat, his grip on me tightening. "I thought you'd turned invisible and left."

And *I* thought he'd never hold me like this again, crushing me against his body like it's physically impossible to let me go. For the first time in my life, I'm ecstatic to be wrong. "I can't do that."

Pulling back slightly, Griffin searches my face. "You can't?"

I cup his jaw, needing to feel his raw masculinity under my hand, and he subtly, maybe unconsciously, leans into my touch.

"I could go for a walk and then come back. Go training. Shopping. Visiting. But if my intention is really to leave you, I probably can't get farther than the castle gate. I vowed to live with you, or die trying. I can't leave you unless..." I audibly swallow, sudden nerves making my stomach flip over. "Unless you release me from my vow."

"*Never* release you." Griffin's stark, harsh, wonderful truth sears me with its intensity. I chose him. I chose us. I don't want to be let go.

"And my vow to you remains, Cat. Just as binding as yours." His words ring with truth, and *forever* sings through me on a ripple of magic—a promise he'll never break.

A hard drumming starts in my chest. It builds, battering the wall I built around my heart until the fragile barrier explodes outward in a shattering of fire through ice.

I spear my hands into Griffin's hair, using his inky locks to hold him tight. "But you said you were done with me."

"How could you think that?" He gives me a shake that's both gentle and frantic. "I love you like a man insane."

My breath hitches. Tears prick my eyes, and I blink them back. "You said you couldn't be with me."

Griffin looks confused. Then angry. "I couldn't be with you *right then*. You were spouting nonsense that was making me crazy—things about us not belonging together. I was fuming and…not in control of myself. I hurt you, so I left. I walked out the door so I wouldn't hurt you again, but that never meant I wasn't coming back."

I gape at him, the most horrible knot unraveling in my chest. "Gods, I'm an *idiot!*"

Shaking his head, Griffin smoothes my hair back. "I'm sorry for what you thought. For what I made you think."

"No. I'm sorry. If I didn't come from a completely deranged and homicidal family, I might actually understand relationships." Maybe I wouldn't have taken the worst possible meaning from Griffin's words. Maybe I'd have given him the benefit of the doubt, and just maybe, I'd have put more faith in us.

Griffin gently holds my head in his hands. His touch is soothing, but his voice suddenly cuts like a knife. "You lied to me. You didn't trust me. I *hate* that."

"I do trust you!"

"Then why? Why hide from me?"

I open my mouth to try to explain, but nothing comes out. Any words that are even remotely sufficient stick in my throat.

"I need an answer, Cat. Don't think you have a choice." Griffin's hands drop away from me, leaving me cold. Flat eyes. Flat voice. When he looks like that, he gets what he wants.

I swallow hard. "I didn't want you to leave me."

If possible, Griffin turns even more stone-faced. "Like I said—no trust."

"That's not true! But look at you. At your family. Then look at me and mine. I'm ashamed. And I should be!"

"You're not them."

I laugh. It's bitter and shaky. "I'm not them. But I'm something." Something I don't want to think about. Denial is an old friend.

He takes a deep breath through his nose, his mouth flattening. His eyes close and then open again, snaring mine. "I'll let this go, Cat. For us. I'll let all these weeks of deception go, and we can move on from here. Just promise me one thing—that there's nothing else. Vow there are no more secrets between us."

My gut clenches, and I look down.

Griffin instantly reacts. "What?" he demands. "What is it?"

Toxic words well up, a poison prophecy. "I'm not ready to talk about it."

His eyes turn thunderous, and that tight muscle bounces in his jaw.

"It isn't about trusting you," I try to explain. "I love you. I trust you. It's about me. About…trusting myself."

He's silent for so long that fear takes root in my belly. Then, so low I almost don't hear him, "Fine."

"Fine?"

He nods brusquely, curt and small, almost like it's against his will. "For now. But at least answer this. Why did you leave the castle? How could you leave?"

I frown. "I thought you didn't want me."

Griffin growls low in his throat. He leans forward and presses his mouth to mine, gently at first, and then much harder. "*Always* want you."

His words are a promise, his kiss a claim. I kiss him

back, hardly taking the time to breathe, and with the first searing slide of his tongue over mine, Griffin conquers my body, my soul, and my bruised heart with no effort at all. They were his all along.

I shift in his arms and straddle him, wedging my knees on either side of his hips. His hands rake down my back to cup my bottom, squeezing in that rough way he knows I love—and he loves just as much. He gathers my nightdress around my hips, bunching it in his fists. When his hands move back up, they take the gauzy material with them.

Griffin breaks the kiss to draw the garment up over my head. Frowning, he tosses it aside. "What's this?"

"A nightgown."

"I know it's a nightgown. Where did you get it?"

"Kaia gave it to me from her collection."

"Kaia?" It's always unsettling the way his voice can turn chilling without rising or falling a notch. "My fifteen-year-old sister, Kaia?"

"Yes, that Kaia. And Jocasta and I are the only ones who have ever seen her dressed like this, so you can stop plotting torture and imprisonment."

"But…Kaia?"

"She's fifteen, Griffin. Some girls are married by then. I'm surprised she's not sneaking around and kissing the pages."

His eyes darken dangerously. "Did you kiss the pages?"

"At fifteen?" I nod. "And fourteen. And thirteen…"

"If you say twelve," he growls, "I won't be accountable for my actions."

I tilt my chin up and look at him through narrowed eyes. I'm learning to appreciate this man's irrational jealousy. "Twelve…"

Snarling a curse, Griffin flips me underneath him. I land on my back, only getting in half a bounce before his weight presses me into the mattress, the hard, powerful lines of his body a delicious counterpoint to all my softer places. Braced above me, he closes his eyes and scrubs one hand down his face. Calluses scrape over stubble. "We'll talk about this—and Kaia—later. Right now, we're talking about us."

I wiggle my hips. "We were talking?"

Heat flares in his eyes. His body answers me—his arousal growing thicker and harder—but his mind is still occupied by less pleasant things. "No, but we should have been." He lifts off me enough to concentrate. "You thought I didn't want you? How could you ever think that?"

The pain of our fight comes rushing back, and I stiffen. "It wasn't an entirely absurd conclusion, you know. Your 'I can't be with you' was a big hint."

Griffin's large hands bracket my head. His gaze troubled, he sweeps his thumbs over my cheekbones in a rough-skinned caress. "You misunderstood. And I wasn't clear, which I'm sorry about. But that was never what I meant."

"But I'm the enemy."

Griffin's eyebrows slam down. "Not *my* enemy."

"A big obstacle, then! You want to take over the realms. You want to turn them into one kingdom and be their king." It isn't easy, but I slip out from under him and sit up, facing him. "That's not what I want. I've never wanted that, and while I live, it's technically not even possible. As a direct descendant of the Origin—Thalyria's *original* king—I will always outrank you. I don't want to rule a kingdom. I don't want to be Alpha. For the Gods' sakes, I don't even want to be Beta. Or the consort. Or whatever!"

Griffin's brow furrows. "I don't care who's officially in charge as long as we do what needs to be done. Together."

I shake my head. "I think you do care. In the end, you will."

"And I think you want to stick your head in the sand and only come out when you have to save someone you love. What about everyone else? The realms are going to the Underworld with these rotten Alphas. They have been for generations. People are suffering. They need help."

"And that's the difference between us!" What makes Griffin good and a leader, and what makes me...*me*. "I don't want to risk war, and death, and destruction, and the total annihilation of every single person I care about for the sake of people I don't even know!"

"That's not true. That's not you, Cat."

"It *is* me. You called me self-sacrificing. You're right. I am—for the people I love. It'll get me killed. I know that. I accept that. What I don't accept is dying for anyone else."

He slices his head to the side. *Stubborn man.* "The Power Bid is here. War will come, whether we court it or not. Innocent people will suffer, and you won't be able to stand it."

I look at him in shock. *Is that really what he thinks? How he sees me?*

My heart starts beating too fast. In my mind, I see armies clashing. I see me in the center of a raging storm and bodies strewn around me. Suddenly, every last one of those bodies is my mother's. Sable hair. Green eyes. A crown of Fisan pearls. *My* crown.

"No, Griffin, I..." I squeeze my eyes shut. She's still there. She sits up and looks at me like I betrayed her.

I open my eyes again. This view is much better. "Andromeda is too powerful. She'll win. She always wins, and when you're dead, and it's all my fault, I will *never* recover." My voice breaks, and I inhale sharply, a fragile, reedy sound catching in the back of my throat.

Griffin understands this fear. It's one I've shared with

him—and yet he persists in not seeing our relationship for the death sentence it is. He gathers me close, smoothing his warm hand up my naked back. His fingers stop on my nape, locking me in place. "I'm hard to kill. And you won't fail. You never fail."

Pressing my lips together, I lean my forehead against his chest. Seeking comfort? Hiding, really. I already failed. I was fifteen. I stole back into my home, armed not only with a knife and my new invisibility and ability to steal magic—gifts from Poseidon's Lake Oracle—but also with a soul-burning hatred after my sister's brutal death. Mother was to blame for that, and for so many other things. It would have been so easy to take my revenge. She would never have seen me coming.

But when I found the cruel and mighty Alpha Fisa chewing her lip to blood, her eyes frenzied because she couldn't find *me*… I couldn't do it. I was weak and stupid because I thought, just maybe, Mother was acting like a normal person for once.

She didn't love me, or miss me. Nothing as pure as that. But I was something to her, something more than just the Kingmaker. I didn't know what. And I still don't. But whatever it was stopped me, and then I hurt her in the only way I could. I ran.

Griffin takes my face in his hands, tilting it up, his grip light but firm enough to keep me from turning away. "Stop looking for things that could go wrong instead of finding things that will go right."

I roll my eyes, huffing a little. "Great. An eternal optimist."

Griffin squashes my cheeks until my lips pucker. "Am I going to have to kiss you into submission?"

I snort. Sort of. It's hard with my face all mashed up. "Submission? When has that ever happened?"

He gives me the roguish half-smile that always makes my heart skip a beat. He winks, and I could swear I'm looking at a Fisan pirate. Something in my chest flutters.

"It was worth a try." Sobering, Griffin lets go of my cheeks. "I know it's hard for you to trust, and always has been, but you should have had more confidence in me. In *us*. You should never have left."

Deep hurt underlies his carefully even tone. Griffin's neutral voice always does strange and painful things to my heart.

"I walked across the courtyard to the barracks." Apparently, the last place anyone thought to look for me.

Griffin levels his hard stare on me. "You shouldn't have left."

"You destroyed our bed and looked like you wanted to rip me limb from limb."

He keeps staring. "You. Shouldn't. Have. Left."

I toss up my hands. "I thought you wanted me to go! I thought I had to. The castle is your home. Your right. Your legacy. I don't belong there."

"Don't *belong* there?" Careful neutrality deserts him. His eyes flash gray fire.

Suddenly nervous, I shake my head. I think I just woke the slumbering Cyclops inside every man—his inner, primal monster.

"Well, if you'd agree to marry me, you bloody well would!"

Uh-oh. That's the one. The colossal, one-eyed, battering ram of a warrior creature. Awake. And livid. "That hardly matters, considering everything else that's going on."

"Hardly matters?" Griffin demands. "It'll matter when we have our first bastard!"

I wrinkle my nose. He's really hung up on that.

"It'll matter when we have realm functions, and I can't claim you in any meaningful way."

I shrug. I don't give a Cyclops's eye about my place in realm functions.

"It'll matter when my sisters tell me they're doing the same thing with some man because they worship you and hang on your every word."

My lips thin. Responsibility rears its annoying head.

"It'll matter if someone steals you, and I can't tell my army we're going to war for my *wife*!"

"No one's going to steal me."

"*I* stole you!"

"Stop roaring at me! I'm not deaf!"

Calm descends like a colossus falling on my head. Griffin goes utterly still, and yet he *vibrates*.

Trepidation skips along my spine. Our eyes meet, and his are like thunder before a storm.

I catch my lower lip between my teeth. "What are you thinking?"

His ominous answer comes seconds after he grabs my wrists and hauls me to my feet. "I'm thinking about teaching you a lesson, *Your Foolishness*."

CHAPTER 3

GRIFFIN SPINS ME AND PUSHES ME UP AGAINST THE WALL. He holds my wrists above my head in one hand, pulling so that my arms are almost fully extended. His other hand palms my naked bottom, its scorching heat a shocking contrast to the cool stone against my front. My nipples pebble against the smooth surface. One of Griffin's splayed fingers dips into my cleft, sending a lightning bolt of desire through me. I might like this lesson.

His hand leaves my body, though. Cool air rushes in to chill my backside, and goose bumps shiver across my lower back. I wait, a thrilling riot of sensations and emotions heightening my anticipation. What will he do to me? If it's anything like usual, I'm all in.

Without warning, Griffin smacks my ass so hard I yelp and shoot forward against the wall. The sting is hot and sharp, inside and out.

"Ow!" I glare at him over my shoulder. "Did you just spank me?"

"Yes." He glares back. *Smack!* "Twice."

I gasp. "Griffin!"

"The second time was for kissing pages when you were twelve," he growls. "The first time was for driving me insane."

I kick back, but my foot barely connects. He's too damn fast. "You'll pay for this," I grind out, stomping on his toes. *Twice.* My bare foot doesn't appear to faze him through the thick leather of his boot. "I swear you'll pay."

"If I pay, I'd better be buying a bride."

"Argh! You're impossible!"

Griffin leans in to me, asking gruffly against my cheek, "Where do you belong?"

"What?" My backside smarts. I liked it better when spanking was a metaphor.

Excitement still surges through me, along with a surprising rush of eagerness when Griffin palms my bottom again. His long fingers delve further toward my core, cupping me completely. I stop struggling, craving his next touch more than I crave air. He gently rocks his fingers through my folds, and my forehead drops against the wall. I moan in total surrender, growing wet for him after only a few strokes.

Griffin's broad front presses against my back. He pushes my hair aside with his face, and then his lips brush the sensitive spot below my ear. I feel his teeth, his tongue, and then his amazing mouth trails lightly over my nape, sending hot little shivers down my spine and arms. He nuzzles and kisses, his breath increasingly ragged against my neck. My blood turns molten. Reckless and ready for anything, I press backward into his arousal and grind my hips.

His free hand slides around my hip to my lower abdomen, holding me tightly as he presses me harder against him. "Where do you belong?" Griffin asks again, his question a gravelly rumble against my neck.

A smile curves my lips. I understand the rules now. I'm ready to play.

I pull on my wrists as hard as I can. Griffin tightens his grip, sending a thrill of danger and excitement through me. Rough and low, he says my name as he lifts his hand from my stomach. Between our bodies, I feel him work his belt free. A moment later, his pants drop, and his metal buckle hits the floor. One-handed, he rips his tunic over his head, leaving it dangling from the arm still holding me against the wall.

His bare torso touches my bare back, the contact scalding. Need burns through me. I lean back into Griffin's powerful body and rub myself against him. Crisp hair tickles the backs of my thighs. I want to touch him, but Griffin is in complete control. I can only feel, and wait, and crave, and the newness and unpredictability of his rough play drive my desire to Olympian heights.

Griffin's free hand comes around me again, grazing up my front until his knuckles skim the undersides of my breasts. Lightning sizzles under my skin, streaking straight to where I long for him to fill me. He touches my breasts—cupping, circling, teasing, squeezing—and my head falls back against his chest. I make breathless sounds, panting. He brushes the callused pad of his thumb over one sensitive peak. Back and forth. He does the same to the other, and I press my legs together, my tightening nerves restless for friction. Griffin tugs on my nipple. Need pulses at the apex of my thighs, and my legs start to quiver.

"You're going to torture me, aren't you?" I ask.

His voice is an erotic promise in my ear. "You have no idea."

Griffin's warm breath whispers over my neck. My wrists are a little sore and my arms are starting to ache, but the dull pain only accentuates the pleasure and exhilaration storming the rest of my body. Heady sensations spiral through me. Desire flares hotter with Griffin's every touch. I shudder when he rubs his rough palm in a slow circle just below my navel. He's barely even touched me where I really want him, but the mounting tension between my legs already has me tumbling toward release.

"Griffin."

"Cat?"

"Touch me."

"I am touching you."

Pleasure and frustration dance around each other inside of me, intense, unlikely partners. I flex my fingers. They're going numb. "Touch me lower. Touch me where I need you."

His hand slides down. I can feel the heat of his fingers, poised to bring me a shattering orgasm. My sex throbs, each needy beat bringing me closer. I groan, and the husky sound is loud in the room that's quiet except for our harsh breathing and the popping of the torch.

Griffin's teeth graze my neck. He nips my shoulder and then growls against my skin, "Where do you belong?"

I squirm when his tongue trails over the spot he just bit. I know what he wants to hear. I don't give it to him yet. I'm just insane enough to want to prolong this sensual torture. "I belong…here?"

Griffin lifts his face from my neck, his stubble a delicious scrape against my nape. A deep rumble is my only warning before he slaps my ass again like he means it.

I gasp, shooting forward. Something clenches deep down, flooding me with wet heat. Griffin stretches me up to my full height, extending my arms above my head. Bracing his forearm against the wall to help carry my weight, he pulls, and my heels leave the floor.

I make a strangled sound. My arms ache, my ass smarts, and *by Gods* I'm about to explode!

"Wrong answer." He cages me, and his thick shaft presses against my backside. He circles my thigh with his hand and then lifts my leg, hooking his free arm under my knee and leaving me spread open and pivoting on the ball of one foot. I don't worry about falling. I'm too focused on the hot, blunt tip of Griffin's erection as he lifts me even higher and slides it between my legs. He slowly thrusts, guiding his iron hardness through my slick folds and then right over my most sensitive spot. I forget to breathe.

"Where do you belong?" He thrusts again, the slow friction driving me wild.

"Oh my Gods…" I moan when he spreads me wider.

"Wrong answer."

"So spank me," I pant. And I mean that in whatever sense.

His chuckle is dark and thick, like a hot summer night. It makes me want to lick salt and sunshine from his tanned skin and worship his sculpted body with my mouth.

Griffin positions himself at my entrance. I'm so wet and ready that the head of his shaft slips right in, and we both shudder from the shallow joining.

The deep groan expanding in Griffin's chest resonates against my back. A bead of sweat drips onto my shoulder. He's as tortured as I am.

I turn my head. Heated silver eyes meet mine. They reach inside me and yank out my soul. If it weren't already Griffin's, he'd have captured it all over again.

"I love you." The words spring straight from my heart. I couldn't stop them if I wanted to.

The look he gives me scorches me to my toes. "Where do you belong?"

I can't wait any longer. I need to feel him fully inside me. I need to know we're one. "With you," I gasp out, starving for the deep thrust I know is coming. "I belong with you."

Griffin drives upward and buries himself to the hilt inside of me with a sound of pure masculine satisfaction. A bright light flashes from me, illuminating the shadowed corners of the room. A long rumble of thunder vibrates in the air. I throw my head back, my mouth open and gasping for breath. He pumps his hips hard, just once, and my inner walls contract. My body gathers sensation, holding it tightly for that potent, suspended moment before racing toward bliss.

Griffin thrusts again, and I shout his name, beginning to pulse around him. He presses deeper, and my toes leave the floor. He holds me up, pinning me at my very center as release pounds through me in powerful waves.

His breath ragged on my temple, Griffin unhooks his arm from under my leg. My feet touch the floor, and my legs nearly buckle. He lets go of my wrists in order to band both arms around my waist. My arms fall like lead weights, and I groan, blood flowing back into them in a stabbing rush. I slump against him, weak and limp, but he doesn't give me time to recover. He pivots and drops me onto the bed on my hands and knees. My arms collapse, and my upper body lands on the mattress, leaving my ass in the air.

"There's a handprint on your arse."

I turn my face so I can breathe. "Are you sorry?"

He grunts. "Not one bit."

I grin beneath a curtain of hair. I'm not either. Not one bit.

Leaning over me, Griffin sweeps the tangle of curls out of my face. He gets ready to enter me from behind, something he's never done before besides those few mind-blowing thrusts against the wall. I twist my head so I can watch him. He looks like a God—massive, handsome, stern, his countenance dark. Torchlight flickers over his face, illuminating some parts and obscuring others. His eyes are in shadow, but they still smolder as he stares down at me.

I start to lift up on my aching arms, but Griffin's hand

lands on the small of my back. He slides it along my spine, pressing me back down. He gives a gentle push when he reaches my nape and then moves his hand to my hip, holding me steady as his other hand guides his arousal back to where we both want it. He goes slowly until he's fully seated and then begins to thrust.

He's not gentle, and he's never been so deep inside me, like he's pounding my heart with every powerful stroke. I whimper, weak and hot, slick and needy. Vulnerable. Pleasure builds—coiling tension, tingling warmth. The sensations aren't just physical. Griffin's behavior since he pinned me against the wall—his insistent question, his barely checked aggression, this dominant position—they all tell me a lot about how he felt when he thought I was gone. I may be the one on my knees right now, but I bring this earthquake of a man to his knees as well. He's big, and strong, and commanding, but he needs me. I'm vital. He's becoming the air I breathe, but maybe that's all right, because I'm the air he breathes, too.

I grip the rumpled blanket and press back with a throaty sound I didn't even know I could make. Griffin's hands tighten on my hips, stopping my rocking motion. He's in complete control, and it makes me wild and greedy and frenzied for more.

"I love you." He drives into me. "I love you more than anything in this Godsforsaken world."

My heart does a hard flip. I believe him. I feel his truth as deep inside of me as he is, hammering me just as fiercely. Griffin would choose me over anything, which is why I can never get in his way of trying to make a better world—of bringing Thalyria back to what it once was.

And if I can't stop him, I'll have to help him.

"I will never leave you," I vow, feeling the magic in my

words bind me. "Only death can tear us apart, and even then, I will wait for you at the edges of the Underworld until you come to me again."

"Cat." His voice breaks. His thrusts falter.

Griffin pulls out of me, flips me over, and then covers me from head to toe, burying his face in my neck and his shaft between my legs. He makes love to me with fevered intensity, no longer dominant or in control. He shudders and rocks, and we chase each other blindly up a wave that builds, crests, and then finally crashes when I topple over the edge with a hoarse cry.

Griffin's eyes capture mine. He holds my face in his hands. "You. Belong. With. *Me*." He gives a final, hard thrust before his seed explodes inside of me, his claim still ringing off the granite walls. A magical tempest erupts from my body. Lightning and words collide in the air, the storm searing his declaration into my heart and mind. I'll never doubt us again.

The room rocks. A crack snakes up the wall near my head, splitting the stone. Plaster dust shivers down from the ceiling. Reining in whatever is happening is beyond me. My emotions are raw and blazing, fanned into combustion by the beat of wings in my chest.

Griffin throws his head back. The sweat-beaded muscles in his corded neck bulge as his whole body goes rigid. It's the most glorious sight I've ever seen. I drink it in. Drink him in—his scent and his seed, his love and his life force. My arms stop aching, and strength infuses every part of me, leaving me bursting with energy. And ready to start again.

Griffin tenses one last time and then slowly relaxes. He settles so he's not crushing me, using his forearms to carry the bulk of his weight. His hands still hold my head.

Brushing hair out of my face, he looks at me with sated, adoring eyes. He kisses me. "*Kardia mou.*"

I wrap my arms around his neck. I'll bet my eyes are pretty sated and adoring, too. "You're my heart as well."

CHAPTER 4

WE SLEEP. WELL, GRIFFIN DOES, AND I WATCH HIM. HE'S clearly exhausted, with dark shadows under his eyes that not even the thick sweep of his inky lashes can hide. Even at rest, there's an unusual tenseness around his mouth. I don't close my eyes. I got plenty of sleep while I was finishing healing, escaping reality, and holed up in what turned out to be the one place no one thought to look for me.

I'm not exactly comfortable. The bed is small for Griffin. For both of us, it's ridiculously tight, but there are worse things than being trapped against and tangled up with the man I love. The blanket is scratchy. The bare mattress isn't much better. And it's hot, but I'm learning to deal with that. Even like it. Sort of. It's Griffin, so I can take it. Besides, whenever I try to wiggle away from him, even just a little bit, his arm tightens around me. Even in sleep, he's not letting me go.

Finally, the torch gutters and dies. Oddly, it's the sudden darkness that wakes him up. With a husky groan, Griffin nuzzles my neck as he sweeps his hand up my back. My leg slips between his, and I cling to his shoulders, loving the feel of all that solid muscle under warm, smooth skin. His already rock-hard arousal presses against my lower belly. When I press back, he makes a low, masculine sound that sets me on fire.

He curves his hand around my hip, holding me firmly against him. "Remind me to do some hiring. I need to employ a legion of poets."

I kiss the underside of his scruffy jaw, rubbing against him. I can't help myself. He feels so good. "A legion? That's a lot of poets."

"It'll be worth it if one of them can possibly come up with the words to describe how much I want you right now."

I'm on my back so fast it makes me dizzy. I laugh, already breathless with anticipation. "You just had me."

"If it wasn't within the last eight minutes, it doesn't count."

"Oh, it counted." It counted so much I'll never forget it as long as I live. My stomach dips at the memory of Griffin spanking me, of his unrelenting grip on my wrists, and of the explosive fullness when he finally thrust into me. Who knew that being so utterly at the mercy of another person—a person I trust—could be so fantastically exciting?

Griffin grunts and sucks hard on my neck, I'm sure leaving a mark. "Why do you always argue?"

I grin, not that he can see in the pitch-black. "Because I'm always right."

He chuckles. "I'll let you get away with that."

Laughing, I wiggle underneath him. "*Get away* with that?"

"Yes. I have more important things on my mind." He demonstrates by sliding down my body. The rasp of stubble, his hands and lips, and teeth and tongue make me forget not only what we were talking about, but how to talk. I grip his hair and mumble incoherently. With his mouth between my legs, he does a dozen different things that turn me inside out. My mind blanks, and pleasure takes over, leaving me throbbing and trembling in its wake.

The strength of my climax unleashes my unpredictable magic, and lightning bounces off the stone walls long enough to illuminate Griffin's face. He looks smug and satisfied under a messy tumble of midnight hair.

He quirks an eyebrow. "Did that count?"

The room plunges back into darkness. "Uh…" I can't think. I'm supposed to talk?

His laugh is a deep, rich rumble. "I guess all that purring and panting wasn't what I thought it was."

"Nope." I giggle, sounding absurd. Or happy. Or both.

He sighs, a smile in his voice. "Obviously, I have more work to do."

"Obviously," I say, feeling amazingly light. Lies must weigh a lot—at least on me.

Never one to waste time, Griffin gets right down to proving he's up to the task.

There's something incredibly sensual about making love in the total dark. Anticipation is magnified, heightened until every touch becomes a heart-stopping mystery waiting to be solved. A whisper of breath across my skin has me tensing in eager expectation. The warm brush of lips leaves me shivering with desire. The subtle tightening of Griffin's grip intoxicates, just like the surprise of a nip, or the low rasp of a groan. In the quiet dark, our breath and our bodies speak a language of their own, weaving a spellbinding story in which only the two of us exist.

Griffin rocks slowly above me, his deep, thorough strokes branding me from the inside out. Sweet tension coils within me, and I cling to him, gasping every breath until I shatter in his arms. He follows me, shuddering, his face in the crook of my neck and his muffled roar a song in my heart.

Aftershocks ripple through us. I sigh into Griffin's hair. It smells of citrus and bright summer sun. I feel changed, once again forever altered by the man still gently pulsing inside of me.

He loves me anyway.

We both sleep this time. I wake up to Griffin striking my stumpy piece of flint to light the oil lamp. With him sitting on the edge of the bed, his considerable weight buckles the small mattress so much that I have to brace myself to keep from rolling into him.

"This wouldn't have lasted long," he mutters, finally getting a decent enough spark to light the wick. "You'd have gotten three fires out of it. Maybe four."

I rise to my knees, slip my arms around his waist from behind, and kiss his shoulder. "I wasn't running away, remember? I could have, you know…gotten more?"

He grunts. "My family is in shock. They think you broke me."

Pressure clamps down hard on my heart, suspending its next beat. He says it neutrally, without accusation, but Griffin only ever speaks the truth to me. For the time he couldn't find me, I broke him.

"I'm sorry. I love you." Words I never used to say, would have never even considered saying, are so easy now. If anyone knows that tomorrow isn't a given, it's me. I'll never hesitate again.

He scrubs both hands down his face and then braces his elbows on his knees. "I should have looked here earlier. I don't know why I didn't. It's just you always…"

"Run," I finish for him. "Of course you'd think I'd run."

"I thought I drove you away." The sudden bleakness in his voice slices straight through me.

I slip off the bed and drop to my knees between his legs. Griffin instinctively reaches out to touch me. His hands delve into my hair, and he runs the long, dark waves between his fingers.

I gaze up at him. Soft light plays over his striking features—the hard planes of his cheekbones, his strong jaw, the slight hook in his nose. "I'll still run, Griffin. The difference now is that I'll run to *you*."

He looks at me for a long time, his gray eyes inscrutable. "You'd better."

I arch an eyebrow. "Or you'll spank me?"

His mien changes. His expression brims with interest, and a little thrill zips like an arrow right to the target between my legs.

His already deep voice drops in pitch. "Possibly."

"I might hit back," I announce, meaning it.

He laughs, hauls me up, flips me onto the bed, and then covers my body with his.

"Griffin?"

"Hmm?" He sounds sleepy again. *How is that even possible?*

"We have to leave our cave."

He has me draped mostly on top of him. His fingers trail lightly back and forth across my bare shoulder, tickling a little in a way that gives me chills.

"Why?" He doesn't sound at all convinced, despite having a realm to run and—I guess we're really going there—invasions to plan.

"Because if I don't eat, I'm going to get very grumpy."

"Ah." There's a beat of silence. "We can't have that."

Finally, blowing out a long breath, Griffin stands, taking me with him. He's speedier at dressing than I am, and I hate every second he spends covering his magnificent body. I frown even harder when he hands me a pair of pants and a high-necked, long-sleeved tunic better suited for the dead of winter or the far north. From the irate looks he keeps leveling on my discarded nightgown, I think the conservative *suggestion* of clothing is a reaction to the nearly transparent dress.

"You didn't like it?" I add the rumpled garment to the pile of belongings I'm loading back onto the sheet.

"You were utterly irresistible in it."

"So what's the problem?"

"Kaia," he mutters darkly.

"She's fifteen. It's only fair she gets to explore...certain things."

Griffin seems to choke on something. The idea of Kaia *exploring things* probably.

"She's not a child, you know."

"I'm going to burn them," he decides.

I roll my eyes at his primitive, overprotective attitude and finish tossing my things into the center of the sheet. "She's behind her own closed door, and she's not doing anything stupid. Let it go."

Griffin plants his hands on his hips. His chest expands on a deep breath as he tilts his head back. He appears to have a long, in-depth struggle with himself before exhaling loudly. His head levels out.

Humph. I think we dodged that knife—for now.

His gaze drops to my mess on the floor. "You took our sheet. Feeling sentimental?"

Yes. Horribly. "It was my bag." I knot the ends and sling it over my shoulder.

Griffin takes the bundle from me, kissing my temple. "Clever, Cat. Always improvising."

"Improvise and survive!" I chant.

He chuckles. "That doesn't rhyme."

"Yes, it does."

"No, it doesn't."

"Yes, it does."

Griffin hits me with his hard stare. "You're arguing again."

"That's because I'm right."

"No, you're not."

"Who's arguing now?"

"Cat..."

I smile innocently. It's hard not to laugh. "Yes, Your Growliness?"

He growls.

I tap my chin, thinking up a rhyme he's sure to like. "There once was a Sintan warlord, who overcame an incredible horde. Even so, he'd be easy to mock, except he has this really huge co—"

Griffin plants his hand over my mouth, his eyes narrowing.

"What? It rhymes," I say, my voice muffled beneath his fingers.

"So do *spank* and *thank*."

I bite his hand, he smacks my bottom, and I shriek as he flops me over his shoulder along with my makeshift bag. With me gripping his waist and laughing, Griffin strides back to the castle, his head held high like the triumphant conqueror he is.

CHAPTER 5

JOCASTA LOOKS AROUND THE ROOM, HER BLUE EYES narrowed and her lips pursed. "You need a new bed."

"Really? I hadn't noticed." Last night, Griffin and I slept on the thick sheepskin rug in front of the unlit hearth—if sleeping is what you can call what we did for most of the night.

Griffin's sister snorts. "I wish I could take a sword and beat the stuffing out of something when I'm upset."

"You can. Here." I hand her my sword. It's short, about the length of a man's arm. The hilt fits my grip perfectly, and the rounded guard is engraved with a decorative pattern of intertwining laurel leaves. I'm thinking about naming it. Swords need names. "I recommend the bed, but I'm not particularly attached to that table over there."

Jocasta glances at the upturned table with its irreparably cracked central board. Her dark hair reflects the morning sunbeams streaming through the open window as she approaches what's left of the bed and then gives the ruined mattress a good whack. Her whole body jars from the impact. She hauls the sword up again and then thumps it back down harder. This time, the blade sticks in the splintered bed frame. By the time she wrestles it out of the wood, she's panting and half her curls have slipped from their pins.

She shoves her almost blue-black hair out of her face. "That was annoying."

I shrug. "Sometimes that happens in bone."

Revulsion crosses her face, but instead of setting down the sword, she strikes the bed again like she has something to prove. She keeps going, avoiding what's left of the frame. Stuffing erupts from the torn-up mattress, and feathers catch in her hair, giving her a savage appearance. With her bright sapphire eyes, flushed face, and a sword in her hand, she looks like a force to be reckoned with.

Since Griffin turned all our chairs into firewood, I stand there, watching, with my arms crossed. "What are you upset about?" I ask.

Jocasta takes a few deep breaths and then props the sword against the wall. "I'm not upset, exactly. I'm restless. The north wall is nearly fixed, and the children don't especially need my limited expertise in construction to finish the job. The pages have all settled into their roles in the castle. I don't have any groundbreaking ideas for improvements to the realm. The new healing centers and schools are Egeria's projects, and she doesn't need or really even want my help, although I keep offering." She brushes goose down from the front of her dress, her mouth thinning.

"You're bored." I get that. If I weren't so in love, which is completely new to me, I'd probably be bored, too. As it is, I'm tired of being confined to the castle grounds. I'm used to living mostly out in the open and traveling with the circus. Sometimes, these walls feel like they're closing in on me.

Jocasta sighs. "Piers is busy recruiting new soldiers, and that's not exactly my domain anyway. Carver has responsibilities that Griffin trusts him with. You have Beta Team. Father reads or sleeps most of the day. Mother concocts herbal sludge that I can already recite the recipes for forward and backward and use to heal most of the usual ailments. Kaia has her tutor—who's an old goat, by the way—but besides a few adjustments to court life, I've already had my schooling and don't need to sit in on lessons." She eyes my sword like she wants to start bashing things again. "I have nothing to do."

"Life is different for you now. As a younger sibling in a royal house, you have no real role. And even less freedom."

She chews on her lower lip, looking annoyed. "I used to be able to go places by myself. Ride a horse. Talk to people. Help them because they knew me and came to me and respected me. Now I'm stuck behind these walls where no one really needs me."

"There are days I feel trapped, too," I say. "But there are worse prisons than this."

"Yes, but everyone needs you. Especially Griffin." Scowling, Jocasta kicks a piece of wood across the room— debris from Griffin's rampage. "Sintans should see their new royals. They were nothing but welcoming on our way north last spring. I asked if I could travel the realm, with a large guard, of course, but Griffin won't let me. He says it's too dangerous."

"He's right."

Her eyes flash a fierce blue. "You, too? I thought you'd understand."

"I do understand. But the realms are entering into a Power Bid now. Fisa is a shadow over us all. Tarvan snakes are rattling their tails. They've attacked us twice, and the last time Griffin nearly died. What do you think they'd do if they got their hands on you?"

Jocasta doesn't answer.

In her silence, I answer for her. "They'd tear apart everyone you love as they came for you, and then they'd tear you apart, too."

"Then I should learn to defend myself!" She starts pacing, her fluid prowling reminding me of a certain Sintan warlord I know. "Teach me to fight, Cat. Make me less of a liability. Then maybe I can have some freedom."

I doubt it. *Overprotective* is Griffin's middle name. "I'm better with knives. I can teach you to stab and throw, but someone else should train you with a sword. Carver's the best out of everyone."

She huffs a laugh that's entirely without humor. "Carver thinks his sisters should be wrapped in glass and perched on pedestals. He'll never agree."

And here I thought Carver was less overbearing than Griffin. "What about Flynn?"

Jocasta stops mid-step and turns crimson. "We hardly speak anymore. I don't think he even looks at me."

"Oh, he looks. He just doesn't want to."

Her flush deepens. "You really think so? Why not?"

"Because you're Griffin's sister. And Carver's sister. And a Sintan princess now." I could probably go on, but I don't want to depress her.

"He's the highest-ranking soldier we have. He's been with us forever. He's not exactly a nobody!"

"You're right. And he's more than old enough to settle down. He's responsible and even-tempered. I'm fairly certain he wants a family. He's perfect for you."

Looking even more annoyed, Jocasta resumes her pacing. I realize too late I should have let her argue her case. It might have eased some of her frustration.

Someone knocks. Jocasta is closer and yanks open the door. Flynn is on the other side, dwarfing the doorway with his size. They both go stock-still, their eyes simultaneously widening. Mine do, too. I've only seen Flynn in the royal wing once before, the morning he burst into this same room with Eneas in tow, the healer who saved me after Daphne's attack.

Flynn unfreezes first and reaches out, removing a downy white feather from Jocasta's jet-black hair. He starts to hand it to her but then drops his arm, folding the feather into his large hand.

Jocasta throws her shoulders back, her color rising again fast. It's nearly a match for Flynn's shock of auburn hair. "Flynn."

"Jo." Flynn clears his throat. "Jocasta."

Her eyes narrow. "You can still call me Jo."

He looks at her for a moment and then frowns. "Your hair is a mess."

Her eyebrows wing up her forehead. "*That's* how you start our first conversation in months?"

Panic flits through Flynn's brown eyes. He looks like he's fallen into quicksand and doesn't know how to get out. He scratches the back of his neck, his face turning a ruddy color. "It's only... I just thought something might be wrong."

"Did you?" Jocasta crosses her arms, the movement thrusting her breasts up and revealing a good deal of skin at the neckline of her low-cut gown. Flynn tries so hard not to notice. *Poor Flynn.*

"Did you need something?" I ask.

He looks at me like I'm his savior. I'm getting that a lot lately. I hate it. *Don't these people know I'm doomed, and that I'm going to doom everyone along with me?*

I guess not. Because I haven't told them.

"Helen is leaving," Flynn says.

"What? She just gave birth."

"She says she can travel, and she looks like Zeus is chasing her with a thunderbolt. The woman is scared."

Of me, of course. Either she thinks I'll accuse her of my near-death—because, obviously, if someone tries to kill me, it must be family—or she knows her husband outed me to Griffin, and she's afraid I'll retaliate.

"Griffin is stalling your cousin and her family in the courtyard."

I swallow, suddenly nervous. "He told you, then?" If Flynn knows Helen Fisa is my cousin, he *knows.*

Flynn grins, surprising me. "I knew you were holding out on us. Knowing you, it had to be something momentous." He claps me on the shoulder, nearly sending me flying. "Glad you didn't disappoint."

Relief unties the knot of worry inside me, leaving me feeling absurdly emotional. "Tell Griffin I'll be right there."

Flynn nods. To Jocasta he says, "Jo."

"Flynn," she answers coolly.

He shuts the door, and she turns to me, dropping her crossed arms. "Well, that wasn't awkward at all."

I shake my head. "Not at all."

"He'll hate me now. I was awful."

"It'll take more than that for Flynn to hate a person he's known nearly his whole life. Besides," I say, thinking about how I treated Griffin for weeks, "men like a little awful. It keeps them on their toes."

She frowns. "You think so?"

What do I know? I'm a disaster at relationships. "Don't listen to me. Kaia would probably give better advice."

Jocasta laughs. Then sighs. Then looks at the door.

I stop with my hand poised over the doorknob, glancing back at her. "I guess you know, too?"

Her chin notches up as she shifts her focus back to me. "Of course. All the family knows. Beta Fisa. *My Gods.*" She shakes her head. "Griffin wouldn't keep something like that from us. Besides, he couldn't have. When you disappeared, he looked like he'd been trampled by a herd of Centaurs and then sat on by a Cyclops. I've never seen anything like it. He was destroyed." Her blue eyes harden as she adds, "It's a good thing you didn't really run away. I would have had to find you."

It takes a direct order from Egeria, Alpha Sinta, to get Helen out of her carriage. I watch from the shaded terrace overlooking the woods. If I'd known it was going to be this much trouble to talk to Helen, I would have just let her go.

Helen leaves her infant boy with her husband and his parents. I'm not a fountain of experience in the matter, but I don't think a woman leaves her newborn unless she thinks the child is safer without her. Once Helen finally starts toward me, she walks with her spine straight and her head high. As she should. She's Zeta Fisa. After me, only three people separate her from the most powerful throne in the realms. And to think, I started out with seven siblings and she with four.

A team of dark horses prances, impatient. Oreste steps down from the carriage, leaving the door open and the baby inside. Preparing for a speedy escape?

I study him as Helen approaches, curious since his family intended him for me. Despite being the most influential and ancient dynasty in Sinta, Andromeda saw them as pretentious pond scum, and no amount of gold could tempt her to send me to them. What must have been a number of years later, they settled for Helen, but as Oreste seems to have guessed, he lucked out. I'm no prize.

He's older, with a head of thick, graying hair, wide shoulders, and an athletic frame, despite being nearly fifty by now. He was in his mid-thirties when his family tried to buy me thirteen years ago. I was ten, and I was more petrified of staying in my own home than of being sent off to marry an adult Magoi in a far-off realm. They would have held off on the actual wedding for a few years. Despite what Mother likes to think, Sintans aren't child-marrying barbarians. And I'd wanted to go. Oreste would have been my escape.

From a distance, I watch grandparents I have no doubt are ruthless and ambitious coo over Helen's baby through the open door of the carriage. I don't need Oreste or his family, but a familiar tightness grips my chest nevertheless. If I'd been allowed to go to them, I'd have less blood on my hands, and Eleni might still be alive.

Helen stops in front of me and offers a small curtsy. "Talia."

I don't curtsy back, even though in Sinta and without my publicly claiming my title, she technically outranks me. Neither of us thinks like that. Once a Fisan, always a Fisan. I wonder if her new Sintan kin offered for my younger sister Ianthe before moving on to Helen. If they did, it happened after I ran away, or else Andromeda never told me. Mother doesn't exactly share.

"You didn't bring the baby." I glance over her shoulder toward the courtyard. "I wanted to see him. He's family, after all."

Helen pales, and I want to kick myself. *Family* is a curse word where we come from.

She steps to the left, blocking my view of the carriage. "My power has grown. I have Elemental Magic you would envy."

Clearly she's not afraid of a confrontation. It must be hormones. And I *do* envy Elemental Magic. I can absorb those powers and then use them until they run out, but permanently possessing a magical form of even one of the four elements would be a huge advantage—one I'm often without.

"I killed Sybaris and stole her Dragon's Breath. Don't threaten me."

Helen's face goes from white to ghastly white. "My baby is innocent."

"Good Gods, Helen, I'm not going to hurt your son. You had nothing to do with my getting stabbed. Believe me, that was entirely my own fault. I should have taken care of a threat weeks ago, and I didn't." *Because I'm in love, and happy, and going incredibly soft.* "And your husband inadvertently telling Beta Sinta who I am wasn't your fault, either. If I understand correctly, you were busy giving birth at the time."

If I didn't know her, I probably wouldn't see the new influx of anxiety sharpening her already angular features. "Oreste has no idea who you really are. I kept your secret."

I like Helen. I always have. She's protective and paranoid, like me. "I know. I believe you. We were friends before." Sort of. We never tried to kill each other. "I'd like to be friends again. I'd like our families to be friends."

Helen stares at me, her expression not giving much away. "Families?"

The word just slipped out. No taking it back now. Rather than backpedal like a fool, I hold out my hand and show her the large, square emerald flashing on my finger. "I'm betrothed to Beta Sinta." *Not that I'm telling Griffin that.*

Helen's jaw slackens, her reaction more marked this time. "He's a southern Sintan Hoi Polloi. You have ichor in your veins. Olympian blood. Titan blood. He's so far beneath you, you'll have to squint to see him."

I shake my head. "He's so far above me, I'll get a neck ache looking up to him."

Helen looks at me oddly, like I just stripped down to muscle and bone and donned a new skin—one she likes much better. She glances toward the carriage. Her baby started crying, and Oreste takes the boy from his mother, Urania, and rocks him. There's something innately shielding and tender in the curve of his body as he tucks the infant against his chest.

"He adores you, doesn't he?" I ask. "You're safe."

Helen turns back to me, and I see her swallow. "I always wanted you to be happy. You and Eleni."

"Eleni never got the chance." I can't keep the bitterness from my voice. And, apparently, the guilt.

My cousin reaches out and grips my wrist. Despite growing up in the same household, I think it's the first time we've touched. "It wasn't your fault."

I shrug. My next breath leaves me empty. "Maybe not, but there are infinite things a person can do differently in the space of just a few seconds."

Helen nods. She knows that, too.

"Go," I urge when the baby's cries turn into wails. "He's probably hungry."

Helen looks over again but doesn't move. "What are you doing, Talia? You're a queen, not a Beta's wife. Is this really where you belong?"

I laugh softly. "You should have seen what I was doing before." Soothsaying at a circus, dressed like a brigand, living in a tent. It was fabulous. Free. "Also, I'm only a queen when Mother dies, and Andromeda isn't going anywhere. Unfortunately."

We both grimace. It's involuntary. Simultaneous. Then Helen's eyes stray toward the courtyard again, small grooves forming beside her mouth.

"What is it?" I ask.

"Tarvans," she answers. "They're up to something."

"Aren't they always?"

"It's just…" She frowns, much of her attention on her baby. "They're going about it wrong."

I cant my head. "What do you mean?"

"Beta Sinta started the Power Bid. Delta Tarva has always been ambitious—serpent charmers often are. She should be making her play for the Tarvan throne. Besides that one murderous blast to northern Kitros, no one ever sees Alpha Tarva using his magic. Maybe he can't control it. Maybe it comes and goes. And his children are still young, with immature powers. But instead of attacking her brother and his kids, Delta Tarva is sending out discreet delegations to visit Sintan nobles. One came to our house, talking about alliances and coveted positions at court. It would appear she's trying to gain support and undermine the new Sintan royals from within."

"And you heard this conversation yourself?" I ask sharply.

She nods. "Three men came to speak to Agatone and Urania. As their heir, Oreste was included in the conversation. I was left out."

"But you listened at the door?"

"Naturally." Helen slants me an arch look. "They gave no answer for Delta Tarva at the time, and after the recent realm dinner, I think your Beta Sinta has seduced them with the strength of his ideas. Alpha Sinta was a surprise, too. They have *plans*." She snorts, a surprised sound rather than derisive. "Any but the most idiotic and prejudiced of Magoi will see that these are good moves. Things that will help bring Sinta out from under the shadow of the other realms."

"Did we derail Delta Tarva's efforts?" I ask.

Helen shrugs. "Fundamentally, we're all crafted from

our own land—made from the dust, and ice, and magic. I may live in Sinta now, and prefer my life here, but I am Fisan. I will always be Fisan. Acantha Tarva will always be Tarvan. I doubt Sintan Magoi would ever truly accept her as their Alpha, and Sintan Hoi Polloi would hate it."

I press my lips together. Herein lies a problem for us, as well. If we succeed in reuniting the realms, will the people across Thalyria accept Griffin and me as their Alphas? At least between us, we've got two of the three kingdoms covered.

"What if Delta Tarva's brother supports her?" I ask. "What if he gives her an army to get her out of his hair? If she wins the Sintan throne, Alpha Tarva gains an ally next door. Together, they more than rival Fisa."

Helen glances away, motherhood pulling her by its intangible thread. "It's possible. I suggest you prepare for battle either way."

A chill slips down my spine. *Bodies strewn about me. Realms destroyed.* "Acantha and her Drakons are coming for us, aren't they?"

Helen shakes her head. She doesn't know. "If they are, I don't think it's imminent. Delta Tarva is still sneaking delegations around Sinta, and the Tarvan royals have the upcoming Agon Games to prepare. As the hosts, I doubt they can make a move until the competition is over. The Games are too huge and popular to ignore."

In other words, we have sufficient time to prepare. "Thank you for the warning."

"What will you do?" she asks, poised to walk away.

I flash a ruthless smile that must remind Helen of the bad old days. "Watch out for snakes."

CHAPTER 6

"Does your cousin really think Delta Tarva is going to attack us instead of making a bid for her brother's throne?"

Piers brings an abrupt end to the usual fun of the family dinner. The brother between Griffin and Carver has permanent ink stains on his hands. He sometimes squints in the evenings because he reads so much. With his height, his black hair, and his slate-colored eyes, Piers would look a lot like Griffin if he gained muscle weight and was out in the sun more. To be fair, Piers takes his Gamma Team on patrol around Sinta City often enough, and he gets involved in training the soldiers from the barracks. He's fit, he knows how to handle a sword and ride a horse, and he's even second in command of the army under Griffin, but he's essentially a scholar.

The others around the table—Griffin and his parents and siblings—all pause in their eating and talking to listen to my answer.

"It makes sense," I say. "Tarvan mercenaries attacked us in the south with a hired Giant, which means spending a lot of gold. And someone tried again at Ios with an entire Tarvan tribe. That takes influence and deep pockets. Acantha Tarva has both. And now she's trying to win over Sintan nobles, according to Helen. If that's true, which I think it is, the realm dinner didn't come a day too soon. The Magoi elite got to see you all in person and understand your goals and what you're like. I think you gained significant support." *Thank the Gods.* "That said, her plotting is still a problem."

Griffin nods his agreement. We hardly had time to greet each other before we were summoned to dinner, and he's still rumpled from two days of travel. He and Carver accompanied Helen and her family home, their escort proving a clear desire for further cooperation between the two families. For Agatone and Urania to throw their lot in with Delta Tarva after the new Sintan royals showed them such a sign of favor would be surprising and stupid. They're not stupid.

"There's a good chance Acantha is gathering her forces while she tries to weaken our position from the inside. If she hits us with a Tarvan army, her own Magoi, *and ours*, we'll buckle." Griffin balls his hand into a fist on the table. "My army is spread out protecting the realm. I lost hundreds of soldiers in a war we just won. You're all vulnerable to magic, even if Cat and I aren't." He looks around the table, his expression shuttered. His ambition has never been selfish, but I sometimes wonder if he ever regrets bringing his family to this point. If it were me, I'd throw half of Sinta under a Cyclops to save the people around this table, but Griffin doesn't think that way.

"Aren't you recruiting?" I ask Piers. Last I heard, he'd amassed a significant number of soldiers, mostly Hoi Polloi eager for the opportunities of advancement and employment available in a newly structured realm.

He nods. "I go to Velos and Kaplos next week. Skathos after that. Then I'll move farther south."

"Having soldiers doesn't make an army," Griffin says in frustration. "Not a good one, anyway. They'll need to be armed, trained, dispatched..."

Piers stiffens. "I know. We talked about this. I have plans. You approved them."

Griffin stares into his wineglass and then moves it away from him, the contents untouched. "It'll take too long."

"Acantha Tarva, assuming it was her, just came off a resounding defeat at Ios." Egeria, with her dovelike nature and quiet gray eyes, calmly passes the vegetables as if we were talking about the weather. I still don't think Griffin's older sister should be Alpha, the role requiring a certain amount of ruthlessness as well as mercy, but she's repeatedly proved herself more capable than I gave her credit for at first.

"Acantha will need time to regroup, and if the realm dinner went half as well as we think it did, we'll have foiled her efforts with a number of Sintan nobles," Egeria continues. "Our most powerful Magoi will look to Agatone and Urania for guidance. We just delivered Helen's baby—their grandchild. That newborn boy landed in *my* hands, and he's healthy and fine. Helen has her husband wrapped around her finger, and if she volunteered this information to Cat, she supports us. They will support us."

"I agree with Egeria," I say.

Everyone looks at me. When I don't add *but* or *except*, Egeria looks pleasantly surprised.

Anatole finishes his last bite. When he's up and about, Griffin's father does everything with lightning speed, including eat. His aging body no longer holds the muscle and power it once had, but it's easy to see how he was once one of the most formidable warlords in all of Sinta. His sly, sparkling gaze holds a wealth of intelligence, cunning, and experience.

"Piers should stick to his plan. Keep recruiting." Anatole looks first at Piers and then at Griffin. "In the meantime, secure the border."

Griffin spreads his hands, leaning back. "With what army? There aren't enough trained soldiers yet. I can't take anyone away from Sinta City, and there are barely enough people stationed elsewhere. If the major cities fall, the rest of Sinta falls, too."

"Invading forces can't get to cities if they can't cross the border," Anatole reasons. "Put our soldiers where we need them the most."

Griffin shakes his head. "Too risky. It's a good idea, but it'll never work. Foot soldiers can't move fast enough to cover the entire border. There'll be huge gaps to get through."

"What if they're mounted?" Jocasta asks.

"There aren't enough horses," Griffin and I say at once.

"I have two horses," Kaia volunteers. Always eager and full of energy, she shifts forward in her seat. "You can have mine."

Her spontaneous offer sends a stab of something hot and twisting through my chest. I wouldn't offer up my horse now, and I certainly wouldn't have done it at fifteen. Griffin's youngest sister is a constant surprise to me. Her straight dark hair and gray eyes mirror Egeria's—although with a touch more blue and a good deal more fierceness in Kaia's youthful gaze, there's nothing subdued about her. I'll bet she battles Dragons in her daydreams.

Next to her, Nerissa takes Kaia's hand. In turn, Anatole takes Nerissa's. Husband and wife. Parents and daughter.

Emotion swells inside of me. Is it envy? Sadness? It expands in a rush, and I don't think it's either. I'm pretty sure it's something much more dangerous and frightening than mere self-pity. I think it's a deep, stomach-hollowing longing accompanied by a terrifying sense of hope. That could be *me*. Not the daughter. That ship sank on Poseidon's sea a long time ago. Not the daughter...but the mother.

"I know two isn't many, but what if everyone around Sinta did the same? We could...rent the animals and then give them back once the danger passed." Kaia's face brightens. "I could be in charge of that."

For reasons I don't fully understand, my throat is suddenly too thick for breath.

Anatole gives her a patient smile. "That's a generous offer, *glikia mou*."

His sweet. I love how the southern tribes retained the old endearments, things that northerners never seem to say.

Kaia sighs. "But…"

"But people depend on their horses for their livelihoods. It's almost harvest time. There won't be a horse, ox, or mule to spare for the next two months. Taking animals now could not only chip away at the goodwill Sintans feel toward us, but also endanger our entire food supply."

Kaia slumps in her chair. "That's what the royals did before. They just took everything, and we hated them."

Jocasta nudges a pair of cheese-stuffed olives around her plate. "So where does that leave us? Building the army and hoping it functions properly before Acantha decides to invade?"

"Yes." Piers reaches over and steals her olives.

"There is something else." I glance at Griffin, sure he remembers our conversation about gaining the assistance of creatures. "Something we could try."

I sense Griffin's mood souring even before his eyes settle on mine like boulders, and he was already pretty tense. I'm undaunted. Mostly.

I hazard on. "If we have magical creatures patrolling the border, it'll send a clear message to the other realms, and even to our own people. Strength. Power. Boldness. It'll be proof of resources they didn't think we had. It'll make them wonder what else we have in our arsenal, which, in turn, will make them hesitant to cross us. Creatures move fast, their hearing is acute, they're huge and intimidating. A herd of Ipotane, for example, could block Sinta behind a nearly impenetrable wall."

Egeria looks bemused. "But we don't have any Ipotane."

"Not yet." I sip my wine. It's white and tart.

"It means going to Fisa." Griffin's voice is like a gathering storm. "I don't want you anywhere near there. Near *her*."

Mother. Yes, she is *a delight.* I set down my glass. "You want to conquer Thalyria. That includes Fisa. What do you expect me to do while you're at it? Ignore my Dragon's Breath? My ability to turn invisible? To detect lies? To steal magic? Sit on my knowledge of creatures and royals and Oracles? Play with my knives instead of using them? Just *wait* for you? I might as well go back to the circus," I say hotly. "At least I'd be entertained."

I glare at Griffin. Griffin glares back.

"Should I lounge around eating sweets and fanning myself all day?" I ask. "Maybe in my nightgown? If I get bored, I'll call in some pages to distract me."

A muscle jerks in Griffin's jaw. Maybe I went too far.

"You can steal magic?"

"Turn invisible?"

"Detect lies?"

The questions come from around the table. *Damn it!* I forgot I was keeping all that a secret from everyone except for the members of Beta Team. Besides Griffin and Carver, everyone in the royal family thinks I'm simply a sooth-sayer, reading people in some mystical way.

In the next second, I realize I don't care. I trust them. Betraying me would mean betraying Griffin, and his family would never do that. I keep that knowledge close, just like the knowledge that Griffin loves me, no matter what.

We both get angry. We both get over it. In the meantime, maybe I can get him to spank me.

I turn invisible to hide a completely inappropriate grin. *Gasps!*

I pop back into sight when my face is under control.

"Really useful," I announce. "In case you were wondering why I showed up so late, I spent half the realm dinner night invisible and detecting lies. I get burned to a crisp on the inside every time I hear a falsehood, and then the truth slams into me like vicious little punches all over my body, especially my head. It was a hoot."

The family gapes at me—which is always satisfying.

I turn back to Griffin. His expression is stony and unreadable, although if I had to take a wild guess, I'd say it was tending toward ominous.

"I'm not staying here to write sonnets to Cerberus," I tell him. "I'm called the Kingmaker for a reason. I go with you."

Griffin's eyes darken. He flashes me a look that promises…*something.*

"The Kingmaker," Piers echoes with a jolt.

Heard of me, has he? I'm not surprised. He reads a lot of old scrolls.

"Go where exactly?" Egeria asks, her now worried gaze shifting back and forth between Griffin and me.

"To the Ice Plains," Griffin replies stiffly. "That's where magical creatures are."

His entire family erupts in unison. It's impressive.

"But we have our own Ice Plains to the north," Carver finally says over all the denials and arguing. "Why go all the way to Fisa?" He shakes his head in confusion, setting loose a few strands of jet-black hair that curve toward his angular jaw.

I think what he really means is *why go anywhere near*

that death trap at all? Carver is an expert swordsman, lean, sinewy, and strong. He's smart and fast, but magic leaves him out of his element—and possibly with no means of defense.

"Because the Ipotane could be anywhere from our northern border with the Ice Plains to Mount Olympus in the far northeast. We need someone to help us locate the herd and tell us how to ensnare it. A Chaos Wizard lives just over the Fisan border, on the south shore of the Frozen Lake. I think he can help us." *Or, more to the point, I hope the Gods will.*

"What are Ipotane?" Kaia asks. She's young, southern, and Hoi Polloi—all good reasons she's never heard of the creatures.

"They're like Centaurs, only fiercer. Bigger." I look sternly at her from under lowered brows. "Something you never want to meet in the dark. Or the day."

Kaia's blue-gray eyes go wide and sparkle with curiosity. She giggles.

"A single blow from one of its massive hooves will crush a man's rib cage. A human skull doesn't stand a chance. One flick of its long tail feels like a hundred lashes from a stinging whip. Two flicks will flay the skin and muscle from your bones. They have glowing, amber eyes that can see farther than a hawk's, and equine ears that can hear a man unsheathe his sword from a mile away. They don't eat meat, but I've heard they bite." I snap my teeth at Kaia, and she giggles again. I probably shouldn't joke. Ipotane are no laughing matter.

"Have you seen one?" Kaia wiggles toward the edge of her chair, as if chasing down a herd of murderous Ipotane sounds like a fine idea to her.

"Not yet."

"Then how do you know?" she asks.

I think the smile that twists my face must scare her a little because her eyes lose some of their eager glitter. "Bedtime stories." I leave out Mother's favorite part—how if I didn't rat out someone's lies, she would stir a herd of Ipotane into a frenzy and then drop me into the middle of it, weaponless and alone.

Nerissa gives me a disapproving look, sweeping it to Griffin next. "These don't sound like creatures you should approach."

"That's why we need the Chaos Wizard," I explain. "So we don't blunder around and get ourselves killed."

"*Chaos.* Sounds like fun. Not very reassuring, though." Carver picks up a goat cheese–filled phyllo wrap and inspects it with a critical eye. "Can't we find a Tell-Them-What-They-Want-To-Know Wizard?" he asks.

I push my own wrap to the far side of my plate because goat cheese—*gah*! "Life would be too easy if we had any of those," I say dryly.

"What about an Oracle? They seem to like you." Carver pops the goaty atrocity into his mouth.

I shrug. "I've seen two, and neither of them killed me." In fact, they were more than helpful. "But Oracles are about judgment and doling out magic, weapons, or death. You can't just ask questions and get answers. And a Chaos Wizard isn't—"

"He has nothing to do with wreaking havoc or creating disorder," Piers interrupts me.

I blink. Set down my fork. "Perhaps you'd like to finish my explanation for me?" I ask sarcastically.

Piers does, as if that were a real invitation. "In this case, the word reverts to its original meaning. Before the cosmos took shape, there was only Chaos—a whirling mass without form."

"I just had this lesson!" Kaia exclaims. "From Chaos, Gaia emerged. Her son, Uranus, fashioned the first world. From the two of them, all life was made."

Piers nods. "Their children, among others, were the Titans. The Titans birthed our Olympians."

"Then the Titans and the Olympians warred. I'm not sure why." Kaia's face falls. "My tutor hasn't gotten to that part yet."

I jump in before Piers can. "The Titan king was so intent on maintaining his power that he started swallowing his babies whole to keep them from growing up and over-throwing him. Poseidon, Hades, their sisters—they all went right down the hatch, unharmed, but gone. No one liked that, especially not Zeus, who escaped being eaten and then freed his siblings. He slipped his father a potion that made the Titan king vomit everyone back up. The New Gods and the Old fought bitterly and for a small eternity before Zeus and his brothers finally killed their father. Their victory ushered in the new age."

Piers looks at me like he can't quite believe I just summed up the longest, most important war in the history of the universe in a few sentences. I smirk. I'm clever like that.

"After winning the War of Gods," Piers adds, apparently needing the last word, "Zeus banished the Titans to Tartarus."

Ah, Tartarus. Those Olympians don't fool around with eternal torment. They have a whole realm just for that. "Actually," I say, because I can't help needling Piers with information he left out, undoubtedly to simplify matters for us idiots around the table, "Cronus, the Titan king, got to go to Elysium, even though he didn't deserve it, and his war leader, Atlas, was cursed to hold up the heavens for all of eternity."

"And that's how the Olympians came to power?" Kaia asks.

I nod. I knew all this and much more by the time I was half her age, but this kind of learning is neither taught nor prized in Sinta. Southern Hoi Polloi are usually about as versed in ancient history as northern Magoi are in farming. But now Kaia has her royal tutor, and I'm constantly filling in knowledge gaps for the rest of the family. Well, not for Piers. With the amount of time he spends in the library, he could probably teach me a thing or two—not that I would *ever* admit it.

"Zeus and Hera took over, and the Dodekatheon was formed—twelve Gods to rule Olympus. Zeus eventually got bored, created man, a few more worlds, et cetera, et cetera." I wave a hand in the air. "He impregnated a bunch of mortal women and at least one Titan princess, and here we are."

Anatole quirks a grizzled brow. "Here we are?"

"What Cat means," Griffin clarifies, obviously remembering a recent conversation we had at the realm dinner, "is that the Titan princess had a son. Zeus took him from Tartarus and created Thalyria for him. He was the Origin of this world—and its first king. He ruled until his own Demigod children struck him down and then warred amongst themselves, eventually splitting Thalyria into three realms—Sinta, Tarva, and Fisa."

Griffin cuts me a sharp look, the few remaining pieces of the puzzle that used to be me slamming neatly into place. "Fisa's royal house is the only one still blood-related to the Origin. That means Zeus is Cat's great, great, great—"

I wave my hand in the air again. "Go back a few millennia."

"Grandfather," Griffin finishes.

I frown at him. "You don't have to sound so put out about it."

"It's just so..." He stops talking, probably trying to

figure out a way to say it's incredibly disturbing without offending me.

"It's fantastic!" Kaia cries, bouncing in her chair. "Cat's a Goddess!"

Heat rises in my face. "I wouldn't go that far." *Really, I wouldn't.*

Anatole leans forward, looking more serious than I've ever seen him. "As shocking, and interesting, as that new revelation is, what does any of this have to do with the Chaos Wizard in Fisa?"

I answer before Piers can jump in and steal my thunder again. "He's a conduit for the Gods, especially Zeus. He's completely insane. His knowledge is essentially Chaos, a whirling mass without form. Everything. Ever. *Forever.* If the Gods are listening, and feeling generous, they can help the wizard to focus. If you go about it the right way, he can tell you anything."

Piers looks skeptical. "So Grandfather Zeus is going to help you out? Tell you where the Ipotane are and how to not get massacred by them?"

I narrow my eyes and lift my glass, tilting it toward Piers in a slightly mocking salute. "Here's hoping." I take a sip.

"What's the right way to get answers?" Griffin asks, always the pragmatist.

Good question. "We'll figure it out." Although the last time I tried, I got stuck with a fate-of-the-world prophecy instead.

My dinner suddenly feels like a block of marble in my stomach. I'm going to have to tell Griffin about that.

"We leave in four days," Griffin announces. "I need to put things in order here, prepare for an absence."

"So soon!" Nerissa pales.

"Are you serious?" Piers all but growls. "Just because Cat suggests something doesn't mean you have to do it!"

"It's a good idea," Carver says. "If we wait too long to act, Acantha Tarva could regroup and attack. Leaving now gives us a chance to get the Ipotane on our border before she makes her next move."

"This can't be the wisest course of action." Piers addresses Griffin alone, as if the rest of us don't exist. "I can build a bigger army. I've already started."

"Our recent successes won't hold off Delta Tarva for long," I say. "A few months, maybe. She'll be distracted by preparations for the Agon Games for now, and tradition dictates that the Tarvan royals attend at least the final rounds and then greet the victors." There's no need to explain what the Agon Games are. The highly popular, bloodthirsty competition only happens once every four years and is slated to begin several weeks from now, hosted by the equally bloodthirsty Tarvan royals. "A lot of people, especially Magoi, take the Games very seriously, and having them canceled because of an invasion could easily stir up trouble and resentment Delta Tarva doesn't want."

Griffin readily agrees. "She wants Magoi support, not anger."

"Helen's right to think Delta Tarva won't take action again before the Games. And then it'll be the rainy season, which might hamper her, too," I add. Storms could buy us time. "But even a few months from now, Piers's army will still be green. With the Ipotane, we don't have to worry about that. With them guarding the border, they'll stop any attack before it even starts."

Piers focuses on me with barely suppressed ire. "*If* you come back. Going to the Ice Plains is rash, even for you. Dragging Griffin and Carver there is even rasher."

Even for me? *Dragging* Griffin? "Should I sit in the

library, read all day, and then dazzle people with my ability to retain information I'll never act upon?"

Piers's eyes glint furiously. "Maybe you should stop being an arrogant show-off and think about the danger you're putting people in."

"Did *I* bring your family to this castle? Did *I* suggest taking over the whole Gods damned world?"

"Cat! Language!" Nerissa says sharply.

I don't look at her. My expression would make her flinch.

Piers holds my stare. His voice drops in anger. "You're making things seem possible that aren't, that would never have seemed feasible before you came along."

"Came along? I was abducted!"

"Semantics." Piers flicks his ink-stained fingers in the air.

My jaw drops. *Words are important!* He'd know that if every single falsehood fried *him* from the inside out. "Griffin took over an entire realm before ever laying eyes on me. He had a vision. He made it happen." I level a frosty look on Piers. "Is hope forbidden now? I didn't get that scroll."

Piers leans toward me, crowding me with his wide shoulders that throw me into shadow. Is he trying to intimidate me? *Ha!*

"It's not *hope*, it's *hopeless*. Almost no one survives the Ice Plains. Surviving them, then a war with Tarva, then a war with Fisa…" He shakes his head. "There's no way."

"There's *always* a way," I say fiercely. "You just might not like it."

"War, Cat," Piers snarls back. "Do you know what it's really like? It's not only the other side that bleeds."

Eleni flits across my consciousness like an iridescent dragonfly under a dazzling summer sun. Laughing. Dying. "You have no idea what I've seen. Or who I've lost."

"Enough!" Griffin's fist hits the table with a startling

thud. "We still build the army. We need it. But the Ipotane would be an enormous asset, especially if we move fast and get them back here before the Agon Games begin. They could spare Sintan blood."

"Or spill yours," Piers mutters.

Griffin silences further protest from his brother with a quelling, full-on Alpha look. The innate dominance in his granite eyes puts an instantaneous end to the argument.

"Who will you take?" Nerissa asks anxiously.

"Me," I say, my tone wholly uncompromising.

"And me." Carver's tone matches mine.

"Beta Team," Griffin says flatly.

No argument. Amazing. Although I am kind of indispensable to the mission.

Jocasta's throat moves on a nervous swallow. Her blue eyes dart to me and then drop to her lap. Is she worried about Flynn?

Kaia bounces in her seat. "I wish I could go."

"No!" the entire table shouts at once.

Her shoulders slump. "You have no idea how boring my tutor is. He's crusty. He has actual crust on him." She frowns. "Like a shell. I'm not sure he's human."

That's it. These girls need rescuing. And Gods help me, I need to get away from Piers, or I might maim him by almost, sort-of accident. "Four days, you said?"

Griffin nods.

"Can I take Jocasta and Kaia out for a while?"

Griffin goes utterly motionless. Never a good sign. "Where? And how long is 'a while'?"

"Not far, and just three days. Into the woods north of Sinta City. One day out, one day to explore an underground cavern I know, and then one day to come back. We'll leave for the Frozen Lake the day you're ready."

"No." Griffin slices his head to the side. "Too dangerous."

Griffin doesn't like me out and about without him because of a not entirely irrational fear of someone trying to steal or kill me. Add his sisters to the mix, and it's even worse. "We'll take Carver with us." I glance hopefully at Carver.

Griffin shakes his head again. "I need Carver here."

"Then give us Kato and Flynn."

His already stubborn jaw hardens. He's about to cross his arms. After that, his eyebrows will slam down, and I don't want to give him time to think of another reason to say no.

"We'll be fine, Griffin. I'm chock-full of Dragon's Breath, and we'll be back before you can blink."

"I just blinked," he says, crossing his arms.

I take a deep breath. This is going to take some finesse, something of which I have very little.

CHAPTER 7

I DON'T GET MY WAY IN THE END. GRIFFIN WOULDN'T budge, and the extent of his stubbornness was about to drive me insane when I realized I don't want to be apart from him anyway. I stopped arguing, but not without a bargain. Three days in the castle woods, safe behind our own thick walls. No questions. No checking up on us. No men. No crusty tutor. We go back to the castle every day before dark, which works just fine for me. I get a bath, a hot meal, and then Griffin.

"I did it!" Jocasta shouts.

I grin at the target. Her knife isn't in the middle, but it's pretty damn close.

"My turn." Kaia positions herself in the way I showed them both, the movement fluid and automatic by now. She completely ignores the way the reddened skin on her hand must chafe and lets her blade fly. It sticks dead center, and she jumps up and down, cheering.

I let out a long, low whistle, making her flush with pride.

It's our final day out, and both of them are hitting the bull's-eye more often than not. It's time to move back a few more paces, or aim from the side.

"I still think we should have used your usual practice range instead of making this new one." Kaia's naturally bright eyes turn dreamy. "We would surely have seen Kato that way. And Flynn," she adds as an afterthought.

Hmm. No wonder she's not running around kissing the pages. She's already in love.

"We're trying to avoid them, remember? This is a secret." Jocasta gets ready to throw again.

Kato already knows. He took me into the city, and I bought the girls each a set of knives the morning we started target practice. The knives are double-edged at the tip and medium weight with sleek metal handles wrapped in sinew for grip. They were hideously expensive because the sinew comes from Kobaloi, gnome-like creatures fond of playing tricks. The vendor said the sinew retains the creature's magic, which is always useful. I bought myself a set, too. I just hope the knives don't play tricks on *us*.

"I don't see why it has to be a secret. They could have taught us, too. With swords." Pink infuses Kaia's cheeks, and I have a feeling she's imagining Kato's strong arms around her and his big body cupping hers from behind as he shows her the right way to move. She's tall for her age, taller than either Jocasta or I am, and as dark-haired as Kato is fair. They'd fit well together.

Gah! What am I thinking? He's way too old for her.

I frown. What is *she* thinking?

"Neither of them actually prefers the sword." I motion for Kaia to stand farther away from the target. She's so good that anything too close range will start to get boring. "And knives are a good start. They're lighter, easier to conceal, and you can defend yourself without letting anyone get too close." Or else they're really close, but we're working on throwing, not stabbing.

While Kaia moves back and gets ready again, I help Jocasta with her position. She tends to throw high and to the right. I reposition her shoulders and slowly extend my arm, holding hers by the wrist. "Let go here," I say when our arms are straight, "when the tip points to where you want it to go."

Kaia listens and makes a minor adjustment before she throws, keeping her wrist stiff to avoid wild rotations. She hits the red hibiscus flower we pinned to the target as a bull's-eye and lets out a shriek. She bounces over and hugs me.

"You're a natural." I awkwardly pat her back.

"I wish Kato could have seen that." She grins so wide I see her molars. "He would have been impressed."

"Kato is more than twice your age," Jocasta points out gently but firmly. "And he wouldn't approve."

Actually, considering the overprotective *grrr* factor of the four male members of Beta Team—which meant I couldn't go shopping without one of them as an escort—he was fairly casual about the whole thing. Then again, I did present it to him as a fun new hobby for the princesses rather than a vital self-defense technique.

"Why not?" Kaia asks. "Would Flynn approve?"

"No, he would not." Jocasta sounds like she just bit down on half a lemon—and broke a tooth on a seed.

"But Cat has knives. And a sword. They fight together. They're a team."

Jocasta looks to me for help. I wish she wouldn't. I don't exactly have a delicate way with words.

I flip a knife in my hand, the sinew-wrapped hilt hitting my palm with rhythmic, dull thuds. I wish I could spin it vertically like my friend Vasili at the circus does, with the hilt twirling on my hand, but it always tilts right off. "The difference is that I came to them that way. A grown woman. Already a warrior. They know I can handle myself, and they've seen me take my fair share of hits and come out stronger for them." I point back and forth between the two of them with the tip of my new blade. "You, on the other hand, came to them as little baby girls, and they've watched you grow up. They've seen you scrape your knees and play in the mud after the first rains. Helped you climb trees. With you, their only thought is to shelter and defend. It wouldn't even occur to them to let you protect yourselves."

Kaia's youthful face scrunches up. "That's obnoxiously unfair."

"That's men. Stubborn." I throw my knife. The blade scrapes against Kaia's in the heart of the flower.

"Does Griffin treat you that way?" Kaia asks.

I snort. "He can try."

They both grin at my choice of words. "You're officially family now. You've adopted our motto," Jocasta says.

My insides take a sudden, violent dive. Griffin would like to make it a lot more official than that.

To distract myself from that alarming train of thought, I whip around, slip my foot behind Kaia, and shove hard on her upper body. With Kaia down, I snake my arm around Jocasta's neck and haul her up against my body, cutting off most of her air. She squeaks and slaps at my forearm.

Laughing, I let go of her and step back, shaking my head. "At the very least, you should have stomped on my toes or elbowed me in the ribs."

Jocasta glares at me, but her mouth moves like she might smile. Kaia gets up, grinning. She doesn't bother brushing herself off. They're both flushed and disheveled.

"We have time before dark. I finally got you two wearing tunics and pants, so let's work on balance and grappling." I shift into a fighting stance. "I'll show you how to take someone down and hold them there. Then you'll have to practice on each other while I'm gone."

They look disturbingly eager, and I wonder what I've started, and whether I should have left well enough alone.

We assemble in the Athena courtyard after breakfast on the fourth day. Griffin and I are already mounted, but the rest of Beta Team—Kato, Flynn, and Carver—are still finishing their good-byes, strapping on the last of their gear, and readying their horses. If I'm not mistaken, Flynn is moving slowly because he keeps shooting discreet glances toward Jocasta from under lowered auburn brows. Carver, his long, leggy gait slower than usual, only just left his family under the shaded arcades that band the castle's ground floor like an ornate marble ribbon. And Kato, all blond hair, blue eyes, and corded muscle, moves with casual purpose and lionesque indolence—unhurried in his stride but powerful and inherently ready for action. Despite the stakes of the journey, none of them seems to feel any real urgency to leave.

I don't like lingering over farewells, and their lagging makes me feel like I have ants in my pants. It's all I can do not to start hopping in the saddle. Panotii is champing at the bit, and so am I. He prances sideways and bumps into Brown Horse. Brown Horse doesn't move an inch and regards us with calm, intelligent eyes. He's so much like his rider that I almost laugh.

Unable to hold back a smile, I drink in Griffin with my eyes. Actually, I look at Griffin all the time. I think about him even more, and every time I do, it's like a wild kick of adrenaline straight to the heart. It's distracting. *He's* distracting.

A tingling warmth spreads beneath my skin. "I can't wait to gallop." I haven't been outside the city walls since Ios. Panotii and I need to stretch our legs, see for miles, and feel the wind in our faces. It's good for a horse. For a person who's been confined to a cage, it's cathartic. Castle

Sinta and its grounds may be big, beautiful, and full of Griffin, but in some ways, it's still a cage. Real freedom is answering to only yourself, and being responsible for no one. Since that's a moral vacuum, none but the truly wicked are ever truly free.

That must be how Mother feels—free.

Panotii keeps dancing, and I stroke his sleek, chestnut neck, trying to soothe him. "Panotii wants to run, too."

"You'll burn yourselves out." Griffin's silver-hued eyes hold a hint of warning. "And you'll burn us out chasing you. We have a long way to go."

I make a sour face. "Did I ever tell you I detest the voice of reason?"

"Did I ever tell you you're adorable when you're riled up?"

I scowl. "I'm never adorable."

"You're right," he says mock-seriously. "You're very scary. Especially with that curl bouncing over your cheek."

I shove the stupid curl behind my ear. My wavy hair is turning even more unruly with the approach of the rainy season. It's overcast for the first time in weeks, and I can smell the moisture in the air, somehow both sultry and refreshing, as if a cloud were about to burst over the scorched land, but the Gods aren't quite ready to stick a dagger in it yet. My hair doesn't know the difference. Anything too short to stay firmly in my braid is now springing out with gusto and frizzing all around my head.

Out of habit, I check my knives. My old set hangs from multiple belt loops. My new set is secured to flat leather straps circling my thighs. My sword is on my back in a sling Griffin had fashioned for me along with the thick boar's-hide armor that hugs my upper body from shoulders to waist in a sleeveless, close-fitting shell. A direct hit will pierce the leather, but it'll provide protection from slices or glancing blows, as will the new vambraces on my forearms.

I told Griffin I'd be too hot and confined, which I am, but he insisted in that steady, intractable voice of his that if I want to ride with warriors, I'd better have the equipment.

He knows I've been fighting without any of this since before I could walk, but I humored him because I love him. Apparently, that's how couples work. *Compromise. Gah!* Now there's so much metal and leather weighing me down that I almost couldn't get on my horse.

That curl bounces back out, and Griffin leans over, tucking it behind my ear again. "Terrifying," he murmurs, and something in his voice makes me shiver like he just trailed a warm, rough fingertip down my spine.

"In a Fisan fishing village, they call me Talia the Terrible."

One midnight eyebrow creeps up. "Do tell."

I settle deeper into my saddle when Panotii swings his back end around again, his hooves banging out an impatient rhythm on the marble of the courtyard. "It was that exceptionally cold winter about ten years back when the Ice Plains swept down into the realms and frosted over land that usually never sees even the barest dusting of snow. The northern forests hung with icicles, and terrifying creatures followed the freeze down into the realms, extending their usual playground by miles. People were scared, cold, and hungry—totally unprepared for that kind of severe weather.

"In this village on the coast, a giant, crazed octopus came down from the magic-filled waters of the north. Its appetite was huge, and it began devouring all their fish and ripping apart the boats that dared to cross into its new territory. The entire village was slowly starving to death. Hands and bellies empty. Hopeless eyes. Wailing babies.

I heard about their plight, traveled there, and caught the gigantic tentacled monster—at great personal risk to myself, as you can imagine—and tore it limb from limb with my bare hands. Pluck." I mime yanking a leg off and tossing it over my shoulder. "Pluck." I toss the next one over the other shoulder and watch the imaginary limb splat in the imaginary dirt. "When I got to the eighth and final leg, the creature looked at me with doleful eyes and said, 'You are truly terrible,' and then it died in a pathetic, gelatinous heap."

Griffin explodes with laughter, the sudden sound making even Brown Horse's ears twitch. It rolls from him in great, deep waves, and I can't help laughing, too, even though my ridiculous grin destroys Talia the Terrible on the spot. It's the first time in days he's looked happy like this. The broad smile, the way his eyes crinkle at the corners, bringing out the silver lining around his irises—it's a different kind of pleasure from the intensity of lovemaking, or the times when it's just the two of us, wrapped in each other's arms. I like seeing him simply enjoy himself. I love being the reason for it.

"Octopuses live in warm water, Madam Terrible. And is *tentacled* even a word?" Griffin asks, still chuckling.

"Of course it is. It rhymes with *manacled.*" I give him a significant look, my mind jumping straight to his big hand gripping my wrists, but my face heats to the point of burning, which ruins the effect.

Fabulous. Catalia Fisa, master of seduction.

Griffin's glittering gray eyes smolder with interest, though. He looks ready to drag me off my horse and forget about leaving for a few hours.

Maybe I *am* a master of seduction!

With a low sound that makes my whole body hum, he

leans down and brushes his lips over mine. When that's not enough, because it's never enough, he clasps the back of my neck and presses his mouth down harder. Our kiss starts to move in a rhythm. His fingers tighten on my nape. I breathe him in and savor his taste, and when he pulls back, I tingle from head to toe.

"You *are* terrible when you need to be. And terribly self-less." Griffin drags his thumb across my lower lip. "Even in that ridiculous story you made up, you were defending people, putting others before yourself. You like to pretend otherwise, but don't you see? You're the shield, and I'm the sword. Together, we'll forge a new world."

My heart hangs suspended for a moment and then beats again hard. Fear mingles with…*anticipation?* "Who said I made it up?"

Griffin grins and kisses me again. Our teeth click softly when I grin back. Then our lips cling until I lower my head.

Do we make a whole? Or do we cancel each other out? What if he's the shield, and I'm the sword? What if I break him, and everything else?

A dull clomping in my ears tells me the others are finally mounted and ready. I look over my shoulder and see the guys moving in our direction.

Carver draws alongside us. Kato and Flynn take up the rear. On Griffin's signal, the gate rises. The rest of the royal family calls out and waves to us again. I briefly wave back but don't linger over another good-bye. The first one was hard enough. I don't turn again as the spiked portcullis finishes its slow crawl up into the high rectangle of the castle's main gate, although I think I'm the only one. I don't know why it's not universally acknowledged that looking back is a terrible idea. It only makes going forward that much harder.

"Now that we're done with the kissing," Carver mutters, "we can finally leave."

I flush and adjust my seat, picking up the reins I'd apparently dropped. Griffin gives his younger brother a withering look and then presses his heels to Brown Horse's sides, setting the big animal into motion.

Panotii follows without any direction from me. "I didn't realize *we* were kissing," I tease Carver, trying to take everyone's mind off the people and place we're leaving behind.

Carver grunts. "Gods forbid."

I arch an eyebrow. He's usually such a flirt, although I've never seen him look seriously at any woman, and certainly not at me. "I'm pretty sure I should be offended, although I'm telling myself you're just doing your best to avoid Griffin's rampant jealousy."

Now Griffin grunts.

"I love kissing women," Kato offers. "I'll kiss hundreds of them." He sweeps his hand toward the tiled rooftops of Sinta City. "The whole city."

"That sounds unhygienic," Carver says without humor.

Kato winks at me. "And fun."

I roll my eyes.

Kato tips his blond head toward Carver and tells me in a low voice, "He's just frustrated because he's not using his sword."

I choke a little. Is that a metaphor again?

"We all know I'm the best swordsman around," Carver comments dryly.

I doubt that. My money is on Griffin—unless this really *isn't* a metaphor again. In actual swordplay, Carver just can't be beat.

"It's not only about the sword. It's about knowing how to use it," Flynn remarks sagely.

"And where to stick it," Kato adds, miming a slow, low stab.

Carver finally cracks a smile. He turns and leers at me, but it's not as authentic as usual. "Show me your sword, Cat, and I'll show you mine."

Griffin's eyes glint dangerously, which goes a long way toward restoring Carver's usual good humor.

"You need the practice, Cat. We should cross swords," Carver says.

I ignore him.

"Work on our parries and thrusts."

I ignore him some more.

"There's really only one good way to jab."

I mash my lips together to keep from smiling.

"But there are a lot of ways to perform without actually getting poked."

I burst out laughing. "Good Gods! Are you trying to get yourself killed before we're even five minutes out of the castle?"

Carver grins, his lean face lighting up. He seems to set his unusual moodiness aside for good. Griffin takes the whole thing surprisingly well, and I'm so happy to be away from the confines of the castle that I'll gladly participate in a lewd conversation.

Actually, I'd do that anyway.

Open farmland greets us as we exit the city, ripe crops lending a sweetness to the air that mixes appealingly with the sharper aromas of sun-baked wild thyme and the huge, rambling rosemary bushes lining the road. Olive groves glint in the distance, silvery-green leaves fluttering on the warm breeze. A slender ribbon of water snakes through the squat, solid trunks like a sparkling thread, reflecting the midmorning sun that's already done away with the earlier cloudiness.

I inhale deeply, breathing in the freedom of the road. I can't quite come to terms with living behind stone walls again, with guards, and gates, and people who look to me to make decisions for them.

I wasn't at all hungry at breakfast. My stomach actually cramped at the thought of food, but I'm ravenous now, so I pull an orange from my saddlebag and drop the reins to peel and eat it. Panotii will keep going in a straight line without my largely token involvement in the steering process.

We settle into a familiar rhythm as the day goes on. Kato and Flynn talk from time to time, Carver hums softly, and Griffin and I ride side by side, our mounts keeping stride with one another. We're rarely more than a few feet apart, almost like we're still attached by the magic rope Griffin used when he abducted me.

I glance at Griffin only to find him already watching me. Maybe we are still attached, but the rope has turned intangible, and the magic runs deeper now.

He doesn't turn away. The intensity in his gray gaze makes my cheeks heat, and his low chuckle conveys pure masculine satisfaction that he can still make me blush with only a lingering look.

We reach Ios at sunset. After a quiet meal, Griffin and I take full advantage of having a bed and a closed door because who knows when we'll have that kind of privacy again. From now on, we'll be sticking to the woods and forgoing inns.

In the morning, we visit the healing center site where Eneas and Calla are. The two healers were recently promoted for keeping me alive—Eneas to the head of Ios's new healing center, and Calla to his personal apprentice—although I'm not sure gaining a dusty construction site and a group of petulant healers is any great gift. Griffin instructs Eneas to hire Hoi Polloi medics if Ios's healers still haven't agreed to take their shifts by the time the building is in working condition.

I smile to myself, just imagining the fits of apoplexy when Magoi realize they're being replaced by Hoi Polloi. Good Hoi Polloi medics have decent skills. Magoi healers can cure just about anything, but if they're too pompous and prejudiced to treat nine-tenths of the people who need attention, they deserve a far worse fate than just getting bumped out of their traditional role.

Times are changing. I have a feeling they'll come around. Eventually. And if they don't, I'll come back here and make them.

CHAPTER 8

SHIFTING IN HIS SADDLE, GRIFFIN DIPS HIS HEAD TOWARD mine. "Something is following us."

My eyes widen, meeting his. At the sudden tension coursing through my body, Panotii's ears twitch.

Griffin puts his hand on my shoulder to keep me from turning around. "Three wolf-like creatures. Enormous. They've been there on and off all day."

"Their eyes glow," Flynn adds softly. He's on my left. Griffin is on my right. They box me in, squashing my legs.

"Am I the only one who didn't know about this?" I ask from between gritted teeth.

Griffin doesn't answer, which is answer enough.

"Why didn't you tell me?"

He doesn't look over at me again. His sharp eyes scan the forest ahead and to the sides. "I didn't want to worry you before I was sure."

I guess he's sure now. *Fabulous.*

We're deep in the vast, uninhabited woods of northern Tarva. Lichen and moss crawl over boulders and fallen logs, cushioning the forest in deep greens, russets, and orange. Long, ghostly tendrils of mist slide like exploring fingers around towering tree trunks and loop over gnarled branches, cooling and dampening the air. The dense canopy is so thick and thriving it shades everything and swallows all sound.

A moment ago, I was soaking up the freshness, glad for the shadows and feeling my magic spark. Now I shiver.

I'm not cold, although the air is cooler here, this far to the north. It's the sudden sense of foreboding that feels like ice melting down the back of my neck.

Griffin's heavy hand is still on my shoulder. "What do you think they are?"

"How am I supposed to know? You won't let me turn around and look."

Griffin gives my shoulder a warning squeeze before removing his hand. "Right now, they're not far behind, and a little to the left."

I draw two knives, leaving Panotii to steer himself. "My left now? Or my left when I turn around?"

"Your left now."

"So my right."

Griffin shoots me a sidelong glance. "This isn't funny, Cat."

"It never is." We're close enough to the Ice Plains now that magical creatures might wander down from the north, looking for food—or fun. Neither option is good for us.

I turn around, focusing on Kato first. He looks shaggy, disreputable, and incredibly handsome. His bright cobalt eyes stand out like jewels in his tanned face. "You're looking rather uncivilized. Did you lose your razor somewhere?" I let my eyes slide to the right and search for movement amid the trees.

Kato scrubs his hand over the thick coating of whiskers on his jaw. Then his arm drops, and his long fingers curl around the handle of the mace lying in his lap. "The beard keeps my face warm. Interesting development with your hair, by the way," he comments back, giving me a reason to stay turned around. "You can borrow my comb."

"Thanks, but I'd probably break it." There's a springy, dark frame all around my face. The dry season is officially over. "It's my Medusa look, minus the snakes."

Quietly scoffing, Kato lifts his weapon to rest it against his shoulder. "I doubt you'll be turning men to stone anytime soon."

"Good to know," I murmur distractedly, catching a flash of gray fur, a distended, barrel-like body, and four thick legs.

Carver rolls his shoulders, warming them up. Flynn draws his ax and the short sword he's taken to carrying as the creature melts back into the woods.

"Thoughts?" Griffin asks.

A pair of blazing eyes materializes from the shadows. Then another. And another.

Bollocks! They know I've seen them. They aren't trying to be discreet anymore.

They approach, and their new proximity brings a prickle of power to my searching senses. The sinister vibrations of magic weaving through the forest along with them sweep over me like a harsh, dry wind. I tense. The power emanating from the creatures is the kind of stuff I wouldn't touch in a million years, a darkness so deep and hungry that no one who gets sucked into it ever crawls back out again.

Suppressing a shudder, I turn back around, but not before something instinctive within me pulses, probing deeper into the dark magic. A yawning pit of immorality overlaps the creatures' own disturbing presence. The familiar essence haunted my childhood and makes my blood run cold now.

Mother's here.

A hard knot forms beneath my ribs, and suddenly I can't breathe. My eyes find Griffin's. She'll rip apart everyone I love—and laugh while she's doing it.

Griffin's eyes widen. I must look as terrified as I feel.

Pressure builds behind my forehead, and then a low, eerie ripple of a voice invades my mind. *"Coming home, Talia?"*

Gasping, I slam down my mental shields so hard and fast that my head goes numb, and I see spots. I hope Mother's brain rings for an hour.

"Talk to me, Cat." Griffin's concerned voice seems to come to me from miles, and seasons, and lifetimes away. "What just happened?"

"Alpha Fisa." I blink, trying to clear my head. "Andromeda is driving the creatures." I tighten my grip around my knives because I don't want Griffin to see my hands shake. How can Mother possibly drive three creatures at once *and* have enough power left over to get into my head?

Griffin eases Brown Horse even closer to Panotii, and the two horses move like they're one.

Swallowing hard, I rub my thumbs over the handles of my knives, warming the metal. Mother thinks she's above everyone. She confuses might with right. Strike that—all she cares about is might. And like the strongest, most vicious animal around, she plays with her prey, wanting to see it cower and sweat.

"I doubt they'll attack unless we make a move. At least not yet. She's just toying with us for now and gathering information, which some creature or other has probably been doing for days," I add bitterly, clenching my knives until my hands hurt. "We didn't hide my blood. What we did that morning Daphne stabbed me—none of it was enough." I almost died trying to dilute the evidence of my heritage in the bathhouse pool. I poured lemon juice all over a gaping wound, and Andromeda *still* found me. Talk about a failure of epic proportions. She knows I'm alive. She knows where I am. She knows where I came from, and there's a very good chance she knows who I'm with. Everything I didn't want.

Carver unsheathes his sword and lays it across his lap. "We were on an open road for days. Nothing followed us from home. We would have known."

"*Something* followed, probably from the air. This is the second wave, and I'll bet they came from the opposite direction." From the Ice Plains above Fisa, where Mother latched on to them like a leech and then sent them to do her bidding.

"You're a threat to her. To her throne. Why is she so Gods damned bent on getting you back?" Griffin asks in a low growl.

I shrug, the casual movement belying the sharp twisting in my gut. "I don't know. It's an obsession I can't even begin to understand. All I know is that if she gets her hands on me, she'll drag me back to Fisa for fifty years of fun and torture. She's evil and insane."

"I won't let her touch you," Griffin says.

He sounds so sure. I look at him, and my heart starts to ache, the pain physical and overwhelming. This is exactly what I didn't want, what terrified me and drove me to push Griffin away for as long as I could—Mother going through him to get to me.

"Is this like with the She-Dragon?" Flynn asks softly. "Some kind of long-distance compulsion?"

I nod, answering in equally quiet tones, despite the harsh drumming of my pulse. "Alpha Fisa gets a relayed impression of what the creatures see—five riders, the woods, our general location. Words are more direct. She can hear through them just like with Sybaris, and speak through them if they're capable of speech. To try to control three creatures at once is risky, especially ones this powerful and malevolent. My read on their magic is that they're incredibly sentient, yet at the same time…empty." I shake my head. "I don't understand exactly. It's like there's something missing."

Griffin pulls a long, straight dagger from his boot and holds it in the same hand as his reins. His other hand carries his sword. "Can you break her hold?"

"I couldn't with Sybaris. And I can't handle three. If I somehow break her hold and then can't control them myself, they'll attack on their own anyway."

I glance back. I'll always refuse to use compulsion on humans, but I really need to gain some control over creatures if Mother is going to keep throwing them at us.

The wolf-like things are closer now, weaving between the trees with no thought to keeping hidden anymore. The yellow glow of their eyes intensifies with each loping step.

I shiver. I don't know what they are. "We can't let them keep following us and hearing half of what we say. We should make a stand."

Griffin nods in agreement just as we emerge into a large clearing, seeing our first direct sunlight in hours. A field ripples before us, mostly flat. No cover—for us or them.

"Don't forget that nothing is ever what it seems this close to the Ice Plains," I remind everyone. Then I turn to Griffin, a bad feeling kicking around inside of me. "I love you."

Griffin scowls. He looks like I just punched him in the gut. "Fight. You *fight*. You can tell me you love me when it's over."

I nod. "When it's over." A heartbeat later, I slip my feet from my stirrups, swing my right leg over Panotii's neck, and then slide to the ground. I land facing the creatures, leaving my horse to continue on.

The monsters stop. And they really are monstrous. A menacing frill of gray-black fur rises along each of their spines from the base of their oversized necks to the tips of their curving, whiplike tails. I don't like the look of this. Knowing Mother is behind it makes it even worse.

"Cat!" Griffin wheels Brown Horse around. Panotii swings back toward me like he's tethered to them.

"Stay back!" I throw out my arms as if that could somehow keep four seasoned warriors from charging into the fray.

"Dismount," Griffin barks. "They're too low to fight on horseback."

"Which part of 'stay back' did you not understand?" I snap.

Like a big, predatory panther, Griffin drops down next to me. He sends his mount to the far side of the clearing with a shove on Brown Horse's rump, and Panotii follows like a sheep. "The part where you fight alone," Griffin snaps back.

I glare at him, but really, what did I expect? "I'm going to incinerate them."

Stone-faced, he says, "Be my guest."

I focus on the wolf-things again, and that sense of foreboding deepens, scraping through me like a sawing in my bones. Their legs and paws are massive, but their bodies are still too big for them, huge and barrel-like, with almost no shape, just mass. They could flatten me in seconds and then rip out my throat.

Good thing I have Dragon's Breath.

The lead creature bares its fangs in a warped smile, revealing splotched gums and razor-sharp teeth. I'd recognize that expression anywhere.

My mouth twists into a smile that's probably just as awful. "It was nice seeing you, Mother. But, really, you didn't need to send gifts."

The monster growls. Mother never did like my sarcasm.

Once the creatures are far enough from the trees—I don't want to burn the forest, and us, along with them—I draw in a deep breath. Magic leaps from the well of power inside me, ready and eager. It sizzles through my veins and then pours from my mouth in a crackling inferno. The torrent of flames blisters the grass between the creatures and me, slamming into them with enough force to lift them off their feet. *Ha!*

But instead of melting into piles of sludge and bone, they snarl and gouge their claws into the scorched ground, crouching low as the lethal firestorm boils over them.

I slam my mouth shut on the Dragon's Breath. They burn, and yet they *don't.*

The monster in the back spins and races for the woods. My heart lurching, I throw my two knives in quick succession, afraid of what will happen if it reaches the trees.

My blades land where the creature's neck meets its shoulder. It skids to a stop at the tree line and howls. The sound isn't one of pain, and it makes my hair stand on end. Dread shivers through me. Gleaming yellow eyes lock on mine, and in that instant, I know Mother lost control.

The flaming monster pivots and smashes into the nearest tree. The dark bark sparks and glows, catching fire. Red and orange lick higher, crawling up the ancient tree trunk and then exploding through the dense canopy above. The sudden roar is deafening. Cracking wood. Pulsing air. The rush of fire through healthy green leaves. The hottest, most dangerous magical flames known to man snap through the forest like twisting acrobats. Within seconds, the entire far side of the clearing goes up in a pounding blaze.

I gasp, and Dragon's Breath explodes from my mouth like someone reached down my throat and ripped it all out. Pain sears my insides. I clamp down and wrap my arms around my middle, but it's too late. My Dragon's Breath is gone, and the destruction in front of me turns into total devastation.

I stumble back and bump into Griffin. My mouth tastes of ash. My throat burns, and an acrid exhalation is all that's left of the greatest weapon I've ever possessed.

Griffin steadies me. "What happened?"

"I don't know." I swallow, my throat so raw it hurts. "It feels like my guts were pulled out. I lost the magic."

Mother's creatures don't move. They seem to be waiting. Watching. *Did she get control back?* Everything burns around them, red-hot and glowing. Flames jump from tree to tree, moving up our sides as Dragon's Breath attacks the woods around the clearing. High above, branches pop. The trees whoosh and whirl. Everything is red, yellow, and orange, and my eyes are so huge they burn along with the forest.

"I have to stop it!" I try to latch back on to the magic as my lungs fill with heat and smoke. Nothing happens. It *ignores* me.

"Leave it!" Griffin shouts. "Let's go!"

I shake my head and concentrate, blocking Griffin out. Finally, after what feels like a dozen ground-down teeth and three buckets of sweat, a smoldering bough groans, and its flames dip toward me. I pull harder, willing my fire back from wood and leaves and burning space. I can steal magic. I can take it from a person. If I'm close enough, I can grab it out of thin air.

The strain is tremendous. My ears start to ring, and the heat is like a constant punch in the face. Dragon's Breath continues to devour the treetops, and the fire I caught doesn't complete its arc to me. The magic isn't obeying me. *At. All.*

On my left, Flynn suddenly slams into Carver, shoving him hard seconds before a flaming branch hits the ground where Carver just stood. The fallen bough erupts in a shower of sparks, catching Flynn's pants on fire.

I drop to my knees and smother the fire with my bare hands. There's the initial, searing pain of the burn, and then my body reclaims the Dragon's Breath and heals. Small dose. Direct contact. Easy, if painful.

Flynn's pants are in tatters. His skin is an angry red, and there are blisters around his knees.

Grim-faced, he hauls me to my feet. "That's the third time you've kept me from burning."

I dart a look around the clearing, fear choking me like the fire. "Don't speak too soon."

Grunting in answer, Flynn tosses me at Griffin, who grabs my wrist and yanks.

"Run! Now!" Griffin barks over the raging inferno.

Mother's creatures still haven't fled, like they don't fear the fire. I stumble after Griffin as he hauls me toward the horses. Panotii's eyes roll so wildly I see more white than brown. He tosses his head, yanking at the grip Kato has on his reins.

I glance over my shoulder. My face hurts. My lungs feel scorched. "We can't outrun this. It's Dragon's Breath. It won't stop until there's nothing left to burn." I pull on my wrist. "I have to stop it. I can!"

Griffin abruptly swings around, and we nearly collide. A flickering bronze, his eyes reflect the firelight. A muscle jerks in his jaw, but he releases his hold on me.

Turning, I fling both hands into the air with a shout I can barely hear over the bellow of the fire, my fingers outstretched and reaching for the magic. I pull so hard that flames rush down and engulf my arms. The shot of agony shakes loose my hold on most of what I've gathered, and the time to reclaim the magic, heal from the burn, and then adjust to the surge of power costs me the initial battle.

My stomach drops. Calling the fire back to me won't work. There's too much, and it's too powerful. But I think I know what to do now—even if I don't like it.

"Keep back!" I shout as I catch more flames with a ferocious mental yank and then slam them into the barren dirt where there's nothing left to burn. The fire writhes, a living thing, searching the charred grass for something to consume. Finding nothing, it burns itself out.

Grimly satisfied with my method, even if it means losing the magic, I do it again, and again, until I'm shaking with fatigue. Choking black smoke rolls over me. I drag more fire from the trees, piercing the growing darkness with glowing streaks and riddling the clearing with craters. The scene is apocalyptic. There's not enough air.

I don't take my eyes off the firestorm. If I can just concentrate hard enough, be strong enough, the magic *will* obey me. It has to.

A powerful arm bands around my middle, and Griffin drags me backward. I dig in my heels, and my boots leave twin scars as they scrape through the ash. Flames snap boldly, and I lose another tree to the fire.

"We're almost boxed in," Griffin shouts, his voice hoarse from smoke. "It's over!"

"We'll never outrun it!" I cry. "You're wasting time!"

"There *is* no time." Beads of sweat roll down his temples and trace the line of his jaw, leaving streaks in the soot. Magic and nature's grim war paint.

As if hearing us and reacting, a twisting rope of flame leaps through the air and ignites the trees behind the horses. Like a door slamming shut, an impenetrable wall rises with a roar, blocking our only exit.

I stare in shock. Fear is a terrible emotion. It strips away hope and leaves a gaping hole.

Griffin curses and loosens his hold. "You're stronger than this." He turns me toward him with sudden ferocity, the terrifying beauty of the fire reflected in his somber gaze. "You're better. You can do anything you set your mind to."

I swallow, my throat painfully dry. If it were just me, I wonder how hard I'd fight, what extremes I'd go to to survive. But it isn't just me, and extremes don't even come close to what I'd do to protect the people I love.

I take Griffin's hand. Energy and vitality pulse where our palms meet, and I squeeze. Strength leaps from the point of contact and thunders through my veins. I know in my gut that I have enough of the power of the Gods in me to bend nearly anything to my will, even this rogue, reactive magic that's burning out of control.

My concentration doesn't falter again, and sheer mental determination pours from me in an almost tangible wave. Little by little, I force the Dragon's Breath out of the trees and into the ground. The long struggle leaves my brain throbbing and my body weak. The world around me blurs into a rust color. Something warm and wet leaks from my eyes. More drips from my nose.

I bow my head and grit my teeth, tasting blood on my lips. Kato materializes on my other side and takes my free hand. I hold on to both men hard enough to feel their bones grind. My knees nearly buckle under the agonizing pressure, but bit by bit, the magic implodes at my feet. The heat lessens. The roar diminishes, and my brain stops feeling like it's being hammered with a burning rock.

At last, the final flames burn themselves to death in a smoking crater, leaving leafless, lifeless trees standing like charred sentinels all around the clearing and as far as I can see. I collapse to my knees, swaying. Liquid, dense and soupy, swims in my eyes. The fire is out, but everything is still red and yellow.

"Is it over?" I croak.

"You did it." Griffin drops down next to me. "I knew you could."

I snort. Sort of. "You tried to drag me away."

"It seemed like the best choice at the time." He takes my face in his hands and then sweeps his thumbs under my eyes. His fingers come away with my blood on them, but it's not just red. It's red veined with shimmering rivulets of gold.

"What is this?" Griffin asks.

I stare, too exhausted to feel much emotion. "Ichor." It's never been visible before. Sometimes, I wondered if it was really there.

"Blood like the Gods," Griffin says quietly, awe in his smoke-roughened voice.

"Diluted." *Unfortunately.*

My body feels like honey straight from the beehive— thick and slow. The more I try to move, the heavier it gets. I close my eyes, and a great void rushes up to meet me.

Griffin catches me against his front as I tip over, utterly beyond caring that my cheek is pressed against hard leather, or that I'm smearing it with the blood of Olympus.

"Tired..." Dimness wraps me up like dusk enfolding the day. The small amount of Dragon's Breath I reclaimed doesn't sit well inside me. I don't want it anymore when I think about what almost happened. Griffin and I would have suffocated. Carver, Flynn, and Kato would have burned. My brave Panotii would have died.

A violent series of coughs makes it impossible to drift

off to sleep like I want to—and to breathe. "This was my fault," I finally wheeze.

Griffin lifts my hand to his lips. "No. You saved us."

An ache spreads through my chest that has nothing to do with smoke and ash. "I don't know what happened." Griffin blurs before me. I blink, but my eyes slide out of focus again.

"Get up. Now." Carver's terse command is like a thunderbolt to my veins, flooding them with adrenaline. I turn. *Oh, no.*

"Hades, Hera, and Hestia," Flynn murmurs, drawing his ax again as well as his sword.

Kato mutters a more violent oath as he and Flynn take up positions next to Carver, forming a wall in front of Griffin and me.

"Up!" Griffin says sharply, hauling me to my feet.

Low vibrations skim my ears, deep with menace. I grab Griffin's arm for balance because my legs aren't ready for this. No part of me is ready for this.

Mother's beasts are alive. Growling. Moving. A few canine shakes send their fire-blackened pelts flying. Tattoos cover the mottled skin underneath, running up and down their drum-shaped bodies in vertical lines. The ink extends down their legs to paint their enormous, razor-clawed paws.

The sight of the primitive, powerful symbols jolts into me with the force of a physical blow. I reel back, and only Griffin's hand on my upper arm keeps me from falling over. I'm no expert in the archaic language of wards. I don't know all the symbols, or even how to put most of them together, but I recognize the ones for lock and fire well enough. Thanos taught me how to bar my door against my brother, although I never did it right. Wards always mutated things when I tried to use them, made my magic—

"Son of a Cyclops!"

Griffin looks at me.

"Impossible," I breathe. Except, not really. My magic backfired on me every time. "Mother saw me steal the Dragon's Breath from Sybaris. She warded her creatures against it, and wards always corrupt my magic. That's why the fire turned on me."

Griffin's big body coils tight, ready to shield me from anything. "That's possible?" he asks.

"Apparently. I've never heard of it happening to anyone else. I'm special, I guess."

He grunts. I guess he agrees.

The lead wolf flashes its fangs, and I pull away from Griffin to stand on my own, drawing two knives from my belt. I can't afford to be weak. Not now. Not ever.

But my head still swims, and my vision isn't quite right. My grip around my knives feels foreign and feeble. Blood drips onto my upper lip, and I wipe the back of my hand under my nose, my blade glinting dully. In the red streak, I see only the faintest shimmer of gold.

How I envy my Olympian ancestors their near inde-structibleness. I'm so destructible that I have no idea how I'm even going to throw a knife in this fight.

CHAPTER 9

KATO THROWS TWO KNIVES. BOTH LAND IN THE LEAD creature's chest. Without even a flinch, it bares yellowed fangs and leaps at him from eight feet away.

Kato pivots and kicks, snapping his leg to catch the catapulting wolf in the head. It thuds into the even larger creature charging alongside it, and the two beasts hit the ground together, rolling and snarling in a tangle.

The third creature lunges for Carver. In a lightning-fast move, Carver springs to the side and slices it from shoulder to tail. The gash runs the length of the monster's body, deep enough to reveal flashes of bone. It skids to a stop, crouching low on its front legs with a growl. Raised skin sweeps down its spine, puckering where its fur should be.

The savagery in the creature's eyes makes my head spin. The wound Carver inflicted closes within seconds, leaving the pseudo wolf's side smeared with a black liquid thicker than blood. A putrid odor hits my nose, and I shrink back from the awful smell.

Carver attacks, and while the creature is distracted, Flynn rushes in and sinks his short sword nearly to the hilt in its barrel-like chest. The deep thrust must have gone through something vital, but the injury doesn't even slow it down. Utterly unfazed, the creature pushes, working its way *up* the blade to get its jaws closer to Flynn's throat. Black liquid oozes from the new wound, carrying more of the rotten stench. Flynn's arm muscles bulge as he grips his sword and leans away.

"Decapitate! Decapitate!" I shout. Decapitation is the one way to kill just about anything, even a God.

Carver's blade flashes, but the other two beasts attack. Every last one of us shouts a warning, and he whirls, swinging out of instinct and hitting the massive body leaping through the air. He severs both front feet from the creature's body and then ducks as it sails over his head, dripping noxious fluids from the severed stumps.

Kato deflects the third wolf with a swing that should have crushed its skull. It somehow evades, taking the bone-crunching head of Kato's mace on the shoulder instead. Short metal spikes rip through sallow skin, and the fetid odor intensifies. We all gag as if punched in the throat by it. I cover my mouth and nose and look at Griffin. His eyes water. Other than that, he's perfectly still, watchful, but I can tell he's twitching on the inside, torn between jumping into the fight and standing guard over me.

With a nightmarish howl, the downed wolf springs back onto *all four feet* and charges Carver again.

Good Gods. Regeneration.

Griffin's large hand splays across my chest, and he pushes me behind him.

"It grew back its feet!" Carver fends off a ferocious attack, his blade whip-fast.

Kato pulls out another knife as he and the third creature circle in a wary dance. He throws well from the right now, but he's rarely accurate with his left hand. He'll only be able to use the dagger or his mace in close quarters, and I don't want the wolf-abomination getting that close to him again.

I step to the side of Griffin and take aim. My tired arm locks as the muscles near my shoulder catch in a painful spasm. I don't have a consistent clear line with Kato between the creature and me, and for the first time in years, I'm not confident I'll hit my mark.

Gingerly, I lower my arm. "Griffin. You do it."

He switches his sword to his left hand and then unsheathes his only short blade. His throw is beautiful, steady and strong. The knife sticks between the wolf's eyes.

The beast swings feral, glowing eyes on us and laughs. It's grating and animalistic, but I could swear it laughs.

Flynn utters a strained grunt. The creature has wormed its way so far up his blade it's almost on top of him now.

Griffin starts forward, but Carver whirls out of his confrontation and, with one sharp, downward slash, tries to sever the impaled wolf's head from its body. The beast jerks back at the last possible second, pushing on powerful forelegs to slide off Flynn's blade. The two swords meet with a jarring, metallic clang. There's the high-pitched, scraping ring of steel on steel as Carver twists back around, leaving Flynn to deal with the beast that just slipped from his blade.

With a fiendish growl, the monster races past Flynn and heads straight for Griffin and me. The one Kato was keeping at bay takes its cue from the other and darts around the blond warrior. The two hairless creatures converge, and my pulse hammers as they barrel toward us.

Griffin's sword crashes into the underside of the closest wolf's neck and sticks, not severing it. His shoulders tense, and it takes a powerful yank to get his weapon free. The creature readies for another attack almost immediately, alarmingly unaffected by the damage Griffin inflicted.

The second creature circles wide to avoid Griffin and then jumps on me. Its massive front paws slam into my leather-clad chest, shoving me back. I cross my daggers and push, catching the base of the monster's elongated jaw between the blades. My arms shake as I work the knives into the softer skin of the neck. Inches away, the beast's saliva-strung mouth opens, and its stinking exhale breaks like a rancid wave over my face.

Balanced on its hind legs, the wolf's front claws scrape at my chest. Only the thick boar's-hide armor saves me from a mauling. Slowly, my knives sink through skin, muscle, and sinew. Black liquid smears my fingers. An overwhelming stench inhabits my nose, coating my senses. My stomach heaves, and I nearly retch.

"Cat!"

Out of the corner of my eye, I see Griffin frantically hacking at a beast that *just won't die.*

"I thought she wanted you alive!" he shouts.

"She does!" I think. The state I'm in when she gets me has never concerned her, though.

My worn-out muscles can't take the beast's weight for much longer. I want to slam my foot into its rear leg joint and hope it crumples, but I don't dare shift my balance. My legs are locked, and that's the only thing keeping me upright.

"Carver!" Griffin's shout is smoke-ravaged and panicked. "Carver! Get Cat!"

Carver tries. Everyone tries, but the third wolf, the biggest and most ferocious of the three, is between Beta Team and us. It wheels and snarls and lunges, keeping them away. Every move one of them makes toward us is countered by an even quicker, more vicious attack from the beast.

My body has already burned up the last of its reserves. Heat crawls up my spine. A chill slides back down. A numbing weight presses on me, and as if the world took a step forward and left me standing there alone, sound and sensation fade, growing distant.

My back cramps, snapping my consciousness back into

place with a ribbon of pain that races from my waist to my neck. I jerk, and the jagged claws of one paw scrape off my leather breastplate and slice into my armpit. The sting is heinous. I cry out, reflexively pulling my arms down.

In the next second, I'm on my back. My head cracks against the ground, and bright spots explode behind my eyes. I blink, dazed. The creature is over me, its front paws planted on my shoulders and the air punched from my lungs.

Griffin's anguished roar overlaps the wolf's triumphant howl. A violent shudder runs the length of the creature's deformed body. Its face twists and pops, moving like there's something alive and churning beneath the skin. The monster turns into a living nightmare before my eyes, and I finally understand what we're dealing with.

No wonder injuries don't affect them, their breath smells of decay, and their skin is the yellow-gray of death. I should have known.

The canine snout, ears, and fangs melt, turning malleable and unrecognizable before sharpening into human-like features. Leathery skin pulls tight over harshly angled cheek and jawbones. The eyes don't change. They're still glowing and soulless.

The heavy paws crushing my shoulders morph into a man's enormous hands and grab my wrists. Muscles and bones in the creature's ropy forearms snap into place and weigh painfully on my bent arms, grinding my elbows into the dirt. The torso transforms, narrowing, and then the hind legs trapping mine become thick thighs, calves, and feet. Every part of the monster is hairless and tough, massive and muscled. The Vrykolakas lowers its face to my neck and inhales deeply.

I shudder. *The living dead. The wolf-men Charon*

won't ferry into the Underworld for any price, leaving them here instead.

The undead creature's entire body drops heavily onto mine. Its unnatural eyes flare brightly as it sniffs once more and then groans a guttural sound that sends a bolt of sheer terror through me. Fear and revulsion spur me into action as the creature grinds what can only be a male erection against the juncture of my thighs.

My thrashing only seems to excite it more, and it ruthlessly rams its swollen member against my groin. "She said *alive*, Princess. All she said was alive."

I jerk my head up, catching it on the side of its chin. I can't move, and that's as high as I can reach. I'm pinned, powerless, and deeply afraid.

The Vrykolakas bites its lower lip with a still lethally sharp incisor, drops its head, and then smears its disgusting blood across my mouth. Griffin shouts my name. I twist away, gagging.

"Fight me. Yes, fight." It breathes in quick, harsh pants against my neck as it switches my wrists into one hand and then shoves its other hand between us, getting up under my tunic to grip the fastening of my pants.

A hollow feeling carves a hole in my chest. It can't end like this.

"Don't let it do this, Mother." A pleading note slips into my voice, and I hate myself a little more for it. I didn't kill her. I didn't kill her all those years ago, and she sends me *this*?

The undead creature barks a canine laugh that mixes with Griffin's wild shouting. "Mother lost control. But I'll still sell you for a mountain of gold."

The Vrykolakas lowers its head and licks my neck, its tongue dry and scraping. Panic spikes impossibly higher when pointed teeth scrape down the column of my throat, pausing over my thundering vein. The creature shudders, grating a harsh sound against my skin. "You're worth a lot, or I'd drink you dry while I rut."

Claws score my stomach and fold viciously inward, ripping open my pants. I scream as the Vrykolakas tears the barrier away. Fear and rage blister through me. I see no way out of this.

Griffin suddenly smashes into the creature's body like a charging Centaur, throwing the monster off me. They both pitch over and tumble to the side. Griffin rolls to his feet first, his face a nearly unrecognizable mask of fury. He lands a punishing kick to the creature's rib cage, flipping it onto its back. Before the Vrykolakas can move, Griffin's sword spirals in a tight, deadly arc and severs its head from its body. Leathery skin collapses onto bones, desiccating within seconds.

The monster Griffin was fighting before he came to my rescue surges over me and then leaps on top of him, knocking him to the ground. Griffin twists, but the creature is still in wolf-form and weighs more than he does. It pins him in the ash, its jaws descending with brutal force.

"No!" My heart vaults straight up my throat.

Griffin shields his neck with his forearm, and the Vrykolakas's teeth latch around his vambrace. I thank the Gods the leather is thick, tough, and boiled into near solidity as the creature snarls and shakes its head, whipping Griffin's arm around.

I stagger to my feet, lift my arms, and plunge both the daggers I still hold into its back. The jolt up my arms tells me I hit the spine. The creature releases Griffin's arm long enough to snap at me, and I reel back, narrowly avoiding a vicious bite.

I look to the others for help, but it's pandemonium across the clearing. One huge creature, the most terrifying of the three, takes hit after hit, keeping its neck out of reach and making it impossible for anyone to get past.

There's no time for weapons, and they don't work anyway. Snarling, I throw my weight forward and ram my hands into the beast's side, frantic because I don't have a chance in the Underworld of saving Griffin like he saved me. He sacrificed himself for me, and I will *never* forgive him.

Lightning leaps down my arms and shoots from my hands with a deafening crack. The twin thunderbolts throw the creature off Griffin and puncture two smoking holes in its side, destroying the wards. It lands with a pained yip and then tries to stand up again—and fails.

It's not healing! Hope rises in my chest. I hold out my hands, willing more lightning to come. I extend my fingers. Shake my arms. Nothing happens.

Griffin regains his feet, disheveled and dirty but miraculously intact. He places one large, warm hand on my lower back. "You can do this," he encourages quietly, although there's steel in his voice.

I try. I really do. The magic just won't come. Something inside me feels off. "Gods damn it!" I explode. "The wards must be doing something again."

"It worked before," Griffin points out. "And the wards were intact."

I shake my head. "I don't understand, then."

"We'll practice." He raises his sword, stalking forward as the creature snaps, twists, and shudders into an approximation of a man, two holes still punched through its oozing side. The Vrykolakas looks at Griffin with defiant yellow eyes. This is a being that even Death won't claim. It has no mercy—and it expects none.

Griffin takes the monster's head, and the undead creature shrivels, leaving behind parchment-dry skin clinging to distorted bones in a sickening parody of humanity.

"Talia!" Mother's voice is a guttural snarl in the final creature's mouth. With just one Vrykolakas left, I have no doubt she's back in control and fully aware of everything that's happened here.

The creature sheds its wolf shape, standing on two legs but keeping the elongated arms, razor-sharp claws, and lethal fangs that continue to hold Kato, Flynn, and Carver at bay. Even in this grotesque half-form, the monster is so huge that it makes three of the biggest men I know look small.

I draw my sword and charge the Vrykolakas in a blind rage, ignoring Griffin's startled shout.

"How could you!" It turns toward me, and I slice the monster's middle, cutting deep enough for rotting intestines to spill out. "How could you do this to me?"

"Talia! Enough!" The creature twitches angrily but doesn't attack.

I swing again, slashing at its throat. It dodges and then just barely misses clawing Carver, who slices the tendons behind the creature's knees from behind. It drops, and Flynn darts in, his ax whistling toward the monster's neck.

The Vrykolakas somehow avoids Flynn's attack. Hissing in fury—or maybe that's Mother—it grows dark claws the size of daggers, wielding them so fast they ping and hum. Carver drops, twists with athletic grace, and then slices from underneath, severing one of the creature's hands before rolling back to his feet. Kato lunges forward, his mace thundering down just as a pulse of blinding green light sends all three of them flying across the clearing. They land sprawled on their backs, stunned.

I lurch when the surge of power ricochets back to me from off the blackened trees. *What is that? She's...telekinetic? From a distance!* I had no idea Mother could channel physical magic through creatures. I didn't even know that was possible, which fills me with an even deeper rage.

"I hate you!" I chop furiously at the Vrykolakas, my hits wild and reckless, made up of impulse, and chaos, and wrath. They open the creature's torso over and over, so the wounds don't have time to heal before I inflict another. This is retribution. Torture, maybe. And I don't care.

I feel Griffin's strong, steady presence right behind me, but it does nothing to calm my savagery. And he does nothing to stop me. The creature evades anything lethal but still doesn't attack. Mother has never wanted me dead. Sometimes I wish she had. Maybe Eleni was the lucky one, ending up in the Underworld instead of beaten, terrorized, and nearly raped. I shake, pitch-black emotion pounding through me.

The undead creature's hand and claws grow back. Black fluid seeps from its open wounds. Needing both hands to lift my sword now, I throw my weight into yet another attack. My body wants to quit on me. It needs to stop, but I keep swinging because the devastation inside of me hasn't even begun to run its course. Was I really stupid enough to hold on to some idiotic morsel of hope that Mother would look at me one day and see a person, a daughter, instead of a vessel to use and mold for her own nefarious gain?

I wipe my forearm across my face, clearing my eyes of splattered blood. Then I slash and hack, knowing that Griffin is watching my back, likely my front, too, and letting me burn through my rage.

Mother knew exactly what kind of monster she was dealing with. She knew that sending three of them at once was a risk, especially from a distance, and that she could lose control. And she knew better than anyone that I never practiced compulsion or creature driving, and that I had no hope of controlling one, let alone three.

Yet here they are. And there I was...

"What are you waiting for?" I cry. "What do you want?"

"For you to cease your temper tantrum," Mother answers. "It's unbecoming."

Temper tantrum? Unbecoming!

"You. Are. A. Monster!" With every word, I carve a deeper gash across the Vrykolakas's chest. Its stinking blood nauseates me, but I don't stop, blind to the gore, insensible to anything but my twisting emotions, my hammering hate.

"Your fits have always been a waste of my time," Mother says. "And now you're wearing men's rags and trolling the Sintan swamps for companions when you could be draped in Fisan pearls and associating with Magoi worthy of our line." The creature's chin jerks toward Griffin. "He pollutes you every time he touches you. Don't think I don't know where he's been, and how it's changed you. Your blood is different."

Ichor—visible for the first time in my life. Did Griffin somehow do that? I'd hardly call that pollution. More like power.

Pointed canines flash in a snarl. "A gutter rat plowing a future queen."

A gutter rat? Griffin? She sends soulless, undead creatures to hunt down her own daughter, and yet she still believes she's the superior person in all this?

Something violent and out of control breaks loose inside of me. I drop my sword and tear into the Vrykolakas with my bare hands, sinking up to my elbows in order to yank out its festering guts. I slap them in its face—*her* face—grinding and watching them smoke as my hands heat with a God-like power I can't seem to control. I scream. I scream, and I keep screaming. I can't stop.

Griffin bands an arm around my waist and lifts me back. I twist, kicking and shouting, spraying everything around me with black sludge. I smell like death, but I don't care. I'm beyond caring. I want to rip my mother apart like I should have done years ago, even if it's not really her, and she doesn't really feel it.

Griffin sets me down next to him. Low and furious, he grates out, "Don't talk to Cat. Don't come near her. Ever."

The Vrykolakas is still standing—and healing—proving it's really hard to kill something that's already dead. The monster takes a menacing step forward, Mother sneering "Filthy Hoi Polloi usurper," in guttural tones from its mouth.

A concentrated line of translucent green, fast and strong, slams into Griffin's chest. My heart takes a sickening dive, but he doesn't even flinch. A circular hole gapes in his leather armor. The skin underneath is perfectly intact. Relieved, I thank the Gods for Griffin's total immunity to harmful magic.

"What sorcery is this?" Andromeda demands.

"The kind that ends you," Griffin says, his voice lethally soft.

The creature's glowing eyes narrow to slits. Neither Griffin nor I move, not giving away the men sneaking up on the Vrykolakas's back. Andromeda must have thought our friends would be laid out longer by her hit. She underestimates them. She underestimates us all, and maybe the fact that I've claimed these men as my family offers them some kind of protection, some small portion of the natural resilience alive in my Olympian blood.

With predatory silence, Carver swings his sword, beheading the Vrykolakas in one clean sweep. Mother's magic implodes from the clearing like a reverse breath, pulling the air from my lungs.

I stagger, and Griffin steadies me by drawing me against him. He holds me tight. I stifle a sob, knowing that when that stupid, irrational ember of hope I never should have kept burning for Mother died like a spark under a careless boot, it snuffed a certain part of me out of existence right along with it. Any lingering naïveté—lost.

"Are you all right?" Griffin's grip is almost painful, leaving me airless, but that's okay because his warm, solid body is still there for me to be crushed and breathless against.

I drop my forehead against his chest. "I love you. I love you. I love you." It's the only thing keeping me sane. Without him, I would shatter.

Holding me, Griffin presses his lips hard against my hair. "I love you, too. I love you forever." His words warm the top of my head. My heart. My everything. I want to crawl on top of him, into him, where I'm safe and treasured.

"Forever," I vow. "In this world, and in the next."

"*Kardia mou. Psihi mou.*" *My heart. My soul.*

I wrap my arms around his waist, clinging to the one thing I'm sure of in this world. Through damaged armor—steady heartbeat, steady breath, steady Griffin. The broken pieces of my soul that are still retrievable start fitting back together again as a breeze blows, silence falls, and the trees rain ashes.

CHAPTER 10

I LIFT MY FACE AND STARE AT THE CHAOS WIZARD'S distant hovel, nerves fluttering in my belly. Cold, blustery air whips across the Frozen Lake. Magic nips at my skin with sharp little teeth, but the slight sting is nothing compared to the rush of power proximity to the Ice Plains brings. I breathe deeply, soaking it in along with the hint of frost on the wind.

After the disaster in the woods, we changed course and headed straight for Kitros, an outlying district of Tarva City. We replaced our ruined gear and clothing, and I used the time to rest and recover. For some reason, Griffin's life force stopped transferring to me during intimacy, and no tingling warmth helped me regain my strength this time. Maybe I finally got back everything I initially gave, or maybe the seemingly increased ichor in my blood is the reason for the sudden change. I don't know, and there's no one to ask.

What I do know is that now that we're finally in Fisa, all I really want to do is turn around and go back to Kitros. It wasn't that bad, even with its nerve-racking proximity to Castle Tarva, its ruined neighborhood that everyone avoids, and the city's entire population going berserk over the upcoming Agon Games.

My gaze leaves the hovel to sweep out over the lake. Whitecaps crash against the icebergs dotting the surface. Somewhere in the vast, deep-blue water, a giant three-tentacled trout trolls the depths. More than eight years ago, instead of swallowing me whole, Poseidon's Lake Oracle granted me the gifts that got me out of Fisa, helped me to hide, protected Beta Team more than once, and saved Griffin from a mortal wound.

On the far side of the lake, a rippling green meadow stretches toward the first great, snow-glazed mountains, their towering sides clothed in patterns of aqua glaciers, crumbling shale, and weathered rock. Whorls form in the lush grass, the blades dipping and swaying like millions of primitive dancers moving to a mysterious rhythm only the wind and valley can hear. I strain and can almost hear it, too, just like I can almost taste the bracing flavor of magic on my tongue and feel the whisper of forces beyond any of our imagining setting my senses alight.

I open myself up to the strong sensations, almost foreign to me after living for so long in Sinta and largely in the south. The glacial shard in my pendant pulses with magic, and power explodes from somewhere deep inside of me. Lightning webs over my skin, crackling and bright, and the whole world suddenly takes on an orange hue, as if consumed by fire.

Gasping in shock, I try to tame the sizzling currents. When I can't hold them back, I vault off Panotii, afraid of hurting him. I back away, and the ground under my feet darkens and smokes.

Griffin spins Brown Horse around and then leaps down, calling out to me. His voice is frighteningly distant even though he's right there.

I hold up my hands to keep him back. His gray eyes widen at my expression, and then narrow when lightning surges out at him, narrowly missing his arm.

Inhaling sharply, I ball my hands into fists and tuck them against my middle. "Stay back!" The grass around me starts to smolder. Hellipses grass. Everywhere. Dry as kindling. Thunder rumbles, vibrating in my chest.

"You can't hurt me." Griffin keeps moving toward me.

"I could burn the field." Memories of the inferno in the woods send panic snapping through me like wildfire.

"You won't burn the field."

"You can't be sure!"

Low and steady, he says, "You can control this."

I scoff. "Do you even know me? Self-control and I aren't friends."

Griffin stops. "I do know you. You're the strongest, most stubborn, most determined person I've ever met. And I'm not talking about self-control. I'm talking about willpower."

My hands shake, jittery with magic I can't contain. Usually, I can't get it out. Now I can't keep it in? "Isn't it the same thing?" I ask.

He looks at me hard. "Is it?"

"I don't know! I just want it to stop." *No, that's not true.* "I want it to come when I need it. I want it gone when I don't."

"You need to master this."

"I don't even know what this is! Half the time, it's not even there!"

"Then figure it out."

"Oh, that's helpful!"

Griffin flashes me his pirate's grin, and my insides shift with something that has nothing to do with the magic storm. "You do know what it is. *I* know what it is. Emotion."

"Emotion?"

He nods. "Fear. You get scared, really and truly scared for someone who is not yourself, and there it is—lightning."

I keep my lightning-charged hands pressed hard against my stomach. "That doesn't mean I know how to control it."

Griffin steps close enough that when our gazes lock, I

see the white-gold web around me reflected in his eyes. He dips his head, and his mouth brushes my ear, his voice a rumbling caress. "Excitement."

I shiver, thunder rolling through me along with his voice. *Excitement*. A heady thrill did course through me a moment ago. The freedom. The wind. The magic-laced air...

Griffin threads his fingers through my tangled hair, cradling my head with both hands. He tilts my face back. "I see you need a demonstration."

"A demonstration?" I echo dumbly, my pulse quickening.

His thumbs skate over my jaw. "Delivered in sign language."

"That's called a distraction, and it's probably not the most effective way to calm me down."

He dips his head and kisses me until my toes curl in my boots. But the soft way his lips move, how he gently holds me—it's a kiss meant to soothe. Soon enough, the lightning dims, and my hands start to cool.

Griffin pulls back, looking decidedly smug as he slides his boot over some blades of smoldering hellipses grass, extinguishing a budding fire.

"You got lucky," I tell him, my lips still tingling and warm.

He grins. "I know just what you need. And you love me for it."

I roll my eyes. "Good Gods, what an ego."

He spreads his hands. "No more lightning."

"That's because you distracted me. Not because I controlled it."

"Maybe that's the key to controlling it," Griffin suggests. "Get your mind off it. Stop being scared."

"Because it's always that easy," I say tartly.

Before he can answer, the others surround us.

"What just happened?" Leading Panotii behind his own mount, Kato watches me with a crease between his brows, his blue eyes dark with concern.

"Well…" I say with exaggerated patience. "It's called kissing. I won't offer to demonstrate, but I can probably find a number of women who will, although"—I look around at the acres of swaying grass, the wind-tossed lake, and the lonely hovel—"probably not right now."

Kato grunts, a spark of humor brightening his eyes. "Because that's exactly what I meant."

"I know!" I flick what's left of my windblown braid over my shoulder. "I'm uncanny like that."

Flynn doesn't crack a smile, although I get one from Kato and Carver.

"There was lightning all over you," the auburn-haired warrior says. "Not just your hands."

I shrug, not nearly as unconcerned as I'm trying to appear. "There's a bright side to everything. My own lightning doesn't burn off my clothes."

"When was the last time you were this close to the Ice Plains?" Griffin asks.

Turning my head, I scan the landscape, hauntingly familiar despite my only having been here once before. My eyes stop on the Chaos Wizard's modest dwelling. "A long time ago. But when I was younger, I was near the Ice Plains a lot, and I never turned into a walking storm. Ios was the first time."

"Doesn't magic mature?" Carver asks. "So tiny Magoi aren't running around setting off earthquakes and floods and fires?"

I chuckle. "That's a good point, especially for Elemental Magic. It doesn't usually manifest until later—early teens or so—and even then, it still needs to grow. The stronger it is, the longer it takes." I think about the ichor in my blood, about the thunder and lightning in my veins. But I'm not an Elemental, so what is this?

I look at the dilapidated house again. I'll bet the Chaos Wizard knows.

As if my thoughts summoned him, a man steps out onto the porch, leaving the front door ajar. Anxiety shoots through me. He's just a form in the distance for now, but I recall every detail about him. Tall and willowy thin. Worn white robes and a twisted staff, the sacred olive wood shiny and black with age. Stringy hair, entirely gray and reaching well beyond his waist, contradicted by a face that doesn't look a day over thirty. Smooth skin, not particularly tanned. Stained fingertips on his right hand, as if he spends his days grinding herbs between them. I remember him as if our last encounter were yesterday, just like I remember his terrifying words, resonating voice, and swirling eyes.

Nerves claw a hole in my stomach. That man knows too much about me, things I don't want to hear, or think about, or tell Griffin. Ever.

Taking a deep breath, I gather Panotii's reins from Kato. It galls me to do it, but I need to say something before we approach the wizard. "Even if the wizard points us toward the Ipotane, without any offensive magic, we have very little chance of making it off the Ice Plains alive. I have a hiccup of Dragon's Breath in me. Without more, or something equally useful, Piers might be right." And the Gods know it makes me want to vomit to admit it. "Maybe we should go home and rely on the army."

"Or you absorb the magic of whatever creatures we come up against," Flynn suggests. "They attack. You steal. We fight back."

"I second that plan." Like he's already itching for a

fight, Carver sweeps his fingers over the hilt of his sword, a nimble dance of flesh on steel.

I shake my head. "It's not always that simple. Cyclopes are colossal and swing a battering ram of a fist. I can't steal that. It's not magic. One kick from a Centaur, and your entire rib cage will implode. Then there are the Gorgons. Medusa could show up anywhere. And Harpies and Giants and Dragons. They're all magical creatures, but that doesn't mean they always *use* magic. They *are* magic. And they're a lot bigger and meaner than any of us."

"I don't know, Cat." Kato looks me up and down, his long blond hair flying on the wind. The teasing sparkle in his eyes takes the sting from his words. "You can be pretty mean sometimes. In terms of size, though…" He winces.

Carver nods his agreement. "Cat is small and weak."

I swing the evil eye back and forth between the two of them. Compared to the Minotaur-like men of Beta Team, I am small and weak, which means Carver can get away with this nonsense without frying me with a lie.

"So glad you're taking this seriously," I grumble.

"What? Life and death?" Flynn shrugs. "Bah!"

"Been there a dozen times," Kato says casually, pretending to buff his nails against his leather breastplate. The idiot.

I glare at all of them, especially Carver. "I am *not* small and weak." *Well, small maybe. And weak only if they decide to wrestle me.* "I have other skills."

Carver eyes me contemplatively for a moment. "You could fit in Griffin's pocket. Well, maybe not your hair."

"Oh my Gods! I feel an outburst of lightning coming on!"

Carver grins. "Do your worst, fuzz top."

Griffin chuckles at that, earning his own dose of my evil eye. He appears unrepentant, even when my well-practiced glower lands solely on him. He winks.

"Gah!" I toss up my hands. "You're all insane!"

"Really?" Flynn glances around, looking confused. "No, no. We're fine," he tells the horses. "Thanks for asking."

I can't help it. I laugh. We all laugh, and it feels like lifetimes have passed since the last time we did.

Griffin curves his warm, strong hands around my shoulders, turning me toward him. "I have faith in you. Our greatest weapons on the Ice Plains are here"—he lightly taps a finger against my forehead—"and here." He taps over my heart.

I make a face, torn between enjoying his compliment and knowing his faith in me is egregiously misplaced. "Then we're sure to die because neither of those functions quite right."

"They function well enough," he says, a small, lopsided smile lifting his mouth and making my heart skip a beat.

"Such high praise," I mumble, ignoring the flutter in my chest.

"I'm learning from you."

"Good Gods, don't," I say. "I'm hopeless."

"You're never hopeless." Griffin gazes down at me, deliberately changing the intent of my words. "When something matters to you, no fight ends until you've won. That's why we can go onto the Ice Plains and live—maybe even come back with what we went there for. We'll change the world, Cat, and we'll do it without the war you fear. I swear to the Gods, we'll do it with as little bloodshed as possible."

My heart drops like a stone. *Harbinger of the end. Destroyer of realms.*

"Now let's go talk to a wizard," Griffin says, drawing me in close first.

I lay my cheek against his chest and wrap my arms around his waist. His body shields me from the brisk,

buffeting wind, and I inhale a familiar mix of citrus, sunshine, outdoors, leather, and man.

We'll do it without the war you fear...

I wish that were true. But it's not, and *my Gods*, is he in
for a disappointment.

CHAPTER 11

W<small>E FREE THE HORSES TO GRAZE AND APPROACH THE</small> hovel on foot, stopping a few paces from the ramshackle porch. The Chaos Wizard doesn't move a muscle for more than an hour. He just stares straight at me with those all-seeing eyes. His timeless gaze is disconcerting, to say the least.

The last time I saw Thanos, I asked if he knew anything about the wizard's swirling eyes. My childhood protector dropped his voice to a reverent whisper and leaned his battle-scarred face close to mine. *"His knowledge is Chaos, infinite but without form. The dark pupils hold all the Gods' worlds combined. The golden irises reflect the whirling of the stars and the passage of time."*

I don't know how Thanos knew about the wizard's mesmerizing eyes. When I asked, he just looked at me in that inscrutable way of his. I was the princess, and he was my guard, and yet I knew better than to question him. If Thanos said *jump*, I jumped because it meant someone was swiping at my feet.

The Chaos Wizard finally speaks, his deeply resonating voice at complete odds with his fragile appearance. "Catalia Andromeda Eileithyia Fisa."

He greets me by my full name, which doesn't bode well for my whole keeping-the-prophecy-a-secret-at-least-for-now ambition. I'll tell Griffin. I will. It's just that acknowledging it to another person makes it that much more real.

Guess what? You want to make a better world? Good luck with that, because I'm going to destroy it.

That conversation is bound to go well.

I lift my hand in a small wave. "Hello." I don't know his name, I don't think anyone does, but I figure it's polite to at least respond. My own name still echoes in my ears, and my pulse picks up—walk, trot, canter—until my heart is galloping under my ribs.

But nothing else happens. Eventually, the Chaos Wizard's eyes glaze over again, although his strange stare stays fixed in my direction. I sit down facing the wizard's porch. I tell the others I think we're in for a long wait—he stared at me for hours the last time I was here, too—but they stay standing, the Frozen Lake on our left and the grassy field swaying around us.

After a while, Kato slides me a sidelong look. "Andromeda? Fantastic second name."

A dry smile lifts my lips. "She stamped me from the day I was born, as if that would somehow make it easier to bend me to her will." I pick a blade of hellipses grass and start peeling the tough layers apart. "Where Mother's concerned, I do love to disappoint."

Kato glances at the wizard. "How does he know?"

"He knows everything. That's why he's completely mad," I say, winding my finger around in circles next to my head.

The men glance anxiously toward the house, but the wizard isn't paying any attention. My antics are of supreme disinterest to a being like him.

After another half hour or so, something cool licks at my skin. At first, I think it's just the wind, but when it happens again, goose bumps break out on my arms. The same persistent coolness dips into my head, probing.

I sit up straighter. I know this feeling. Two Oracles have demanded my thoughts and tasted me with their frosty tongues. This is both subtler and more powerful, and my fingers tense reflexively around the torn-up grass in my lap, all of me stiffening. After one slightly panicked breath, I force myself to relax and open my mind. I'll lay myself bare in a way I rarely do, even for myself, if it means helping Griffin avoid a war.

The feeling of icy habitation recedes just as a gust of wind blasts through the valley. It's chilly, even for me. Next to me, Flynn shivers. His brown eyes flick to mine.

"Shouldn't you stand?" he whispers nervously.

"You whisper really loud," I whisper back really loudly.

Flynn scowls. "I feel like we should light candles and pray. Like this is a temple."

"That," I say, pointing to the hovel, "is a hovel."

Flynn gasps. It's funny, especially since the wizard seems to have finished exploring my mind, and we're not dead.

"Do you see those marks?" I point to the grassless depressions littering the field around the shack. "Those are from God Bolts. The wizard has a direct line to Zeus, whose favorite weapon is the thunderbolt. If he wanted us gone, we would be. Permanently. As in *disintegrated*. Poof. Nothing but ash."

Flynn's eyes dart from side to side, taking in the dozens of charred pockmarks scattered all around us. "People the wizard, or Zeus, decided shouldn't be here?" he asks.

I nod, and he looks suddenly grumpy. Or like he has an upset stomach. Or maybe both.

"You failed to mention that before we got here," Flynn says tightly.

I shrug. "I was pretty sure we'd be fine."

Carver snorts. "'Pretty sure' is a pretty big gamble."

I wave off his concern. I wasn't worried. Not really. "Not killing us doesn't mean helping us, though."

Griffin sits down next to me, his eyes on the impossibly still man and his creepy black staff. "'Pretty sure' from Cat are odds I'll take any day."

I offer him a small smile. His confidence both warms and scares me. "Zeus is my ancestor. I think, I *hope*, he'll point us toward the Ipotane." I can't explain exactly why I think Zeus favors me, and I have no real proof that he does. Except maybe that booming voice at Ios, that crack of thunder and flash of lightning. I think Zeus may have helped me heal Griffin and then chastised me for praying to his brother Poseidon, my go-to God, when I should have turned to the king of Olympus instead.

I'm here now, Zeus. What's next?

Glancing north across the lake, I give myself an inward shake. *Great. Catalia Fisa. Humble as ever.* I almost wonder if the sky *will* open up and rain down lightning bolts.

Evening approaches, and the biting wind dies down as the sun sinks in the west. The wizard, motionless as ever, looks like he grew right out of his porch. I'm not nervous anymore, I'm bored. Luckily, Griffin chooses to be bored along with me. The guys, starting to finally relax and act normal again, play dice games where they set up camp a few dozen feet away. Two rabbits cook on a spit over a fire in one of the God Bolt pits, and Flynn tends to the evening meal, as usual.

The smell of roasting meat makes my stomach growl. "I'm hungry."

Griffin retrieves the saddlebags and unloads bread, cheese, cured meat, and a plump orange. I try to hand back the meat, but Griffin won't take it.

"Just a little," he says. "To keep up your strength."

I wrinkle my nose, dangling the dried strip between my thumb and forefinger. More disgusted than usual by it, I drop it in his lap. The smell of aged cheese reaches me next, and my stomach turns over. Grimacing, I push away everything but the bread and fruit.

Griffin frowns. "I thought you were hungry."

"I'm starving." I tear into the orange, free a quarter, and then ram the entire thing into my mouth.

Griffin watches me inhale the orange, an odd expression on his face.

"What?" I lick pulp and juice from my fingers. I'm a mess. I hardly stopped to chew. My eyes widen. "Did you want some? Was that the last one?" He's not fond of fruit, so I didn't think to ask.

"No. And no." He sweeps his thumb under my lower lip, catching a drip. He licks the juice from his finger, and the intimacy of the simple act thumps me in the chest.

He hands me the dried meat again, but I shake my head.

"Eat it," Griffin says, "or I'll sit on you until you do."

My mouth drops open in what I'm sure is a very attractive way. "I knew you were overbearing, but don't you think that's taking it a bit far, Your High-Handedness?"

"I knew you were stubborn, but don't you know you can't survive on oranges alone? That's practically all you've eaten for days."

"I have bread!" I hold up the bread.

"Bread fills the belly. It does little to nourish the body."

I start to argue, then stop and scowl. "It's annoying when you make sense."

"Would you rather I were a fool?" he asks.

"Yes."

"Meat." He slaps it into my hand. "Eat."

I roll my eyes. "You could rival Calliope with poetry like that."

"My ability to get what I want is legendary." It's not a

boast. It's fact. "I'll do this every day if I have to, all day, until you stop arguing and eat some damn meat."

I glower at him, secretly enjoying his gruff concern and domineering ways, something I'll never admit to—not on my deathbed or beyond. "Fine. But I'll wait for the rabbit. We should save our dried supplies for the Ice Plains."

Griffin gives me a hard *I'm holding you to that* look before putting the cured meat away.

Compromise. I guess it's not so bad.

While the rabbits hiss and cook on the spit, I settle against Griffin's side, breaking off bits of bread to eat and also feeding some to Griffin. My mind wanders to our time in Kitros. Too close for real comfort to Castle Tarva and the enemy royals who live there, Griffin and I rarely left our room at the inn while Carver, Kato, and Flynn took care of replenishing supplies and replacing damaged items.

Heat blossoms low in my abdomen at the memories that flood to mind. Staying out of sight and "resting" extensively furthered my understanding of Griffin's thorough and inventive nature. I never knew what to expect when his eyes turned that stormy gray and he prowled toward me, clearly intent on stripping me bare. His lovemaking can be long and slow with soft touches and gentle words. Or it can be fast and hard with fevered hands and shuddering breath. I've had my back against the wall—and my front. I've had his mouth between my legs until I scream and thunder shakes the room, and I've been naked on my knees with my hair gripped tight in his fists doing things that definitely don't require a bed.

I lift my face and kiss his scruffy jaw, the heat from Griffin's big body matching the warmth now swirling through mine.

A smile curves his wide mouth. "What was that for?"

I flush, certain my heart and my thoughts are in my eyes. "Kitros."

"Ah, Kitros." His silver gaze glitters like the first stars at twilight. His arm tightens around my waist, and he lowers his head, his breath warming my neck as he presses a lingering kiss to the sensitive spot below my ear. His lips are firm but soft. His stubble rasps. Tingles ripple down my spine.

I slide my fingers into his windblown hair, desire licking through me. "If we were alone, I'd want you inside me right now."

He groans softly. "Right now?"

"Right. Now."

"With only a kiss on the neck?" His rough whiskers lightly scrape the shell of my ear.

I shiver, shifting closer to him. "I was ready without the kiss on the neck. Now I'm desperate for you." I grip his hair, keeping his dark head close to mine. Our cheeks brush as I whisper in his ear. "Just thinking about the things we did in Kitros makes me hot and wet. You'd slide right in, and I'd clench you so hard your mind would go blank."

Griffin's hand convulses on my hip. His grip is possessive. Deliciously hard. I hear him swallow. His voice comes to me a shade deeper, and a good deal rougher. "You have no idea how much I want that."

I moan quietly. "I want it more. I want you. There's a pulse between my legs. If you touch me, I'll explode."

He tenses, like he's holding himself back. "We have an audience."

I move restlessly against him, nearly in his lap, mostly sheltered by him. "The guys aren't looking, and the wizard is probably in a trance."

"We can't leave in case he decides to talk."

"We don't have to leave. We don't have to undress. Just touch me. I need you."

Griffin curses softly. His eyes searing, he straightens away from me. "I love you to the point of desperation, but it's a mood, and it'll pass."

I reach for him again. "I'll be quiet."

He grabs my hand. "You're never quiet."

"I can try."

He chuckles at that, but it turns into a husky, almost pained groan. Squeezing my hand, he exhales slowly. "You'll be the death of me, Cat."

And just like that, my blood freezes over. Lust crashes, leaving behind a tangle of foreboding and fear.

Griffin senses the change in me instantly. "It's a figure of speech."

I draw back. "And in our case, horribly fitting."

He shakes his head. "Stop doing that. You're not responsible for everything that happens around you. Whatever the Fates have in store for us is decided before we're born. Whatever happens to me, to any of us, it will *never* be your fault." He tilts my face up, forcing me to meet his now steely gaze. "And I have no intention of dying."

"That's what we all say. That doesn't stop it from happening."

"Eventually, yes. But for now, don't add shadows to the dark."

It's hard to believe that just moments ago, I was so wild with desire I was ready to disregard our surroundings. I do like to put on a good show, but not *that* kind of show. Now, there's a chasm in my chest. "My sister died because of me."

"Your sister died *for* you. It's not the same."

"And if you die for me, will that make it any easier? You'd do it. Don't deny it. We both know it's true."

His mouth flattens, his jaw hardening until it seems carved from stone. "What worries me is your sacrificing yourself for *me, agapi mou.*"

I gape at him. "You can't have one standard for yourself and another for me!"

"And you can't keep living your life like everyone matters except for you!"

"That's…" *Damn, that's a good argument.* "I don't want to die any more than you do. But I've been on borrowed time for years. Sometimes, I can't believe I even made it this fa—"

"Stop. Don't finish that thought." Griffin's eyes glint dangerously, reflecting the moon's first rays. "If you won't put yourself first for you, then do it for me. For our family."

"We don't have a family."

"We *are* a family!"

The vehemence in his voice slaps me so hard that I jerk. Tiny daggers start stabbing at the backs of my eyes, making them sting and water.

Griffin takes my face in his hands. His fingers press into my head. "I may not be holding you with a magic rope anymore, but I will *never* let you go, and I will *never* leave you. I would defy creatures, and Gods, and terrible, brutal queens to keep you safe and by my side. I would move Mount Olympus itself to hold you in my arms and feel your heart beat against mine. You are my soul, and *yes*, I will fight for you and protect you until my dying breath."

His vow stuns me into silence. I swallow hard as the force of it ignites the magic in my blood, proving its utter truth. A quiet sob rattles my chest. I gulp it down, but that effort goes to waste when Griffin pulls me into his lap and wraps his arms around me. All the knots inside me unravel, and a floodgate opens. It's loud. And ugly.

His jaw brushes my temple. "I thought cats didn't cry."

I sniff. "They don't." *Usually.*

Griffin slides his hand up and down my back, letting my uncharacteristic breakdown run its course. *"Ee-lee-thia,"* he says after a while, his pronunciation of my second middle name hesitant. "That's nice."

I let out a watery snort. Kind of a hiccup. *Is this what love does to a person? Uncontrollable emotion?*

"Eileithyia's not bad," I agree. It's a lot better than Andromeda.

"Goddess of childbirth, right?"

I nod, wiping my eyes with the backs of my hands. "Prepare yourself. With a namesake like that, chances are I'm really fertile."

Griffin has the good sense to look like that doesn't bother him at all.

Flynn brings us a rabbit to share, not commenting on my strange behavior, if he even noticed it from over by the campfire. While we eat, Griffin cuts some of the longer hellipses grass around us, stacking the wide, dry blades into a neat pile next to him. He eventually binds the stalks with a leather cord and then carefully slips the whole stack into the bottom of his saddlebag.

"What's that for?" I ask around a bite of admittedly succulent rabbit. Flynn's a good cook. The meat is never dry. He even carries herbs.

Griffin smiles faintly. "There's something I might want to make. And the grass here is good. Strong."

I'm curious about his ability to create. I saw the grass crown he wove for Kaia. It was beautiful and intricate even though it was just for play, and I'm sure it pleased her more than all of her new jewels combined.

"Why didn't I ever see you weaving when we spent all those weeks traveling together before?" I ask.

Griffin turns slightly and looks out over the darkening meadow. In profile, the rugged contours of his face and his aquiline nose stand out more prominently. There's nothing delicate or bland about his strong-boned face; he's a magnetic, masculine work of art. His gaze stops on the lake, its now smooth surface a vast shadow splashed across the center of the valley. The moon hangs low and yellow in the sky, already lighting a shimmering path across the water. Icebergs reflect the moonlight, the hulking, jagged mounds like a Giant's stepping-stones to the snowcapped mountains beyond.

"If there's one thing Sinta doesn't lack, it's dusty plains and dry grasses. There's never a shortage of hellipses grass. It's even here, in Fisa, and so far to the north." He looks at me then. "Weaving reminds me of all the times our tribe had to make everything we could from something that costs nothing at all."

"Because royal soldiers kept stealing everything and burning your homes?"

He nods. In the fading light, his features are like the granite peaks in the distance, angular and hard. "Tax collecting wasn't just about taxes in the south. It was about pillaging, meaningless destruction, and instilling fear. My father built an army big enough to get them to finally cease those types of raids, at least in our corner of Sinta, but no victory will ever make me forget those endless days of weaving after the royal soldiers came. The stinging cuts. The bloody hands. The work songs with their plaintive, sliding tones. The smell of sheaves upon sheaves of freshly cut hellipses grass in whatever was left of the house." He brushes his long, strong fingers over the thick blades next to him, watching them bend. "The lifeless. The mourning. The girls, some younger than Kaia is now, leaving for the nearest city to sell whatever they could, even their bodies, for Charon's obol to pay their loved ones' passage to the land of the dead."

I unconsciously press my hand against the coin that's always in my pocket, the one I'll never spend. We all carry one. With the lives we lead, we'd be insane not to. There's no crossing the Styx without paying the ferryman first, and the Shadowlands are no place to end up for all of eternity.

I've sometimes wondered how the Griffin I know could have slaughtered Sinta's entire royal family, men and women alike. Luckily, they were an unfruitful lot, and there were no children in the castle because when he brought his army to their gates, he wiped them out, just like they'd callously wiped out so many people before that, victims of royal greed and senseless violence, people who weren't just nameless and faceless to Griffin.

"Why weave at all if it brings back those memories?" I ask.

He shrugs. "It's a part of me. It always has been. I don't know how to stop."

"Then why didn't I see you weaving before? There was hellipses grass everywhere. You could have made an entire supply of household goods in the time it took us to reach Castle Sinta," I tease, trying to take some of the new grimness from his expression.

Griffin's teeth flash briefly in the growing dark. "There was no time. You were distracting—and that's putting it mildly—and I was always busy making sure you didn't escape or maim me for life."

I roll my eyes, although he does have a point. "Then what are you making now?"

He looks at his empty hands, studies them, flips them over, frowns... "Nothing, as far as I can tell."

Giving him a sour look, I turn my voice as dry as Sintan dust. "You're a thespian wonder."

Griffin leans back on his elbows, sighing dramatically. "It was a sad day when I had to choose between being a warlord and having a career on the stage."

I have to bite my lip to keep from laughing. "I still want to know what you're doing with that grass."

He looks over at me in a way that makes my heart start fluttering like a damn butterfly in my chest. "Patience, Catalia Eileithyia Fisa. I'm not doing anything yet."

I scowl. Patience is *not* one of my middle names.

CHAPTER 12

I JOLT AWAKE TO THE SHRIEK OF AN OWL. THE FIVE OF US surround the campfire, and Griffin and the others are on their feet before I can blink. I'm just tossing off my blanket when a deafening noise makes me curl in on myself. I duck my head and cover my ears as a bone-jarring, body-seizing boom rolls through the valley.

When power stops warping the air, I stagger to my feet and look for the Chaos Wizard in the dark. The moon is high and bright, reflected off the lake, and I can see him just fine. He hasn't moved. He's right where we left him after several hours of waiting for a big, fat nothing.

He looks straight at me—maybe he never *stopped* looking at me—and thumps his staff on his crumbling porch. The same debilitating, magic-heavy sound rends the air and shatters my head. I double over, gasping, and Griffin leans protectively over me, not affected in the same way at all. I find his waist and hold on, my head buried against his abdomen.

The Chaos Wizard's deep voice resonates along with the last of the terrible noise. "Harbinger. Approach."

Dazed, I try to shake off the aftereffects of those two thundering blasts of pure Olympian magic. Somehow, I step away from Griffin, my head still spinning. Griffin automatically moves with me, and the wizard thumps his staff again. I cry out, crushing power nearly putting me on my knees.

"Harbinger alone," the wizard commands.

Frowning, Griffin helps to steady me. In a low voice, he asks, "Why is he calling you that?"

Straightening, I press my lips together and don't answer. I have some explaining to do. *Later.*

The awful noise subsides, and I move cautiously forward, my tunic flapping in the wind that picked up again as if in answer to the wizard's magic staff. By the time I cover the short distance to his porch, I feel almost normal again, only a slight hum in my veins reacting to the residual power in the air. I dip my head, attempting humility, although I don't think we're in any real danger—except of total hearing loss.

The Chaos Wizard doesn't bang his staff again, thank the Gods. "Zeus and his daughter Athena choose to aid you in your quest to secure the herd of Ipotane."

My eyes widen. *Fantastic!* No explanation necessary *and* two Gods on our side. I could dance a Fisan jig.

"You must make a worthy offering to the herd Alpha, Lycheron, to keep him from killing you on sight."

Huh. Cancel the jig.

"Propose a challenge. The Ipotane cannot resist a competition, but Lycheron will only play male Alpha to male Alpha."

For the first time, the Chaos Wizard's swirling eyes land on Griffin, and I have to resist the urge to jump in front of him and shield him from the wizard's unsettling gaze.

"A bargain must be struck."

Uh-oh. A bargain means us promising something, too.

"Zeus has spoken."

My jaw drops. *What? That's it?* "What offering? What could Lycheron want?"

The wizard doesn't answer. He just stares at me like before, his eyes infinite and so immeasurably full they're void.

Turning, I stomp back toward the others. They meet me halfway.

"We waited hours under that frankly disturbing stare; I just got a thumping headache and a magical ass-kicking; and *that's it*?"

Griffin seems at a loss as well. "What do we do now? Leave?"

The owl I heard earlier swoops low over our heads, lands on the wizard's shabby roof, and then hoots.

Griffin's eyes sharpen on the bird. "The owl is the symbol of Athena."

"Climb the northeast needle of the Deskathi Mountains," the wizard abruptly continues. "The glacial caves hide a treasure that will please the Ipotane Alpha."

Shock hits me like a Giant's fist. "But those caves are a labyrinth!" One I've hardly ever heard of anyone going into. I've never heard of anyone coming out.

The owl hoots again, and a ball of twine appears in the wizard's hand. He tosses it to me with an awkward, under-handed throw, the gift barely reaching me from not even twenty feet away.

"Ariadne's Thread. It will not end. It will not tangle."

I grip the coiled string, feeling its magic nip at my palm. "What will we find there?" I ask.

"Only the Harbinger and the fair one must enter the caves. The other three must not."

Kato. Me.

"Beware Atalanta's bow. Find the lyre before the three-headed beast. Heed the Goddess's needs."

Well, that's not vague at all! "Why only us? What's the treasure?"

"Athena has spoken."

"Wait!" I cry. "Where do we find the Ipotane?"

The wizard just stares, his gaze whirling and vacant again.

I look at the owl, my eyes pleading. "Athena? Please."

The owl cocks its head and looks at me like I'm a rodent it might eat for dinner. Round, amber eyes pulse with an inner light. It's perfectly still. Not even its feathers ruffle in the wind. Its sharply curved beak snaps once, the menacing click loud in my ears. Goose bumps spill down my arms. I keep looking at the bird, but for all I know, I'm being a fool, and it's just an owl.

Nothing happens. Frustrated, I pocket the thread, wondering what to do next. After a while, the wizard turns and shuffles into his house. The weathered door swings shut behind him, the snick of the latch hitting me like a sucker punch to the gut.

I glare at the closed door in disbelief and then mutter a curse that probably makes Flynn want to wash out his ears. "Everything he said is completely useless without the actual location of the Ipotane! Bloody useless, crazy, swirly-eyed son of a—"

Griffin's hand lands on my shoulder, and I whirl.

"That didn't help us at all!"

"It did." His voice is calm and reasonable. I hate calm and reasonable.

"A few fuzzy suggestions and a ball of string?" I fume, outraged.

"A ball of string that will keep you from getting lost in a labyrinth. I hold one end. You hold the other. It will not end. It will not tangle." He takes both my shoulders and squeezes. "With this, you can find your way back out."

"That's if we avoid Atalanta's bow, find a lyre before some three-headed beast, and heed an unknown Goddess's needs." Scoffing, I step back from him. "No problem at all!"

"It's better than nothing," Griffin argues.

"No. *Nothing* would have sent us home." The word *home* sparks an unexpected ache in my chest. I meant Sinta, but having my feet on my own soil again must be doing strange things to my head because a sea of nameless Fisan faces with fierce eyes and olive skin butts into my thoughts, their expressions full of accusation, and worse—hope.

I quell what's only my imagination. And guilt for abandoning them. "This," I say, disgusted with everything, especially myself, "gives us just enough to keep going and get ourselves killed."

I glance around me. Carver, Flynn, Kato. Griffin. I can't risk their safety—their *lives*—with only this to go on.

"Who's Atalanta?" Carver asks. Dark hair, dark clothes, all lean muscle and deadly grace, he's one with the night. It strikes me suddenly how little I've seen him smile lately, as if the darkness he wears so naturally is shadowing him on the inside as well as out.

I shake my head. "I have no idea."

He huffs quietly. "That's never good."

No. My lips thin. Another epic failure. First Mother finding us. Now this. "Yes, well, I'm only mostly all-knowing."

No one laughs, which is fine. It wasn't really a joke.

The Chaos Wizard's door creaks open again, and the five of us turn as one. Adrenaline surges through my veins, sudden hope leading the charge. My eyes widen as the strange, powerful man steps back out onto his porch, something flame-licked and glowing floating out after him. It's a long, sweeping garment of some sort. *A cloak?* Four others follow, their flickering light softly illuminating the night.

I watch in utter fascination. *Cloaks made of fire?* Then my breath catches. *Cloaks made of fire!*

Darkness swallows the insides of the garments, making

them just deeper shadows in the heart of the night, but the outsides… The outsides are spectacular. Undulating softly in the frost-scented breeze, the flowing folds race with the swift, scintillating currents of thousands upon thousands of thin, delicate threads enrobed entirely in flame. Mesmerizing like the glowing embers of a dying fire, the cloaks give off a steady pulse of red, gold, and heat.

No matter past encounters, there's no denying the savage beauty in the element of fire. The white heart. The twist of yellow. The sudden surge of orange, and the occasional snap of blue. Exquisite. Treacherous. Flames make you want to wrap your hand around them, only to come away with nothing but a burn.

Even from a distance, the smoldering cloaks warm my night-chilled skin with a subtle heat that smells faintly of wood smoke, incense, and burning herbs. Is that what the Underworld smells like? I open my mouth to tell Beta Team where I think these gifts came from, but no sound comes out. I'm amazed beyond words—and it's hard to stun me speechless.

Five cloaks float above the porch in an eerie, sweeping dance. Wavering patterns of brightness and shadow play over the wizard's young-old face, reflecting fire off his eddying eyes.

"Harbinger. Approach."

I can't move. I can hardly drag my jaw off the ground.

Kato shoves lightly on my back. "That's you, Cat."

I stumble forward, somehow making it up the crumbling steps without falling on my face. There's only one person— well, God—that can be responsible for this, and he's already helped me more than once. He sent Cerberus to my side and kept the terrifying three-headed hound there for years, making sure my watchdog was with me when I needed him most.

The Chaos Wizard's booming voice sounds like it should come from a sturdy, young man, not a gray-haired, willow-framed stick of a person of indeterminate age. "Forged in the eternal furnaces of the Underworld. Made from the same fire used to keep the fruits and flowers of Elysium forever in bloom."

Emotion and gratitude thicken my throat as the shortest and narrowest of the cloaks settles over my shoulders, my braid tucked safely against the dark, waxy inside of the ample hood. The heat is nearly overwhelming for the split second it takes Hades's gift to sense my needs and adjust. The glow dims until only a soft splash of light brightens the space around me and a hint of warmth erases the chill of the night.

Zeus. Athena. Hades. The support of three key Gods is more than I ever hoped for, and yet I can't help wondering where Poseidon is. Poseidon and his Oracles have never failed me, and his absence now leaves a restless feeling deep inside me that I can't quite dispel.

Cloaked in living fire—which I can't believe I even remotely like—I slide the warm metal buckle at my collarbone closed and then march back down the stairs. The remaining cloaks float after me like a glowing regiment. With or without Poseidon, our path is officially set. There's no turning back after such a clear sign from the Gods that we're meant to continue on to the Ice Plains. First Ariadne's Thread. Now the cloaks. This is survival gear.

The gently blazing cloaks settle over the men's shoulders, wrapping them in the flame-free insides. Every single one of them lets out a deep, masculine sound of contentment. The heat coming off their garments intensifies. Apparently, they were cold.

"This is amazing." Flynn pulls his cloak closed over his wide chest, his big hands tucked safely inside.

Griffin sighs in pleasure, hesitates for a moment, but then slips his cloak off with a look of utter longing that almost makes me jealous. Flames race up and down the outside, jumping from thread to thread. "And a beacon in the dark," he says. "These will attract attention from miles around."

I frown. There's no way Hades didn't think of that. He's a God, after all, a deity of the first Olympian generation, even if he doesn't live on the mountaintop. He may stick to the Underworld, with its amazing and its awful, but he knows what's around here, too, and the last thing anyone traveling the Ice Plains wants is to attract attention.

I unhook the buckle and shrug out of my cloak. After being cocooned in its subtle warmth, I'm more aware of the icy wind and actually shiver as I inspect both sides of the cloth. Unlike the exquisite, delicate, flame-licked fibers of the glowing outside, the thicker threads on the inside seem to absorb the dark.

Wary of any kind of fire at this point, but figuring I'll heal fast enough if anything magical burns me, I flip my cloak around and then throw it back over my shoulders, the glow on the inside now.

A curse exploding from him, Griffin lunges for me like he's going to rip off my cloak. He draws up short when I grin and latch the buckle again.

"It's reversible!" All I feel is the same comfortable warmth.

"You should have let me try that first," he growls.

I adjust the folds of my cloak, hiding the flames. "We can't test magic on you. You're immune to anything harmful."

"Someone else then," Griffin bites out.

I frown at him. "How is that a good idea?"

"It's a *better* idea," he snaps, "because it isn't *you*."

My eyebrows shoot up. I get it now. And if he thinks for one second he's wrapping me in glass and pushing me up onto the pedestal along with his sisters, he needs his head examined. "I don't toss my friends to the Cyclopes," I say hotly.

Griffin's nostrils flare on a clipped inhale. His eyes spark with anger. "I'm not asking you to. I'm asking you to think before you act. Use caution."

"I did think. I thought 'Hades isn't an idiot. This is probably reversible.' And guess what? It was."

Round one to Cat! Ha!

"You could have just touched it. You didn't need to jump to extremes and cover yourself from head to toe!"

Huh. Round two to Griffin.

Ducking out of an argument I might not win, I pull up the hood and draw it low over my forehead. "Well?" As far as I can tell, I'm completely shrouded in black.

Kato breaks the tense silence. "Decent camouflage. Still some brightness around the neck."

I glance down, thinking the small glow isn't worth worrying about.

Kato claps a hand on Griffin's shoulder, saying to me, "You just shaved ten years off my life with that stunt. Since you do that often enough, it probably puts me close to the grave."

I look at him, something thorny twisting through me. "That's not funny."

Kato looks straight back. "Sometimes, Cat, neither are you."

A hot dart of betrayal stabs me in the chest. Kato just chose sides in my argument with Griffin, and he didn't choose mine.

Carver turns his cloak around, putting the fire-bright

threads on the inside now. "Keep in mind that I'll kill anyone who admits we needed Cat to tell us we were wearing our clothes inside out."

"Who would have thought of putting the fire on the inside?" Flynn wonders out loud.

"Someone who's not afraid of getting burned," Griffin says, his tone still laced with fury.

I glance up, my surprise hidden by the deep hood. Does he think I'm not afraid? I'm terrified. Constantly. I just do things anyway and hope for the best. Admittedly, that's not always the best strategy, but sometimes there really isn't much choice.

"Hades wouldn't hurt me," I announce. "And now we're sure they're safe."

Griffin looks like he wants to wring my neck, which is just unnecessary.

"I do what needs to be done," I say stiffly. "Just like you."

"Put yourself in my place, Cat. In all our places." Griffin roughly pushes my hood back, and I get a good idea of how angry he is from the hard glint in his granite eyes. "Keep throwing yourself into the fire first, and I'll kill you myself."

Heat crawls up my throat, and not only because that was a blatant lie. "That's an empty threat if I ever heard one."

"Fine. Then I'll tie you up and leave you at home."

No burn this time. "You wouldn't."

"You know I would."

"You can't. You need me!"

"I need you alive!"

I stare at him in shock. "You're overreacting." I'm a warrior, just like him, and he *knows* it. My skill set is simply different from his. It includes burning to a crisp one minute and coming back from it the next. "I didn't do anything reckless."

"You are *synonymous* with reckless," Griffin growls.

My hands clench at my sides. That was low. And kind of true. I lift my chin. "I trust in the Gods."

"The Gods' motivations are rarely clear," Flynn says. "You should have been more careful."

Flynn, too? I expect this kind of overbearing nonsense from Griffin, but not from the others. I take a shallow breath, feeling another attack of completely uncharacteristic crying coming on.

When Griffin takes my shoulders and swings me back to him, my eyes must betray something of my distress because he abruptly softens his hold. "Don't you get it, Cat? You're the key. I knew it the day I laid eyes on you and couldn't take them off again. Didn't want to." He gives me a gentle shake, his eyes burning into mine. "Every single one of us would fall if it kept you standing. *You are not expendable.*"

"And none of you are expendable to me!" My voice cracks, brittle with unshed tears.

Griffin breathes deeply and then pulls me against him. My arms automatically rise, and I cling to him, my emotions so close to the surface they hurt my skin.

In a deep rasp, he says, "Enough of this. We've both made our points."

I nod. I don't move. I don't want to. I lean my head against Griffin's chest, surprised when the Chaos Wizard's resonating voice disrupts the fraught quiet of the night. I'd thought he was in a trance again. Done.

"Persephone sends her blessing to the Harbinger. Hades has spoken."

I lift my face, puzzled. "Persephone? That's new."

Griffin's expression seems to say nothing surprises him anymore. There's also a stoniness to it, and I can practically read the questions on his mind.

Harbinger. My stomach suddenly rolls like a pitching ship, and I move out of Griffin's arms. He releases me except for keeping one of my hands in his.

"We still don't know where to find the Ipotane," I call to the wizard.

Silence. Blank stare. I don't know why I bothered.

I start to turn away, thinking we're finished here, but then the conduit to the Gods opens his mouth to speak, surprising me yet again.

CHAPTER 13

OPENS HIS MOUTH TO SPEAK? SCRATCH THAT. IT'S NOT words that come out of the wizard's mouth. That would be too simple, and when did the Gods ever do simple? Drama is their collective middle name.

A shiny, dark snake head rises from the man's thin throat, and my stomach starts to kick its contents around in disgust. A forked tongue flutters out to lick the air. Lidless eyes and gleaming scales reflect the moonlight as the reptile slowly emerges, swaying slightly in the way of the most deadly and venomous of snakes. Deep green or black—it's hard to tell in the dark—the creature has a row of diamonds on its glistening back, the pattern alternating between crimson and gold. It keeps coming until two and then three feet of snake dangle from the wizard's slack-jawed mouth. The Chaos Wizard convulses every now and then. His bottomless eyes are a whirling tangle of other-worldly light as he heaves up more and more of the snake, distressed sounds rattling in his chest.

Completely horrified, I stare at the long rope of reptilian muscle arching toward the porch. The snake keeps its triangular head raised, its unblinking eyes shining an eerie reddish-yellow as its tongue darts out again, vibrating.

I'm fifteen feet away, but a quick, stinging lash seems to whip the side of my face. I flinch, touching the icy path smarting across my cheek. *Is it an Oracle? Or something else?*

"Gods on Olympus," Griffin murmurs under his breath. I guess he can still be surprised after all.

Kato curses softly when the snake hisses in his direction.

The Chaos Wizard gives one last heave, and the creature drops to the porch with a slap of scales on wood. Raw, choking coughs rasp in the wizard's throat. Then he stares blankly again, his eyes a spinning, iridescent mix of golds.

The serpent slithers down the steps and then glides soundlessly toward us. I despise snakes. I'm about to back away when it stops and forms a nest of coils, settling into a bed of its own body to observe each of us in turn.

I have no idea what to make of this, but I do know one thing… "Snakes are mean and unpredictable."

"Sounds like someone I know," Carver tosses my way.

"Har, har," I respond dryly, keeping my focus on the snake.

"Don't go near it, Cat." Letting go of my hand, Griffin steps in front of me. "Don't," he repeats, as if I need the extra instruction.

I lean around Griffin's arm, tracking the creature's movements and the direction of its eyes. It gives us all another piercing once-over, that two-tined tongue shooting out again.

A chill ripples through me that has nothing to do with the frosty wind. I slip a Kobaloi knife free, weighing it in my hand. If there is any surviving magic in the sinew wrapping the hilt, it doesn't nip at my palm. I don't know why the snake is here, but I don't like it. Snake symbolism ranges from very good to very bad, but it's not as though anyone keeps a pet adder around, and this snake is clearly dangerous.

Torn, I can't quite bring myself to throw the knife. Is this somehow another gift? It might not be. The Gods are a vengeful, spiteful lot. They rarely get along, and they can be opportunistic. Whoever sent the snake may simply be implementing a straightforward, time-old strategy—the friend of my enemy is also my enemy—that has nothing to do with us.

My eyes don't leave the serpent as I call out, "Who sent the snake?"

The wizard doesn't answer. *Of course.*

The creature rises from its nest of coils, hissing softly. Its roaming glance is sly and subtle, sliding over Kato without any real pause, but instinct screams at me that the serpent just found its mark. My heart hammers a frantic beat, and I stop hesitating. My knife flies from my hand and lands...*in the dirt?*

I gasp. I never miss.

The snake strikes so fast it's hard to see. Kato somehow sidesteps the sudden explosion of movement, twisting out of the way. His fiery cloak billows as he spins, splashing light over sharp, curving fangs and glistening scales. I see the glassy surface of a predatory eye, and then nothing as the snake drops to the ground with a soft thump and disappears into the long grass.

"Where is it?" Kato whirls, drawing his mace.

Flynn turns in a slow circle, his battle-ax ready in one hand, a knife in the other. The rest of us don't move, as if going perfectly still will help us find a shadow in the dark.

Apparently, it does. "There!" I shout, pointing to Kato's left.

I lunge, ready to grab the snake with my bare hands if I have to, but Griffin catches me around the middle and hauls me back, his sharp "No!" ringing in my ears.

In the next second, the creature propels itself upward with otherworldly power and snaps its jaws closed around Kato's neck.

My heart stops utterly. I blink. I don't believe what just happened. I *refuse* to believe.

Fear and guilt rob me of my breath. *I brought them here.*

Kato's eyes dilate, turning dark and huge. His arms drop

heavily to his sides, and the mace he was holding thuds to the ground. He takes an unsteady step back, and then another, his tall, broad body going stiff. Under the serpent's powerful jaws, his throat works, convulsively grabbing for air. Twin rivulets of blood slide down his neck, hissing when they hit the racing embers of his cloak.

The sight of those thin, dark lines shuts down all rational thought. I tear at Griffin's arm. "Let me go! Do something!"

"I'm not letting you go until that snake is gone, or we know why it's here." Griffin's rough words hit my temple like a warm punch. "You're not getting in the middle of this. I will not let you."

Flynn grabs the snake's tail and yanks, stopping when Kato staggers and gurgles a pained sound.

Fury boils my veins. Dread ices them. Hot. Cold. About to explode. "Kill it," I shout to the others. "Kill it!"

Flynn hovers with a knife in his hand, but Carver whips his head around. "You just told us to trust gifts from the Gods!"

"We don't know who sent it! It's biting Kato!"

"And it came out of him!" Carver flings his hand toward the Chaos Wizard.

Out of the corner of my eye, I see the wizard. He's immobile. Impassive. Not reassuring. Not unusual, either.

Kato's throat stops moving, and his cobalt eyes go blank. He falls like a tree. Flynn catches him before he hits the ground, easing him down. Laid out, unmoving, Kato is so rigid he looks dead to me. Terrified, I go numb from the scalp down as the blood crashes from my head.

Flynn rears back, nearly falling over when the serpent releases its bite. The creature springs up and then dives into Kato's open mouth, disappearing down his throat faster than I can blink.

CHAPTER 14

Flynn crouches and lays his hand on Kato's chest. When it doesn't move, his head bows, and his fingers curl into a white-knuckled fist.

There's total stillness for too many breaths. My heart throbs, each painful beat fracturing me a little more until something inside of me shatters, and I scream. Raw grief shreds my throat. Griffin tucks me inward against his body, as if the feel of his heart hammering against my back could somehow keep mine from breaking.

Kato opens his eyes, and I choke on my scream. He blinks, sits up, and I forget to breathe.

"Kato?" Flynn grips the blond warrior's shoulder, steadying him.

Grimacing, Kato gently rubs his throat. He coughs, and then his voice rasps like a wire rake over stones. "That was one of the more traumatizing experiences of my life."

There's a heavy beat of silence while we all stare at him, struck dumb with relief. Then Flynn chokes out a laugh and claps Kato on the shoulder. "I thought you were dead, you Gods damned idiot."

"Not dead. Possibly deaf." Kato gives me a wry look. "You're really loud for such a small person."

A strangled noise escapes me, a sob trying to disguise itself as a laugh. I push on Griffin's arms, and after a slight hesitation, he lets me go.

I drop to my knees next to Kato, my fingers trembling as

I reach out and cautiously touch the twin puncture wounds on his neck. Kato sucks in air through his teeth.

"Sore?" I ask, inspecting the angry red circles.

He nods, his lips forming a bloodless seam.

I gently press again, and he grabs my wrist, pulling my hand down. *Reflexes—normal. Speed—excellent.* But there's still a snake inside him, which can't be good. "I have to see if there's venom."

"There's venom," he says. "The whole left side of my neck feels like a Giant took a spiked club to it."

"Then we have to draw it out."

Kato doesn't let go of my wrist. His grip loosens, but the way his strong fingers curve around my bones makes me think I'm grounding him, when really, he's grounding me.

His throat bobs. "How?"

The almost imperceptible catch in his voice punches a hole between my ribs. "I've seen it done in Fisa. We have lots of venomous snakes. I know how to suck it out."

There's an immediate, fierce rumble of denial from behind me. "No poison *anywhere* near your lips."

"I won't swallow anything." I glare over my shoulder at Griffin, my tone promising fury and savage retribution if he tries to stop me again.

A muscle pops in Griffin's jaw. His eyes are frightening, but he doesn't move.

I turn back to Kato, shifting forward and angling my head toward his neck. "Hold still."

The moment my lips touch his skin, a blast of magic knocks me on my ass. *That bloody wizard thumped his staff and sent me flying!* The boom rattles my brain and leaves it ringing so hard I have to curl up on the ground and cover my ears again. Then Griffin is beside me, and I roll into him as he buffers me against the magic and the torturous pounding in my ears.

"If he thumps his staff again," I gasp out, "I'm going to grab it and whack him over the head."

"No, you won't," Griffin says flatly. "Let's not give Zeus a reason to smite us where we stand. And I think he did that for your protection."

I glare up at him. It's annoying that he makes sense—*constantly*. But I suppose I wouldn't be wildly and irrevocably in love with him if he were an idiot.

"The Drakon Titos's venom is incompatible with the Harbinger," the Chaos Wizard thunders.

I lurch back up, gripping Griffin's arm for balance. "Now you're just ganging up on me."

Griffin smiles tightly. It doesn't reach his eyes. "You're too rash by half. You terrify me. If I had a staff that could stop you in your tracks, I'd be thumping it all the time."

"Then it's a good thing you don't," I say acerbically. Narrowing my eyes, I look around me. "Now, which one of you is going to suck the venom out?"

The wizard's deeply resonating voice crushes any response. "Seek the Ipotane along the Phthian Gap."

I must look like a Centaur just kicked me in the face because Griffin's eyebrows slam down. "What? What is it?"

"That's the last mountain pass before Olympus. Deep, deep into the Ice Plains. There's a lake at the mouth of the gap. According to legend, it's guarded by the Hydra."

Griffin's eyes widen. "The Hydra is real?"

Gods, I hope not. I turn back to the wizard. "How do we get past the Hydra? Is it really there?"

"Poseidon has spoken." The Chaos Wizard turns, his worn robes swirling, and then the door to his hovel closes behind him with a hard click. I hear him throw a heavy lock.

My mouth snaps shut. I stare in shock. At least Poseidon finally showed up, albeit with a parasitic snake and a casual *By the way, why don't you head on over to the Phthian Gap!*

Kato stiffly regains his feet. Turning, I reach for him, grip his arm, and perch on my toes to inspect the snakebite. The twin holes have closed over, leaving two red, raised bumps on his tanned skin.

"They've closed," I say. "We can't draw the venom out."

Kato touches his neck, wincing. The whole left side of his throat is enflamed, and I can feel the heat radiating off the bite like a fire in front of my face.

"I'm not sure we're supposed to," he answers.

Maybe he's right. I let go of his arm and drop back onto my heels. "If this was Poseidon's gift, why would it go to you?"

Kato shrugs. "You're incompatible."

"I've never been incompatible before."

"Maybe it's because you were yelling 'Kill it! Kill it!'" Carver suggests, a wry arch to his brows.

I purse my lips. He has a point. "I loathe snakes. They have that lidless stare, and you can just tell they're thinking about dinner. As in *you* are dinner. It's creepy."

"Snakes are a symbol of healing. Asklepios's rod and all that," Kato says, obviously trying to make himself feel better about having just swallowed one whole.

Where is that thing, anyway? How can it fit?

"And protection. And rebirth. And God-like power." I shake my head. "I still don't like them."

"But giant carnivorous fish and sea serpents are okay?" Griffin asks.

"Oracles? Sort of. Not really. To be honest, before they helped me, I was pretty sure they were going to eat me."

"Poseidon's Oracles—*all* scaly creatures—have only

ever helped you," Griffin points out. "You just wrapped yourself in fire and said to trust the Gods. The cloaks didn't harm us. Even without knowing why the snake was here, it stood to reason it wouldn't harm us, either."

"Don't bring logic into this!" I lift my hands and shove his chest. "And Kato didn't look 'unharmed' a few minutes ago."

"I thought, *hoped*, it would be okay," Griffin says.

Okay? Okay! "In that case, why were you holding me back?"

"Just in case," he answers.

Just in case! "So you figured we'd sacrifice Kato on the altar of 'wait and see'!"

A small muscle contracts under Griffin's eye. He never gets the chance to say something like "better than sacrificing you"—which would have made me explode like a hundred Harpies flying from a burning nest—because Kato suddenly grunts in pain. I whirl and see him slap his hand over his swollen neck.

My eyes widen. "What? What happened?"

His lips draw back in a grimace. "Don't know," he grates out.

I pull his hand down and suck in a sharp breath. A snake tattoo is starting to take shape and coil up the column of his neck. The inflammation disappears under the quick progress of the dark ink. Incredibly lifelike, glossy black scales undulate with Kato's every breath and swallow, making the tattoo look like it's alive and in constant motion. A forked tongue paints itself onto his skin and then curls behind Kato's left ear, licking up into his windswept hair. Faultless crimson and gold diamonds chase each other up the serpent's gleaming back.

"You've been marked," I say, uneasy.

Panic flashes in Kato's blue eyes. "What does that mean?"

"You have a snake tattoo. It looks just like our new friend Titos, only smaller."

"But what does that *mean*?" he asks again.

I shake my head, feeling a stab of panic myself. "I'm sorry. I don't know."

Kato's eyes only stay wild for a moment. Then he takes a deep, bracing breath and slowly nods. He actually smiles at me. "We'll figure it out. You're Cat the Mostly-All-Knowing, right?"

Something twists in my chest. He's reassuring *me*? I'd be clawing my throat out and trying to vomit up a magic snake by now. And if that didn't work—dagger, meet gut. *Maybe.*

"How do you feel?" Flynn asks, handing Kato his dropped mace.

"Better." Kato slides the hilt back into the leather harness on his back. He rolls his shoulders a few times and then moves his head from side to side. Something pops in his neck. "Stiff, but better."

"Do you feel Titos?" I ask.

He presses the flat of his hand against his chest and then lower, running it over his abdomen. He shakes his head. "So, riddles and serpents," Kato says.

The tension inside me starts to unwind. Men are mysteries. But I love the way they can move on from things, even giant snakes.

"And these." I raise my arms under my cloak, lifting the sides like a set of darkly burning wings.

Griffin's hand settles on the small of my back. "Do you think the wizard is coming out again?"

I glance at the hovel. No light shines from within. "I don't think so. That seemed pretty final." *And awful.*

Griffin drops his hand, and I feel the loss of his warmth

like some vital part of me being torn away, missing it instantly. Or maybe I've gone cold because I know what's coming next.

Swallowing, I turn to him, and Griffin's hard stare hits me like a ton of marble.

"Then it's time to fill in the missing pieces. Harbinger."

CHAPTER 15

MY STOMACH TAKES A SICKENING DIVE. GRIFFIN'S shadowed features turn rock-hard when I just stare at him, mute. But my silence isn't belligerence anymore. It's dread overpowering speech.

His eyes glint ominously. "You asked for time, and I let things go. Right or wrong, I can't do that anymore."

My first instinct is to lie, but I can't do that to Griffin again. To us. He'd find out, and he might never trust me again. He might not forgive, and that's not a life I want.

"It's a long story." I glance toward our abandoned camp. "We should sit." Kato could probably use a rest, and right now, even I want the comfort of the fire.

Nodding, Griffin herds everyone away from the wizard's house. Carver throws more wood on the fire in the God Bolt pit, and then Flynn gets down low to blow on the dying embers. When a small blaze is dancing again, lighting our pocket of the night, we settle in a circle, pulling our new cloaks around us.

At my side, Griffin looks at me, expectant. He wants answers. I can't blame him.

"I..." The words stick, and I clear my throat, trying again. "I was here before."

"For Poseidon's Oracle, in the Frozen Lake," Griffin prompts when I don't go on.

I nod. "The magic I was born with was the occasional flash of foresight, the ability to detect lies, and through them, to learn the truth, and a powerful predisposition for compulsion, which I refused to hone. I learned to fight with my body and my knives, to defend myself and survive. My brothers..." I flinch a little.

"Ajax just needed to live. He was already on top just by right of birth, Beta to Mother's Alpha. Thaddeus was the ambitious one. He murdered Ajax, and he tried to kill me." Just thinking about Thaddeus makes me relive his magic all over again, his searing power locked deep in my muscle memory. I force the phantom pain away. "He would have killed me when I was just a little girl, but Thanos always got there in time. Thanos or Eleni." Saying my sister's name out loud is like getting kicked in the chest. For a moment, I can't breathe.

"Thanos?" Griffin asks.

"My guard. My only friend besides Eleni." A not-so-gentle giant of a man, Thanos taught me to fight. And win. "It was always Thaddeus or me, just like with Otis when he came after us. So I...killed him."

Thaddeus tortured me—repeatedly—and yet my unalterable act is still like an open wound. I flex my fingers in my lap, for once trying to get rid of the feel of a knife in my hand instead of wanting the cool comfort of the metal there.

"I surprised him one night when he attacked me. Fire needles. A piercing, deep burn," I explain. "He let up to gather more power, and instead of just kicking and screaming until Thanos got there, I stuck a dagger in his throat. He bled all over me." I swallow with an audible click. "I can still feel his blood."

Griffin's brow creases. "That's self-defense."

"We were children," I say, a tremor in my voice. "He might have changed, but I chose to end his life."

"Do you regret killing Otis?" Griffin asks.

"Never." The very idea is laughable. "I was protecting you. Avenging Eleni."

He looks at me long and hard. "You'll protect us without a second's hesitation and without regret, but you can't justify protecting yourself?"

I glance away, not answering. I don't like where that question is leading. It hits too close to our earlier argument.

"Thaddeus targeted me after Ajax was gone because he could never get the jump on Eleni. She was too fast and smart. And she could make these flaming birds... They'd swoop, and peck, and claw, and burn. Along with her natural goodness, they made her my ray of light and righteous fury. She protected us from Thaddeus—the younger ones and me. She even protected Otis, which makes his betrayal even worse." My breath hitches. "Fisans loved her. I loved her."

When I look at Griffin again, it's through a sheen of tears. "She was like you. She would have changed everything."

He reaches over and squeezes my knee, encouraging me. To my relief, he doesn't pressure me about the question I evaded.

"Eleni and I grew up, got stronger. She could fill the sky with fiery birds, and I could put a knife into just about anything. We ran away. Constantly. Sometimes along the coast. Sometimes straight west or south. Mother's soldiers always found us and dragged us back, but not before we'd snuck through villages, handing over coins and jewels." I look down, blinking rapidly. "Just like in Sinta, the royal tax collectors always took too much, leaving too many people with little, or nothing at all." And I abandoned them. I lost Eleni, and then Fisa lost us both.

Growing up, Eleni and Thanos were my true kin, blood

related or not. Then I had Selena and my friends at the circus. And now these men.

My eyes skate over the faces around the campfire. *Family*. Not a curse word anymore. But still so easily lost.

"I was just Eleni's shadow. She was the one who dared. Dared to steal from the royal coffers. Dared to defy Mother with more than just sarcasm and aggression." A dry laugh escapes me. "We collected allies without even realizing it. It wasn't the goal, but people rallied to our names."

"You were loved." Griffin says this like it doesn't sur- prise him. Like it shouldn't surprise me.

I shoot him a wary look. He doesn't understand. "Fisans still hold vigils to pray for the Lost Princess. All these years, they've prayed for my safe return while I kicked up my heels in Sinta, as far away as I could possibly get."

Griffin doesn't say anything. I didn't expect him to. He can't possibly defend me now.

"Otis grew up, too, and jealousy warped him. Mother always seemed so focused on me, and everyone else loved Eleni. He could never get the better of us in a fair fight, so he perfected underhanded moves." Flashes of pain, red welts, searing burns. I suppress a shudder. "His fire whip could bend around corners. I'd never see it coming."

A low sound rumbles in Griffin's throat. Everyone looks somber. They saw Otis and his fire whip. They saw me turn the magic back on my brother and then flay him alive before I stabbed him in the heart, just like Otis stabbed Eleni.

"Laertes, Priam, and Ianthe were still young, their magic immature. They sometimes squabbled amongst themselves, but they never bothered us."

Sudden pain slices deep into my chest. This knife has cut before, but the blade twists harder now. Ajax, Thaddeus,

Eleni, Catalia—gone. What did Otis do to the little ones once I left?

Carver tosses blades of grass into the fire. They glow and then curl up, burning. "This gives us insight into your cuddly personality, but what does it have to do with the Chaos Wizard calling you Harbinger?"

Griffin slants his brother a warning look. Carver has been acting differently lately. One minute he'll joke and spar with Beta Team, laugh with Griffin, or flirt outrageously with me, and the next he'll shut down, turning irritable. Lately, he's had that edgy look.

I take a deep breath. Secrecy is a hard wall to tear down, especially when the stones are cemented with guilt. "Griffin has already heard, or guessed, a lot of this, but I want you all to know the whole story now."

Flynn smacks the back of Carver's head. "So stop being an ass."

"Sorry, Cat," Carver mumbles, rubbing the spot Flynn just whacked.

I wave his apology away. There's no need. "With Ajax and Thaddeus out of the picture, Eleni was Beta Fisa. I was Gamma. But Mother always wanted me to be next in line. She saw herself in me, I think—no Fire Magic, sly powers like compulsion and hearing the truth in people's lies. She tried to train me to drive creatures and encouraged me to latch on to people's minds, but I refused, and nothing she did could make me." I laugh bitterly. "Just to spite her, I ignored my advantage over nearly everyone—then and now."

"No one should be able to control another person's mind," Griffin says.

"No, and there aren't many who can, but I still should have learned to control creatures. I know the basics. I could probably do it if I didn't have to fight Mother's hold at the same time, like with Sybaris and the Vrykolakas." I twist my fingers in the warm folds of my cloak, fidgeting in a way I never used to. "Learning doesn't mean doing, and it doesn't mean using the power maliciously like she does. But I was afraid she was right, and that I'm just like her. She was always telling me that."

"You're nothing like her," Griffin says fiercely. "Just having that fear should tell you you're not."

I want to believe him. And maybe I do. A little. "My stubbornness enraged her. I reveled in infuriating her until I understood where it led." Sorrow and regret are millstones on my chest as I admit, "She blamed Eleni for holding me back."

Griffin's deep voice simmers with anger. "She forced you and Eleni apart. Forced you into an arena to fight."

I nod. I already told him this, pretending those horrible days trapped in the sweltering arena weren't about me. "She wouldn't feed us. She wouldn't give us water. She got into our heads, pounding away with lies and images of betrayals that never happened. We resisted." And *Gods*, did it hurt. "We fought back until we were weak and bleeding and not sure of anything anymore. I finally lost all sense of myself, all sense of the truth. *I* cracked first. My heart was never as pure as Eleni's, and Mother knew it. She counted on it, because she wanted me to be the one to walk out of that trap alive."

"So you fought each other in the end," Griffin says quietly.

"Fought hardly describes it. We kicked and bit and clawed at each other like animals in the dirt. Mother must have been so happy to have finally gotten what she wanted that her concentration wavered, and we snapped out of it." I swallow, my throat thick. "Eleni crouched over me and held me and promised that nothing would tear us apart."

I press my lips together, my eyes burning. "But then a shadow fell over us. It was Mother. And Otis. She dragged Eleni off me. Eleni twisted and fought with whatever strength she had left, keeping herself between Mother and me. Mother told her she was weak. I could hardly move, but I started screaming because I knew weakness never went unpunished. I somehow got to my knees, but I was too late. Mother handed Otis a knife, and he stabbed Eleni through the heart." My voice trembles and turns raw. "I couldn't stop it. She died right next to me, and I didn't *do* anything."

Shifting closer, Griffin presses his lips to my temple. "I've changed my mind. You don't have to go on. Not now, not ever if you don't want to."

I reach over and grip his hand. He squeezes mine back, and I take that small comfort, even though I don't deserve it. "But Carver's right. I haven't gotten to the Harbinger part."

"You have the right to your past, Cat. It doesn't have to be a part of our future."

I close my eyes, my heart aching. I meant it when I said I wasn't fit to lick Griffin's boots. He should have believed me.

"It is our future," I say. "It's everyone's."

Griffin's hold on my hand tenses. This is the start of losing him. But he deserves the truth, so I force myself to go on.

"I don't know how I got back to the castle. I think Thanos carried me. I stayed in bed for three days, physically recovering. Mother came to see me. She was excited that I was Beta at only fifteen, just like her at the time. She grinned, and I slapped her. You should've seen the look on her face." I stare into the fire, remembering. "It was the only time I ever raised a hand against her, despite everything she'd put me through. Later that night, I snuck into the cellars, crawled into a pile of garbage, and got taken out with the rest of the trash."

"Don't call yourself trash," Griffin says in a deceptively soft voice.

My eyes jerk to his. "I've killed two brothers and a sister. I've outdone them all."

"You defended yourself, and you did *not* kill your sister. You're brave." He squeezes my hand. "You're good."

I twist out of his grasp, feeling like an imposter. "I could have ended it all, and I didn't."

Griffin's eyes search mine. "What do you mean?"

"I ran away, with no intention of ever going back. I came here, stripped naked, and dove into the lake. I swam straight out. I swam until my muscles cramped and I couldn't feel myself anymore, until my heart didn't know how to pump the frozen sludge in my veins, and I didn't care if I lived or died."

Something dangerous flashes across Griffin's face.

"Poseidon's Oracle grabbed me just when I started to sink. It had three long tentacles that kept me from drowning while it probed my mind and tasted me. I was frozen to my core, but I still felt every one of those icy suckers on my skin." I shudder. "I thought it was going to eat me. I couldn't wait for it to end."

"I don't believe that," Griffin says. "You're a survivor. That's not you."

"I was fifteen. I'd just lost Eleni. I hated myself. I was Beta Fisa, and I had grief and rage and a hole in my heart where my sister used to be."

I can see Griffin struggling to understand my feelings, but wanting to give up isn't something he truly comprehends. Conceptually—maybe. In practice—never.

"But the Oracle didn't eat you," he finally says. "It gave you a gift."

My heart starts to pound. I've never said this out loud before. "It gave me *two*."

His eyes widen. The others murmur in astonishment. Even magic-deprived southerners know that's unheard of.

"Turn invisible. Steal magic and heal." That's actually three, but the second two go hand in hand.

"What happened then?" Flynn asks.

I rub my forehead. "The next part is hazy. The Oracle brought me here. Well, there…" I point toward the shore. "I got these horrible shooting pains all over my body when I started to thaw out. Somehow, I was inside the hovel, covered in blankets in front of the fire. The Chaos Wizard was sitting in a rocking chair, staring at me. I didn't know who or what he was at the time. I tried to talk to him, but all I got was that swirly, vacant look. You know the one." I wave vaguely toward the wizard's house.

"My clothes were there, so I got dressed and left. I turned invisible to test out my new magic, walked back to Fisa City, and snuck into the castle. I had questions that needed answers, and that meant going back. I found Thanos—who, oddly, didn't seem worried about me at all—and asked him about the man in the hovel. He's the one who told me about the wizard and how he channels the Gods. That explained a lot. The infinite gaze, and…other things." I chew on my lower lip, anxiety twisting my stomach into a hard, painful knot. "But I didn't only go back for Thanos."

"Then why did you go back?" Griffin asks.

My expression must turn ugly. It *feels* ugly. "I was going to kill my mother. Maybe Otis, too."

Griffin watches me. They all do. I can't tell how they feel about that, or what they're thinking.

"Why didn't you?" Griffin finally asks.

"Because I'm a coward."

"You are not a coward," he growls softly. The others echo their agreement.

I can't look at them and settle my gaze on the slowly dying fire instead. "I could have ended her reign of terror. Fisa needed one thing from Eleni, and if not from Eleni, then from me. End it. End her. There could have been peace, security, prosperity. I held it all in the palm of my hand, along with a dagger. I was invisible. I kept telling myself to just do it. Then I could move on to Otis. I could cut them both down without ever showing my face."

"But you didn't." I know Griffin is looking at me. I don't look back.

"Otis must have guessed I'd come for him. He locked himself behind so many wards I couldn't get through. He probably stayed in his room for a year." I snort, but it sounds hollow. "I wouldn't know. I was long gone by then because I didn't do any of it. I did *nothing*. I watched Mother for days. She was frantic when no one could find me. In her own warped way, she *hurt*. I'm not sure why she was so out of her mind, but do you know how that made me feel?"

Griffin seems to choose his words very carefully. "You were fifteen, confused and hurting. You can't spend your life blaming yourself for a child's decisions."

"Fifteen is not a child!" My voice lashes out, slicing loudly through the night. "You know that as well as I do." Especially in the south, most girls are considered women from their first cycle, ready for a home and family of their own. Just because Griffin is absurdly overprotective doesn't change the rest of the world's standards.

"For the first time ever, Mother looked uncertain, and I

thought maybe she actually did care about me. That maybe in her twisted mind, everything she did was to make me stronger, to groom me to rule." I turn halfway, finally facing Griffin again. "I did immeasurable harm just by being the Kingmaker and caving to Mother when she wanted to get people's truths out of me. I murdered Thaddeus. I got Eleni killed. Without Eleni, I thought—"

Griffin shakes his head. "You did *not* get Eleni killed."

I scoff. "I'll believe that when the Underworld freezes over and Centaurs fly."

"Don't hate yourself for giving your own mother a second chance. You wanted to see good in her."

"I was stupid, Griffin. There is no good in her."

"None of this is your fault."

"Argh!" I snarl. "If you can't admit I'm a terrible person, I'll never believe another word you say!"

He laughs. *Laughs!*

"Sorry," he mutters gruffly, capturing my hand once more. "What you did, or rather *didn't* do, proves something you shouldn't have so much trouble believing," Griffin says.

I debate twisting my hand out of his again. In the end, I leave it where it is. "What?" I reluctantly ask.

"You're the exact opposite of your mother."

I snort.

"You know I'm right."

"You're never right." Which is a colossal lie. "You can't even rhyme."

His low chuckle warms something in my chest.

"He's right," Flynn says.

"He's right," Kato agrees.

"He's right."

Carver, too? I sigh. "You're all delusional. And I didn't let Andromeda live just because of some idiotic hope that she'd change and the first fifteen years of my life could be blood under the bridge." I take a deep breath. *Now for the hard part.* "It's possible that killing her will end the world."

Griffin's face goes utterly blank. "What?"

"The Chaos Wizard... He, uh, said something. Before I left."

His eyebrows dive together. "What?" Griffin repeats, his voice sharpening.

"A prophecy." I shift nervously. "One of those fun, fate-of-the-world kinds."

Staring at me, Griffin goes disturbingly still. My heart slams a hard beat against my ribs.

Carver sits up straighter. "That sounds dire."

"It is dire." Glancing around the campfire, I see all eyes on me.

"What did the wizard say?" Griffin asks.

I feel short of breath, and I have to rip the words from my throat. "He said I'm going to destroy the realms. That I'm the Harbinger of the end."

Griffin still doesn't move, and a painful ache spreads across my chest. He's shutting down. What he felt for me is frosting over on this chill wind, and I'll never get him back.

And why would I? I'm the diametric opposite of every-thing he stands for. Everything he wants.

His tone flattening, Griffin says, "Details. Tell me everything."

"Details don't change the outcome."

"Humor me."

My heart lurches. The last time he said that, I told him evasive half-truths and made myself out to be someone I'm not. He probably thinks I'll do that again. But I've changed, and I won't.

Dread still rises like a riptide to drag me under. "Catalia Andromeda Eileithyia Fisa—no mistaking it's about me," I add dryly. "Harbinger of the end. Destroyer of realms. Origin magic takes Alpha blood. Kingdoms crumble with the fall of the scourge."

Griffin studies me hard. "And you think that means what, exactly?"

"Isn't it obvious?"

"Is it?" he asks.

"Don't make this harder than it already is." I stand, starting to back away.

Griffin snags my wrist, stopping me, his grip tight but not hard enough to hurt. "You're interpreting it wrong."

"What are you talking about? I have Origin magic. It's my heritage. I spill Alpha blood, my mother's, *the scourge*—you even called her that yourself once—and therefore somehow destroy the world."

Griffin's mouth breaks into a slow smile.

I glare at him. "There's nothing funny about this!"

Leaping up, he grabs me and swings me around.

"Griffin!" My heart swoops wildly.

"Cat. Cat." Lowering me, he buries his face in my neck, inhaling deeply. "You've spent eight years imagining the worst, haven't you?"

"Uh…" Of course I have. Who does he think I am?

"Magic and mayhem? Floods and earthquakes? Death and destruction?" he asks.

I nod. "Thunderbolts from Olympus, creatures running amok…"

Griffin lifts his head, his eyes dancing. "You have no idea of your own worth."

I frown. "You really are delusional. You need help. Maybe your mother has some herbs."

Griffin gives me a horrified look.

"Fine. No herbs."

He squeezes my waist. "You need to stop with the pessimism. No more self-pity. You're better than that."

My jaw slides unhinged. That stung. "Then what do *you* think the prophecy is about?" I've always been terrible at riddles. Could I have gotten it *that* wrong?

"The Gods have been watching over you for years. They've helped you, given you gifts, magic, advice. Saved you. Why would they go out of their way to keep you alive if you were nothing but a means of base destruction?"

"I don't know! The Gods are weird. Maybe they're sick of Thalyria and want to start over again."

"*Finally.*" Griffin nods. "You're getting it now."

My eyes narrow. "Are you being sarcastic?"

He shakes his head. "I took Sinta. The Gods brought us together to take the rest of Thalyria. It's just like we thought. We're going to unify the realms."

"Unify. Destroy." At a loss, I look around at the world I'm apparently going to make crumble. "It's not the same thing."

Griffin challenges me with a stern look. "Poseidon brought us together so we could do this. Origin magic." He lightly taps my chest. "Alpha blood—which you *took*, multiple times, and not only blood." He winks and taps his own chest.

"You're not Alpha." Only he is.

"It's just a word," Griffin says.

"Words are important in a prophecy!"

"Fine. I hereby declare myself Alpha Sinta. I'll send Egeria a scroll."

I laugh. I can't help it.

Griffin lifts his hands and pushes my hair back from my face, holding the fluttering strands against the sides of my head. "The scourge isn't just your mother. It's everything. The way the realms are run, what the Alphas have become. You broke the mold, you and Eleni, when you refused to take part in the race for power."

My nostrils flare. "I ended up on top. What's worse than that?"

"Stubborn to the core," Griffin mutters, pressing his fingers into my scalp. "You defended yourself. That's all."

I open my mouth to argue but then snap it shut. Nothing I did was ever to gain power. I've always run from responsibility, which makes what Griffin is saying even scarier. If we succeed, I won't just have Fisa to deal with, I'll have everything.

"You *are* the Harbinger of the end of the realms. We'll destroy them. We'll break down borders, create a new kingdom, and make it a place worth living in again—for everyone, if we can."

"Your idealism is nauseating." But something foreign and bright streaks through me. *Optimism?* It's nauseating, too.

Griffin looks more certain than ever. "The Gods created us for *this*. The Fates wove the threads of our lives around *this*."

I stare at him. "You can't know that. We don't know."

"*I* know." Lit by moonlight, Griffin's steady gaze tells me a story of devotion—and utter conviction. "You should trust me. Trust me, Cat."

Trust me. I swallow. One breath. Two. My stomach flips over and then crashes through a tangle of nerves. "Okay."

Griffin's eyebrows fly up. He abruptly straightens, dropping his hands from the sides of my head. "*Okay?*"

I smile at his obvious shock. "Yes, Your Persuasiveness."

"Good." He nods once. "When a crumbling house

reaches a certain point, there's no fixing it. You tear it down. You clear the rubble, and then you build something better." The silver linings around Griffin's irises draw me like a magnet. "You may be the Harbinger of the end, but do you know what else you are?"

I shake my head, half dreading the answer still.

"You, *agapi mou*, are the new beginning."

CHAPTER 16

PANOTII LOOKS PUT OUT ABOUT BEING LEFT BEHIND AND dogs my steps as I stow his tack under the deep overhang on the south side of the wizard's hovel. There's plenty of grass here, water at the lake, and it's not that cold yet, despite the shift in seasons. If the rains start before we get back, the horses can take shelter under the overhang. I'm not worried about them wandering off. Not one of them has stepped outside of the large makeshift corral of God Bolt pits since we got here.

"You can't come with us," I tell him. "It'll be cold and slippery. And big monsters will want to eat you."

He tosses his head, snorting.

"Really big monsters. There might be Dragons. And the Hydra. And I can't vouch for the friendliness of the Ipotane toward regular horses." I blow gently into his nose. Panotii chuffs back. "You'll be safe here, and if anyone tries to steal you, Grandpa Zeus will throw down a thunderbolt. *Boom!* No more horse thief."

"Zeus may have better things to do than babysit our horses," Flynn says, stowing his own equine gear next to mine.

I glance northward toward the Gods' mountain home and speak loudly. "In that case, I'm announcing right now that I'll make an Olympian stink if anything happens to my horse."

Flynn looks nervous and moves away from me like he's expecting a God Bolt to come thundering down.

"She's not kidding." Sunlight glints off Griffin's wind-blown hair. Thick black stubble darkens his jaw. He flashes me a smile that brings out the slight hook in his nose, and something tightens in my belly.

I turn back to Panotii and scratch under his jaw. "You're in charge here." His enormous ears flick my way. "You keep the others in line."

Panotii nods. I swear to the Gods, my horse nods.

Brown Horse raises his head and pins me with a gimlet stare.

I roll my eyes. "Fine. You can help. You're both in charge."

Apparently satisfied, Griffin's horse goes back to grazing, shearing the grass around him with neat, orga-nized efficiency. Griffin and Brown Horse were made for each other.

Panotii shoves his nose into my shoulder, knocking me back a step. Taking a handful of his chestnut mane, I stretch up on my toes to whisper into one of his donkey ears. "Seriously, you're in charge. I'll bet you can even rhyme."

Carver and Kato chuckle as they walk past.

Griffin bands his arms around my waist from behind, surprising me. "I heard that." He hauls me back against his chest and buries his face in the crook of my neck with a warning growl.

I laugh, a heady burst of awareness racing through me. He nuzzles that spot below my ear, giving it a lingering kiss and then a soft little nip. Hot shivers cascade from my nape to the small of my back, pooling at the base of my spine.

"We're never alone anymore." I hear the huskiness in my voice as I press against him and lift my arms, curving my hands around his neck. "I haven't seen you naked since Kitros. Haven't felt your skin on mine."

He groans. I feel him hardening behind me. "I miss that. I miss being inside you."

Desire spills swirling warmth through my middle. The pleasurable feeling moves lower, tightening. "I love the way you touch and kiss me everywhere and then again. As if you can't get enough."

"Can't *ever* get enough." Sheltered from view by Panotii at our front, Griffin skates his hands up my rib cage until his thumbs tease the undersides of my breasts. He draws rough knuckles along the curves, and toe-curling tingles radiate from his touch. Muscles heat and clench in my core. Under my cloak, Griffin palms both breasts. When my nipples stiffen, he gently rolls them between his fingertips, and I stop breathing. I want to tear off my tunic so he can touch bare skin.

"You're torturing me," I murmur.

He tugs, and a jolt of sensation arcs straight to the space between my legs. "Then we're even, because I'm torturing myself."

His whiskers rasp my neck, sending a wash of goose bumps down my body. The delicious chills heat me up until I'm simmering with need. Before he can drive us both even crazier, I turn and slip my arms around his waist. The accelerated beat of his heart drums beneath my ear. Sometimes, I want to be so close to Griffin that I think only crawling inside him will satisfy me. I don't understand that—this overwhelming need to be one.

I grip him hard. "I love you. I need you. It's a constant ache."

Griffin buries his hand in my hair, holding my head against his chest. His other arm circles my back. The evidence of his desire is thick and hard against my belly. "I know, *kardia mou*. I feel it, too."

A heavy longing settles in my bones. I tilt my face up, he lowers his, and the searing kiss that follows leaves me feeling claimed all over again.

"There it is. The northeast needle." My breathing is ragged from another endless trudge through thigh-deep snow. I point to an intimidating peak, the last of the icy spires before the Deskathi Mountains finally taper off into the long, twisting valley leading to the Phthian Gap.

Even with my underdeveloped sense of direction, we would have been hard pressed to get lost. The mountain range practically grew out of the far shore of the Frozen Lake, and all we had to do was follow it northeast, sticking to the cols and valleys, and watching the peaks around us grow taller and spinier with each passing day. With the way this direction tugs on my magic, I could probably have done it blindfolded. The farther we venture onto the Ice Plains, the more I'm aware of the magical compass inside of me, and the needle only seems to point one way—toward Olympus.

A gust of wind lifts fresh powder from the slope beside us and sends it swirling through the air. The sun reflects off the frosty particles, turning them into a whirling cyclone of glittering gold. Squinting against the dazzling brightness, I pull my cloak more firmly around my head and neck to block the biting cold.

I glance at Griffin. He and the others are holding up well in the harsh climate, or at least they're not complaining. Thank the Gods for Hades's cloaks.

Well, thank Hades, really.

Griffin scrapes a cold-reddened hand over his thickly bearded jaw, cursing softly as he takes in the sheer mountain face. His gaze narrows on the shadowed entrance to the high-up caves. "How in the name of Zeus are we supposed to get up there?"

I grin, giddiness sweeping through me to have gotten this far with so little trouble. The few skirmishes we've had with magical creatures ended quickly and in our favor, and the weather, while frigid, has been free of storms. "There's a path, of course."

Silvery eyes meet mine. "I see no path."

"It's there. Thanos told me."

"And how did *he* know?" A low, particular growl edges into Griffin's voice whenever I talk about Thanos. I may come across as overenthusiastic in my admiration, at least for Griffin's taste.

I shrug. "I can't think of anything Thanos *didn't* know. I suppose he came here. He'd been pretty much everywhere."

"And yet he was your guard?" Griffin asks.

I nod. "He taught me more than all my tutors combined. I was in awe of him." Thanos, with his broad cheekbones, deep-set eyes, hammer-like fists, and colossal build. "I was convinced I was going to marry him when I grew up."

Griffin goes completely stiff, and I bite my tongue. I forgot. I still haven't agreed to actually marry Griffin yet.

I reach for his hand beneath his cloak. "He didn't take me seriously. I didn't even reach his waist when I was thinking things like that."

I stop there, not adding that at fifteen, when I left, my head just barely reached Thanos's chest—or that I begged him to leave with me. I'd wanted us to stay together. Forever. Despite what I just told Griffin, I'd been half in love with Thanos for years, and if it had been up to me, it would have turned into more. But Thanos just set me on his gigantic knee like I was still a child and told me I'd be fine without him, and that once I was safely away from the castle, he had other things to do.

Other things to do!

I was devastated. He sent me on my way as if he hadn't spent my entire life up to that point being my friend and protector.

"None of that matters now," I say more easily than I feel, a time-dulled shard of hurt still alive inside of me. "We don't see the path because it's on the northern slope, which isn't as steep. It only winds around to this side at the very top. Look—just below the cave. Do you see that darker line? It's the end of the trail, coming around from the back."

Griffin nods and squeezes my hand. He doesn't let go as he angles his body into the wind and starts walking. There's still a long way to go.

Dawn breaks over the Ice Plains, turning the icicles lining the mouth of the cave into a jagged row of fiery daggers. Around us, a landscape of white, gray, and glacial blue slowly emerges from the night like a cautious beast leaving the shadows—still, monumental, treacherous. In the silence of daybreak, Griffin takes steel to flint, lights one of our two torches, and then hands it to Kato.

I peer to my right. The glacial tunnel leading into the labyrinth is as dark as a Cyclops's heart. Griffin hands me the second, unlit torch, and I slip it into a loosened dagger loop in my belt. Two blades are missing, both melted down by the Dragon's Breath.

In return, I hand Griffin Ariadne's Thread. He holds the silvery ball of twine while Carver ties the loose end around my wrist, tugging hard on the knot to make sure it's secure.

Griffin rechecks it, twice, his expression grim. "Remember what the wizard said."

"Only Kato and I go in. Beware Atalanta's bow. Find the lyre before the three-headed beast. Heed the Goddess's needs."

His eyes bore into mine, dark and troubled. "I don't like being separated."

My chest aches. I lean into him. "I know."

"Don't you dare cut this thread. For any reason." Griffin's arms clamp around me, hard as rocks. "If you do, I swear to the Gods I'll come in there, find you, and give you a spanking you'll never forget."

My shaky laugh is muffled by his cloak. "I find that a lot more tempting than I probably should."

Griffin squeezes me. "Come back to me. Don't do anything foolish."

Me? "I'm never foolish."

He grips me until my bones creak.

"I'll be careful," I promise, feeling my magic spark with the pledge.

Griffin eases his hold, pressing his lips to the top of my head and inhaling deeply. When he lets me go and offers his hand to Kato, the other man shakes it, absorbing Griffin's long, hard look with a solemn nod. The silent communication has "protect her with your life and then some" written all over it. A few weeks ago, I would have dismissed it as a lot of overprotective male posturing. Now, I only wish I could convince them that dying for me is *not* an option.

As Kato and I enter the labyrinth, I have to convince myself to put one foot in front of the other. About thirty feet in, just before the tunnel curves to the right, I stop and look back even though every instinct tells me not to.

My heart seizes, tumbling painfully at the sight of Griffin. Ariadne's Thread trails from his tightly fisted hand. His big frame is taut and still with the kind of coiled tension that hovers on the brink of explosion, as if he's barely restraining himself from coming in after me.

Our eyes collide across the frost-blanketed entrance of the cave. "I swear I'll cut this thread, drop it, and leave it behind me if any one of you steps past this point in the tunnel before we're back." The vow jolts through me, sealing itself in my skin, my blood, and my bones.

Griffin's face twists. He curses violently.

Fighting the burning rawness inside me, I say, "You can take shelter in the cave's entrance, but if you come after us, I'll be physically compelled to cut the rope and not pick it up again." The magical chain reaction will hit me no matter where I am, not leaving me any choice.

"I release you from your vow," Griffin says.

"It's not a vow to you; it's a vow to myself. You can't release me."

"Cat. Be reasonable. What if—"

"Just wait for us," I call. "We'll be back."

My pulse thuds wildly as I back away under Griffin's livid stare. A muscle jerks in his cheek, ticking hard enough to send a ripple through his beard. His eyes blaze, and my heart wrenches as I turn away.

"Cat!" he roars.

I turn the corner without looking back. My eyes burn, and every shallow, quick breath shudders in my throat.

Kato waits until the light from the cave's entrance fades entirely before asking gruffly, "Are you all right?"

I sniff and press my chilled fingertips to my stinging eyes, stemming the hot prickle of tears. "No."

He doesn't try to talk to me again, which is for the best.

With only the light of the torch and the dim glow from our cloaks, we wind our way deeper into the labyrinth, ducking pointy icicles and slipping on mirror-smooth patches of ice. When the tunnel splits into three branches, we peer into the darkness. Which reveals nothing. Because it's dark.

"What do you think?" I ask, my voice rough from disuse and swallowing tears.

Kato lowers the torch, scanning the tunnel floor for footprints or signs of passage. There are none. The ice is even and unmarked underfoot, and so cold that the chill is already seeping through my thick-soled boots.

He shrugs. "Straight?"

After that, there are so many offshoots that we simply take turns deciding which way to go. Twice, we stumble back onto Ariadne's Thread and know we've gone in circles. We're debating whether or not to backtrack while picking up the thread when a dim light beckons us from a distant tunnel on the right.

Curious, cautious, we follow the light and find a cavern, bright and high-ceilinged—if you can call the enormous sheet of ice filtering in the sunlight from outside a ceiling. Far above our heads on the frozen roof, zigzagging patterns of windblown snow splash swirling shadows across the cavern floor.

Kato looks up, frowning. "How thick do you think that ice is?"

I scrunch my nose. "Thick enough?"

Voices carry differently in the cavern, amplified by the smooth walls and towering ceiling. When we're not speaking, it's quiet enough that I fancy I can hear my own heartbeat echoing back to me off the sheets of ice.

It's quiet enough that there's no mistaking the distinctive twang of a bowstring when it vibrates in my ears.

CHAPTER 17

W<small>E BOTH DUCK ON INSTINCT, AND THE ARROW SLAMS</small> into the milky-white stalagmite behind us, embedding itself deep into the mineral deposit.

Kato reaches for me, but another twang sends us diving in opposite directions. I scramble toward another stalagmite, slipping on the ice and skidding beyond my mark. The bowstring hums again, and my right foot gets punched out from under me.

I hit the ground hard on my side and slide. Grunting, I flip onto my stomach and then scrabble back over the ice until I crash into the back side of the mineral tower. Another arrow clatters across the ice just as I snatch in my trailing foot.

"Cat!" Kato is ten feet away, behind a stalagmite that's not even as wide as his shoulders. "You're hit!"

A colorfully fletched arrow sticks out from the heel of my boot. "It's in the sole." I yank it out and drop it next to me. "I'm fine."

"Not for long," a singsongy voice croons from a gallery of caves high up along the opposite wall of the cavern. "You're oh-so-wrong."

I take a quick look out from behind my shield, trying to discern the archer's form. "Atalanta, I presume?"

There's a pause. "She knows my name. That's not part of the game."

Twang. Crack!

She aimed high. I look up and see a huge, lethally sharp icicle speeding toward my head.

I jump out of the way, forced to forsake my shelter. Another arrow flies before I can take cover again and slams into my shoulder.

I gasp, staggering back. Then Kato has me. He shoves us both into the debris of the shattered icicle behind my stalagmite an instant before another arrow skids over the ice where I just stood.

Fuming, I grab the shaft and yank the arrow from my shoulder. Kato looks horrified.

"It hit a buckle. The armor blocked it." Mostly. Under the tough leather, warm liquid dampens my tunic, making the material cling to the side of my breast.

His eyes close briefly in relief. Then, setting me behind him, he calls out, "We're here on a mission from the Gods. We don't want any trouble."

Atalanta laughs. It's a light, airy sound, like wind through trees. Preternaturally fast, she flits from cave to cave along the far wall. "So handsome. I think I'll hold you for ransom."

"What?" I say through gritted teeth.

Kato looks at me. The wariness in his cobalt eyes doesn't color his arch tone. "Now *she* can rhyme."

My jaw drops. "I can rhyme!"

"Live among bears, get covered in hairs!" Atalanta sings.

I roll my injured shoulder, testing it. It stings, but that's all. "She makes no sense. She's trying to kill us. We have to get past her."

Drawing a Kobaloi knife, I rub my thumb over the sinew while I watch the way the archer's silhouette moves. When I think I've nailed down the pattern, I throw the blade into an empty gallery, counting on her to flit through it at the same moment. She does, but she *catches* the knife, stopping it right in front of her armored chest before twirling back into the shadows.

I blink. Titos and now *this*? Those Kobaloi knives were the worst purchase of my life!

Atalanta pops into the next cave, flips my knife in her hand, and then throws it back. The blade sticks in a mini stalagmite an inch from my foot. I jerk back, thumping mad.

"It's not with a knife that you'll take my life."

I pry my knife free and then sheathe the blade again.

Twang. Crack!

Kato yanks me against him and spins to the side as another icicle falls from the roof and smashes down next to us. Shattered ice blasts our legs and scatters in a chiming wave.

"Nock an arrow, hit the marrow," Atalanta chants, letting another bolt fly.

Too late, I realize Kato isn't entirely behind the stalagmite anymore. He slaps his hand over his neck, right at the base of his skull.

Fury gathers inside me like a storm as he moves us both closer to the mineral deposit again. I reach for his wrist. "Let me see."

He lowers his red-stained fingers, and I rise to my toes, using the arm he still has around me for balance.

"It's just a scratch." But mini Titos's forked tongue is *lapping up* the blood.

I pat Kato's chest in what I hope is a reassuring way, trying to keep my eyes a normal size and my voice steady. "You're fine." Animated tattoos and vampiric snakes are *not* something he needs to worry about right now.

I pull my tunic from my pants, rip off the relatively clean hem, and then wrap the strip around Kato's neck, securing the ends with a knot. "There. Good as new."

He gives me a tight smile. "This stalagmite isn't big enough for the two of us. I'll go back to mine."

"Don't." I grab his arm. "She's too good. She'll pin you in seconds."

He hesitates and then gets behind me, pushing me right up against the frosty surface. Stuck, I can't even give Atalanta the evil eye anymore.

"I can't breathe," I eventually protest.

"Good. Then you can't move."

"And that's ever so helpful in a fight!"

"Atalanta!" Kato calls, not moving an inch. "Zeus and Athena sent us. We're meant to bring a treasure to the Ipotane Alpha."

I roll my eyes. "Fantastic. Just tell her we're here to steal her treasure."

"It might not be hers."

"She might be guarding it," I argue.

I feel him shrug behind me. "Or she could say she was expecting us."

"Expecting to kill us," I mutter.

Kato inhales sharply, moving enough for me to lean over and see what he sees. Atalanta has stepped out onto a ledge. Framed against the gallery of caves above, she's magnificent. Wild and dark. Silky hair falls to her knees, spilling over her arms, hands, and lowered bow. Diaphanous skirts cover her long, shapely legs only to mid-thigh, and gleaming, golden upper-body armor illuminates the smooth, pale skin of her neck and face. Dark brows wing across her forehead, arching delicately. Her full mouth looks like it's been stained by kalaberries, offering an exotic splash of color against her flawless, almost translucent complexion. She's as cold and perfect as the ice crystals adorning the cavern.

Thick-lashed, elongated eyes send a shock through me. They mirror mine, glinting with the pure light-green of magic and the north.

She moves forward, her long hair swaying. "The Gods sent you to me that I might be free?"

Free? From what? "Yes!"

Kato gives me a warning squeeze, and I stick an elbow in his ribs.

Atalanta cocks her head in a perfectly savage way, reminding me of a wolf let loose in a field of sheep. "Please Artemis, and you may depart from this."

Artemis is the Goddess? Heed the Goddess's needs.

What does that mean?

"We don't have an offering," Kato whispers in my ear.

"I know!" I grate back.

Atalanta steps so close to the edge of her perch that the tips of her boots kiss empty air. "We'll take the warrior to serve as courtier."

My insides plummet. *Is that why the Gods sent Kato in here?*

"You can't have him." I search frantically for an alternate offering. "You can have a magic cloak."

Atalanta laughs.

"Fine. Two magic cloaks."

Kato grunts. I don't think he wants to give his up.

"I'm not just handing you over!" I snap.

"Your worry can end, for we will not keep your friend."

I look sharply at the other female. "Then what do you want from him? And for how long?"

She wets her berry-colored lips. Her hands curl at her sides. "Mistress and I, we've decided to try…"

Her words trail off, an intense, heated look coming over her face. I know that look. I look at Griffin that way all the time.

Scowling, I wiggle enough to turn around and face Kato. "She looks like a wild animal in heat. I have a good idea of what they have planned for you."

"Me too."

I smack his arm. "You don't have to look so happy about it!"

Kato shrugs. "What's not to like?"

"She shot me!"

"She shot me, too."

Gah! Men! "Artemis is sworn to virginity. Her...disciple might be, too. You can't touch them."

"Heed the Goddess's needs." Kato spreads his hands like he can't help it if Artemis wants a man.

"That's not a need, it's a want! She can live without."

"She's immortal. That's a long time to live without."

"Maybe she is sick of her eternal virginity." *I would be.* "But what if you're wrong and Zeus strikes you down with a God Bolt for deflowering his daughter?"

Kato looks less keen about that. "This is part of what the wizard said. I have to go with her. What happens next..." He frowns. "I'll figure it out."

"It's a test." I start to panic. I don't like it. "It's a test to see if you'll hold out, if you'll keep the Goddess pure."

"If the woman is brave," Atalanta calls down, "she'll find her man in the second large cave."

"What second large cave?" I glance at Kato. "It took us hours just to find this one."

"She thinks I'm your man," Kato says, surprised.

"And yet she has no problem dragging you off for an Olympian orgy!"

"Two women is hardly an orgy," he points out.

I glare.

Kato takes my shoulders and squeezes. "This is why it was me, Cat. Why they said only I could come into the caves with you."

My eyebrows slam down. "What do you mean?"

"I'm the only one of us who can do this without damaging something. I'm the only one whose heart isn't engaged."

"What? Oh…" Griffin loves me. Jocasta is clearly something to Flynn, even if he's not sure what. And Carver… Obviously Kato knows something about Carver that I don't.

"There are always consequences," I say darkly.

He shrugs. "Sometimes more. Sometimes less."

My mouth flattens. I don't like this. "Who is Carver pining for?" No wonder he's been moody and a little solitary lately. Whoever she is, he had to leave her behind. "I can't be the only one who doesn't know."

Kato smiles faintly, something sad edging into his eyes. "A ghost."

I wince. *Oh, Carver.*

Kato drops his hands from my arms. "Don't worry. I've been in the back room of a tavern or two. I know what to do."

I don't doubt that. "You don't have to. We'll find another way."

"This was written, Cat. You know that as well as I do." Kato steps away from me. "Find me in the second cave."

My heart clenches hard. "What if I can't?"

"You can."

I grab his wrist. "Have you seen me try to read a map? It's pathetic, and I don't say that lightly."

"You don't have a map."

"Well, that's even worse!"

Atalanta drops from her perch, landing lightly on the balls of her feet despite the impact fracturing the frost in a wide circle all around her. She strides toward us, tall, confident, and poised, possessing an animal's natural grace. Her arms are loose. Her hips sway. Her hair swoops. *Gods, it's annoying.*

I've got animal grace. I've got plenty. Definitely enough to claw her eyes out.

With a last look at me, Kato steps out from behind the stalagmite.

I jump after him, trying to pull him back. "What about the three-headed beast?"

He rubs the back of his neck, his blue eyes swimming with shadows. "I don't know, but I don't think she'll wait."

Atalanta's avid gaze is already bright with lust. She's practically foaming at the mouth. "Strip!" she commands, not bothering with a rhyme.

My jaw drops. Kato looks rather shocked himself.

"Now?" he asks, for some reason directing the question at me.

I shrug helplessly. "I guess."

Atalanta slings her bow over one shoulder and then starts rapping her fingernails against her armor. The impatient tip-tapping grates on my nerves. Everything about her grates on my nerves—the rhyming, her agility, the way she caught my knife, and how she intends to use Kato, although *he* doesn't seem to mind.

Kato strips, handing each item of clothing to me. He starts shivering almost immediately.

"The temperature won't exactly enhance my performance," he mutters.

I take his pants, trying not to glimpse what they used to be covering. "I have a feeling she'll keep you warm," I say sourly.

Atalanta claps, apparently delighted with what she sees. I don't look. I *refuse* to look.

"The treasure you need, you'll receive after the deed. As you depart, it will"—she looks Kato up and down with unabashed libidinous craving, her tongue sliding along her lower lip—"warm your manly parts."

I glare at her. "That does *not* rhyme!"

She unslings her bow, nocks an arrow, and shoots me. Sort of. If she'd meant to kill me, I'd be dead. I think I lose some hair, though. In any case, Kato is faster than I am. He spins me out of the archer's path again and deposits me back behind our stalagmite. In the time before he lets me go, my face is buried in his chest. Crisp, golden hair tickles my nose and brushes my lips. His skin is still warm, and smells of man, and frost, and leather. He turns almost as fast, leaving my face against his back. I exhale, and goose bumps spread across his skin.

"I go with you now," he tells Atalanta, "and you leave her alone. You will not harm her. Ever."

Atalanta makes no response that I can hear. Maybe she nods. I don't know. I can't see around Kato and about a mile of naked back.

He seems satisfied, but then adds, "I'm keeping my boots."

I can't help it. I look down. Before I get to his boots, though, my eyes snag on a very fine backside. I've only ever seen one naked male bottom. I tilt my head to the side. There's no real harm in seeing two.

Kato half turns, looking at me over his shoulder. My eyes jerk back up, a ridiculous blush hitting my cheeks like a thunderclap.

"Griffin will kill me for leaving you alone in here," he says.

"Griffin will kill you for being naked in the same room with me," I answer.

He grunts. "Believe me, I'd rather be dressed. It's bloody cold in here."

"Go, then," I reluctantly urge. "Atalanta will warm you up." My tone could curdle milk, and the words almost stick in my throat. It's hard not to choke on them.

The muscles in Kato's bare arms ripple as he balls his hands into fists. "There's still the lyre, and the monster."

I push on the middle of his back with the flat of my hand. He needs to go before he freezes to death. The warmth is already seeping from his skin. "That's my part, I guess. You just heed the Goddess's needs when you see Artemis. *Needs*," I remind him. "Not wants."

"Heed the need," he echoes, looking less enthusiastic now that he's freezing cold and actually parting from me.

Kato suddenly turns and grabs my wrist, crushing Ariadne's Thread into my skin. "Keep the string tied. No matter what, *you* find your way out."

Does he really think I'd leave him in here? "I find *you*, and then we *both* find our way out."

He looks ready to argue. He looks ready to turn this whole plan on its ear.

"Go." I give him the hard look Griffin is always giving me. "Go before I give in to my base feminine curiosity and look at your 'manly parts.'"

Kato slowly drops my wrist. "I've seen you naked. We'd be even."

"Being even isn't high on my priority list."

He grins. Then he sweeps his big hand over the top of my head, turns, and walks away.

There's a long moment when my heart forgets to beat. Atalanta takes hold of Kato's arm and drags him toward a shadowy tunnel. As she turns back to me, her long hair sweeps over his bare skin, and I wonder what she'd do if I took out a knife and sawed it all off.

Shoot me, probably. For real.

"Don't follow us. Go that way." She points to the third tunnel on the left.

No rhyme this time? I bare my teeth, a horrible pressure building beneath my ribs. I'm terrified of never seeing Kato again.

They enter the dimly lit passageway. Rows of uneven icicles hang from the rounded entrance of the tunnel, making it seem as though they're disappearing into a monster's gaping maw. Sharp teeth. Dark gullet. Ready to swallow them whole.

I shudder as they disappear from sight. To keep myself from chasing after them, I fold Kato's clothes and then tuck his things into our satchel before strapping his leather armor to the outside of the bag. His cloak is too big to fit inside, so I throw it over my shoulders and fasten it at the neck. The heat of my own cloak diminishes as the two fire-wrought garments balance their warmth together.

There's a cold spot deep in my chest, and nausea plagues my stomach as I walk toward the third tunnel on the left—into my own gaping maw. More than a foot of cloak drags on the ground behind me, sweeping my footprints from the frost.

CHAPTER 18

FIND THE LYRE BEFORE THE THREE-HEADED BEAST. *No problem. I'll get right on that.*

My fingers and toes are icy. I rub my hands together, muttering to myself just to hear the sound of a voice. By the number of times I've gotten hungry, I estimate that three days have passed since Atalanta separated us, which means we've been in the labyrinth for almost four full days. A few days of being utterly on my own have validated one thing about me that hardly needed proving: I hate being alone.

Solitude, cold, and darkness are wreaking havoc on my mind and body. Despite resting and eating at regular intervals, I'm exhausted like never before—weak and even woozy sometimes. I slept twice because my body was telling me to stop in a way I simply couldn't ignore, but both times I woke up screaming, my raw shouts echoing off the frozen walls, and not feeling rested at all.

Kato left me everything we brought with us, and I've eaten sparingly, but if we can't be on our way out of here soon, meals will get truly sparse. He also left me our torch, but it burned out ages ago. After a while of seeing only by the faint light of the two cloaks, I broke down and lit the second one. Since then, I've gone up, down, and around, stumbling onto my own path eight times so far. *Eight!*

The tunnel I just left has Ariadne's Thread on its slippery floor three times over. Who was the idiot who thought it would be a good idea to leave me alone in a labyrinth?

That's right! Grandpa Zeus.

He obviously doesn't know me at all. And for all of Griffin's and Beta Team's praying to Athena, she was in on this, too. So were Hades and Poseidon.

Bloody Gods. They could at least *try* not to make this so hard. You know, throw me a lyre or something.

I come to yet another fork in the tunnel and frown, worry a bitter taste on my tongue. There's a thread to the left. It's icing over, which means I was already here hours ago.

Grumbling, I go right, knowing Kato and I will walk every same, useless circle on the way back out again. Worse, we'll do it in the near pitch-dark. The torch won't last much longer, and the cloaks, even turned flame-side out, aren't actually that bright. With my luck, I'll probably stumble onto the beast just as soon as I'm blind.

A scraping noise puts an abrupt stop to my low mumbling. I pause and listen, hearing a scrabbling that sounds a lot like claws on ice.

Adrenaline dumps into my system. My pulse roars, and my muscles tense. I try to steady my breathing as I silently draw my sword, keeping the torch in my left hand. Before, I would have drawn a knife, but I haven't had much luck with them lately.

Click. Click. Chuff.

Great. I have the beast. I do not have the lyre.

I round a bend, moving as quietly as I can. The tunnel brightens by degrees, and a thought kicks my already thundering heart into overdrive. *Is the beast guarding the second large cave?*

I'm desperate to see Kato again. And to get us both out of here.

My blood drumming in my ears, I inch toward what can only be described at the moment as not total dark, my sword leading the way. I swear to the Gods, when this is over, I'm never going underground again. It's horrible, black, quiet, and incredibly lonely. I have no idea what's happened to Kato—well, *some* idea—and Griffin and the others must be freezing cold and out of their minds with worry.

The scratching sound gets louder. I want to turn around and find another tunnel, but there's light this way. And a three-headed beast was part of the Gods' warning. I need to face it, whether I want to or not. Unfortunately, I'm minus one lyre.

Ariadne's Thread trails from my wrist, and I wish I could somehow sense Griffin on the other end. What if something's happened to him? What if I don't make it out?

A desperate sort of anxiety constricts my throat, making it hard to breathe. I clutch my sword, feeling each ridge of the grip press into my palm. Fear usually makes me angry. I need to get back to that.

I plaster myself against the icy wall and creep forward just enough to get a look at what comes next. The passageway opens up, but not enough for what I'd call a cavern. It's a bigger, wider, higher tunnel, with multiple offshoots, some of which are not utterly dark.

What do those offshoots lead to? The second cavern? The first? The top of the needle? At this point, I'm completely turned around. I could be anywhere inside the mountain. Maybe it's the exit. I could be closer to Griffin than I thought!

Quietly, I hurry toward the light until I slip on black ice and nearly land on my back. Then I step on something uneven, and my left ankle twists. Ignoring the twinge of pain, I lower the torch to see what my foot just landed on.

It's bone. Old, crunchy, dried-up bone.

Thump! Scrabble.

I jerk my head up.

Scrabble. Thump! Thump!

I whirl to face the darker tunnels. Something's coming down one of the passageways, but I don't know which one.

Thump! Thump! Chuff.

The middle! I dive to the right.

Wrong! The three-headed monster explodes from the right-hand tunnel.

A shot of pure fear detonates inside of me. I drop and roll under a lethally clawed foot. Something razor-sharp slices my thigh, and I hiss in pain as I shove my torch up into the beast's underbelly. It bellows and skids to a stop.

I jump to my feet, my injured leg howling in protest, only to drop again when a powerful clubbed tail whizzes over my head and smashes into the side of the tunnel. Ice shatters, and I duck as a shower of cold, sharp shards splashes over me.

The beast pivots. One of its huge heads lunges for me, and I spring back, pain pulsing in my thigh. Its jaws snap, and I back away. Six black eyes track me. They're as dark as the rest of the beast, only with a shiny, liquid gleam.

"We don't have to fight." So saying, I raise my sword.

The middle head attacks. I shoot to the side and then bring my blade down hard on that skull. The impact jars me from teeth to toes.

In the flickering torchlight, I see a flash of dark horns— long, smooth, and curved low over the beast's skulls. Like a ram's horns, they spiral back around to protect the vulnerable necks.

Massive. Three heads. Too many teeth. Horns like helmets. *Uh-oh.*

While I'm assessing the situation, the monster brings its clubbed tail around again like a battering ram. There's just enough room in the tunnel for the maneuver and nowhere for me to go. The cramped quarters work in my favor, though, because the thick, muscular part catches me in the middle while the bony club scrapes a deep furrow along the tunnel wall. I have just enough time to curl inward and throw myself backward to better absorb the impact.

I fly through the air and land sprawled on my back, the wind knocked out of me. I slide what feels like a mile down the slippery tunnel before the top of my skull cracks against the wall. Bright lights explode behind my eyes. Pain rips through my head as momentum carries me around in a hard arc, and the rest of my body slams into the icy barrier.

For a second, there's nothing. No air. No light. No sound. Then I suck in a huge breath, and my stunned body jolts back to me. Groaning, I roll to my knees. Pain grips my head. Everything spins. I touch the sorest spot and feel the start of a huge knot, warm and wet.

I tighten my other hand around a familiar hilt. Somehow, I held on to my sword. The torch lies far down the tunnel, dimly illuminating the advancing monster from behind. I blink, trying to chase away the dizziness, but my head throbs, and the pounding ache doesn't stop there. I can't focus on the beast, but I know it's coming for me, hulking, huge, and snarling snorts and growls that remind me of Cerberus.

Hades left me his guard dog for eight years, and I needed him a grand total of once. The Hound of the Underworld would come in really handy right now, and yet he's nowhere to be found. I'll never understand the Gods' sense of humor, or irony, or whatever it is.

Real fear, the kind I recognize like an old enemy, takes root inside of me. I'm so completely outmatched right now that there's a good chance I'm going to die.

I slide backward on my hands and knees, still trying to clear my vision. A growl reverberates around the tunnel, and then the beast catapults forward. Straightening, I grip my sword with both hands and swing in a wide, wild arc, somehow keeping it at bay. Every bruise and abused bone aches as I swing again, gaining myself the time to get to my feet.

Dizzy, I stagger and almost fall into one of the beast's mouths. Gasping, I stumble back as another head grabs for me at the same time. The two fang-filled faces collide with a thump. The beast roars, and the competing heads snarl at each other, growling and biting.

I spin and run. Pain streaks through my head, and suddenly up is down. I lose my balance and hit the ground with a full-body smack, my chin bouncing off the ice. Stunned, I roll onto my back only to find all three of the monster's heads looming over me.

Instinct makes me swing with all my might. I hit horns again, and my sword flies from my grasp. My frozen fingers bark in pain, and I pull them back, clutching them against my chest as my sword clatters away.

Oh Gods! I can't stay here. I have to get up.

Desperation and panic give me a burst of strength. I flip over and pop up running. I skid on the ice and career off the side of the tunnel, using it like a frozen springboard. Sharp teeth snap behind me.

The beast charges, its claws scraping on the ice. Despite the risk to my balance, I dart a look over my shoulder. It's gaining on me.

Light sparks in my head, radiating out from the throbbing pulse point at the top of my skull. Gritting my teeth, I twist and throw two knives. It's too dark to see what happens, but the ping and clang as I face forward again tell me they didn't stick.

I sprint for the fractionally brighter end of the tunnel, my head pounding like my blood. Hot breath slams into the back of my neck as I jump, breaking an icicle off the mouth of the passageway.

I turn in the air and land facing the beast, already swinging the icicle with a vicious upward thrust. Just before the frozen dagger connects with the soft underside of one jaw, another head swoops in and snatches the weapon from my hand. There's a crunch. *It ate my icicle!*

I sway on my feet. All three heads lunge at once, and I leap back, turning to flee.

A horrifying, empty feeling rushes up through me. I gasp, flailing. It takes only a split second to realize there's nothing under my feet.

Fear punches me in the gut. My stomach flies up into my mouth, and my terrified shriek almost drowns out the sound of Kato frantically shouting my name from across an immense, dark hole.

CHAPTER 19

I DROP. I'VE DONE THE UNTHINKABLY STUPID AND stepped off a cliff. I can still hear Kato's panicked bellow, and it's almost as heartbreaking as knowing I'm going to die.

My life flashes before my eyes. I don't like a lot of what I see. But there's Eleni. And Desma, Aetos, Vasili, and Selena. There's Beta Team. And Griffin.

My heart explodes at the thought of Griffin. My scream turns raw. Cold wind buffets me. The two cloaks flap above my head, their buckles digging into my chin. Their glow does nothing to pierce the vast darkness. Below me, everything is black.

I'm completely unprepared for total, icy submersion. Freezing water closes over my head, expelling the air from my lungs and bruising me straight to my bones. My scream cuts off, bubbling around me. Reflexively, I fan out my aching arms and legs, trying to slow my descent before starting to kick.

Kicking is useless. I keep going down. The weight I'm carrying pulls me in the wrong direction.

My lungs scream for breath as I wrestle the strap of the heavy satchel over my head and then drop Kato's clothing and all of our supplies. I'd rather starve than drown. One happens a lot faster than the other.

It's not enough. I kick furiously, yanking at the cloak buckles and trying to shed the heavy garments. The dark water is numbing, and my stiff fingers slide off the latches. Panic beats through me as I reach for a knife. My mind races for solutions, but my body is sluggish, the marrow-deep cold preventing my hand from closing around the hilt.

I sink, my head and ears throbbing from the pressure. My lungs spasm, my chest convulsing as I deny myself the right to breathe. The light from the smoldering cloaks illuminates the steady stream of bubbles rising around me. Soon enough, that decreases, fading until there's nothing.

Reflex finally overwhelms me, and I breathe. Water floods my lungs, painful and wrong. I can't cough. There's no air for that, so I just breathe more water, sucking it down and choking on it, the cold invading me, inside and out.

Numb to my core and yet filled with a burning desire to live, I shout a liquid scream. I scream for Griffin, for my friends, for myself, and maybe even for Fisa, the home I abandoned to a monster.

My scream heats my throat, heats it until my neck burns, my skin catches fire, and...*splits?*

Grimacing, I slowly lift my hand to my stinging neck. The pressure in my ears disappears, and I breathe. Sort of. I breathe water, but it doesn't hurt. And it doesn't feel wrong anymore. It clears my head of the shadow of death an instant before my feet touch solid ground.

Unsteady, *confused*, I try to catch my balance and my breath. Instinctively, I draw more liquid in through the slashes in my neck.

I didn't drown. I have gills.

I didn't drown.

I have gills!

My thoughts jump to Poseidon. I start to shake, as much from shock as from cold. I'd bet my knives this lifesaving magic has something to do with my vigilant, many-times-removed uncle watching over me—although he might have thought about intervening *before* I fell over a cliff.

Gradually, I get used to the feel of freezing water in my eyes and the idea of breathing underwater. There's no current, giving the unsettling impression of being shrouded in a cold, dark, weighty cocoon. The silence is eerie and absolute, making the abrasive sound of my own clattering teeth almost deafening. I wrap both burning cloaks tightly around myself to gather their heat. They flare brighter, and their warmth starts seeping into my frigid skin.

I spot my satchel in the cloaks' dim circle of light. It fell right next to me. Not stopping to look a gift Centaur in the mouth, I pick it up and start toward what I hope is the opposite shore of the lake. Kato sounded like he was somewhere over there. The three-headed beast… Hopefully not.

Walking through water is a slow and arduous process, especially after being thoroughly trounced by a monster and suffering what I suspect is a severe head injury. The heated cloaks chase away the worst of the numbness, leaving me feeling battered again. Anxiety over underwater creatures doesn't help matters any. What could be down here? This is the Ice Plains, so pretty much anything.

I shut that thought down. Griffin is always trying to get me to be more positive. I'll be positive for once. *Positive. Positive. Positive.*

Something slithers between my legs, thumping my ankles. I squeal a mouthful of water as my heart throws itself against my ribs. Spinning in a tight circle, I peer into the murky depths—and see nothing.

Hunching over, I trudge on, worn out and heavy. Intensely nervous. I have no sense of time. Both it and I seem to move incredibly slowly. Colorless fish, some big, some bigger, swim by, ignoring me for the most part. Eels slink past as well, smooth, long, and gray, their beady eyes seeming to track me long after I've lost sight of them. I see a flash of teeth every now and then and try to make myself as small as possible. Unfortunately, I still glow. I'm the only light down here, a bright beacon that might as well say "Big fish, chomp here."

My strange breathing accelerates when the lake floor begins to slope upward. I push myself harder, cupping my hands and pumping my arms through the water. The incline sharpens, but it's so dark above me I have no idea I've reached the shore until my head pops out of the water.

For a moment, my body doesn't know how to react. The gills stop providing air. My lungs are full of liquid. The lack of vital sustenance is sudden and alarming, and then I double over and spew water from my lungs. Heaving violently, I brace my hands on my thighs and cough until my throat hurts and my head spins again. Finally, I take my first real breaths in I don't know how long.

Exhausted, weak, and trembling, I collapse on the rocky bank and just breathe. I'm iced through and dripping wet. Despite the fiery cloaks, the sleep of the irretrievably cold is calling to me. Sleeping is a terrible idea, especially when you add a massive blow to the head into the mix. I might not wake up.

I need to keep moving. I'm still trying to convince myself to get up even as I drop my head into my hood, tuck my booted feet up under the blazing folds of the cloaks, and then sink heavily—and maybe irrevocably—into darkness.

I groan. I'm definitely not dead. I hurt too much for that. I have a headache to end all headaches, but I'm not shivering anymore, and my clothes are dry under my gently smoldering cloaks. I must have slept for hours, long enough for the cloaks to dry even my boots.

I touch my neck, my fingers bumping over four raised slashes under each ear. The gills have closed over, leaving the skin on either side of my throat rough and tender. *Fabulous*. More scars.

A wave of dizziness washes over me when I sit up. One whole side of my body feels bruised—well, more bruised than the rest—and I know I hit the surface of the lake tilted to my left when I fell in.

Pushing my hair back from my face, I feel something that barely resembles a braid anymore. More worrisome is the huge knot on the top of my head. I wince when I hit the sore spot and then take a deep breath, making my ribs ache. A monster tail to the middle will do that.

Needing to get my bearings, I drop my hands and look around, seeing mostly nothing. Considerably higher up, there's some light.

I sigh. I need food, something to get me going.

Pulling my satchel closer, I pick through the water-logged offerings until I find a hunk of cheese and strips of cured meat that are still edible, discarding the rest. But I end up battling myself for every bite—as soon as the food gets anywhere near my mouth, my stomach rebels.

Nauseated, I fill my waterskin and then drink. The lake water is so cold it shocks my mouth and clears my head. It even settles my stomach, probably icing it over.

Steadier than before, I spread Kato's wet clothing out on his smoldering cloak to lighten my load and let it dry while I explore. Pebbles and stones line the bank under my feet. Torches burn high above me. And I mean high. I'm going to have to climb to get back to the level of the tunnels. Unfortunately, I don't see a way up.

My own cloak burns brightly as I strike out to the right. The torches start lower on that side and then climb upward in a spiral, giving the impression of being inside a cone—or the tip of the needle.

The footing is precarious, and my balance still isn't right. I fall down twice, first bruising my backside and then opening the skin on one elbow. I don't bother binding the cut and let my blood drip onto the rocks. Maybe Mother will come looking for me here and never find her way out.

I refuse to wonder if Kato and I will make it out. I have Ariadne's Thread, which is currently dragging through the water and pulling on my wrist. I have a little food left. I have warmth. I have Griffin to get back to. I have stubbornness a donkey would kill for. I have—

The lyre!

I snort, incensed. There it is, propped up against a rock.

I squat and run my fingers over the strings. The sound they make is beautiful, beyond harmonious—music worthy of the Gods. I reach for the frame.

"Good Gods, that's heavy." I wrestle the instrument up against my chest. The lyre appears to be made of solid gold. It definitely feels like it. I'd leave it here if I didn't think there was a good chance of running into the three-headed beast again. And even then, what am I supposed to do with it? Choose a head to throw it at?

Carrying the lyre awkwardly in front of me, I continue my struggle over the shifting stones, staggering and slipping like a drunkard. Before I can fall down again and break something, probably with the lyre on top of me, likely pinning me forever until I die of starvation, I come to a solid wall of ice.

Foreboding trips through me as I crane my neck up. And up. The cliff is soaring. Sheer. "How in *Hades* am I supposed to scale *that*?"

An arrow sings through the air and lands an inch from

my boot, sticking between the loose stones. I jump, nearly drop the lyre, and curse like a warlord. Griffin would be proud. Or shocked. Either would be fine.

"She'll use the stairs if she dares."

I scan the cliff top for Atalanta, seeing no one.

"I climb, you rhyme?" I call back acerbically.

An arrow knocks my hood back from my head and probably slices off a few frizzy hairs. I shut up and look for the stairs.

They're not far away, but they climb out of the shallows of the lake, which means I'll have to get my feet wet to reach them just when I was getting used to being dry and a relatively normal temperature again. Worse, they're narrow and nearly vertical, and there's no handy railing. Doubly worse, I don't trust my balance at the moment. If I fall, a foot of water won't save me like the deep side of the lake did.

Atalanta seems to have disappeared, and I'm not making this climb twice, so I leave the lyre and follow the shoreline back to Kato's cloak and clothes. I pack up and then pick my way over to the cliff again, wondering how to get everything up. I need my hands to steady myself and climb, and the lyre won't fit in my bag.

After some deliberation, I end up making a back sling out of Kato's cloak. I pin the cloak behind the lyre against the cliff wall, sit down in front of it, and then draw some of the material up between my lower back and the lyre to fashion a sort of pocket for it. With the instrument pressing into my back, I latch the neck clasp above my breasts and then bring the bottom edges of the cloak around my waist, tying them in a tight knot.

Getting up again is a nearly herculean challenge I hadn't really considered, but I eventually manage to stand with the lyre tucked safely against my back. My contraption works and has the advantage of putting most of the instrument's weight onto my hips.

Praying my head doesn't start spinning again, I sling the heavy satchel across my upper body and then step into the lake. A full-body shudder rolls through me when liquid cold seeps into my boots. The climb takes a small eternity, leaves me panting like a dog in the sun, and scares the magic out of me every time I slip on the ice. A bashed shin is the worst of the damage, though, and when I finally haul myself—and the lyre—over the top of the cliff, all my muscles are quivering from fatigue. I thank every God and their pet Pegasus it's over. Stairs are my new enemy.

I move toward the torch-lined wall, staggering under the weight of the lyre. There's a good chance I'll pitch the bloody thing into the lake if it doesn't end up being useful. I get my shaking under control and then look around, still breathing hard. The cavern consists of galleries and tunnels shooting off into darkness, all of them bordered by a slippery ledge of rock that can't be more than three feet wide in most places, and sometimes less. The ledge circles a giant pit, and far below, the lake.

Exhaustion weighs as much as the lyre. I don't let it get the better of me this time. I'm on the same level as the beast now. I'm sure of it after picking up the slack in Ariadne's Thread and seeing the line coming out of a tunnel about a third of the way around the cavern from where I stand. Atalanta is running around somewhere as well, probably rhyming about an arrow with my name on it. And I need to find Kato more than I need to sleep.

Closing my eyes for just a second against the relentless throbbing in my head, I jiggle the lyre into a more comfortable position. Opening my eyes again, I start toward the only thing that looks different in this dim, inhospitable cave. One spot along the wall is a whole lot brighter than anything I've seen since Kato and I stumbled onto the first cavern together.

I'm convinced a snarling, three-headed beast is poised to jump out at me from one of the tunnels, so it's a nerve-racking walk along the ledge. Finally, I reach a wall of thick but transparent ice caging off what looks like a plush boudoir with an enormous bed, two long couches scattered with colorful cushions, platters of food, softly flickering torches, layers and layers of thick flokati rugs covering the icy floor—and Kato.

My heart takes a painful dive at the sight of him sitting cross-legged just beyond the wall, his head in his hands and his big shoulders slumped. He's wearing his boots and what appears to be a large, golden fleece. His mace, which he held on to even when he was naked, is on my side of the enclosure, sitting on the ledge.

He doesn't move. Maybe he didn't hear my footsteps through the ice.

"Kato?"

His head jerks up, revealing a face I hardly recognize. Pale and drawn, his eyes hollow, he looks more like a wild animal than the man I know. Hanks of long blond hair shadow his eyes and tangle with what's becoming a very shaggy beard. The little I can see of his expression underneath his disheveled mane speaks of utter devastation.

Panic wells up in me. *What happened here?*

I peer through the ice. Bloodshot eyes stare back at me, deep-blue bleeding into red. Kato's hands drop, open and limp, on his knees.

Dread explodes through my chest. Those women did something to him. I'll kill them. Bludgeon them. Slowly. With my bare hands. Or maybe the lyre.

I bare my teeth in an involuntary snarl, and Kato's whole body jerks in reaction.

His throat works, bobbing and then eventually producing a voice that's rough and broken. "I'm sorry. I'm so sorry."

I frown. What does he have to be sorry for? He did his part, although it obviously took its toll. That golden fleece covering him from neck to knees is clearly the gift we're supposed to present to Lycheron.

Kato swallows. It looks painful. "How will I tell Griffin? How can I ever tell him?"

He utters a hoarse curse, and something inside of me cracks. Heat crawls up my throat.

"I'd rather die in here. I'll die here instead." Bleak eyes sweep over me, taking me in from the top of my head to the tips of my boots. The total defeat in his reddened gaze pierces my heart like a lance. "We'll be together. You and me, Cat. That'll be okay."

I stare at him. Honest to Gods, I have no idea what he's talking about, but he's breaking my heart.

"Haunt me all you like, just don't haunt Griffin. He... he couldn't handle it. Not you. Anyone but you. He loves you too much. It would drive him mad."

I snort. "I fully intend to haunt you, Griffin, and whomever else I please, but that'll have to wait until I'm dead."

A sudden sheen glasses over Kato's bloodshot eyes. They start to glitter in the torchlight. He doesn't even blink. "You are dead."

I look down at myself and then bounce as much as I can with the lyre on my back, shaking out my aching arms. "No, I'm really not."

His voice lowers, raw in his throat. "Don't do this to me, Cat. I saw that...*thing*. I watched you fall. Heard you scream. It went on for—" He chokes on the words, his face contorting. "Then there was nothing. Two days have passed. Atalanta told me. There's no way you walked away from that. Even you."

Two days! Well, I did have head trauma, drowning, and gills to deal with. I could hardly jump right up and scale a cliff.

"Now, I either have to find my way out of here and tell Griffin, or die in here with you." His sunken gaze locks onto mine with a rather desperate spark of hope. "I shouldn't leave you, right?"

He looks far too keen about the possibility of dying under the mountain, which is a testament to how much he doesn't want to tell Griffin I'm dead. Which I'm not.

"I know how much you hate to be alone. You should have gone to the Underworld, with your sister. Or to Elysium, with heroes and warriors. I don't know why you didn't." He gives a bitter shake of his head, and the tawny ends of his hair drag through the thick, curling wool of the fleece. "Since you're still here, we can be realm-walking spirits together. Maybe you won't have nightmares if you're with me."

Tears flood my eyes. That's one of the nicest, most selfless things anyone's ever said to me. I want to shake him for it. Maybe punch something. "I do hate being alone, I would never ask you to bury yourself alive for me, and I'm not bloody dead!" I kick the wall of ice so hard it cracks, and a webbed pattern splinters out from where my foot connects.

Kato's bloodshot eyes shoot wide. He jumps about a mile and then springs to his feet. His posture transforms as he raises himself to his full height. Gone is the defeated man. In his place, a raging bull. He launches himself at the ice, slamming into the sheer wall with the force of the

Minotaur. He does it again, then again, bellowing like a lunatic the entire time.

The sound of his huge body crashing into the ice is brutal. I yell and pound my palms against the frozen barrier, but it's like he doesn't even hear. He keeps coming. Fissures form, turning the ice jagged and obscuring my view of him. Blood smears the other side, but the wall holds fast.

I race farther down the side of the ice room, suck in a breath, and then exhale my last bit of Dragon's Breath. There's barely enough magic to melt the ice—just enough for a Cat-sized hole. I launch myself through it and land in a heap on the rugs, squashed by the lyre. Pushing up on my arms, I look through clumps of tangled hair and see Kato whirl, his blue eyes frantic. Then he's on me, wrapping his arms around me and pulling me hard against his body.

My heart nearly shatters my ribs. I make a sound frankly not worthy of myself and throw my arms around him, holding on, my ear against his thundering chest. At least a minute goes by before I can talk without embarrassing myself. "You're not a battering ram, you know."

"I don't care."

"Your arm is bleeding."

He squeezes me harder. "I don't care."

Kato finally steps back from me enough to grip my face in his hands. His fingers are cold. "I thought you were dead."

"I could tell," I say, holding on to his thick wrists. "I am *so* hard to kill. There's a lake down there. I sank to the bottom and grew gills. Look!" I tilt my head, showing him. "I thought I was going to drown. It was creepy down there. And cold. Thank the Gods for these cloaks. Thank Hades, I mean. He's turning out to be a fabulous uncle. There were eels. I hate eels. Are the scars ugly?" Vanity crashes through my verbal tidal wave, and I self-consciously touch my neck.

Looking slightly dazed, Kato shakes his head. "You can hardly see them."

Meant to reassure me, his lie burns through me instead, igniting my Kingmaker Magic. The scars are pretty damn noticeable, it turns out.

"Thanks for warming me up," I say from between gritted teeth. Sarcasm should be one of my middle names.

"Sorry." Kato pulls me back in for a gentler embrace. "They'll fade. Scars always do." His hands brush the bundle on my back. "What's this?" he asks.

"The lyre. The one I was supposed to find *before* the beast."

"Where was it?"

"At the bottom of the pit." I angle my head toward the black hole on the other side of the boudoir ice cage.

Turning me around, Kato supports the lyre while I untie the sling. The moment the instrument's weight is off my back, I groan and stretch my sore muscles.

"I wondered how you got so heavy," he says.

"Not with spice cakes, although that would have been more fun."

The line of his mouth stays flat as he turns the lyre over in his hands. He strums a few chords of hauntingly beautiful music, the purity of the sound making my chest ache. "You couldn't kill the monster?"

"Kill it? It kicked my ass three ways to Olympus, sliced my leg, threw me into a wall, and drove me over a cliff. And that's the short version."

Kato looks up from the lyre, his eyes troubled. "You're resourceful. And tough."

"Why, thank you. But it had protective horns, a clubbed tail, and—oh, that's right—*three heads*!"

Kato's expression shifts into something I could almost call a smile for the first time since I found him. He plucks the chords again in the beginnings of a tune I recognize, a ballad popular in southern Sinta. His fingers move with skill and subtlety over the strings. I had no idea he was musical.

"Maybe we're not meant to kill it." He keeps playing. "Doesn't music soothe the beast? I'll play, you sing."

"I sound like a strangled Satyr when I sing."

He smiles. "Somehow that doesn't surprise me."

"There's no need for mudslinging," I say with a huff.

He chuckles softly. "I can carry a tune."

"Great!" I pat his arm. "That'll be your job. I'll stand back—waaaaay back—while you calm the beast. I'm confident you'll sound as good as you look."

His chest puffs out. "How do I look?"

"Terrible." I grin. "You needed a bath, a shave, and a comb before we even set foot on the Ice Plains. Now, I can just barely make out your eyes and your nose. The rest is all"—I flap my hands around—"hair."

His chest deflates. He eyes me wryly. "I could say the same about you."

I gasp. "I grew a beard? Do you think Griffin will like it? I've been trying to keep it neat, but I may have picked up an eel."

Kato laughs outright, and he really is unbearably handsome. Some of the grimness evaporates from his eyes. "I was talking about this." He gives one of my tousled waves a light tug.

I once saw Griffin do that to Kaia. It's brotherly. Affectionate. My heart squeezes in my chest. My love for Griffin is completely different, but Kato has a piece of me that no man ever had, not even Aetos. Kato *sees* me, and accepts. In that moment, I realize he's slipped inside my soul right next to Eleni. They're a blond-haired, blue-eyed, sunny pair—my light in the dark.

Clearing my throat doesn't drive away the thick lump in it, or dispel the sudden tightness, so I make a show of smoothing down my hair—a lost cause at this point. "Ah, that. It's getting to the stage where it deserves a name. The Knotted Nest? The Twisted Tresses?"

"What about the Terrible Tangle?"

I nod. "That has serious possibilities."

"The Matted Mess?" he suggests.

My jaw drops. "It's not that bad!"

Grinning, Kato pats my head. "Let's get out of here."

Yes, please! "I have your clothes. They're even dry, thanks to your Eternal Fires of the Underworld Cloak."

He quirks an eyebrow, taking the things I hand him. "That gets a name, too?"

"I should think so," I answer loftily.

"Have you named your sword yet?"

I shake my head. "Your mace is outside." His knives are tucked into his boots, like always.

"I know." He looks me over, frowning. "Where is your sword?"

"In the beast's tunnel, along with two knives." I bite my lip. "I have to warn you... I may have, uh, gone in a few circles. Here and there."

Kato barks a sudden laugh. "Of course you did."

I give him a halfhearted evil eye and then turn my back while he changes. The God-sized bed and other low, lavish furniture have fruit bowls and filled platters all around them. I gather food, devouring a bunch of grapes while I'm packing up the rest.

"What happened here? To you?" I try to sound casual and fail miserably.

Kato comes up next to me, grabbing a huge handful of nuts, which he manages to fit into his mouth all at once. The golden fleece hangs from his shoulders, the excess bulk making him feel like a Giant by my side. He takes the heavy satchel from me as he chews, loops it over his shoulder, and then holds it open for me to finish filling with provisions.

"Atalanta..." He clears his throat and then reaches for a cup of water near the bed, drinking deeply. "When she talked about being free, she meant of her virginity. But she didn't just want it gone, she wanted it annihilated. For two days, she made sure I wouldn't stop."

I gape at him. "How does *that* work?"

A flush works its way across his masculine cheekbones. "She gave me a potion. Some kind of herbs. It tasted vile."

"You couldn't..." I wrinkle my nose. "You know?"

The flush deepens. "There was relief, thank the Gods. But I was always ready to start again."

I glance at his groin. I can't help it.

Kato tilts my head back up. "The effects wore off. Eventually."

It's my turn to flush. "Well, that's good." I look around. "Is there any left?"

He chuckles, but the sound is strained. "It isn't fun. Believe me."

With Griffin, that sounds like it could be a lot of fun. "It wasn't?"

His expression shutters. "It was exhausting. Empty and exhausting."

I don't like the sound of that—or how Kato sounded when he said it. "What about Artemis? You have the fleece, so you must have passed her test."

"She watched."

My eyes widen. "The whole time?"

He nods.

"That's…" I have no words. Kato on display? Forced to repeatedly mate with a woman he holds no affection for?

"She was stunning. A million times more desirable than Atalanta." A faraway look hazes his expression, but there's nothing dreamy about it. He looks pained. "She wanted what I could give. She wanted it so much she called for me, over and over, and it was like…like a siren's song, you know? Especially in my state. But I remembered what you said about needs and wants. I didn't go to her, and it must have been the right thing to do because she gave me the fleece in the end. Gave me the fleece, took Atalanta, and left."

I reach out and squeeze his forearm. "You denied a beautiful Goddess who wanted you while you were in the clutches of a drug-induced sexual frenzy. That makes you incredibly strong."

Kato shrugs, like it wasn't something heroic.

"And Atalanta just left? She doesn't strike me as the type of woman to give up a man she wants."

"Artemis didn't give her a choice." He frowns. "Atalanta nearly defied her Goddess over me, and I didn't even want her. Didn't even like her."

A gloomy weight settles over me, despite my joy at seeing Kato again. "You did what you had to do, and you got what we needed. We don't have to tell anyone what happened here."

Kato stares at something above my head, or maybe at nothing at all. "Atalanta told me she was raised with bears. She only knew of one way to copulate and didn't want anything else." He looks at me again. "I'm pretty sure there's no hair left on my knees."

I snort a laugh. It just bursts from me. It must make Kato happy, though, because his features soften.

"I don't care what we tell the others. That's not important. This is." He thumps the golden fleece. "And you."

"Me?" I shake my head. "I'm useless. I walked in circles, lost my weapons, and fell off a cliff."

"At least you had a bath. If it weren't cold enough to freeze off my balls, I'd be tempted to do the same."

I laugh again. "It's a long way down, and a long way back up." I move toward the hole I melted in the ice and then start kicking at the edges until it opens up. "Besides, your balls have proved useful. Let's keep them intact."

A low laugh follows me out onto the ledge. Crouching, Kato steps through after me. "Good point, although they might shrivel up and fall off anyway if I ever hear another rhyme."

CHAPTER 20

KATO NOT ONLY LOOKS LIKE ADONIS, BUT HE HAS THE voice of a God. He puts the beast to sleep within minutes, filling its tunnel lair with the melodious vibrations of the golden lyre and the haunting, sliding tones of a southern lullaby.

Half mesmerized myself, I gather my blades, pull up the slack in Ariadne's Thread, and then find the torch, relighting it. Neither of us wants to carry the lyre, so we leave it at the entrance to the sleeping monster's den. When the torch eventually dies, we stop to eat and drink by the dim light of our cloaks, although neither of us has much of an appetite. Before we move on, Kato ties a new knot around my wrist, and we cut off the excess twine.

"I know what you're thinking," he says when we pause again some hours later.

My heart does something unruly in my chest. I'm thinking about Griffin. Loyal, selfless, determined, domineering, overprotective Griffin—a man of action, consigned to waiting. He's probably aged a decade in a week.

I swallow hard. "What then?" My voice is almost steady.

Kato turns his back to me and then relieves himself against the tunnel wall, probably melting a line down the ice. "That it's a good thing we're not eating much because pissing is one thing, but there's no way you want to share a latrine with me for anything else."

Expecting anything but that, I burst out laughing. "Gah! You're such a man."

Kato turns back around, grinning. "Last time I checked, I had the right parts."

And the last time I checked, my feet were dragging, and I was missing Griffin so much I was close to tears.

I shove Kato's fleece-covered shoulder, still smiling. "You go first. Your cloak is brighter."

We walk, and walk, and *walk*. Time moves slowly in cold, dark monotony, broken only by Kato telling me stories, mostly about Griffin, and by my sharing whatever thoughts come into my head. When we stop, we do so huddled together against the chill, taking turns sleeping, although Kato doesn't get his fair share of rest, and I seem to need more than I ever have before.

Not having any clear sense of the passing of the days, it's a shock to see the light from the first cavern, not only because it's so bright to our unaccustomed eyes, but because it means we're less than a full day's walk from the exit.

My heart starts pounding so hard it steals my breath. "We're close."

Squinting into the light, Kato scans the gallery for Atalanta and her bow. Tension and wariness roll off his big frame. "The archer got me to her bed in about twenty minutes."

I point to the tunnel we just exited. "She told me to go *that* way. So I did."

"And you have the navigational skills of a four-year-old."

"We're inside a mountain! It's pitch-black! And a labyrinth!"

"True," Kato concedes.

"You didn't freeze?" I ask.

"Atalanta had Fire Magic. Kept me warm."

I'll bet. I drop another armful of thread onto the frosty ground, cut off the excess, and then hold out my wrist for Kato to retie the knot. With the added light, he can see that my skin has been rubbed raw. Frowning, he reaches for my other wrist. When he's done tying the knot, I unbuckle my leather armor and then strap it to the bag he's carrying. I have plans for later today, and I don't want the extra layer between Griffin and me when I see him again.

I start walking, eager to leave the labyrinth at last. "Let's go before the archer shows up and starts shooting at us. I doubt she'd hit you. Me, I'm not so sure."

Kato growls from somewhere deep in his throat. "If she comes anywhere near you, I'll take one of her arrows and stick it through her eye."

Well, I guess that's settled, then.

We walk faster and don't stop again. The closer we get, the longer the journey seems to take. Anticipation keeps me in an anxious, breathless state. The next time the tunnel brightens, my pulse roars, seeming to pound Griffin's name through my veins.

"Come on!" I cut the knot around my wrist and then sprint down the tunnel, sliding and bumping into the icy walls at every turn. I don't even feel the impacts, or maybe I just don't care. "Griffin!" I shout.

After a terrifying moment of silence, Griffin's deep bellow answers me back. "Cat!"

He's there! Relief nearly makes me stumble. His voice is still far away. Always too far.

"Cat!" he roars.

"I'm coming!" And I swear to the Gods, the moment we touch I'm going to crawl inside him and never come out. I never want to be apart again. We'll make love, eat, and sleep. Forget about ruling the world. That means nothing to me. All I want is Griffin.

Tears stream from my eyes as my vision tries to adjust to the increasing light. Sheer joy and relief add to the flow.

I round a bend, bounce off the wall, and leave the tinkling of shattered icicles in my wake. My shoulder throbs, but I welcome the pain. Enduring it means getting to Griffin that much faster.

I finally see the men moving inward from the mouth of the cave, three large shapes silhouetted against the blinding light of day. We meet somewhere in the middle of that first tunnel, and I throw myself at Griffin, suddenly shaking uncontrollably.

His arms close around me, strong, hard, and almost crushing. Griffin's inhale shudders, and then a hoarse sound catches in his throat. He exhales my name like he feared he'd never speak it to me again, like he was almost sure he wouldn't.

I wrap my arms and legs around him so tightly that wild Centaurs couldn't drag me away. Our lips collide in a frantic tangle of words and breath.

"I love you. I love you. I love you." I can't stop saying it. Our teeth bump because he's talking, too.

"*Kardia mou. Psihi mou.*" One steely arm circles my hips and the other my back. He strides into the tunnel.

My heart filled to bursting, on fire for him, I cling to Griffin, my hands tangled in his hair and my legs locked around his waist. We pass Kato, and Griffin looks away from me only long enough to give his friend a nod.

I grin like an idiot, and Kato winks back.

Low and fierce, Griffin says, "I'm never letting you out of my sight again. That was the longest ten days of my life. I thought—" His voice falters in a way that jolts my heart straight into my throat. Then he forgets about talking and slants his mouth over mine as we round the first bend in the tunnel. There's nothing sweet or soft about his kiss. It's fear turned into aggression. Possession. His tongue sweeps into my mouth, claiming every inch of it, and I thrust back, greedy for more.

Finally lifting his mouth from mine, Griffin stops, looks around, and then sets me on a shelf of ice. He settles his hips between my legs, and with my cloak under me and Griffin at my front, I don't even feel the cold. His chilled hands grip my head as he angles my face back to ravage my mouth again. Soft black whiskers lightly scrape the tip of my nose, my lips, my chin, and a husky moan rises in my throat. I trace the delectable curve of his upper lip with my tongue and then suck hungrily on the fuller bottom one.

Griffin's ragged breath fans my fevered lips. "I thought you were never coming back. The days... They just kept going by, and you never came."

I curl my fingers into his hair, holding him tight. "I will *always* come back to you."

With a gruff sound, he settles his hands on my hips. "You should know better than to make promises you might not be able to keep."

He's right. He always is. But that's a vow I'll keep—in this life, or in the next.

Not answering, I lean forward and kiss him because he's my hunger and my food, my thirst and my water, my air and my every breath.

Griffin drags me closer, and the feel of his arousal between us sends heat rushing up my spine. I wiggle to the very edge of the shelf, rubbing against him.

A soft groan resonates in Griffin's chest. His fingers tighten on my hips. "This isn't the place."

His steely length is flush against my core, and white-hot desire is coiling deep in my belly. "This is definitely the place." I tilt my head back, flicking a tangled mess of hair off my neck.

His face dips toward my throat. He stops. Pulls back. "What's this?"

Uh-oh. "Nothing?"

Frowning, Griffin gently explores the tender ridges of my new scars with his fingertips. "What happened?"

There's no use pretending he can't see. Between our smoldering cloaks and the daylight filtering around the bend, it's far from pitch-dark.

I take a deep breath. How does a woman tell her almost, maybe, probably husband she's part fish? Apparently. "Do you find mermaids arousing?"

His eyebrows slam down. "What?"

"I almost drowned."

"What!"

I wince, his near-roar still echoing around the tunnel.

Griffin clears his throat, trying again more calmly. "Would you care to explain?"

I consider. "No?"

"Cat..." he growls.

"Fine." My shoulders slump in defeat. Not that I put up much of a fight. "The three-headed beast chased me over a cliff. It was really dark, and I didn't know what was behind me. I was busy trying not to get eaten, or crushed, or clubbed, and then I fell. I turned to run because I was getting my ass kicked, but then there was nothing under my feet. Luckily, there was a lake at the bottom of this huge, black pit, which means I didn't..." I decide not to finish that thought. Griffin's expression is turning more frightening by the word.

"I hit the water, but I was too weighed down to swim. I had my clothes and cloak, Kato's clothes and cloak, my satchel—which I dropped. But after that, I could hardly move because it was so cold. My fingers were numb, and I was woozy anyway because I'd just hit my head." My hand automatically rises to the sore spot under my hair. "I couldn't get anything else off me."

Silent but clearly seething, Griffin runs his fingertips over my scalp, lightly moving them from front to back. Feeling the sizeable lump still there, his lips thin. "You sank."

I nod.

Griffin takes a calming breath. Then another. It takes three to actually work. "I'm going to skip over your having Kato's clothes and get right to the new scars on your neck."

I glance down, fiddling with my belt. "I didn't drown. I, uh…grew gills."

"Gills?"

Nodding, I run a self-conscious hand over my neck.

"Did you pray to Poseidon?" he asks. "Call on an Oracle?"

I shake my head. "I was too panicked. Too muddled. No air. The cold…" I shrug. "I don't know what happened."

Gripping my waist, Griffin lowers his head and then carefully kisses the slashing scars on one side of my neck. "What happened after that?"

I shiver when he shifts to the other side, and his lips brush a soft, warm kiss over the first raised ridge. "I hit the bottom, wrapped both cloaks around me to keep from freezing to death, picked up my satchel, and then walked to the other side of the lake."

A puff of breath hits my neck, and I think Griffin smiles a little against my skin. "My brave, brave Cat." His mouth gently traces another scar.

"Definitely." I shudder. "There were eels."

"Where was Kato?" The careful levelness of his voice does nothing to hide its sharp edges from me.

"He was getting the golden fleece for the Ipotane Alpha. We'd already been separated for three days. Maybe more. It was hard to tell in there."

Griffin straightens. His nostrils flare as he looks down at me. "He shouldn't have left you."

"He got what we needed. We both made it out. That's what's important."

His eyes spark with anger in the dim light. "What's important is keeping you safe."

"Stop." Sharp, the one word rings out loudly in the icy quiet of the tunnel. "Stop with this obsession. It's not fair to anyone, especially me, and for the first time ever, I can honestly say you're being a hypocrite."

"A hypocrite?" he grates out, stiffening away from me.

"If your goal is to keep me safe, then take me back to Castle Sinta. We'll dance, feast, spend hours in bed together, get fat, and have babies. Don't take over the realms. Don't try to change the world. Don't throw us all into the paths of power-hungry, bloodthirsty Alphas. Don't be responsible for anything except for me."

Griffin blinks. He looks like I slapped him. "Are you asking me to choose between you and everything else?"

Shaking my head, I lift my hands and spear my fingers into his overlong hair. I don't know how his hair stays silky and soft when I'm going to need a vat of olive oil to untangle mine. "I have a feeling you'd choose me, and I won't do that to you. You'd end up hating me for it, and I'd hate myself. But I'm not a princess in a gilded tower. You have to let me do my part."

"You're on the Ice Plains. You went in *there*." A tight jerk of his head indicates the dark tunnel leading into the labyrinth.

"I know. And I know that was hard for you. For everyone. But don't be mad at Kato for doing his part."

Griffin mutters a harsh curse and then stares at me, his expression like a herd of Centaurs on the verge of charging—explosion imminent.

I lightly cup his cheek in my hand. "I'm here. I'm safe."

His eyes close. Slowly, he leans into my touch, and the anger and the stress start to drain from him. "It killed me. Every day, every hour, every minute, every bloody second, it killed me. Waiting for you. Not knowing if you were alive."

"I know." I lean forward and press my lips to his.

Griffin holds on to my waist, anchoring me to him. "There's nothing left of you," he rasps between kisses.

His large hands cover most of my sides. His fingers splayed wide, I know he can feel every bone.

"I can fix that by eating nothing but spice cakes for a year when this is over," I tell him.

He chuckles. It turns into a groan when he slides his hands up to palm my breasts. I arch into his touch, and he increases the pressure. My belly tightens. Desire shivers through me.

"Then these would be a handful again." The huskiness in his voice makes me think he's really looking forward to that. "Plump and round."

I laugh a little, the sound tangling with a rough exhale when his thumbs brush over my nipples. "Those would be plump and round, but my ass would be, too, and probably my hips."

"Perfect," Griffin growls, lowering his head to plunder my mouth again.

He steals my breath and melts my bones. Gripping my nape, he deepens the kiss. Urgency jumps from his tongue to mine. My spine curves, and he bends me even farther back, his fist tightening in my hair. My hips angle up, reaching for him, and our bodies connect right where they should. Griffin moans at the contact. A hot, liquid pulse throbs to life between my thighs.

Tension and need gather like a heady storm. "I want you."

"Cat..." He groans low.

My legs clasping his hips, I push Griffin's cloak aside and then run my hands over his torso, finding hard leather instead of a familiar chest. On a frantic quest for skin, I drop my hands to his belt, unbuckle it in record time, and then artlessly tug at the laces of his pants. His arousal springs free, and I curve my hand around the warm, hard flesh, squeezing as I stroke him from base to tip.

Griffin makes a guttural sound, biting out, "Cold hands," even as he rocks into my grip.

"Fill me." I kiss his scruffy neck and jaw as I swirl the pad of my thumb over the liquid pearling at the crown of his erection. "I'll be hot."

He shudders. "You feel so fragile in my hands."

Is he afraid he'll hurt me? I nip his earlobe. "I am not, never have been, and never will be fragile."

Griffin lifts his head. His eyes flash with silver heat a second before he grabs my boots and tears them off. My pants follow, ripped down my legs with one hard jerk as I wiggle, helping to free them from underneath me.

Cold air sweeps across my bare skin. Griffin wraps my legs back around his waist, tucking them under his cloak again. Then his cool palms slide up my thighs and around my hips. He pulls me hard against him, and I gasp. This is what I want.

He kisses me again, his thumbs skimming along the creases of my thighs. Then one callused finger lightly traces the seam of my folds. The teasing touch gradually turns bolder, circling, pressing down. An explosion of sensation riots through me. I arch back, catching fire.

Griffin bends over me, kissing me senseless while his touch leaves me trembling and hot. I grip his shoulders and hang on, raising my hips to meet his hand.

"Griffin!" A storm races under my skin. I whip my hips, trying to spur him on.

"Patience, Princess."

"*Now*, Your Stubbornness, or I swear I'll start biting."

Griffin slides one long finger inside me. "Is that a promise?" he asks, his voice low and gravelly soft.

A tremor ripples through me. "And kicking."

"So hot." His eyes slide closed.

"And screaming my head off," I threaten breathlessly.

He looks at me again, his storm-cloud gaze half hooded by thick, inky lashes. "Then I must be doing something right."

A second finger ratchets up my need to a nearly unbearable level. Griffin's wide palm puts pressure where I need it most, and my breathing quickens.

"I want you inside me."

"You're making it damn hard to make sure you're ready," he says, sounding almost harsh.

"I'm ready!"

"Cat…"

I push his hand aside, take hold of his shaft, and then practically impale myself on his erection.

Griffin inhales with a hiss. Then he grips my hips and pulls me forward, joining us fully with a slow, deliberately measured thrust. Exquisite pressure builds low in my abdomen. He's barely finished pushing himself inside me when my release hits. My thighs tense. The breath stalls in my lungs, and then I kick back my head and let out the loudest, throatiest, most breathless moan in the history of all history, going boneless in a blissful rush.

"Gods, I missed you," Griffin rasps, holding me as I throb around him.

The high-impact tremors fade into sweet, lingering aftershocks. I look up at him with heavy-lidded eyes. My lips part, but no words come out. Even the drag of frosty air over my kiss-swollen lips is almost too sensual to bear.

Griffin quirks a dark eyebrow, looking smug. "That was easy."

I grin, falling in love with him all over again. "Then do it again."

Heat flares in his eyes. His lips curve in a slow, carnal smile as he slowly withdraws. Pleasure licks up and down my spine, the feel of him moving inside me thrilling me from my head to my toes. He thrusts forward again, and my exhale shudders between us. Griffin's hoarse groan is all I need to rock my hips. He answers by rocking his. Our eyes meet with steady, burning intensity.

"You're mine." He strokes into me again, and thunder cracks in my heated veins. Lightning flashes around us. "I'm yours. Nothing will ever come between us."

"Nothing," I vow, the binding magic snapping in my blood.

Griffin pulls me off the ice shelf, holding me in an iron grip while he thrusts upward again and again. I wrap my arms around his neck, finding his mouth to claim his lips, his tongue, his breath, and more. He moves faster, harder, driving up into me as I grind down. Release swells inside me again, cresting like a great, unstoppable wave.

I start to shout, and Griffin clamps his mouth down on mine, muffling the sound as I tumble over the edge of another shattering climax. My muscles clench his shaft, begging him to join me as hot bolts of pleasure spark and twist through my body. Griffin's grip turns crushing. He goes still, shudders, and then groans against my mouth, finding his own release just after me.

Our lips cling. Neither of us moves. I couldn't even if I tried. Only Griffin's arms are keeping me upright. When he finally lifts his head, my lashes flutter up.

Dreamily, I say, "If you put me down, I'll fall."

Griffin smiles faintly. "I would never let you fall."

Overwhelming love pushes at the confines of my ribs, making my heart feel too big for my chest.

A shrill whistle comes from somewhere beyond the curve in the tunnel, a sudden reminder of the others waiting for us. "If we want to get off this mountain today, we have to leave now," Carver calls.

"How do you feel?" The concern in Griffin's eyes is evident even in the dim light. Or maybe it's his voice that gives it away.

"Honestly?" I grimace, touching the bump on my head. But instead of saying, "Occasionally dizzy with mild to not-so-mild bouts of nausea," I just say, "Exhausted," which is also true. Oddly, I was feeling much the same even before I got tossed headfirst into a wall.

"We camp here until tomorrow," Griffin calls back.

Carver grumbles something unintelligible in assent.

"We should get dressed." I yawn, utterly unmotivated to move.

"Then I'll have to put you down."

That is a drawback. "All right, but only for a second."

Griffin slides me off him and then deposits my cloak-protected bottom back onto the ice shelf. Still half hard, he rights his pants and buckles his belt. On his way down to retrieve my clothing, he stops to inspect the healing cut on my left thigh. "What happened here?"

I yawn again. "Monster claw." The slice wasn't deep and healed over quickly, leaving a line across my leg that's only a little sore. "I don't even feel it."

His sudden, tense silence speaks volumes, but I ignore it. Griffin chooses to let it go, probably because there's no point arguing with a person who is half asleep and who doesn't care about the cut anyhow.

Mostly thanks to Griffin, I end up dressed again before he gathers me into his arms and then sits, settling his back against the tunnel wall. With me in his lap, he wraps our smoldering cloaks around us both. The soft light flickers over the hard angles of his face.

I lift a heavy hand and trace my finger along the prominent bridge of his nose. "I love your nose."

His mouth curves in a dubious smile. "It's big and hooked."

I sigh. "I know."

I let my hand fall and then tuck it between us, resting my head under Griffin's chin. I fall asleep almost instantly, warm, happy, and safe for the first time in days.

CHAPTER 21

THE HYDRA IS REAL—UNFORTUNATELY—AND JUDGING
by the scattered bones, clearly an effective guardian for
the narrow entrance to the Phthian Gap. The creature sits
half submerged in the shallows of the lake, its gigantic,
oblong body only partially visible. At the tops of a dozen
towering necks, heads whip and twist and tangle and roar.
The snarling gets louder the closer we get. I'm guessing
humans aren't welcome here.

I push my cloak back from my shoulders, already sweat-
ing from the balmy temperature. The Hydra is no fool. In
a land of snow and ice, it lives in a place riddled with hot
springs. No wonder magical creatures winter here. With
the Hydra in front and formidable mountains protecting the
entrance on either side, the Phthian Gap then descends into
a wide, verdant valley. The inviting vista winds its way
from where we now stand to not-so-far-off, cloud-capped
Mount Olympus, rising majestically in the north.

Nerves jangle in my belly. "I need more heads," I con-
clude after conducting a thorough inspection of the Hydra.

Griffin angles himself in front of me. So does Flynn.

Next to me, Carver says, "Do I even want to ask?"

Of course he does. "If we're going to keep facing creatures with multiple heads, I need more. You know, just to
make things fair," I explain.

"One head is enough." Griffin stops me with a steely
arm in front of my chest when I try to come up next to him
again. "And I told you to stay back."

I stretch up on my toes and whisper for Griffin's ears only, "I could get creative with my extra mouths."

He ignores that. The grump.

"You know what I love about you, Cat?" Carver draws his weapon. We all do. It's for the best—big monster and all.

"Is this a trick question?" I ask.

He smiles. "You can make jokes while looking a creature like that in the eye."

"Which eye?" I cock my head and study the Hydra. "There are a lot to choose from."

That earns a chuckle from everyone except Griffin. He's still being a grump. Probably because he knows I get flippant and verbally reckless when I'm scared.

I nudge his arm. "Do you have a plan, Your Grouchiness?"

Griffin levels a flat look on me. "Do you, Princess?"

I shrug. "Tiptoe? Go around? Quietly?"

"On that?" Flynn eyes the one-person-wide, narrow strip of ledge butting up against a sheer cliff that appears to be the only way around the Hydra and the steaming lake. "You do know it's already seen us?"

"Plan B, then," I say.

"Which is?" Kato asks.

I grimace somewhat. "Chop off its heads?"

As if in response to that idea, one huge head disengages from the rest of the whirling, serpentine mass and lunges in our direction. Gargantuan jaws snap way too close for comfort.

Cursing under his breath, Griffin grips my hand and leads me thirty feet back. His glare seems to be some kind of silent, masculine command to stay put.

I glare back. "I'm not a bloody dog."

"A dog would listen better," he grates out.

"Five of us. A dozen heads." Carver looks back and forth

between the Hydra and us. "If we consider each head an enemy, we've fought our way out of worse odds than that."

"Except each of those heads is the size of five men grouped together," Kato says. "Or ten Cats."

"I heard that," I mutter indignantly. It doesn't matter that it's true.

"Let's not get technical," Carver says. "It's bad for morale."

"*Four* of us." Griffin looks pointedly at me. "You have no magic left to fight with, at least not any magic you know how to control. You *will not* be foolish." His deep voice resonates with that authoritative quality I find intriguing in a number of situations, particularly in the bedroom, but which lately, usually coupled with his nearly pathological overprotectiveness, I could do without.

"I have knives," I counter. "And a sword. I'm not exactly useless."

"If you throw any blades, do it from back here." I open my mouth to argue, and Griffin's eyes narrow. "We both know you're not too far away to hit your mark."

I close my mouth with a click.

"Kato, Flynn, take that side." Griffin points to the left. "Carver, you're with me. Cat, don't move."

They all charge at once, leaving me high up and alone on the spongy bank. I unhook my cloak, drop it, and then race toward the fray. Did Griffin honestly think I wouldn't?

The fight is a blur, and not one of us even comes close to severing a Hydra neck. I dart away from sharp teeth and whipping heads, getting soaked by the waves the Hydra's ferocious gyrating generates. Otherwise, I avoid Griffin. He's spitting mad and won't stop yelling at me.

Too focused on me, Griffin gets blindsided by a sweeping head. It smashes into his back and propels him into the water. He goes down face-first, and my heart stops dead in my chest. A wave crashes over him, and the strong backward pull drags him into the Hydra's body.

I bolt forward. This is my fault. If I'd let him be effective in battle instead of worrying about me, he never would have left himself open.

The Hydra snaps and hisses, forcing us to scatter as Griffin staggers to his feet. His wet cloak tangles around him, hampering his movements. Terrified, I hold out my hands and aim my fear at the Hydra.

No lightning. Not even a tingle of power ripples down my arms. Only the pendant around my neck pulses with cold, as if reaching for my magic along with me.

Filling with dread, I watch the man I love dodge wide-open jaws. Hydra mouths smash into the lake, sending plumes of water jetting into the air. Currents churn around him, pushing and pulling. But Griffin's agility is his own magic. With strength and coiled efficiency, he spins and brings his sword down hard on the closest neck, severing it.

The Hydra screams. All the mouths shriek at once, and the nightmarish sound echoes off the mountains.

The rising triumph in me crashes the instant two new appendages sprout from the severed stump. The fresh necks and heads grow fast. I blink, and they're the size of me!

"New plan!" I shout. "Do *not* chop off its heads!"

Griffin struggles through chest-high water, swinging his sword defensively. When a full-sized head dives for him, I throw a knife and bury the blade between its eyes. The head jerks back and then falls, sloshing a wave up the shore that helps propel Griffin out of the water. While he's scrambling up the soggy shelf, a set of teeth snags the bottom of his cloak, tearing it. A ball of fire erupts in the mouth, and the Hydra howls, plunging its head into the water.

Griffin races to my side. I throw every knife I have,

felling heads until I'm out of blades. Flynn and Kato follow my lead and drop all but two of the remaining heads.

"I need more knives!" I cry.

"We're out!" Kato yells back.

Griffin hands me his. "Only one." Breathing hard, he slicks his dripping hair back from his face.

I take aim, throw, and hit my target. Only one head left.

Flynn gets ready to throw his ax, but the remaining Hydra head starts ruthlessly biting off its limp counterparts, severing its own necks so that two heads replace every one that was lost. Blood floods the lake. Within seconds, the monster mushrooms into a creature twice as deadly and terrifying as it was before.

"Retreat!" Griffin shouts.

I hesitate. Two severed heads with my knives in them lie just at the water's edge. We'll need those blades. I'm sure we will.

Ignoring Griffin's panicked shout, I race for the weapons, rip one free, whirl around, and then grab the other.

Most of the newly matured heads lunge in my direction. My heart pounds frantically as I sprint back up the bank. A shelf of mud collapses under my feet, and I pitch forward, losing my knives in the muck. I reach for them, but a wave crashes over me, thumping me into the ground and then dragging me back. I claw at the bank, but it's slippery and unstable. There's nothing to hold on to. I slide toward the Hydra and the lake. Bone-deep terror hits me a second before razor-sharp teeth close around my upper arm and shoulder.

Searing pain brings my thoughts to a grinding halt. Griffin's horrified yell slices through my shock, and his stricken face flashes through my field of vision as the Hydra whips me high into the air above the lake. The creature's jaws clamp down, and my skin pops like a ripe olive. Blood gushes. Bones crunch.

Blazing heat explodes down my left side. Darkness pulses through my mind. The Hydra shakes me like a dog with a rope, and muscles tear. More bones snap. I don't scream. I stiffen, trying to hold myself together as the Hydra shakes me apart.

The creature suddenly releases me mid-swing, hurling me toward dry land. My stomach spirals up my throat as ground and sky blur, tumbling over each other in a nauseating rush.

Impact knocks the air from my body. Stuns me completely. There's a split second of all-consuming agony before I descend into the utter dark.

I awake disoriented, feeling outside of myself. Griffin is hovering over me with my head in his hands. His eyes are wild, his expression beyond horrified. He's blank-faced with terror.

My eyebrows draw together. I don't like seeing Griffin scared. It's not normal.

A thunderclap of pain hits me, and I hiss. It rattles through every bone, every muscle, every inch of my skin. The Hydra attack comes rushing back. Everything throbs so horrifically that I know I'm shattered. There's no way that I'm not.

Even short and shallow, my breathing sets my rib cage on fire. Jagged bones must scrape my lungs and probably other things inside me. Ribs. Broken. *All of them?* Left arm… I can't even feel it. I'm terrified to look because it may not even be there. I try to move my legs. The right one does nothing, but the left one jerks up, jarring me with a whole new round of pain. The movement sets off a flare of heat inside me, and then an agonizing cramp tears through my lower abdomen. I let out a hoarse cry, and my right hand flies to my belly.

Griffin's face goes bone-white. "Hang on, *agapi mou*. You have to hang on."

"I'm sorry," I gasp out. "I'm so sorry."

"Stop." It's an order, Griffin's unyielding voice the one that commands armies and wins wars. "You only apologize when you think you're going to die."

I shudder in agony. I am going to die. Doesn't he know that?

I don't want to leave Griffin so easily, so stupidly, but my eyes still close. I can't keep them open.

I sense the others around me. I don't want to leave them, either. Kato—my brother. Flynn. Carver. My family. But I'm being swept along. Pulled away. Something strong is beckoning me. Something nice.

A sharp sting hits my cheek. I open my eyes and meet Griffin's. He slaps my other cheek. "Wake up! Stay awake."

Something hot and thick fills my mouth. I gag and then cough, spraying blood onto Griffin's chin. It's bright red. No handy immortality there. I don't see even a hint of the golden ichor hidden in my veins.

Griffin's eyes turn frantic. "Say your chant. The one for the healing salamander."

I can't focus. The sky is spinning. "Need…running… water." *Need a real healer. Need my voice to keep working. Need help.*

As gently as he can, Griffin picks me up and then lays me back down next to one of the streams feeding into the Hydra's lake. He sticks my right hand directly into water that's warm and stinks faintly of sulfur.

I start chanting. It takes a colossal effort to push the words out, breathe, and not choke on the blood in my mouth. The sounds are easy even if the spell is in the ancient language of the Gods, and Griffin starts saying the incantation along with me, learning it. The others are just shadows in my blurred vision, but I hear them, too, lending volume and clarity to my increasingly slurred words. Magic sparks inside me and my necklace flares to life, but it's their voices that keep me going until the ten repetitions are done.

Griffin plunges his hand into the water. I close my eyes again. His voice fades, and whatever he was saying doesn't make sense anymore. I drift on a dark haze. It sucks me down, down, coating me in a pain-numbing balm. I feel so much better here, but something still tells me I don't want to go where it's taking me. My lips part to call out for Griffin, but no words form, and no air crosses them again.

A murky, shadowed land rises up to meet me. Or maybe I rise out of it. I glance down. I'm upright, whole, and free of pain. I know what I've left behind, but the ache of loss is buffered and indistinct. I turn in a slow circle, gradually accepting what's happened. I'm still me. I still love Griffin. Time is irrelevant. My thoughts adjust surprisingly fast, my new reality just a flip side of the old.

The trees around me are dark, the land gray, with only a few stumpy hills and rocky outcroppings to break up the colorless monotony. Dense fog swirls around my legs as I begin to walk in the direction calling to me, toward a wide, mist-shrouded river curving in a slow-moving buckle. On the far side of the water, the fog burns off and the silvery surface glints under a brilliant sky.

The opposite shore is breathtaking. I've never seen colors so vibrant, grass so thick, or trees so full and high.

A golden pathway leads away from the river and into a lush valley that slopes downward and out of sight. The path is empty now, maybe a little lonely, but my feet long to walk it. It leads to all things better and bright.

Across the river, a boat slips into the sparkling water. I need it to carry me across because this side is dreadful. A clawing weight presses on my shoulders. Hopelessness leaves a sour taste in my mouth and coats me in misery. The air smells musty and stale, and tendrils of damp fog cling to my arms, making me shiver.

Unease ripples through me. I turn to see hunched figures emerging from the dark trees and ghastly mist. They shuffle toward me, their heads bowed, their hands held out to beg for an obol. Their despair is an actual stench, and I back toward the river, both crushed and overwhelmed by it.

More shapes uncurl from the gray landscape. As opposed to the first figures, these ones shake the coin they already have in anger and frustration, but the ferryman crossing the river ignores them. Malice radiates off their hollowed frames, some vibrations of cruelty fresher than others. As my steps instinctively draw me closer to the water, I understand their punishment. Everything becomes clear. An eternity here, or however long the ferryman deems necessary, to atone for evil deeds. With a sickening drop of my stomach, I realize I'm on the Plain of Asphodel.

Am I doomed to stay?

I turn back to the river, my heart clenching in fear. The boat makes not a whisper of sound as it plows through the drab reeds and then butts up against the dismal bank. Charon is bathed in night, wearing a somber cloak that floats around his gaunt body in the nonexistent breeze. His deep hood swallows his face, so I see nothing of his features. A long pole juts from the shallows, and he holds it at the top, primed to push off again. *With me? Without me?* Has my past doomed me to Asphodel?

The obol I always carry burns a hole in my pocket while I stare in fear and desperate longing at the silent, shrouded ferryman. After a long, terrifying wait, Charon lifts a skeletal hand and beckons.

A shaky sound leaks from my throat. But the chorus of wails that swells behind me taints my relief. I want to take the people without a coin with me. Surely I've done and caused things more hideous than they?

I look back at their outstretched hands and mournful faces. There are children. Why should I cross to the other side while they suffer along with the punished?

I reach for my coin, my heart heavy with the knowledge that I can't help even one of them without condemning myself. But a power beyond my control doesn't leave me the choice to sacrifice my obol, even if I could bring myself to give it up. My feet carry me toward the ferry, drawn inexorably.

The drooping figures and their sobbing fade, and as I walk, a girl crests the hill on the opposite side of the river. She emerges from between two soaring cypresses, hurrying along the golden path. She's small and lithe, her long blonde hair shining like the morning sun.

My breath hitches, and I start to run, holding Charon's payment tightly in my hand. It strikes me as odd considering I've only just arrived, but I want her and that golden path more than anything I've left behind, even Griffin. He'll get here eventually. We'll be together again. I'll just wait for him, as long as it takes.

I race through the mist, wondering if this is Hades's gift to the people who pass into his land—to make them yearn for their dead more than they ache for the living.

Across the river, Eleni holds up a staying hand. "Eat," she calls.

Slowing, I look around. There's no food here. Only fog and shadow and the promise of something better on the other side.

I suddenly ache all over. My steps falter, and the vapor creeping around my legs starts to feel like a tangle of giant spiderwebs, holding me back, weighing me down.

"Eleni!" I shout, alarmed.

"Eat!" she yells back. The panic and sternness in her tone shake me to my core. Her voice... It's not quite hers. It's deep and fierce. It reminds me of—

My eyes prick with tears. I don't understand. I scream my sister's name again, but she waves me away. She doesn't want me.

Charon lowers his hand. He pushes on the pole, and his boat slips backward through the mist.

"No! Don't leave me!" I struggle to get him the obol, to reach the shore, but I can't move. *Oh my Gods, what's happening!* "Eleni!"

"Eat!" she screams from across the water, her voice overlapped by a terrified, masculine roar.

Pain lances through me. Breath stabs my lungs. I open my eyes and gasp.

Griffin! My heart explodes as thoroughly as my body, agonizing, inside and out.

"Yes! That's it!" Griffin pries open my jaws and then stuffs something into my mouth. "Eat! Damn it!"

He forces my mouth closed and then holds his hand over it, sealing it shut. My eyes widen and my nostrils flare, drawing in short, panicked, painful puffs of air. The salamander is smooth and slimy and tastes of sulfur and mud. Tiny claws scrape my tongue. A flat tail whips the roof of my mouth.

I gag, wrenching my destroyed body, but then nature forces me to swallow, and the creature and its magic slip down my throat.

Increased consciousness slams into me almost immediately along with the painful throbbing of broken bones. My vision darkens from the sheer force of it.

"Cat?" Griffin leans over me, his expression filled with petrified hope. His gray eyes start to glisten.

Magical warmth coils through my middle, and suddenly I can breathe again without wanting to crawl into a hole and die. "I'm here," I croak.

He exhales slowly, unsteadily, his eyes swimming now. "I got you back."

He saved me. He stole me from Death. "Need more," I say.

"Then start chanting," he replies gruffly, blinking hard.

From the side, Kato shouts, "I did it! I made one!" I hear a splash and turn my head enough to see him pull a bright yellow salamander from the stream. *How did that happen?*

"Open," Griffin orders, pinching my jaw.

Kato stuffs the creature into my mouth, and then Griffin pushes my jaw closed.

My eyes water. It takes some gearing up and a few tries before I manage to swallow. After I do, I start feeling my left arm again. It's still there, thank the Gods.

"Carver? Flynn? Anything?" Griffin asks.

They both answer in the negative.

"Kato. Again." Griffin moves his hand so that it hovers over the water. "Cat, go."

Kato and I start chanting. My second salamander is brown, like always, while Kato's is bright yellow again. I force them both down, and the pain inside me lessens.

Kato's has more impact. The shock begins to wear off. I start to warm up and shake less. It takes two more of the magical creatures and a concentrated effort not to throw up for my leg to begin healing, and before that, Griffin has to hold me down while Flynn sets the bone. Not even a great healer can fuse a bone back together without at least pointing it in the right direction first. Sticking up through my thigh was definitely not the right direction, and the sight of the jagged, bloodstained bone turned my stomach worse than the salamanders did.

As soon as I'm able, Griffin helps me sit up and drink from the stream. The water tastes awful. It's full of minerals, but it calms the twitch in the back of my throat enough to keep me from losing the salamanders. I don't know what would happen if they came back up.

"You're amazing," I say, wiping warm water from my chin. "You all are. Thank you."

Gruff mumbling is my only answer.

"Let's move you away from all this blood." Griffin picks me up even though I could probably limp on my own and then sets me down where the grass is thick and dry. Pain still crawls up and down my body. Repeating the spell drained me, leaving me dizzy and weak. And that's on top of the near-death.

"Should we dilute the blood?" Griffin asks.

I look at him, a surge of emotion making my heart turn over hard. I'm so glad I didn't get in that boat.

I shake my head. "Let Mother come here looking for me. She can have fun with the Hydra now that we got it to grow twice as many heads."

Carver plants his hands on his narrow hips, frowning in the direction of the lake. "There's no way we're getting past that. At least it stays in the lake."

I eye the enormous creature. "If it didn't, we'd be dead. More dead. I mean, really dead. For real."

Griffin's hand tightens on my lower back, and I stop talking. Everyone still looks whey-faced, as if I scared the color out of them.

"How do you feel?" Griffin asks.

I don't meet his eyes. I'm great at exaggerating. Not so good at downplaying. "Nothing to worry about." I stand to prove it, ignoring the shooting aches in my bones. As long as I don't have to run, fight, or move very much until we find a real healer, that'll be true. I hope.

Griffin's expression tells me I'm not fooling him. But I'm upright and not bleeding to death, so that'll have to do.

"So that's it? No Ipotane?" Flynn's auburn hair is soaked through and plastered down. It's darker that way, the color of a peat-stained stream. His brown eyes are three times as dark and charged with frustration. "After all this?"

I glare at the Hydra. "I wish I could fry it. I have God-like power, and I can't even make it work. How worthless is that?"

"If you would take your own safety seriously," Griffin says sharply, "maybe it would."

Guilt keeps me from answering, or even looking at him.

"So now what?" Carver asks.

Before anyone can answer him, Kato reels back. Hissing, he slaps his hand over the serpent tattoo on his neck.

CHAPTER 22

"WHAT?" WE ALL SHOUT AT ONCE.

Kato's lips pull back in a grimace. Smoke rises from under his fingers, and the smell of burning flesh strikes my nose like an acrid punch.

He doubles over and retches violently. Saliva drips from his open mouth, and a horrible groan resonates in his chest. His blue eyes turn huge and watery. Then he heaves again, his entire body bucking with the effort. Titos's head pokes up from Kato's throat.

"Mother of Zeus!" I jump back with more energy than I thought I had, lose my balance, and land on my ass.

Just like at the Chaos Wizard's house, the snake slowly emerges, shiny and black, with vibrant crimson and gold diamonds chasing each other down its back. Its forked tongue shoots out and flutters in the air. It licks again, seeming greedy for the taste of the warm, magic-charged air. The serpent scans the area, unblinking, before dropping to the grass with a flat thud.

Kato staggers back from Titos, hacking out a series of coughs that rattle like dust and gravel. In between, he gulps down half-strangled breaths, his chest rising and falling like bellows. The tattoo is still on his neck, the flesh around it raw and red. Almost immediately, though, the burn starts to fade, and the tattoo settles into healthy-looking skin again, more realistic and lifelike than ever.

Wary, my jaw still slack, I turn back toward Titos. Slowly, like he doesn't want to startle me, Poseidon's

Drakon slithers toward me. He lays his head across my boot and stares at me with those lidless eyes. Still sprawled on my backside, I cringe and tense to kick him off me, but his tongue shoots out and curls around my calf.

Adrenaline spikes in my blood. I think the snake just hugged me. I'm disturbed. *Very* disturbed.

"If you jump down my throat, I *will* cut myself open to get you out," I say with surprising conviction.

I could swear the word *incompatible* whispers through my mind on a soft hiss. The small hairs on the back of my neck prickle upright, and I shiver.

Titos slithers up my recently reset leg. Heat suffuses my thigh. Griffin steps forward, not looking at all comfortable with this, and I hold up my hand. "Wait. It's okay. I think."

From between locked jaws, he says, "You *think*?"

I nod, and then, through the tear in my pants, we all see the jagged, puckered, barely closed-over skin even out, losing all evidence of recent injury. The pervasive ache in my bone disappears.

Griffin lets out a soft grunt and visibly relaxes. So do I.

Titos wriggles into my lap, curls up, and then lays his shiny dark head on my lower abdomen. His tongue flutters out with leisurely vibrations against my belly, and a tingling warmth spreads through my pelvis and higher, soothing away the cramps and aches. Next, he coils around my torso, and my breathing turns completely pain-free. After that, Titos slides his head over my left shoulder and then wraps his sinuous body around my arm. It stops throbbing instantly.

"Titos is healing me," I whisper.

"Then why do you look like you're about to vomit?" Flynn whispers back.

"I'm trying to overcome my visceral dislike of snakes."

I speak through my teeth, not opening my mouth just in case Titos gets any ideas about a new host, despite my apparent incompatibility.

To my relief, Titos eventually slithers off me. I breathe deeply for the first time since the Hydra caught me and twist this way and that, testing my body and stretching my limbs. I grin. "I feel great!"

Squatting down next to me, Griffin squeezes my knee. His return smile looks strained and doesn't reach his eyes.

Kato chokes on something, maybe leftover snake, and then neatly sidesteps a slow-moving Titos. Kato's eyes shift from the serpent back to me. His expression turns incredulous. "I carried a Drakon around all this time on the off chance—no, the *good* chance—you'd get yourself nearly killed and need extreme magical healing?"

I grimace, apologetic. "I guess so. Titos couldn't have survived the Ice Plains on his own. It's too cold for snakes." I look around. "This place is perfect for him. The hot springs will keep him warm, and there are bound to be frogs and other sources of food in the lake."

Kato snorts. "So if something like this had happened when we were still on the glaciers, the snake would have jumped back down my throat?"

I have trouble meeting Kato's eyes and pluck at my boot instead. I don't like how the Gods have been using him. First the labyrinth, and now this. "Maybe." I shrug. "I don't know."

Without even a last look in our direction, Titos slips into the warm lake. Gentle ripples form, spread out, and then melt into the water as he disappears under the surface.

"That was anticlimactic," Carver says with a frown.

"Not for me," Kato mutters, rubbing his neck.

"Titos must have helped you conjure the healing

salamanders." I look at Kato, my eyes drawn to the dark spiral of the tattoo peeking out from under his fingers. "That's why they were so powerful."

Frowning, Kato drops his hand. "I guess that's the end of that."

His tattoo gleams in the sunlight, still lifelike. *Who knows?*

Griffin tenses beside me. He rises, and I follow his gaze toward the lake. My eyes widen just as Griffin reaches down, grabs my wrist, and pops me off the ground with strength that still somehow surprises me. We all run away from the lake, Griffin towing me at breakneck speed. Part of me registers that I don't hurt—anywhere. *Amazing.* The rest of me focuses on the next disaster. Something huge enough to displace massive amounts of water is hurtling straight for the shore.

I glance over my shoulder. Every Hydra head is turned toward the gargantuan disturbance. The frightening creature spins and splashes frantically for deeper water.

Uh-oh. When monster number one is terrified of monster number two, it's definitely time to move faster. Unfortunately, I'm the slowest one here.

The Hydra shrieks, and I turn again. And stop dead. Griffin is still going and nearly rips my arm from the socket before he stops, too, whipping around.

Titos is rising from the lake. Only Titos grew. *A lot.* His black head flares, so high and huge it blocks the sun and throws the entire lakefront into shadow. He towers above the Hydra, an ebony mountain of muscle and fangs. Water cascades down his enormous, overlapping scales, hitting the lake with a tumbling crash. The lake froths and foams, bubbling around his giant column of a body as Titos unhinges his enormous jaws. They widen with a loud, dreadful click. The inside of the serpent's mouth is wet and pink and bottomless. Plenty of room for the Hydra.

Titos drops his head straight down, and the entire screeching Hydra disappears into his monstrous gullet—gone in one gulp.

"Good Gods," Griffin murmurs.

I drag my jaw off the ground. "Well done, Titos!" I cheer. "Good snake!"

Titos looks in our direction and then sets his massive head down on the waterlogged bank, leaving his huge body to bask half in the sun, half in the warm lake. He looks for all of Olympus like he's settling down for a nap and a long digestion. The Hydra is a giant lump in Titos's even more gigantic throat. The lump is *moving*.

I clap. "Onward to the Ipotane! This day is turning out *great*!"

Griffin levels a flat, dark look on me, not amused.

Kato looks ill. "I... It... Me..." He stares at the massive snake. "Big."

I squeeze his arm. "Don't worry. You'll speak in complete sentences again soon."

His brow creasing, Flynn looks out over the now-calm water. "Actually, before we move on... Since Titos has made the lake safe, I wouldn't mind a bath."

The others murmur in agreement, and it sounds like a good idea to me. I'm covered in my own blood.

"Wash and rest." Griffin nods. "We'll camp here until Cat is at full strength again."

As anxious as I am to reach the Ipotane, he's right. I'm pumped up on adrenaline right now, but everything that just happened is bound to take its toll. Better to rest and recover with Titos watching over us.

We return to where we left our gear and supplies, and Carver rummages for soap and a change of clothing. Flynn and Kato do the same.

"We'll take that side," Carver says, and he and the

others move off toward the right, between Titos and the cliffside path, leaving Griffin and me alone.

Griffin grabs his soap and satchel and then reaches for me, swinging me up into his arms.

Smiling, I loop my hands loosely around his neck. "I can walk."

"Or I can carry you."

I arch a brow at his flat, unbending tone, but I like it where I am, so I don't argue.

Griffin carries me toward the steaming lake, heading for a scattering of boulders to the left of Titos. Staring straight ahead, gruffly he says, "I need you."

Anticipation leaps in my belly. I need him, too. I bury my face in his scruffy neck and inhale deeply. I choke a little. "What you need is a bath."

He grunts.

"And a shave." I rub the tip of my nose over his whiskered cheek. "Can I shave your beard for you?"

"No."

I stretch up and nip his earlobe. "Why not? I'm good with knives."

Griffin's grip tightens. "Concentrate on your own hair. It might take a while."

"Ah, the Knotted Nest. That *will* take some work."

Griffin almost smiles. I think. "You named it?"

"Of course. It's worthy of a name. Actually, it's got two. That and the Terrible Tangle. Which do you prefer?"

"I prefer 'I love you and you're beautiful.'"

I grin. "Charming, Your Highness."

This time his lips twitch. I'm sure of it. Almost.

"No sarcasm?" he asks.

I slide my fingers into his smooth, dark, still-wet hair. "You're learning, Beta Sinta."

He growls deep in his throat at the name I used to call him, when I was a conflicted prisoner and he was a stranger I didn't understand. "That's *Alpha* Sinta to you, Princess."

I laugh, shamelessly in love. "What about Husband?"

Griffin stops. Actually, I think he trips. He tenses, and his breathing turns fast and shallow, scaring me a little.

I grab his face and turn it toward mine. "Are you all right?"

He stares at me. His jaw hardens into marble under my hands, and his gray eyes flicker with hints of something explosive and unnerving. "Are you serious?"

"What?" I frown. "Um... Yes?"

His nostrils flare, and his stare turns blistering. "You say that now? You agree to marry me *now*, when I'm so bloody *angry* with you that I can barely hold on to my temper, and I don't know whether to make love to you until I finally can't see you lying there broken and bloody every time I blink, or to spank you senseless!"

My stomach had been spiraling viciously downward, but at "spank" I feel my eyes light up.

"And not in a good way!" Griffin practically shouts.

"You wouldn't."

"My hand is itching for your reckless little arse."

"You were fine two seconds ago!"

"I *wasn't*!" Cursing, he sets me down behind a large rock. In no time, I'm completely naked, most of my clothes simply ripped right off. They were ruined anyway, but I still blink in shock. Griffin strips out of his own wet and bloody clothing as well. He looks like a God—hard, chiseled, powerful, *livid*—and I shiver with slightly wary excitement as I step into the almost-too-warm lake. Steam curls up my body, turning my skin damp and pink. Griffin prowls in after me.

Silt squishes between my toes as I move back. "If you try to spank me, Titos might eat you."

He stalks me. Griffin's arms hang loose at his sides, but his expression is shuttered and stiff. There isn't an inch of him that's relaxed.

I back up until I'm trapped by boulders and the water reaches my knees. When Griffin stops in front of me, his naked body, even vibrating with barely leashed anger, is too tempting to resist. I reach out and slide both hands down his sculpted torso, stopping only when my fingers dip into the indents near his hips.

The taut skin on Griffin's lower abdomen twitches. He sucks in a breath. I sweep my hands toward his growing arousal, but before I can wrap my fingers around it, he grabs my wrists and forces them behind my back.

I look up. He looks down at me with such fierce intensity that my breath catches, and my heart starts to pound. In his severe expression, I see aggression that won't hurt me, and love that will always heal.

Groaning like he's in pain, Griffin drops to his knees in front of me and then cages me in an almost violent embrace. His beard rasps my stomach, and his harsh breathing sends a rush of sensation across my ribs. He stays there, his face buried below my breasts. I want to hold him, touch him, comfort him, but when I try to move, his grip tightens on my wrists. And so I stand there, my heart so full it hurts, staring at the tense line of his broad shoulders and the top of his dark head.

Griffin's entire upper body eventually lifts on a deep breath. He tilts his face up and kisses the hollow between my breasts. The kiss is gentle and lingering, almost reverent, and something inside me heats and then melts. He turns his head and trails his lips over the inner swell of my breast. When his mouth closes over my nipple, a little earthquake trembles beneath my skin.

I restlessly shift my legs when Griffin sucks hard enough for me to feel the pull all the way to my core. Pleasure spikes, soaring through me, and I arch into him, already hopelessly aroused.

Slowly, Griffin drops back onto his heels. Still holding my wrists, he kisses a fiery path down my belly, stopping just above the apex of my thighs. Everything under his mouth tightens, throbbing with want.

"Cat?" His voice is rough. He doesn't look up.

I'm still helpless and caged, and I *ache*, expectation leaving me coiled tight, needy, and panting. "Griffin?"

He pulls on my wrists. My back arches, and my pelvis tips forward to meet his lips. "Marry me." He kisses me lightly and then more deeply, his tongue parting my folds for a long, slow caress. "Marry me soon."

"Yes," I answer, breathless.

Griffin makes love to me with his mouth until tremors shake me, and my legs quiver. "Is that 'yes' more of this, or 'yes' you'll marry me as soon as humanly possible?"

My bones are liquid, my body on fire. "Both."

He growls his approval, and the low vibration pushes me tantalizingly close to the edge. Griffin lets go of my wrists and catches my hips instead.

I sway, sinking my hands into his hair for balance. "I want you inside me."

He groans, drops lower, and then pushes his tongue into me.

I gasp, the first hot waves of release rolling through me. The climax grows, and I cry out, helpless to hold anything back. My fingers tighten in his hair, and Griffin's shoulders and arms flex, tensing to hold me up because I've gone limp in his hands.

He clamps me to him, his mouth coaxing trembling aftershocks from me that I can barely take. I feel weak, my skin flushed and thin. I'm achingly aware of Griffin's big, strong body, of its pure, masculine vitality, and of the power it holds over mine—the lust, the trust, the over-whelming pleasure. My senses spin, so heightened that I feel every drop of moisture beaded on my skin. One slips down my inner thigh, and Griffin follows its path with his tongue. My lips part, and I moan.

He looks up. Warm steam replaces his even hotter tongue, licking over me. Storm-gray eyes glitter from under thick lashes, clumped and spiky from condensation. His face is flushed with heat, and damp hair sticks to the sweat on his temples.

"Turn." One word, the command so deep and sexy that my stomach flutters wildly.

I don't even consider disobeying. I turn, and Griffin grips my waist, his large hands nearly circling it. He feath-ers kisses over the small of my back, and I shiver, goose bumps flaring on my skin. Then he bites one rounded side of my bottom hard enough to make me squeal.

He licks where he bit. "Brace yourself against the rock."

Catching my lower lip between my teeth, I do as Griffin asks. My hands touch the warm, moist boulder.

He rises and sweeps my hair aside, kissing my shoulder and then my neck. His hands splay over my ribs, and my breasts grow heavy, aching for his touch. Griffin leaves his hands maddeningly still on my sides, not sliding them up. Desire and heady tension gather inside me again, coiling deep in my belly. I push backward with my hips, needing to feel him.

Griffin presses back with a low, masculine sound that sets my whole body alight. "Spread your legs," he rumbles in my ear.

I widen my stance, and he drags my hips back. He leans over me, his fingers pressing into my sides. "You are my heartbeat and my every breath."

I exhale, the air leaving my lungs with a soft whoosh.

Griffin wraps one arm around my waist, lifting a little, and uses his other hand to position himself. He enters me with one long, slow stroke. Then he surrounds me, holding me against him with one arm and bracing his weight against the rock with the other, his hand right next to mine.

My head falls back against his shoulder. I turn my face, he turns his, and our lips meet.

He moves slowly, his rhythm far from steady but heartbreakingly intense. The rawness of his lovemaking overwhelms me, just like everything his great, trembling body is telling me along with the pounding thump of his heart against my back.

"Do you remember the first time I told you that you were mine?" Griffin asks.

I drag my cheek over his jaw, drinking in his ragged breaths. His slow, deep thrusts leave my head spinning. "You forbade me to die." His declaration terrified me. Secretly thrilled me. Maybe even made me feel safe for the first time in my life even though I'd just been shot.

Griffin's much larger hand curls over mine on the boulder, lacing our fingers. "It wasn't about the vow I bargained out of you, forcing you to stay with me." He lets me take back my weight, and his now free hand slides up my abdomen to cup my breast. He teases my nipple with the tip of his callused thumb. When he pinches the pebbled peak, giving it a wicked little tug, sensation erupts inside of me.

He starts to move faster, turning our joining harder. His skin slaps mine in the damp heat, the sound incredibly erotic. He dips his head and presses his lips to that spot below my ear that always turns me into a hot, jumbled mess. "I knew from the moment I laid eyes on you that you were meant for me. That I was never letting you go."

I flex my fingers under his, grasping for balance as my heart pounds and my whole world tilts. "That makes one of us," I gasp out.

Griffin rocks into me hard, pushing me up to my toes. My heavy heartbeat thuds between my legs.

"You knew, too," he rasps in my ear. "You knew the second our gazes locked across the crowded fair. Your chest rose. Your lips parted. Your green eyes shimmered like emeralds, and they were all I could see."

I envision myself through Griffin's eyes—flushed, nervous, excited. Maybe some part of me did know that night, and then I denied it for weeks, refusing that instant, visceral spark.

"You were full of spirit and daring, and you made me laugh. I loved you from our first conversation. I yearned for you to love me back."

I want to answer, to tell him that I've loved him for far longer than either of us knew, but I'm too caught up in the feel of him moving inside me. His confession and his body drive me toward a shattering release. Pressure builds until I can scarcely breathe. I moan, and Griffin shudders behind me.

His hand squeezes mine on the rock. He thrusts into me and roughly tugs my nipple again. Pleasure blazes through me. The assault on my senses is too powerful. Gasping, I slam my free hand against the boulder and then cry out when the spasms rock me.

Griffin's guttural groan and the tightening of his muscles around me send a wash of heat down my spine. He clutches me hard through his own climax, and I want to give and give and give to him until I almost cry with the need.

Still trembling in his arms, unraveled, I realize there is something I can give him, something he needs. "I swear to you I'll be more careful. In dangerous situations, I won't take unnecessary risks." Magic jolts in my veins, binding the vow into my blood and my bones. Now I'd better remember it.

"Cat." Griffin drops his face into the curve of my neck. Both his arms circle my waist. "My wife."

A giddy, nervous sort of elation bubbles up through me. "Not yet." I try to turn in his arms, find my legs useless, and simply drop. Griffin catches me and then picks me up. I lean my head on his shoulder. Now that the danger has passed, adrenaline has been absorbed, and desire has been thoroughly slaked, it's hitting me—the nearly dying and then healing process. It'll take its usual toll, and for the next few days, all I'll be able to do is eat, sleep, and watch Titos digest the Hydra.

"Soon," Griffin vows.

I feel his promise, too, and smile as he walks us both out into deeper water.

CHAPTER 23

IPOTANE ARE BEAUTIFUL. *WHO WOULD HAVE GUESSED?*

The entire herd is stunning—powerful, arresting, with fluid, predatory movements and a volatile edge that makes them utterly impossible to ignore. No wonder there are so many Wood Nymphs hanging around. Scantily clothed, if dressed at all, the female creatures vie for the attention of the male warrior beasts. I can hardly blame them, especially since the female Ipotane don't seem to care. Even I feel more than just common curiosity toward the strikingly handsome males escorting us into the heart of Ipotane territory, and I have no interest in discovering the intricacies of interspecies contact.

My mouth still goes dry at the sight of the Ipotane Alpha. Only a blind or severely deranged person wouldn't admire Lycheron's sculpted torso, thick, corded arms, and fearsomely handsome visage. There's even something devastating about his sleek horse body, jet-black and muscled for war. Not even the equine ears poking out of his waist-length ebony hair detract from the raw beauty of his masculine face and form. His chest is a work of chiseled art. It's hard to take my eyes off it, not only because it's jaw-droppingly gorgeous, but because there's a huge, hoof-shaped scar imprinted into his left pectoral.

I resist the urge to fan myself, hoping my sudden spike in body temperature is due to the hot springs and steaming fountains peppering the sultry Ipotane vale and not to the blatantly sensual creature giving me a more-than-thorough once-over.

Lycheron saunters over, leaving behind two pouting Dryads. The Nymphs shoot dirty looks in our direction, particularly at me. I glare back. I'm so good at making friends.

"Hand over your weapons." Lycheron's command rolls out of him like a rumble of thunder, deep and threatening.

"You have us surrounded," Griffin answers coolly. "Isn't that enough?"

I have to hold back my smirk. With a few words, Griffin challenges the other Alpha male's ego just enough to leave us with our weapons but not provoke an attack. *I knew I was marrying this man for a reason.*

Lycheron doesn't like being outmaneuvered. His lips draw back in a snarl, and he rears, pawing the air.

My eyes drop—and widen. "Good Gods, look at the size of his—"

Flynn elbows me in the ribs, and I choke back my words. But it's huge. *Huge!*

Lycheron's hooves hit the ground again. He tosses his long black mane of hair over his shoulder, and then his eyes land on me. They're not a frightening color, or glowing, or horrible at all. Mother had no idea what she was talking about, and it maddens me to no end that I let her scare me half to death with her stories. Lycheron's eyes are a warm honey-brown, almost tawny in color, and rimmed with the longest, thickest, darkest eyelashes I've ever seen on a man.

Horse.

Whatever.

"If my guards let you into the valley, you must be bearing a gift for me." His slow perusal of my person from the top of my head to the tips of my toes sets off a series of nervous explosions in my belly. "She is acceptable."

Acceptable? Acceptable!

Griffin steps in front of me. Flynn boxes me in on my right, and Carver gets so close to my left that our arms brush. Lycheron's eyes narrow at the muscular wall of *no* standing between him and me.

Kato steps forward, lifting the golden fleece from his shoulders. He tosses it to the Ipotane Alpha.

Lycheron catches the treasure and then turns it over in his hands, his fingers sliding admiringly over the springy wool. A slow smile spreads across his face.

"Artemis gave this up?" His chuckle is low, pleased, and genuine, and Gods help me, awareness ripples through me, puddling in every place it shouldn't. "I've long coveted the fleece. Rumor has it the archer brought it from Attica centuries ago, before the people there eschewed the Gods and magic collapsed in their world."

My ears perk up. *A world without magic?* It's hard to imagine.

Lycheron throws the fleece over his broad back, leaving his magnificent, scarred man-chest completely naked. The bright gold garment on his glossy black coat is eye-catching, to say the least. "Did you steal this from the Goddess?"

Kato shakes his head. "Artemis gave it to me of her own free will."

The Ipotane Alpha arches ebony eyebrows, saying without irony, "You must have pleased her greatly, then."

Kato's expression doesn't change, but a flood of color hits his cheekbones.

"Why are you here?" Lycheron asks.

"I am Alpha Sinta," Griffin announces, officially usurping Egeria. "I need you and your herd to guard the Sintan border while I seize the Tarvan throne."

There's a beat of surprised silence. Then Lycheron throws back his head and laughs. His laughter goes on long enough for a muscle near Griffin's eye to tighten ominously.

"The Power Bid already?" Lycheron keeps laughing. "Petty humans asking me to get involved in their petty wars."

Having already moved up next to Griffin again, I cross my arms and glare. "Petty humans don't make it this far onto the Ice Plains bearing a Goddess's gift."

Lycheron leans in and sniffs me. It's unsettling. He cocks his head. "Magoi. Strong. But still human, girl."

Girl? My eyes narrow. I open my mouth.

Griffin's hand circles my wrist, squeezing. "I propose a challenge."

Interest flickers in the Ipotane Alpha's eyes. "What sort of challenge?"

"A battle of wits," Griffin answers. We talked about this, preferring brains to brawn since we all figured Lycheron would be bigger than Griffin, which he is. "Answer my riddle correctly, and we'll leave. Answer it wrong, and you and your herd will protect Sinta until my task in Tarva is complete."

Lycheron doesn't answer straightaway, and nerves start hopping inside me like living things. Finally, he says, "I accept your challenge if it's a best of three, and I'll name the tasks. To begin with, it will be *my* riddle that *you* answer without any help from your companions."

A shadow flits across Griffin's face. This time, I think we're being outmaneuvered. "And the other two?" he asks stiffly.

Lycheron smirks. "I'll name them as they come. I only anticipate needing the first two."

"If I win, you'll come to Sinta?"

"If you best me, I will protect your insignificant border

for no longer than six months." Lycheron's bored tone tells us how likely he thinks that is to happen. "If I best you, you must pay a forfeit."

"What type of forfeit?" Griffin asks warily. The Chaos Wizard warned us that a bargain must be struck. I guess this is it.

"You'll give the Magoi girl to me."

I stop breathing, my insides contracting hard.

Griffin refuses flatly.

Lycheron's mouth lifts in a small but confident smile. "Are you really in a position to say no?"

"I am," Griffin bites out. "And I refuse. Categorically."

Lycheron's smile fades into a flat, penetrating stare, focused entirely on me. "Her scent intrigues me."

Well, that's just disturbing. I lay my hand on Griffin's arm and shrug almost apologetically. "I swore I'd stay with him. Magoi blood… Binding vows… What a pain." *Literally.*

"He can undo it," Lycheron says.

"Never," Griffin growls.

Lycheron doesn't look amused. At all. His lip curls slightly, and then his shrewd gaze slides over Kato's tattoo. "Then I'll take his snake."

Kato rubs his neck, frowning. He's been doing that a lot lately. "The snake is gone."

Lycheron stamps a hoof in irritation. "If you have nothing to offer me, then the bargain is off."

"Fine," Griffin snaps, "as the challenge you're proposing in no way resembles my original offer."

Lycheron scoffs. "No girl. No Drakon. I have nothing to gain. Only the fleece on my back is keeping me from crushing you where you stand." He leers at me. Winks. "Except for you, *matakia mou.*"

My little eyes? I'll show him eyes—the evil kind. I

glare. Too bad we didn't keep the golden lyre. We could have offered it up for the bargain. I'd have happily thrown it at him if I could lift it.

"Are you on friendly terms with the Hydra?" I ask.

Lycheron's ocher eyes spark with rage and take on a sudden, luminous quality. "The Hydra ate two of my Nymphs last week on our migration. It mistook them for human women."

I guess that's a no. "If we lose, we'll kill the Hydra for you."

Lycheron snorts, clearly skeptical, but then his eyes gleam with interest again. "How did you get past the Hydra?" he asks suspiciously.

"Very quietly," I answer in the same bored tone the Ipotane Alpha used earlier.

"Do we have a deal?" Griffin asks quickly.

Something like reserve clouds Lycheron's expression for the first time. Is he suddenly seeing more to us than he did before?

Nevertheless, he nods once. Bargain struck.

"I run but never walk. I have a mouth but never talk. I have a head but never weep. I have a bed but never sleep."

As soon as Lycheron says his riddle, my mind goes completely blank. It's the strangest thing. I can't think of *anything*. All I can do is stare at Griffin, holding my breath and hoping his brain is still functioning, because mine isn't.

Luckily for us, and Sinta, and likely all of Thalyria, our minds don't work anything alike.

"A river," Griffin answers almost immediately.

Lycheron swishes his tail, a low rumble resonating in his throat. He demands they arm wrestle for the second challenge, unsportingly assuring himself a win. Griffin's defeat isn't immediate, but it doesn't take long.

Griffin ducks his dark head toward mine, cursing softly under his breath. "Flynn's the only one who's ever beaten me."

"That was like you arm wrestling me. It was hardly fair."

His mouth a flat line, he shakes out his arm. It must be aching.

For the third challenge, Lycheron wants to summon Artemis, pay homage, thank her for the golden fleece, and ask *her* to set the final task. Not only do I not want the Goddess, undoubtedly followed by the archer, anywhere near Kato, or Griffin, or any of us for that matter, but... "There's a reason people don't just casually summon Gods!"

Lycheron shrugs his massive shoulders. The human ones. Well, male anyway. Entirely, hugely, beautifully male.

"'Call a God, lose a soul,'" I quote. "Sound familiar?"

Lycheron's eyes meet mine with new interest, and I shiver. His previous interest was already more than enough.

I turn my back on the disturbingly virile Ipotane Alpha and gather my group. "Even the most powerful Magoi don't use those spells. The scrolls holding those chants were hidden centuries ago because even Hoi Polloi can do them, but they were almost never educated about the consequences. It's not actually magic, it's just words. But string the words together, and you get a death trap. People finally understood how dangerous it was and locked the knowledge away. Gods always take someone as payment for being summoned. They come, but they never leave alone. It's risky, treacherous stuff."

Lycheron chuckles behind me, and I stiffen, hating the

visceral impact the sound has on my body. Warmth washes up my back. My nape prickles.

"The Magoi female is right. But we're on the Ice Plains, *matakia mou*. Different place, different rules."

I spin around, treating the Ipotane Alpha to my death stare. "What does that mean? Different place, different rules?"

Lycheron eyes me like a bug. A bug he's seriously considering dragging off to his horse den, but still a bug. "I live in the shadow of Olympus. I am not some human dabbling in matters I don't understand."

"That doesn't answer my question."

His ears flatten tetchily. "You doubt my skill? I am a creature created by the Gods."

"Aren't we all?" I ask.

He bares his teeth. "Some are created better. Humans are so…breakable."

Was that a threat? I'm pretty sure that was a threat. "Double-cross us, and I'll show you just how breakable I am *not*." My right hand goes to the hilt of a knife. Since the Hydra chewed off its own heads before Titos ate it, I got my blades back.

With a firm and distinctly proprietary hand on my elbow, Griffin draws me back into the circle of protection Beta Team is always forming around me. I guess we're Alpha Team now. I'm not sure I can get used to that.

"Is Lycheron bound by vows like Magoi are?" he asks. I nod.

The Ipotane scoffs. "Of course not."

Searing pain rips through me, robbing me of my breath. Burning explosions snap through my blood and bones, scorching me with the falsehood and branding me with the truth. "Don't listen to him," I gasp out. "He's lying."

Lycheron looks at me sharply. As the inferno in me

fades, he sniffs me again, long and deep, like he's trying to learn me through scent. As he slowly pulls in air, his thick lashes lower, his nostrils quiver, and his full lips part. To my horror, a full-body shiver hits me just as everyone looks.

Griffin's large hand squeezes my arm almost painfully now. "Do you vow that no harm, disappearance, or any other unexpected ill will befall one or any of us due to your summoning Artemis for the challenge?" he demands of Lycheron.

Lycheron never looks away from me. With my Kingmaker Magic still gently flaring, it's almost like he can't. "Yes."

"Satisfied?" Griffin asks me curtly.

I do my best to ignore the intensity of Lycheron's heated gaze and move into Griffin's rigid side. Some of the tension leaves him when our bodies touch. "Not even close," I say.

With a peevish flick of his tail, Lycheron stops staring at me and repeats the entire phrase, swearing to it.

No lie burns through me, which means he was telling the truth. Different place. Different rules.

CHAPTER 24

I CAN'T HELP LISTENING TO THE WORDS OF THE SUMMON-
ing chant, even though I don't want to know them—
especially since they work.

Artemis appears, dressed for the hunt, armed with a
quiver of golden arrows and a stunning bow. I feel oddly
breathless as she glides toward us, shadowed by the archer,
who is never more than a few steps behind. Tall and regal,
Artemis moves like a shimmering river, fluidly cutting a
path through the greenery of the lush Ipotane vale.

Scenery that seemed vibrant and striking just moments
before now dulls in comparison. The Goddess is magnificent, with a long, graceful neck, a firm, supple body, and
skin so smooth and cool it reminds me of a moonlit pearl.
Shapely legs flash beneath the slits of her diaphanous skirt.
She floats more than walks, her arms gently swaying with
every step, her elegant fingers loose at her sides.

Atalanta keeps pace behind her, her long hair swinging, her steps prowling, her hand on her bow. Her grace
is different—animalistic—her beauty more earthy than
ethereal. Her green eyes land on Kato and instantly flare
with unchecked heat.

Kato stiffens beside me.

"Your dislike doesn't appear to be mutual," I murmur.

His mouth turns down. "There were mixed signals
before the drug wore off."

I'll bet.

Atalanta isn't the only female whose focus lands on

Kato. Artemis's lips part. Pink tinges her high, delicate cheekbones, and her stunning blue eyes widen in surprise. The longing and desire that infuse her suddenly unguarded expression make sympathy bloom in my chest. What a life—eternal virginity. I can now say with absolute certainty she's missing out.

Kato's hands clench into fists. I wrap my fingers around his forearm, squeezing. Atalanta glares like she wants to claw my eyes out, and I smirk. Artemis notices, too, and her dreamy gaze comes into focus with a flash of something dangerous and fierce. Then she seems to recognize me, and her anger dissipates.

The Goddess of the Hunt stops a few feet away, tilting her chin in a way that softens the long lines of her neck. A golden crown adorned with a crescent moon pulls tight, dark curls back from her striking, straight-nosed face. The rest of her hair spills down her back, the glossy spirals gently shifting on the warm, sultry breeze.

Beside me, Griffin looks completely thunderstruck. I can hardly blame him. I'm feeling pretty awed myself. It's not every day you meet an Olympian—and she *is* gorgeous—but the hot knife of jealousy slices through me nonetheless.

I glance at the others. Flynn has stars in his brown eyes, and Carver needs to pick his jaw up off the ground. Only Kato looks like he might still be able to form a coherent thought, but from the look on his face, I'm not sure it would be nice.

Artemis greets us, her voice like a song on the wind. "Lycheron. Humans. I trust there is a reason to have called me from my mountain home."

Mount Olympus? Or the northeast needle?

"Of course, my most exquisite moonbeam."

Lycheron's voice holds a subtle mix of both fawning and charm. "And may I express my most humble gratitude for the superb golden fleece. It is, without a doubt, my most treasured possession."

My jaw unhinges. He sounds like a different man.

Horse.

Whatever.

Artemis frowns slightly. "I did not gift it to *you*."

Lycheron goes very still. I think he stops breathing. *Ha!*

The Goddess's eyes suddenly twinkle with merriment. "But it does look stunning on you, *moro mou*."

My baby? She could even mean that endearment literally—in the creationist sense. I get a sinking feeling in the pit of my stomach. These two know each other. Well.

Son of a Cyclops! Lycheron set us up!

The Ipotane Alpha snaps his fingers, and a pair of huge males rushes over with two luxuriously cushioned chairs, placing one just behind the other. Other Ipotane bring platters of fruit and cheese and goblets of wine. While Lycheron explains the challenge so far, Artemis and Atalanta recline on the plush furniture, nibbling on grapes and hard cheeses and sipping their wine.

Artemis accepts her role as judge for the third task, giving no outward sign of favoring Lycheron for any reason of long-term acquaintance or shared circumstance, although plainly both apply, and Lycheron obviously thinks they'll work in his favor. She's a millennia-old Goddess, and yet there's nothing bored or apathetic in her manner. In fact, her blue eyes shimmer with interest as she sets forth the final task.

"I helped set this challenge in motion by giving up the Attican fleece. Now give me something in return, and I will decide whose gift pleases me more."

"Anything," Lycheron says. "Name your desire, and I will go to the ends of all worlds for it."

I scowl. *Now that's just not fair!*

"In the interest of fairness, and speed, since humans do not have eternity as we do, you must give me something now, something you already carry with you."

I'd found myself rather admiring her until that last part. Since Lycheron carries nothing but his own hide, hair, and, *um*…impressive anatomy, I'm thinking he'll go with the thick, hammered gold cuffs around his wrists—worth far more than anything Griffin is carrying.

Griffin must be thinking the same thing. Grim-faced, he shifts from foot to foot, his hand hovering over the flap of his satchel. I know for a fact there's nothing in there except for food, spare clothes, and a bunch of hellipses grass. His sword is worth something, but I'd hate for him to give it up. There's Hades's cloak, but Griffin's was ripped by the Hydra and has a chunk missing from the back—hardly a fitting gift for a Goddess.

As I suspected, Lycheron removes the heavy gold cuffs from around his wrists and then presents them to Artemis with a flourish. She runs her long, elegant forefinger over the ridges and hollows of the hammered gold, humming softly in pleasure. The metal reflects the setting sun on her face, giving her cool, pearly beauty a warmer, more radiant glow. Nodding her head in acceptance of the gift, Artemis places the cuffs beside her and then looks expectantly at Griffin.

For the first time ever, I see Griffin blush. "What I have in mind will take a moment." His voice is gruff. He's nervous. I suppose he should be. A lot is riding on this, and he is talking to a Goddess.

"How long?" Artemis asks.

He doesn't meet her eyes. He looks somewhere lower. "Twenty minutes?"

Artemis inclines her head in assent before sweeping her gaze back to the Ipotane Alpha. Lycheron straightens. His tail flicks.

"Bring musicians," she commands.

He gives the order, and a bevy of half-naked Dryads appears with flutes and lyres. Some play. Others sing and dance, moving with agility and astounding flexibility. I get why Lycheron keeps them around. Clearly, they provide all kinds of entertainment.

One particularly lissome Nymph twirls to the edge of the circle, her eyes meeting those of a male Ipotane tracking her every move. On her next swirl around, he grabs her around the waist and gallops off into the trees. They disappear, leaving behind the Dryad's breathless cry of delight.

I arch a brow. *Yes, clearly all kinds.*

In the meantime, Griffin lays out the hellipses grass he took from the Chaos Wizard's meadow. He's going to make something, which doesn't surprise me, and yet it does. What could he possibly create that Artemis would want?

With strong, nimble fingers, he separates the stalks and then begins to weave. Even though his head is bowed to his work, I can see the tense lines around his mouth and sense his concentration in the stiffness of his shoulders. I sit next to him and watch him work, supporting him in the only way I can—by quietly being there.

The circle Griffin makes turns into a cone. He extends it downward, each full turn around slightly tighter so that there's a gradual but constant progression toward something narrower. I have no idea what it is, and I desperately want to ask. Being quiet is hard.

When the object is about eight inches long, Griffin ties

off the ends and then neatly tucks them into the weave to
hide them. I chew on my lip to keep my mouth shut. I'm
worried. And I don't understand. I saw the crown he wove
for Kaia. It was beautiful and intricate. This is plain. The
weave is tight and even, the form is regular, the grass is
supple and strong, but it's just an open-ended cone.

Griffin humbly presents his offering to Artemis. "An
arm guard, to protect the Goddess of the Hunt from the
sting of the bowstring."

My eyes widen. *What a good idea!*

Silent and unnervingly expressionless, Artemis takes
the brace. She tugs the arm guard over her left wrist and
up. The top of the cone lies just below the crease of her
elbow. The bottom hugs her wrist. A perfect fit.

She bends her arm and twists her wrist. The grass makes
a soft creaking sound when she moves, and Griffin murmurs, "It will soften. With use."

The Goddess's eyes meet Griffin's, and he goes very
still. I don't like the awe-struck look on his face, or the
way his tanned cheeks color in the least. It takes all my
willpower to not jump on his back, wrap my arms and
legs around him, and snarl "mine, mine" like some kind
of crazed octopus.

Quadropus.

Whatever.

Artemis reclines in her chair, sipping her wine with
absolute calm. She still wears the brace. The cuffs are next
to her. Her flawless face gives no indication of what she's
thinking, or whose gift she favors.

Finally, her cool gaze swings toward Lycheron. "I
already have gold and riches aplenty. However, I have no
objection to more." She slips his wrist cuffs around her
upper arms because they more or less fit her there.

My heart starts to pound. Griffin looks ill.

After a casual dip of her ruby-toned lips to her jeweled goblet, she turns to Griffin. "In my long life, my bowstring has hit my arm exactly five times."

My stomach hollows, and my insides drop through the hole. In other words, we just gave her something completely useless.

Artemis flexes her arm again, making the grass creak. A small smile lifts the corners of her mouth. "That's five times too many, and yet no one has ever offered me one of these."

My heart kicks wildly. Hope nearly shatters my chest.

"This is neither particularly aesthetic nor entirely comfortable, but it took thought and effort, and for that, I will award you the point."

I gasp in astonishment. Griffin smiles brilliantly, his handsome face lighting up, and even Artemis looks a bit dazed by the amazing curve of his lips. Knowing how starved she is for male affection, I throw my arms around Griffin's neck and pull him down for a claim-staking kiss. And then another—just in case.

Griffin swings me up into his arms and kisses me soundly back.

Lycheron stamps his front hooves, bucking in agitated protest. "If he wins, do you have any idea what I'll have to do?" he demands.

Artemis arches perfect, dark eyebrows. "Of course. I know everything."

My head snaps around. *Really?*

"Then you can't possibly—"

Artemis stands, causing Lycheron to fall abruptly silent. "I suggest you gather your Nymphs"—the Goddess offers the Ipotane Alpha a sly smile—"to make Sinta more bearable."

Lycheron swishes his tail, the whiplike ends stinging the

air much too close to Griffin's arm. "The Hydra is restless, attacking when it shouldn't. The herd should stay here until the creature settles."

"The Hydra won't trouble your Nymphs—or anyone—again." Artemis tilts her head in my direction. "Her snake ate it."

An amber sheen rolls over Lycheron's eyes, lighting them with something primal and powerful that roots me to the spot. His chin dips, his nostrils flare, his muscles bulge and almost vibrate with fury, and I take back what I thought before; he *is* terrifying.

"Wait." I'm confused. "*My* snake?"

"It's always about you, Harbinger. Everyone keeps telling you that, and yet you refuse to believe."

The blood crashes from my head, leaving my face numb. "No. No, you're wrong."

Everyone gasps, even Lycheron, who then stamps angrily again, glaring at me with those glowing eyes.

I swallow uneasily, still reeling from the Goddess's words. "That is to say... Thank you for your vote. We're forever in your debt."

Artemis laughs, a beautiful chiming sound that reminds me of something I can't quite place. "Poseidon was right about you."

Do I dare ask? "What did he say?"

"That you're reckless, hot-tempered, and irreverent in the extreme."

I grimace. That sounds about right.

"Zeus has plans for you," the Goddess continues.

"Plans?" I ask, suddenly finding it hard to catch my breath.

"It's best you don't ask." Artemis glances briefly at Griffin, her brow creasing, and that scares the magic out of me.

My fingers tighten on his arm. "If anyone tries to harm him, I will personally see to their bloody and painful demise. Man. Monster. ...Or God."

Artemis's blue eyes ice over. "The sharp-tongued Origin should be more interested in making friends. She may need them."

Origin? A cold slab of marble seems to settle heavily on my chest. Breathing gets even harder. "The Origin has been dead for thousands of years. He's barely a memory, and, to most, not even that."

"Strange, then, that Zeus keeps saying it's you." Artemis's tone remains frosty.

"I... But..." My ribs feel like they're folding in on me. *Breathe. Breathe.* "How is that possible?"

"Not reincarnation, if that's what you're thinking. But you're more a child of the Gods than you realize."

I stare at her, my heart pounding. "What does that mean?"

"Don't you understand you have a destiny?" Artemis frowns. "I suppose not, or you might not have made it so difficult to keep you alive."

I lose the battle not to hyperventilate. Tachycardia—also a check. Griffin's arm comes around me, and I brace myself against his side.

"Gills." Artemis suddenly snorts with mirth, and even that's beautiful. "Poseidon primed you once already, time was running out, and Persephone was having a fit about your drowning." Artemis laughs, like drowning is funny. "He was trying to think of another way, but she grabbed his trident and poked him until he did it." She slashes her fingertips across her neck. "Persephone's quite fierce, you know."

"Primed me?" I echo.

The Goddess waves a graceful, slim-fingered hand in

the air. "That other time you almost drowned. Quite recent. Not a good habit," she adds offhandedly.

So this is Artemis opening up? Her people skills are as good as mine. "Persephone?"

Artemis looks at me like I'm a little damaged in the head. Or maybe a lot. "She sends her regards, by the way."

I nod. Sort of. Mostly, I just shake. I have no idea why Persephone keeps sending her regards. Artemis is talking to me like I'm one of the family, *her* family, which I guess I am in a way about a thousand times removed. And she just called me the Origin. By definition, that means I am the beginning—the start of something new.

My eyes meet Griffin's, and I know they're scared and wide. It's not that I wanted him to be wrong about everything, it's just that I could never really make myself believe he was right. Now, all I can do is keep breathing, which is harder than it should be. It's like someone cracked the world over my head. It's falling all around me, and everyone's looking at me to clean up the mess.

A memory hits me hard. Eleni and me high up in a leafy tree, our hands sore and raw from gripping the rough bark, our legs swinging, our guards combing the woods for us. Thanos whistling loudly enough to cover our whispering because he knows exactly where we are, of course. My twelfth birthday is approaching along with the rainy season, and Eleni is all that's good in my life.

"Look, Talia. What do you see to the east?"

I squint into the morning sun. "The ocean." Blue vastness rolling in. A distant horizon where sea creatures make themselves at home.

"And to the west?" Eleni asks.

I shrug, twisting a hank of long, windblown hair around my grubby finger. My nails are a mess from digging up stones to throw at Cousin Aarken when he chased me into a ravine the other day. He shot me with an arrow, but I knocked him out. "Fisa? The lakes?"

Eleni shakes her head. Her loose blonde hair slides over her slim shoulders, and her clear-blue eyes sparkle with a hidden joy I've never understood. "That's the entire world. And it's yours."

CHAPTER 25

I KICK OFF MY BOOTS AND THEN FALL BACKWARD ONTO our new bed in Castle Sinta. A satisfied groan rises from deep within my chest. I spread out my arms and legs, wiggling into the softness of the feather mattress and relishing the feel of high-quality linens.

After settling comfortably in, I turn my head and watch Griffin splash water over his face, rinsing away the dust of travel. The room is fully furnished again. There's even a new window seat and a grand total of eleven rugs on the floor. *Eleven!*

"You're very clever to have ordered a new bed before we left," I tell him. "And the rest is nice, too."

Griffin threads his wet fingers through his hair, slicking it back. He flashes me a roguish grin and prowls over. "You're very clever to recognize my cleverness."

Awareness licks through me at the marauding gleam in his eyes. "I wish I'd thought of it. I would have ordered a bed twice this size."

One midnight eyebrow creeps up. "How many people are you planning to fit in it? It's already big enough for Lycheron and his Nymphs."

I make a face. "Let's not bring them into our bed. They were hard enough to deal with on the road." Talk about temper. And libido. The Ipotane make Griffin and me look tame.

I grab the pillows above my head and drag them down next to me, finishing my complete destruction of the neatly made bed. "When we dropped them off, they made such a stink that the entire border must smell like horse manure by now."

Griffin laughs. The rich, deep sound melts into me, warming my insides. He smiles easily enough, but he doesn't often laugh outright unless it's with me. I love being the one to make him happy.

I smile back—a wide, idiotic, joyful grin.

"They were great protection," he points out. "Not a single creature bothered us on the way back."

"True. Some even ran the other way." I toss the pillows aside and then lock my gaze with Griffin's. "So what's next?"

His eyes heat up. "You. Me. Bath. That new bed."

Desire whips through me on a web of white-hot lightning. It's been days since we were last alone together. Still, I can't help teasing. "Poor old man. So tired he needs to sleep. No more adventures for you."

I prop my head in my hand, watching Griffin's eyes narrow as he stalks the last few steps toward me—predatory, confident, all strong, loose limbs ready to snap into action.

"Old man?" he growls, looming over the bed.

I grin. "If I'm going to marry you, I should probably know how old you are. I'm guessing really old. Just look at you." I poke his rock-solid abdomen. "So soft."

Griffin moves fast, seizing me around the waist and lifting me high into the air. I shriek, my hair flying and my arms flailing as he turns, sits on the edge of the bed, and then drops me into his lap with me straddling him.

Laughing, I spear my fingers into his damp hair and grip the jet-black locks, tugging a little. His eyes turn hooded, silvery-hot, and he makes a gravelly sound in his throat. Griffin slips his hands under my tunic, settling them over my hips and backside. He yanks me hard against him, showing me just how soft he definitely is *not*.

His thumbs skate over the strip of bare skin above the waistline of my pants. "Are you asking for a spanking?" he demands quietly in my ear.

Heated shivers branch out from the base of my spine. I pretend to pout, which feels ridiculous. "Poor dear. You've forgotten already. I *asked* how *old* you are." I enunciate carefully, since he's obviously hard of hearing and going senile.

Griffin's gorgeous, distracting mouth twitches. "Thirty-four."

I gasp. "You *are* old!"

He chuckles. "And you? I should know, too."

"What's the date?" I have no idea. All I know is that it's raining outside for the first time in months, and the sound of the heavy drops hitting the marble below is like the constant, steady beat of a drum. The air smells steamy. Damp. Renewed.

Griffin tells me, and I laugh. "I turn twenty-four tomorrow."

He frowns, stopping the light stroking around my middle that was driving me to distraction. "You weren't going to tell me?"

I shift in his lap, trying to recapture the tightening and tingling in my lower body. "I forgot. It's not important."

He frowns harder. "Stop wiggling, or we won't make it to the bathhouse."

"Stop doing this?" I grind down on him with a leisurely swirl of my hips, moaning at the exquisite spark of sensation where our bodies meet.

A breath hisses between Griffin's teeth. "Cat..."

My eyes sweep up, and Griffin's molten gaze collides with mine. I arch my back, lifting up on my knees and slowly sliding along his thick, hard length. Heat spreads through me like sunshine on a summer day. His lips part, and he seems to stop breathing, his dazed reaction ratcheting up my need. I don't want anything between us.

Griffin blinks, then his fingers tighten on my hips. In a low rasp, he asks, "How should we celebrate?"

I lean forward and kiss him hungrily, sliding my tongue along his full bottom lip. "How about we find a holy man and take some vows," I whisper against his mouth.

Griffin makes a rough, masculine sound that scorches me to my toes. I'm on my back in two seconds flat, and we never make it to the baths.

"Happy birthday." Griffin brushes a warm kiss across my temple. "What kind of ceremony do you want?"

It takes a moment to process what Griffin is talking about. Our wedding.

I've only just opened my eyes and found myself in my favorite place—sprawled half on top of him, my arm across his broad chest, my legs tangled up with his. Crisp hair tickles my thighs and calves. My breasts are pressed against skin as smooth and hot as sun-warmed marble. He smells like man and home, and I nestle in, nowhere near ready to get up yet.

Griffin's large hand covers most of my back. His fingers move in an idle pattern. "A public ceremony would make a statement. Show you to your people."

My insides lurch, waking me up like a thunderclap and eradicating the pleasant warmth spreading through my body. My people. Fisans. Sintans by the end of the day. *Tarvans, too?*

"A public ceremony will make me run away," I croak, my voice still hoarse from sleep.

Griffin's chest rises on a deep breath, lifting me, too. "You can't run anymore, Cat. Fate caught up."

Shuddering like I just got doused by a bucket of ice water, I sit up, pushing tangled hair out of my face. "Fate can bite me, and so can you if you try to make me do this in front of thousands of people."

Looking at me from under his thick, inky lashes, Griffin loops an arm around my waist and drags me back down, making sure I land mostly on top of him. "Then it's a good thing I've been planning a private ceremony."

"Planning since when?" I pinch his side to let him know I'm annoyed.

He scoots out of my grasp, grinning. "Since the birds woke me up about three hours ago."

"What?" I sit up again, kneeling on the rumpled sheets and finally noticing how bright it is outside. I'm an early riser—or I used to be. "Why did you let me sleep?"

"Why not?" His knuckles graze my thigh in a slightly rasping caress, and he looks at my naked body with an intensity that makes me shiver. "I knew you'd wake up when you weren't tired anymore."

I huff. Sort of. "Well, would Your Logicalness care to take me to breakfast and tell me about your plans?"

Meeting my gaze, Griffin slowly drags his knuckles up the sensitive skin along my inner thigh.

"Would Your Nakedness care to get dressed first?" he asks.

My eyes drop to his formidable chest, his ridged abdomen, and the trail of inviting dark hair leading from his navel to under the impressively tented sheet. I lick my lips, suddenly dying to taste every inch of him. "Not really."

Griffin's mouth spreads into a wide grin. He sits up in one quick, powerful surge and then reaches for me, his eyes glittering with intent. With his wild black hair, shadowed jaw, and storm-cloud eyes, he looks so determined and dangerous that I twist and lunge across the bed, narrowly escaping him.

Griffin pounces, catching my ankle. He hauls me back and then rolls me beneath him, pinning my hands on either side of my head. I squirm and pretend to fight, loving every second of it. He grips me harder. Looking fierce and stern, he lowers his face until our noses almost touch. Then he slides down my body, leaving a trail of hot kisses, wet licks, and soft little nips. He doesn't let go of my wrists. He just drags them down with him, holding me fast.

"Breakfast in bed?" he rumbles against my hip.

I grin as his mouth settles over my most intimate place. My knees fall wide. He's not talking about food.

We do eventually get dressed and look for food, although we only make it to the dining room in time for lunch. Egeria accepts her ousting as Alpha Sinta without a hint of anger or regret. Clearly, it's what she was expecting all along. Piers is away on a recruitment trip, but the rest of the family is here and overjoyed by our wedding announcement. Jocasta decrees that we have to go shopping, *now*, and Kaia bounces in her seat, beyond excited about any outing that will actually get her on the other side of the castle gate.

Shopping requires money, so I dig around in Griffin's pocket under the table, letting my fingers wander enough for him to nearly choke on his stew. I find four gold coins and hold on to them. "You never pay me."

He looks aghast. "I can't pay you anymore."

"We're about to get married. No one's going to confuse me with a prostitute."

Kaia spits out a grape. It bounces across the table and then lands in her mother's lap. Kaia slaps her hand over her mouth, her blue-gray eyes huge, and Nerissa gives her a quelling look. The look finishes on me, and I might have felt a little quelled myself if Carver hadn't suddenly made a noise like a donkey, finally belting out the laugh he'd been holding back.

Anatole bangs his hand down on the table and bursts out laughing. He sounds like a donkey, too. It's contagious, and the whole table erupts, snorting and braying until most of us are wiping tears from our eyes. I shake my head, grinning. I haven't laughed like this in...well, ever.

Nerissa eventually gets up, comes over to me, and then kisses my cheek, something that would usually make me squirm. Today, it somehow feels normal. "I always wanted to have four daughters." She squeezes my shoulder. "Now I do."

I keep smiling like a loon even though my throat suddenly feels thick, and heat stings the backs of my eyes. I have a family that loves me. I would protect them with my life.

Well, maybe not Piers, but I have a feeling he would return the sentiment.

Thoughts of Piers kill my smile and leave me feeling oddly queasy. Or maybe that's the explosion of emotion. Or the lamb.

I lay down my fork, not hungry anymore. Griffin pushes his chair back, signals for Carver to follow him, and then drops a kiss onto the top of my head. Things like that are natural for him—for everyone here except for me.

"Meet me at the Athena temple at sundown," Griffin says.

Excitement and nerves twist my insides into a knot. I slide a hand over my churning stomach. "What should I do?"

"Get ready for your wedding." Griffin's smile makes my heart skip a beat. Or maybe three.

"Besides that. For the preparations, I mean."

He tucks some flyaway hair behind my ear. "Nothing. I'll take care of everything. Trust me, *agapi mou*."

I nod. I do. I really, really do.

I make it back to our room in time to throw up my entire meal. Talk about wedding jitters. *Gah!*

I'm feeling better by the time Jocasta and Kaia knock on the door. We collect Kato and Flynn, two of Sinta's most exalted warriors, to carry packages for us—something which not so secretly makes me laugh.

Flynn gruffly insists they're there for protection, and I roll my eyes when he straps on about fifteen extra weapons just to prove it.

I take up the rear with Kato, leaving a silent and vigilant Flynn to walk in front of Jocasta and Kaia. The princesses nod and wave to smiling merchants and shoppers as we weave our way through the agora toward the more exclusive shops at the top of the hill. I choose the same place we went to before the realm dinner so I can watch the young, handsome shopkeeper fawn all over Jocasta again and see how Flynn reacts.

His response is exactly what I thought it would be— quietly seething. Jocasta keeps her head high and appears not to notice Flynn hovering and glowering.

"You've mastered the princess thing," I murmur behind a display of gowns. "Adoring populace. Surly, overprotective guard. You above it all."

"Flynn's not my guard."

My eyebrows wing up at her prickly tone. "He is whenever we go out."

"Which is twice in almost never." Jocasta plows through the gowns, not even really looking. "And he only notices me when someone else does."

Unfortunately, considering the shopkeeper's obvious admiration and Flynn's sudden grumpiness, it's hard to argue with that.

"I've had enough." Jocasta turns to me, her blue eyes blazing. "I've waited too long already. I'll give him six more months. After that, I'm looking for a husband. Preferably one that looks just like him."

My eyes widen. "Jocasta!"

She sighs, and her shoulders droop. "That was a joke."

I frown. I don't think it was a joke. "Why rush? You have plenty of time."

She absently runs her fingers over a bolt of butter-yellow fabric. They snag on the delicate weave, and I take a closer look at her hand. There are calluses that weren't there before.

"I'm old," she finally says.

I snort. I can't help it. "How old?" Apparently, it's the question of the hour.

Day.

Yesterday.

Whatever.

"Twenty-four."

I scoff. "You're not old. We're the same age."

She gives me a pointed look. "As of today. And *you're* getting married."

"It's not a race," I say.

"I know." She shakes her head. "You're right. I'm sorry. I'm just tired of waiting."

"Then stop waiting and tell him how you feel." My whisper is loud enough to turn Flynn's head. Jocasta shushes me, her cheeks flaming.

Kato and Kaia don't notice. She's draped herself in ribbons and is trying to get Kato to tell her which color looks best. Since Kaia is gorgeous, has the kind of striking, dark coloring that goes well with anything, and would look pretty even in a grain sack, it's a tough choice.

He scratches his chin, looking earnest and interested. Finally, he gathers up the entire lot of ribbons, wraps them around her waist, and then ties a crooked bow. "I can't decide. You should take them all."

Kaia turns bright pink. *Poor Kaia.* She should really fixate on someone her own age. I'll have to take a closer look at the pages.

"I think he knows how I feel," Jocasta says stiffly, drawing me back to her dilemma with Flynn. "He just doesn't want to deal with it."

"Maybe he doesn't want things to change."

She glances down, her voice softening. "Maybe he doesn't feel the same."

"Then he's an idiot." It feels disloyal saying that about Flynn. He's almost always in my corner. "About you," I add, qualifying my earlier statement.

Jocasta takes a deep breath. Her exhale is a little shaky.

A breeze carries moist air and a rumble of thunder through the wide-open window, stirring my unruly hair. It's enough to make Jocasta shiver, and the merchant rushes over with a delicate, expensive-looking shawl. He wraps it around her shoulders, earning a glare from Flynn that has him swiftly backing away again.

I look Jocasta up and down, smothering a laugh. "That shawl is an excellent match for your tunic and pants."

Jocasta smiles faintly, not missing the irony in my voice. "It's better than Kaia—dressed like a boy but covered in bows."

I glance at Kaia. With her narrow hips and only budding curves, her body is still relatively straight, the effort of growth having gone into height so far rather than softness. If she put her long hair up under a cap and kept her delicate-boned face down, she could probably pass for a boy.

Jocasta, on the other hand, has a figure a lot like mine used to be before all the running around, fighting, and nearly dying—lush, with a little extra just where men seem to like it. She fills out her fitted tunic and thigh-hugging pants in a way even *I* notice, so it's no wonder Flynn is pretending to find the display of gold buckles halfway across the shop so utterly fascinating.

"I like boots, at least for going outside. They're better suited to the rainy season." Jocasta pulls out a light-blue gown, holds it up to me, and then puts it back.

I look for something more snugly fitted. There's no time to have a dress sewn to my new measurements, and now that there's less of me, I need to better display what I've still got. "What color would Griffin like?"

"I believe he's partial to red," Jocasta answers.

"Hmm. Hardly appropriate for a wedding."

"What about white?" she asks.

I wrinkle my nose. "Too virginal. There's always ivory." I always end up with ivory.

"Too boring," she says.

Sighing, I flop into a nearby chair, suddenly exhausted. "I should just get married like this." Old boots, brown pants, a dark-green tunic, my worn belt, and the Terrible Tangle to top it all off.

Jocasta shakes her head. "You'd regret it forever."

I hardly agree, but on the off chance she's right, I finally choose a gown with extra draping at the hips. It's a mix of alluring blues and subtle greens, the color so much like the inviting, clear water off the Fisan coast that a strange pang hits my chest. Feeling curiously emotional about it, I make a special request of the merchant regarding the shoulder clasps. He goes into the back room to heat the unadorned gold and then imprint it with the stamps I asked for.

"What about you and Kaia?" I ask.

Jocasta waves a dismissive hand. "We don't need anything new. This day is about you."

"And Griffin."

She rolls her eyes. "What bride ever said *that?*"

"You're right." I grin. "Let's spend the rest of the afternoon at the Aphrodite Baths and see what the women there can do about my hair. I hear they work wonders with milk."

CHAPTER 26

I'M NERVOUS. I'M ACTUALLY SHAKING, WHICH IS ABSURD. I've faced down monsters with more courage than this.

Griffin stands proudly by my side. Dark linen hugs his long, strong legs, and a snowy-white tunic offsets his jet-black hair and striking gray eyes. He's freshly shaved, and his hair is neat and tamed, although it's still overlong—evidence of the warlord who will forever underlie the king.

"The Sintan crest." Griffin lifts his hand and traces a warm finger over my shoulder next to one golden clasp.

The butterflies that colonized my belly the moment I saw him at the temple take flight. "It seemed appropriate."

"It is," he says, love, approval, and something hotter in his eyes.

Just then, the sky opens up outside the sanctuary, and rain starts falling in sheets on the other side of the fat marble columns. Day fades deeper into night as the holy man blesses my veil. My unbound hair stirs on the damp breeze, already curling again.

Griffin brushes a heavy coil over my shoulder. "So smooth," he murmurs, his fingertips lingering on my skin.

Heat spreads through me as cool, humid air breezes in. The combination provokes a pleasant shiver. Then I hear music and singing and freeze.

My eyes widen in accusation. "You promised me a private ceremony. Only family."

Griffin's steady gaze holds mine. "I would never betray you."

I turn, and the people who enter the temple in a soaking-wet display of color and completely irreverent pageantry *are* family. Everyone I used to live and work with at the circus is here, my dearest friends leading the way. Desma weaves rainbows around the temple. Aetos pounds a drum, dancing with wild grace. Tadd and Alyssa spin and leap down the central aisle, twisting and shouting in the air while Zosimo and Yannis twirl flaming batons and toss them back and forth to each other. Vasili and his wife sing a joyous southern melody, their rich voices carrying as if they were twenty instead of two. Thunder rolls during the refrain, like Olympus itself is accompanying them. My eyes blur, and my heart starts pounding to the same stirring tune.

Selena walks alone, utterly dry. The moment our eyes meet, a lump lodges in my throat. My breath stutters, but I blink my tears away, not wanting to miss a second of this. It's too unexpected. Too perfect.

I look at Griffin, overwhelmed. "I'm taking Hoi Polloi vows." I'd already decided, but I want him to know. Hoi Polloi make a verbal pledge of love, protection, devotion, and fidelity. Most Magoi don't dare lock themselves into something so permanent and simply go through the ceremony without saying a word.

Griffin's mouth curves, and it's the most devastating smile I've ever seen. His chest expands. "You won't regret it."

I nod. "I know." If there's one thing I'm sure of, it's him.

Selena stops in front of me, sparing Griffin a brief glance that's surprisingly neutral. He must be growing on her.

She unsheathes an ornate golden knife, lifts a lock of my hair, and then shears off the bottom few inches. She places the lock in my palm, and my skin tingles where our hands meet.

I turn and drop the lock into the flaming chalice next to the holy man. "May Persephone bless our union."

The holy man looks shocked. We *are* in a temple dedicated to Athena. But Persephone's name came to me and stuck. Springtime, renewal, the land's rebirth. In a way, Persephone represents Griffin's and my goal—a purpose I'm still struggling with, but trying to accept.

I glance at Selena, hoping she doesn't mind. The two women share Hades, after all.

Selena nods her approval, and I face forward again, relieved.

Still frowning his displeasure, the holy man puts the blessed veil over my head. It's too thick to see clearly anymore, and I reach for Griffin. His hand is warm and dry and a comfort as the rest of the world fades around me. He says the vows first, his voice strong and sure, the truth in each word anchoring him deep into my bones.

When it's my turn, the binding promises race through my blood. The moment I finish, a powerful jolt of magic nearly knocks me off my feet. Griffin steadies me with a firm hand on my waist and another on my elbow as lightning flashes beyond the stone columns and thunder rumbles overhead.

Griffin removes my veil, handing it back to the holy man. My *husband* smiles down at me, his eyes brilliant, and my heart gives an elated thump. He's mine. Forever. In this world, and in the next.

Carver appears at Griffin's elbow with two rings. Griffin slides the smaller one onto my finger and then gives the other one to me. They're gold and completely simple. I love them. I love him.

I slip Griffin's ring onto his hand, short of breath from sheer happiness. "I can't believe you did all this in one day. You must be exhausted."

He flashes me a tingle-inducing grin while the holy man lays my veil at Athena's feet. The statue is ten feet tall and dominates the back portion of the temple. "I've still got plenty of energy"—he winks—"for an old man."

Giddiness swoops through me in a light and heady tumble. "I'm breathless with anticipation." Flippant doesn't work. I sound ridiculously eager.

Griffin chuckles softly, obviously knowing exactly what he does to me. "How did you spend your day, Wife?"

A spasm hits my chest, a shock of pure joy. "Buying this dress and soaking in milk."

Griffin's eyebrows lift. "Milk?"

"Yes. I'm very soft. Everywhere."

His eyes smolder in the torchlight. "If there wasn't one more thing to do, you'd be over my shoulder and we'd be headed for the nearest dark alley right now."

"In the rain? In my new dress?" I gasp, mock-horrified, completely on board.

"A cyclone couldn't stop me."

Heat dances up my spine.

Looking like he almost wants to cancel whatever else he has planned and find that alley, Griffin finally waves Egeria over. She unwraps a cloth, revealing a crown nestled in the protective folds. Just one. Fiery red gemstones. Sleek uniform pearls. Gold.

The symbolism is instantly clear to me, and my heart drops with a hard thud.

Griffin places the circle on my head. "Sintan gold. Tarvan rubies. Fisan pearls." His voice carries to every corner of the temple, and I break out in a wash of goose bumps. It's almost a cold sweat. He just made a statement about a unified future. He crowned *me*. There aren't many people here, but not one of them is stupid.

My breathing turns erratic. I feel ambushed. "This wasn't part of the plan."

Griffin lifts my chin, gently but firmly forcing me to look at him. "This *is* the plan. This is our family, your closest friends. These are our allies." His knuckles glide along my jaw. "I was wrong when I talked about you being the shield and me being the sword."

I swallow. That's when he said we'd forge a new world. Plan in motion. Apparently.

Griffin's eyes capture mine and don't let go. His steadiness grounds me when it feels like all of Thalyria is tipping sideways, and I'm sliding off. "You're the shield *and* the sword."

I stop breathing, but something in his words and the deep, even cadence of his voice realigns me, helping me to find balance again. An unfamiliar calm suffuses me, replacing both air and blood. It spreads within my body— quiet, inevitable—the kind of calm that heralds the breaking storm.

My lungs fill again, and my voice comes out surprisingly steady. "So what does that make you?"

He smiles, his expression sure. Unflappable. "Whatever you need, *agapi mou*." Griffin raises both my hands to his lips. His breath is warm against my skin, and his quietly spoken promise crushes the lingering fear inside me, compressing it into a small but unbreakable nugget of hope.

CHAPTER 27

"THERE IS A WAY TO GET INSIDE CASTLE TARVA WITHOUT anyone knowing why you're really there." Frowning, Aetos swipes a huge hand over his blue head, rubbing the back of his tattooed skull.

"And that is…?" I prompt when he doesn't go on. The circus residents stayed overnight in the castle after the wedding feast. This morning, everyone but Aetos, Desma, Vasili, and Selena returned to the venue, leaving me the day to more or less reveal all, including my true identity, my Kingmaker Magic, my destiny to tear down borders and unify the realms, and the serpent's nest Acantha Tarva has been stirring up.

Cool and composed, as always, Selena processed the information better than the others, making me wonder how much she already knew. Griffin's family is here, too, and now that everyone has wrapped their heads around me being Beta Fisa and apparently the new Origin according to (*pffft!*) Artemis, ideas are starting to flow.

Sort of.

Aetos keeps his mouth shut, clearly regretting having said anything at all, and I glance out the deep-set windows, attempting patience. The courtyard is already darkening beyond the row of marble arches, each day closing faster than the last with the now usual show of rolling wet clouds racing each other toward the horizon. A damp, storm-charged breeze hits the back of my neck, lifting the wisps of loose hair there.

Turning back to the room, my gaze settles first on Kato and Flynn before moving on to Griffin's parents and sisters. Griffin is next to me. Carver is on his right. Along with Selena, the members of Beta Team, technically Alpha Team now, are the only ones who don't look like they've been kicked by a Centaur for the better part of the day. Griffin's family already knew who I am, but Fate just added a whole new aspect to things. Vasili has been stoic, if worried. Desma's eyes are red and puffy, and Aetos mainly looks thumping mad.

"Aetos!" Patience is not my strong suit.

"If I say it, I'll be as bad as him." Aetos indicates Griffin with a jerk of his chin. "Dragging you into something you might not come out of."

Griffin bristles beside me. His voice hardens, turning flinty. "Are you saying I don't protect *my wife*?"

A thrill rushes through me despite the seriousness of what's going on. I don't think I'll ever get used to Griffin calling me that.

His large hands braced on his thighs, Aetos leans forward and engages Griffin in an epic stare-down. "I'm saying you *can't*. Do this, and you'll die, too."

"Do what?" I toss up my hands, exasperated.

Desma pops out of her chair, the sudden movement breaking the men's tense eye contact. "There's no reason to do anything. Delta Tarva will back off now that you have the Ipotane on the border, and the Power Bid will blow over. She'll just have to oust her own family if she wants a throne. You don't have to get involved. Let Acantha have Tarva. Let your mother have Fisa. Just be happy for once. Love your husband. Live in a castle. Eat spice cakes. You're not responsible for the world!"

I sigh. I wish that were true. "Apparently, all of Olympus

thinks I am. Griffin thinks I am. Gods help me, even *I'm* starting to think I am. There's no more burying my head in the sand."

Selena sits up straighter. "Sand." She turns, and her eyes narrow on Aetos.

I rock to the edge of my seat. "Do you know what Aetos is talking about?"

She nods. "Risky. It could work."

When Selena doesn't offer anything else, I glare at Aetos. "Start talking, or I'll start fighting. You know I will."

He blows out a long breath, rubbing his knees. "You'd think of it yourself anyway." His big shoulders slump. "The Agon Games."

The idea hits me with the force of a solid blow. *Think of it myself?* I should have thought of it weeks ago when we were in Kitros and the entire city was vibrating in anticipation of the upcoming competition. "The winning team goes to the castle. It's tradition." I beam at Aetos. "That's a fantastic idea!"

"It's a horrible idea!" he snarls back.

Griffin's reaction is just as violently negative. "You're not going anywhere near an arena and fights to the death."

"It's not always to the death." Only usually. And for the last few centuries. In the beginning, the Agon Games were about healthy competition—poetry, music, dance, grappling, running, discus throwing, and other physical contests. Athletes and artists vied for the attention of the Origin and the chance to serve in his court. But after the kingdom split, generations of depraved royals corrupted the spirit of the Games, turning them into something else entirely. They became brutal and bloodthirsty, just like the sovereigns themselves. These days, all that remains of the tradition are the central location in what used to be the seat of the Origin's kingdom, the four-year interval between Games, and the invitation for the winners to humbly bow before the nearby ruling family—now the Tarvan royals.

I jump up, turning to Griffin. "It's the perfect solution. We get access to the Tarvan royals without having to invade, without endangering anyone but ourselves, and without creating dissent between two armies and two populations we're aiming to combine."

Griffin stands, too, towering over me. Glowering. "That's *if* we win."

"How can we not? The Gods are with us. You know that!"

Something restless and almost violent seethes in his expression. "Sometimes the Gods are barely fast enough to keep up with your blatant disregard for your own safety. Even Artemis said you're hard to keep alive."

Guilt wrings my chest like an iron fist. "I told you I'd be more careful. And Artemis and her stupid archer can kiss my—"

"Even if you survive, the rest of your team may not," Selena cuts in coolly. "Is that a risk you're willing to take?"

I whirl on Selena and then take an involuntary step back. She has a pretty epic hard stare herself, and it hits me like a God Bolt.

Risk my team to save thousands of people from what could be a long and bloody war? Every face I love comes sharply into focus. They're all here.

My heart starts to pound, but I refuse to deflate. "It's a good idea. I won't lose my team."

"You're sure?" Selena asks.

I deflate a little. I can't help it. "Do you think I will? Do you know something I don't?"

Selena shrugs, which isn't an answer.

"Do you think we should do this?" I ask outright. If Selena says no, I'll listen.

She hesitates, seeming to choose her words carefully. "You could try."

I go very still. Griffin looks over sharply. How does Selena know about his family's de facto motto? I can't tell anything from her tone. It wasn't ominous. It wasn't teasing. What is she telling me to do?

I reach for Griffin's hand. "I can steal whatever magic our opponents have. There's nothing they can throw at us that I can't counter."

"What about that moment it takes you to adjust?" Flynn asks.

I flash him a smile that's all teeth. "That's when you'll be watching my back."

"It's not only about magic," Selena interjects. "There are many ways to win the Agon Games."

"These men are good fighters," I say. "The best."

"I don't doubt their skill," she responds. "But sometimes it's purely a question of size."

That draws me up short. Last time, a team with two Centaurs on it won. They simply had more muscle, pounds, and raw physical power than anyone else. The time before that, a Giant crushed everyone in the arena without the rest of its team lifting more than a halfhearted blade. The accounts of mangling turned my stomach.

Kato catches my eye, his cobalt gaze carrying more weight than usual. "We'll figure it out. We always do, and Cat's never led us astray."

He nods to me then, a solemn message of confidence in the slow dip of his chin. My heart knocks hard against my ribs. *Did I suddenly become the leader of this group?* I spin toward Griffin. He's in charge. He's always in charge.

With an almost imperceptible nod, Griffin cedes the decision to me. My stomach cramps. *Sintan gold. Tarvan rubies. Fisan pearls.* Yesterday, with six words and a crown, he put the world in my hands, and I didn't run away screaming when I had the chance. In fact, the only screaming I did yesterday was underneath him in our bedroom. And on top.

My pulse hammers, pumping adrenaline and anxiety through my veins. The choice weighs too much. It hurts my chest. *Can we do this?* Should *we?*

I curl my hands into fists at my sides to stop their visible shaking. "We'll need one more person. The Agon Games only takes teams of six."

"Piers," Carver says. "You haven't seen it, but he can fight."

My instincts rebel. I don't want my life in Piers's hands. He may be a decent warrior, despite his scholarly tendencies, but he may also be tempted to throw me under a Cyclops or straight into a Harpy's nest. I don't think he'd do it, but any hesitation in the arena could cost us too much.

I shake my head. "He's not due back for two weeks. The Games start in one. We should have already left to register and scope out the competition. We don't have any time to lose."

"There's an advantage to arriving at the last minute," Griffin says, astounding me that he's truly considering this. "The other teams can't get a feel for us, either. I'll send my fastest rider for Piers. He'll meet us there."

Disquiet churns in my gut. Justified or not, I don't want Piers on the sand with us.

"I'll go."

I turn to Aetos and find him watching me closely. Huge. Skilled. Fire. Flight. He survived the Ice Plains. He vanquished a Mare of Thrace. For most teams, he'd be an enormous asset.

Desma stares at him in shock, her face going so ashen even her lips turn white. There's something beyond fear in her eyes, beyond panic. It's utter desperation.

But even without her pale face and petrified eyes making a knot tighten below my breasts, I'd turn Aetos down. Our best survival strategy isn't to gain a hulking Magoi; it's to be wholly underestimated.

"You know how the Games work," I say mainly to Aetos. "The spectators get rowdy when it's over too fast. The weaker we seem, the better chance we have of facing a weaker team in the first round. The Gameskeepers need to make sure the fights are interesting, and that they last, even if it means pitting favorites against each other in the early rounds. Without you, we're Hoi Polloi and one Magoi woman with no combat magic. With you, we'd be in a different category altogether."

"After the first round, they'd take your measure anyway," Aetos argues. "We all know they shuffle the grid. That's why it's never announced."

"Maybe. But that's one less round that's a real danger to us. If we go into this anonymous and underestimated, I can practically guarantee we'll walk through the first round. That means less injury and fatigue going into the second fight, and even the third." There's rarely a fourth. There aren't that many people willing to risk everything for glory and gold.

Aetos stands, his anvil-like fists clenching at his sides. "Do you really expect me not to fight with you? Not to protect you?"

"I expect you to listen to me," I answer.

"And I expect you to make wise decisions not based on sentiment," Aetos growls back.

It's on the tip of my tongue to scoff and say, "When

have I ever been wise?" but I can't do that anymore. I can never do that again.

"Cat's reasoning is sound," Griffin says. "The weaker we appear on paper, the easier our first round will be."

"The weaker you appear on paper, the weaker you are," Aetos snaps. "What's the point of surviving the first round if you have no hope in the second?"

"Because it's a ruse," I say. "We *are* strong."

"And you'd be stronger with me!" Aetos snarls.

Desma squeezes her eyes shut. "I'm pregnant."

"What?" I cry.

"What?" Aetos roars.

She stares at her feet, not saying another word.

Aetos wraps his arms around her, lifts her up, and then holds her at his eye level until Desma finally looks at him again. When their eyes meet, he grins. It's the biggest, widest, happiest smile I've ever seen on his blue face. "I love you." He kisses her soundly.

Desma smiles back, rainbow tears glittering in her eyes. "I love you, too."

Aetos lets her feet touch the ground again, and Desma leans in to him, the top of her head just reaching the bottom of his chest. He strokes her hair, his great, strong hands gentle on her. "But I'm still going."

Desma's face crashes like an avalanche, turning just as white.

"No, you're not." I cross my arms. I hate responsibility. Leadership is the pits. Disappointing the people you love is inevitable, and who knew it would start so soon?

Aetos faces off with me, keeping hold of Desma's hand and swallowing it in his enormous grip. "You're smart, Cat, but you never think. Turning down my offer is short-sighted. Stupid even."

I lift my brows. "Please, tell me how you really feel."

"I don't want to die in some blood-soaked arena. But even if I do, it's not just about you, or me, or any of us anymore."

I stare at him. People keep saying that. It's like a Giant beating me over the head with a club. *All. The. Time.* "Since when do you care about the greater good?" Aetos cares deeply for about a dozen people. As far as I know, his emotional ties end there.

His shoulders turn rock-hard, like a bull getting ready to charge. "Since I realized there might *be* a greater good. Last night, the man who took over Sinta put a crown on *your* head. Today, you told us who you are. I know where this is going. I'll help you get there."

Aetos's glacial-blue eyes bore into mine. *Queen of Thalyria* they seem to say. His trust and belief in me are staggering. I haven't even stepped up. Not really. I don't deserve that gift. I can't imagine how I'll live up to it.

I hold his gaze, my own eyes hardening. "I want another woman on the team. Hoi Polloi. We'll walk through our first combat that way."

Aetos makes a derisive sound. "And after?"

Griffin moves closer to my side. "That's when we'll show them what we're really made of, and what Cat's magic can do."

I look at him, my nerves in a tangle. It's not just my own life on the line here. "I thought you didn't want me anywhere near the arena."

Lines bracket Griffin's mouth. His eyes fill with shadows. "I don't. I don't want any of us there. But it's a good plan. If you think we can do this, then I believe you."

Panic licks through me. I don't want to be the one making these decisions now. Part of me was actually hoping Griffin would talk me out of it, or even manhandle me into giving up the idea. Part of me still is.

"Then you agree with me on this?" I ask, not even sure I agree with myself.

Griffin doesn't answer right away. He looks torn. Then, "*Objectively*, it's a smart move."

I glance at Nerissa and Anatole and wish I hadn't. I'm about to drag two of their children into a bloodbath, and they know it. Piers's accusations come flooding back. Jocasta looks like she's seen a ghost. Kaia's eyes are huge. Egeria seems like she might vomit.

I can't blame her. I feel that way myself.

Swallowing hard, I turn back to Griffin, trying to banish my doubts along with the acidic sting in my throat. "And ruling well is about doing what's best for the most people?" I ask.

His nostrils flare. He nods once, looking rather enraged by his own principles.

"Then we'll go," I say more confidently than I feel.

"On one condition," Griffin says, his eyes landing on Selena. "We take the best healer there is with us."

Selena inclines her head. With the slight angling of her delicate chin, she agrees to come.

"I'm going, too," Jocasta says briskly, standing. "I'm very good with herbs and dressing wounds."

"No way," Carver growls. "Not a chance in the Underworld."

Jocasta glares at him. Her eyes spark a brilliant blue. "It's not your decision."

"Fine!" Carver pivots in his chair to face his parents. "Father?"

Anatole opens his mouth but apparently doesn't know what to say. Nerissa squeezes his hand until the whole appendage turns white, but then he closes his mouth again without uttering a sound.

"Griffin…" Carver all but snarls, turning to his older brother.

"She can come," Griffin says.

"*What?*" I'm not sure who shouts louder—Flynn, Kato, or Carver.

Jocasta's triumphant smile lights her entire face, returning some of the color to it. "Thank you, Griffin, although it's no longer your decision, either." Her final words and her eyes land on me.

Good Gods, is she saying it's mine?

"She needs a guard," Flynn grates.

"I second that!" I say far too loudly.

"Cassandra," Kato suggests. "I saw her today, so Piers didn't take her with him."

I've met Cassandra. Quick, tall, strong, pretty in an unassuming way. She's Piers's number two.

"Cassandra should be your sixth teammate," Jocasta says. "She's fast and smart. An expert with a blade and a bow."

A curt nod from Griffin, who knows Cassandra better than I do. "A good idea. If she accepts."

"Then who will guard Jo when we're not there?" Flynn asks. He's turning red. It's hard to tell where his face ends and his hair begins.

Selena's voice is like a splash of cool water in the rapidly heating room. "I will."

Flynn's head whips around. "No offense, but I don't know you."

Selena's eyes brighten to a striking, luminous blue. The power that suddenly roars around her makes my hair stand up at the roots and vibrate. A shiver ripples down my body, coursing from my head to my toes.

"Do not question me." Her words aren't liquid calm anymore. They rumble like a mammoth waterfall.

Flynn stands, blindly undeterred. Or recklessly determined. Wide and muscled, he seems to take up half the
room. I'm not sure he'll back down, and I don't know
whether to block him or to stand in front of Selena. Not
that I could even begin to hold back Selena. It would be
like trying to cage a hurricane in the palm of my hand. The
magic in her eyes is immeasurable, and not a soul in the
room moves.

Jocasta finally puts a neat end to the thickening tension
by walking straight through it. Flynn follows her with his
eyes, his mouth a grim line.

At the door, Jocasta throws the entire room a defiant
look, sapphire fire in her eyes. "I have tonics to prepare.
When do we leave?"

"Dawn," Griffin replies stiffly.

Jocasta nods and then sweeps from the room, the hem of
her dress snapping around the doorframe.

Flynn stares after her. His jaw could cut marble. Everyone
looks uncomfortable. I know I am. Then Aetos starts arguing with me again, which makes Desma miserable.

I grit my teeth, the start of a headache coming on. I want
to grab Griffin's hand and make a break for it. I'll jump
through the window if I have to. Except I can't. *Gah!*

Deep breath in. Long breath out. The Gods are telling
me I'm some sort of new Origin, which apparently means
it's my job to give Thalyria a fresh start. Griffin crowned
me with the symbols of the three realms, joining them
together on one circle that perfectly fit my head. If I'm
supposed to be not just *a* queen but *the* Queen, I'd better
start acting like it.

My voice rings out, surprisingly firm. "Flynn, sit down.
Aetos, I said no. Kato, Carver—find Cassandra and bring
her here. We might have some convincing to do."

Flynn sits. Aetos clamps his mouth shut. Kato and Carver get up and go. *Huh.*

The pride in Griffin's unwavering gray gaze makes me feel a little dizzy and alarmingly warm inside. I shift restlessly until Vasili catches my eye. His thick mustache lifts with the hint of a paternal smile, and I remember how all those years ago, he found me starving and drifting through the dusty southern grasslands. He took me to Selena, half carrying me in his arms.

He lifts the blunt end of a knife to his forehead now in a silent salute, but his eyes are troubled, like he fears he might be drinking in his last sight of me.

CHAPTER 28

CASSANDRA IS EXACTLY WHAT I HOPED FOR — GOOD AT following orders. I need practice giving them, so that works out well for everyone. She's also exceptional at reconnaissance. All lean muscle and agility, she moves like a shadow and blends into walls. When she asks questions, people answer. Not because she threatens, but because of a rather disarming smile that includes a healthy set of teeth and a dimple in her right cheek. Piers found her in Mylos three years ago guarding the main temple housing the knowledge scrolls. I don't know how she ended up being his right hand, but he was smart to hold on to her. Piers may be a lot of things, but stupid isn't one of them.

"Three teams are camped outside the city." Cassandra draws a map in the dirt and marks the spots to the north and northeast. "They're each missing a team member, which makes me think they're hiding creatures in the woods."

My stomach performs a nervous flip. "Any idea what?" I ask.

She shakes her head. "They could have magic, or just brute force."

"Don't forget venom," Kato adds dryly.

Cassandra nods. "There are eight teams in all. The remaining five, including us, are all housed in the arena. We're in the middle of the living quarters, with two teams on our left, and two on our right."

As soon as a team registers for the Agon Games, they're offered a "suite" in the bowels of the arena, which consists of two rooms with cots, a fully stocked apothecary area, a small privy, and a private bath. The only light comes from torches and oil lamps. The floors are dirt, the ceilings high. *Monster*-accommodating high. On the eve of the Games, every combatant has to be in the underground rooms, Giants and all. Most participants never leave the arena again.

"Physically, we're on par. Maybe even better." Cassandra's eyes stray to Kato. Of course. She's female. "But there's no telling what's beneath the surface. The teams are heavily Fisan, which probably means more Magoi than Hoi Polloi. I've only seen one other woman in the hallways around the suites, but others could be staying in their rooms. I also learned from a talkative Gameskeeper that we're the only Sintan team—with the exception of the Origin."

I force myself not to grimace. When Cassandra agreed to risk her life, it was only fair to tell her why. She immediately started calling me the Origin and Griffin the Alpha. And not Alpha Sinta, just Alpha, which is a statement in itself.

"You did well." Griffin nods his approval, his mien somber. "Anything else?"

Cassandra shakes her head, making her shoulder-length hair bounce. It's shorter, but curly and brown like mine. "They're lying as low as we are. No one wants to show their hand."

Lying low is an understatement. Only Cassandra has left the suite since we got here. The next time I show my face, it'll be covered in cosmetics, just like it was when we arrived. People come from all over to see the Games, many of them Magoi or Magoi nobles. I can't risk anyone recognizing me until we're inside Castle Tarva with a knife to Galen Tarva's throat. And preferably to Acantha's, too.

Flynn squats and uses his finger to draw a tournament bracket in the dirt. "Eight teams. That means three rounds, one less than in the last Games."

I nod. "And sometimes teams kill each other off completely. We might get a pass into the final round." I sound disturbingly eager about the possibility of twelve people slaughtering each other.

Well, better than slaughtering us.

"Unlikely," Kato says, studying the rudimentary grid.

Carver winks at me. "But we can always hope."

Flynn sweeps his bracket from the ground and then rises, brushing the dirt from his hands. "Too bad we can't watch the other rounds. Get an idea of what we're up against."

As of tonight, all the teams will be inside. As of tomorrow morning, we'll all be under lock and key and only let out when it's our turn to fight.

Carver throws a lean, muscled arm around my shoulders, ignoring Griffin's narrow-eyed stare. "If Cat's strategy worked, we've made ourselves out as weak enough to avoid the more terrifying teams in the first round."

"Hopefully." I frown. "Although *weak* is a misnomer. There are no weak teams in the Agon Games unless six people want to collectively commit suicide. But they'll look for teams that don't have an obvious advantage, like magical creatures or a known Magoi. Well-matched teams put on a better show. Pit Hoi Polloi against Magoi and creatures, and it's over too fast. The spectators want gore, and they want it to last. Apparently, that's more fun."

"So where does that put us?" Carver asks.

And that's the crystal ball question. Too bad those things don't work. "It's hard to say without more knowledge of the other teams. Probably not with creatures in the first round, but I doubt there's a single team without at least one Magoi with offensive magic."

"Except for us." Kato glances at me. "In a manner of speaking."

I shrug out from under Carver's heavy arm. He ruffles my hair as I go, setting loose the shorter strands I'd managed to tame into my braid for once.

"I was absolutely truthful when I told the head scribe my magic is defensive." If I still had my Dragon's Breath, I would have had to say offensive and list all my individual abilities. I would also have had no problem winning these Games; there would have been very little show, and my team wouldn't have had to lift a finger.

Once more, I can thank Mother for the colossal shafting and, in a roundabout way, putting myself and everyone I love into mortal danger. Again.

"Can they eliminate us on a technicality when they see you turn the magic around?" Kato asks.

"I don't see how. The magic won't come from me. My defense is to grab it and then turn it back on the other team."

"Are you ready to reveal your talents to the world?" Griffin asks.

His question brings the imminence of my new reality to the fore. I fight my visceral response to run and hide, and press my ice shard necklace against my chest. Cool for courage.

"A stubborn"—I roll my eyes—"albeit wise man once told me that someone has to decide what needs to be done, to make decisions and not turn back." At the time, I told Griffin he didn't have the right to choose for everyone else. But a corrupt, oppressive system should be challenged. And changed. I see that now, and I'm starting to feel the weight of the responsibility in my bones. Unfortunately, ambition isn't limited to the noble and sane.

"No turning back." Griffin's gaze is potent on me, his words almost a question. We both know I can change my mind until the moment we walk out onto the sand.

I take a deep breath. I used to be so good at ignoring things. Then obligation crept up on me, along with everyone saying "Harbinger this" and "Origin that." I gained gills and lost the ability to disregard the inevitable. *Fate. Gah!*

One by one, I look at my team. Warriors. Family. Friends. Jocasta and Selena are part of our effort, too, but they're in the other room, preparing salves and potions for when we come back from our fights. Because we will come back. All of us.

"I brought us to the Agon Games. I'll do whatever I have to do to keep everyone alive and win," I say firmly. "Then we'll walk into Castle Tarva—*invited*—and we'll take over this realm without a war."

Griffin nods. "When the Tarvan royals expect us to bow down before them, they'll find they have to surrender to us instead."

Yes!

That's the plan, anyway.

What if it doesn't work?

Griffin's hands close around my waist, and my heart gives a swift little leap as he lifts me onto a nearby stool. It's effortless, and his strength sends a ripple of awareness through me. Or maybe that's nerves because I'm suddenly the tallest person in the room.

I swallow. *Good Gods, a pedestal.*

"You've admitted who you are. You've accepted what you'll become." Griffin lifts his face to look at me. He's striking, tanned, and utterly masculine. Shadowed jaw. Pirate's nose. Eyes the color of a storm. His gaze knocks into me with the force of a granite punch. "The minute you

cease being afraid of yourself, there's nothing in this world
that can stop you."

A thud rouses me from sleep. Carver's violent oath snaps
me fully awake along with everyone else in our two rooms.

I jump up and race toward the noise. My hand flies to
my mouth, stifling a shocked cry.

"Cassandra!" Jocasta stops dead, sways, and then
reaches for the wall, bracing herself.

Torches flicker both inside our suite and out. The
door to the hallway is wide open, and Carver is lifting
Cassandra's limp form. He carries her to the nearest cot
while Kato shuts the door again, throwing the inside lock
with a savage curse.

I feel Griffin next to me and grab his arm, squeezing hard.

Selena leans over Cassandra to check for a pulse. When
her eyes find mine, they're filled with sympathy. "There's
nothing I can do."

"Nothing you can do?" I repeat, desperately wanting to
have misheard.

Selena shakes her head. "She has her obol. Hades will
take care of her now."

The possibility of denial, intangible to begin with,
ceases to exist. Reeling in shock, I stare at Cassandra. Of
course there's no pulse. Her neck is split from ear to ear.

As if wading through a nightmare, slowly I turn to
Carver. He was on watch. "What happened?" I ask.

"I heard a bang. Someone must have thrown her against
the door. I opened it, and there she was. Like that." His
expression twists into something terrible. He looks down.

"Why was she out of the room?" I ask sharply.

Carver's eyes crawl back to mine. "The three teams that were camped in the woods came in tonight. She thought she could get a look at them."

"By doing *what*?" My voice hardens with anger. Distress. Disbelief. "Breaking into their rooms? If anyone snuck into our suite, we'd kill first, ask questions never!"

Carver looks at Cassandra's bloodless face, his own face turning completely blank. My heart pounds furiously against my ribs a dozen times before he meets my eyes again. "She said she'd stay in the hallway, see if anyone came out. I don't know if she did more, or if someone came out and didn't like her being there. Whoever it was must have been fast and quiet to get the drop on her."

"Fast and quiet? That's the least of it! We're not up against amateurs. What were you thinking, letting her out of the room in the middle of the night? No Gameskeepers around. No servants. No one! And if she wouldn't listen to you, you should have woken me. Or Griffin. Or anyone!"

Carver's lean body stiffens. "I thought it was a good idea. I let her go."

My fury shakes the room. Literally. Guilt is layered on top. Cassandra had no reason to be in this arena except that I asked her. *I* brought her here.

The ground beneath my feet blackens. Lightning coils down my arms and webs between my fingers. Griffin makes a soothing sound and lays his hand on my shoulder, but that just enrages me more. I don't deserve his comfort.

A jagged bolt shoots from my hand, wild and blinding in the dim room. It flies toward Flynn. His pained grunt mixes with the harsh crack of thunder, and my eyes widen. There's a hole in his pants. His leg is smoking.

Both my heart and the storm implode at my feet. I rush to Flynn. "I'm sorry! I'm so sorry."

Flynn grits his teeth, backing away from me with a limp. "It's fine," he grates out. "I'm fine."

He's not fine. Shame and remorse leave me rooted to the spot as Flynn puts more space between us. I want to help him, but I'm afraid to touch him. I think he doesn't want me to.

Jocasta slips her shoulders under Flynn's big arm, staggering under his weight and looking at me like she's never seen me before. I guess she hasn't. Kato jumps in to help, and they guide Flynn toward a chair.

Selena sweeps past me and then sits next to Flynn. "This, I can do something about."

She takes out a knife, cuts his pants off above the lightning strike, and then pours clean water over the wound. I can see straight to the bone. Flynn hisses, and my throat closes over. I can't move. I can't breathe. I can't believe what I've done.

The sharp sting of magic bites my skin as Selena gently touches the seared flesh. Flynn's nostrils flare, and his normally tanned face turns bone-white. She increases the power, and he throws his head back, the muscles in his neck and jaw straining.

Jocasta holds his hand, never looking away from his face. Perspiration dots Flynn's brow. His eyes close, squeezing tight against the pain. He grips Jocasta's hand so hard it must hurt her, but Jocasta keeps murmuring encouragement in a low, steady voice while I stay frozen in place. I know exactly how much this hurts. It's ten times worse than the actual wound.

Finally, Selena draws back. Flynn lowers his head, his grip easing on Jocasta's hand. He breathes deeply, filling his whole chest, and then gingerly flexes his leg. His brown eyes are fatigued but clear of pain.

I let out a wobbly breath and say a silent prayer of thanks, mostly to Selena. When I step back, my boots scrape over my charred footprints. As I look down, something troubling occurs to me. Lightning—offensive magic.

"Son of a Cyclops! If this pops out of me in the arena, we'll be eliminated."

Selena slants me an arch look. "Then don't let it *pop*."

"I can't control it!"

She scoffs. "Of course you can."

"Really? How?"

Her indigo eyes narrow. "Sarcasm and belligerence won't help. Try concentrating."

My jaw drops. Does she think I haven't tried?

"It's not an issue," Kato says glumly. He gently closes Cassandra's eyes and then crosses her hands over her chest. "We're out of the competition. We lost our sixth."

Oh my Gods. He's right.

Unless... I look at Selena. "Can you take her place?"

Selena shakes her head. "You registered a female Hoi Polloi. There's no way I can pass for Hoi Polloi, no matter how I mute myself."

Mute herself? My stomach cramps. I feel sick. "Of course. I wasn't thinking."

I turn to Griffin, barely able to look at him. "Then it's over. I didn't protect my team. We'll have to forfeit the Games. I just started, and I've already failed in every way possible." My hands ball into fists. I want to hit something, break things, tear something apart. Mostly myself. "This isn't me. I can't do this!"

Griffin pins me with his hard stare. "Don't make this about you."

I gape at him. "You're always saying it's about me. Now suddenly it's not? Make up your mind!"

A whisper of apprehension over the back of my neck is my only warning before I'm off my feet and over Griffin's shoulder. The world dips, my insides roil, and acid burns a line from my stomach to my throat. He sets me down in the next room. My feet hit the ground hard, and I swallow, tasting dinner and bile.

Griffin slams the door shut and then turns on me with a frown so fierce his eyebrows turn into one furious slash across his face. "This happens. You think I haven't lost people? You think I haven't seen dead men and women and known that parents no longer have their children? That children just became orphans? That husbands and wives and lovers and friends will never see each other again because they believed in me? Because they followed me?"

My jaw clicks shut.

"It's time to be the person you were meant to be, Cat. You don't just have to make decisions and stand by them now. You have to live with them."

My anger erupts like a volcano. "You live with them! I don't want this! I never wanted this!"

"The Fates don't care what you want! You were born for a reason. Most people have to figure out their role in life by themselves. Some never do. You had yours handed to you when you were fifteen. Harbinger of the end. Destroyer of realms." He advances on me even though we're only a step apart. "*You* end the scourge. *You* rebuild the kingdom. You've had more than eight years to think about it. Now stop hiding and do something!"

If he'd hit me, I couldn't have been more stunned. "I tried to do something! Look how well that turned out!"

"We have the Ipotane. Sinta is behind a locked wall. That's a win."

I shake my head. Scoffing, I look down. "It's over."

Griffin pinches my chin and forces my head back up. "You're the leader. You don't get to look down. You look straight ahead and acknowledge the damage you cause."

My eyes widen. Blur.

"And the good you do," he says more gently, easing his grip. "Nothing ends in this arena. If we have to, we invade. Good options don't exist. Only choices."

My throat burns with rising tears. "I made one, and Cassandra's dead." Her lifeless face is all I can see. Her gruesome second smile. "Oh Gods. Piers already hates me. He's going to kill me."

"Piers doesn't hate you." Griffin wraps his arms around me and draws me in close. I resist at first but then realize that's not what I really want. I lay my cheek against his chest, letting my weight sag and wishing I could somehow settle our burdens back onto his shoulders again.

"This isn't your fault." His large hand moves slowly up and down my back. "Cassandra shouldn't have left the suite at night. Not here. Not in this place."

An ache unfolds under my rib cage. "Did he... Were they...in love?"

"Piers? In love?" Griffin shakes his head. "Not to my knowledge. He cared about her, though. They were comrades. And friends."

The hot sting behind my eyes gets worse. I take a deep breath. Let it out slowly. "Plan B?" I ask.

"Plan B," Griffin agrees.

I sniff. "I don't have a plan B."

Jocasta throws open the door. "No. Plan A." She frowns. "You do realize we can hear every word you say?"

I blink at her. "And?"

"We can go through with the Games." She points to herself. "Woman. Hoi Polloi."

My pulse takes off like Pegasus.

Griffin tenses beside me. "You can't be serious." He uses his calm, scary voice. "You have no idea how to fight."

Her chin lifts. "I trained with Cat before you left. I trained with Cassandra every day until you got back."

Oh no. This is one more thing I did. It explains the calluses on Jocasta's fingers, and how close the two women seemed. "I'm sorry you lost your friend."

Jocasta's expression doesn't change. If anything, it hardens. "Me too."

Griffin's eyes narrow, but not on me. "How long did you train with Cat?"

"A few days."

He stares at his sister. "So overall, you've trained for a matter of weeks and have no combat experience. That's like throwing a toddler into a race and expecting the child to keep up."

"I can keep up," Jocasta says.

A big, masculine mitt grabs her wrist and pulls her from the doorway. Griffin and I storm after her just as Jocasta twists out of Flynn's hold with impressive efficiency. He's changed his clothes. You'd never know he'd been severely burned just minutes ago.

Flynn's face is a portrait of rage. "Jo…"

She turns her back on him and faces Griffin and me again. "I'm a grown woman. I make my own decisions."

"Think about Mother and Father," Griffin says.

Jocasta's chin notches up again. "They raised us to think for ourselves."

"They didn't raise us to throw our lives away!" Griffin snaps.

"And I'm not planning to!" Jocasta's sapphire eyes glint

in the torchlight, determination off cut stone. "I'm from a family of action. Do you expect me not to act?"

"I expect you to act wisely," Griffin responds.

"I don't answer to our parents anymore. I have no husband or children to consider. I don't answer to you, either, Griffin."

Good Gods, I hope she doesn't expect me *to decide.*

"Jo—" Flynn tries again.

She swings on him, livid. "You"—she pokes him in the chest—"don't get an opinion."

"I bloody well do!" Flynn snarls.

He takes a step forward, towering over her, and Jocasta slaps him hard enough to stop him in his tracks.

Her voice lowers, almost masking the tremor in it. "You forfeited your right by ignoring me for the last six years."

Flynn sucks in a sharp breath. So do I. Griffin looks floored. Carver looks miserable. Kato looks uncomfortable. Selena looks mildly interested, which means she's paying attention to every word. And Jocasta looks downright dangerous.

"Do I get an opinion?" Carver is slumped against the wooden door, his arms crossed. There's no lightness in his tone, and he looks bone-weary.

Jocasta nods.

"We should knock you out cold and make sure you don't wake up again until after we've forfeited the Games."

I snort. I doubt *he'll* get an opinion again.

Something close to violence flares in Jocasta's eyes. "Try it, and you'll see what I've learned."

Carver peels himself off the wood, looking more than ready to oblige.

I hold up a hand to stop him. "What *have* you learned?" I ask Jocasta.

"Knife throwing. Swordplay. Some grappling and self-defense."

"How are you with a target?"

"Excellent."

"And with a moving target?"

"Average."

"And with a sword?" I ask.

"Mediocre."

So she can lift and swing. Great. At least she's honest.

The muscles at the back of Flynn's jaw bounce out like they have a life of their own. "I seriously hope you're not considering this."

And I seriously hope he's talking to Griffin and not to me.

Jocasta's expression turns stony with resolve. "I understand your doubts. I'll stay out of it as much as possible. I'll simply be your sixth body in the arena."

"Sixth *dead* body!" Flynn explodes. "This is madness!"

Jocasta whirls on him. "Do you want me to hit you again?"

Flynn's brown eyes catch fire. Then, in the space of a few breaths, his face shuts down completely. "If she walks out there, I don't. We'll have to forfeit anyway."

My heart sinks. He means every word.

Griffin levels the same piercing stare on Flynn that he's always using on me. "I know my sister. She'll forgive just about anything. She won't forgive a selfish choice."

Flynn looks at Griffin like he's possessed. "Don't tell me you condone this!"

Griffin looks torn. How could he not?

"Can you be my shadow?" I ask Jocasta, knowing I should really keep my mouth shut. "Stick to me like the Minotaur to its maze? Do whatever I say? No hesitating. Not even a second. And if not me, then someone else?"

She nods. Not eagerly. Not enthusiastically. She just nods.

"Cat—" Flynn gears up to argue again.

"Stop." I slice my head to the side, silencing him. "We've all chosen to put our lives on the line for a reason. For a cause. Jocasta isn't less of a person than we are. She doesn't get half a vote. She made a noble offer, and you're spitting in her face."

"I'm not spitting in her face! She isn't really trained. How can you even consider this?"

"Do you think I was truly trained the first time my mother threw me into an arena with people twice my size and honed to fight?" I laugh, and it's as brittle as winter leaves. "Trial by fire. It forges a heart of iron."

"And that's what you want for Jo? A heart of iron?" Flynn scoffs. "You're hard and mean and a little bit crazy, Cat."

A warning sound rumbles in Griffin's chest. My own chest tightens painfully, and even though I feel the truth in his words, I try to remember that tomorrow Flynn could tell me I'm fun and selfless and brave. He's angry now. I look him in the eyes and see he already regrets what he said. He knows me well, though. I am hard, and crazy, and mean. But not always, and that's not the sum of who I am.

I step toward Flynn, my voice low and trembling with the kind of ungovernable emotion that only comes from arguing with someone you truly care about. "A heart of iron means *I do not break.* You *cannot* break me. I may not be the strongest, or the fastest, or the best, but I will *fight.* I will fight for everyone I love. I will fight for myself. You can beat me until I'm bloody. You can break my bones. You can tear my skin. You can burn me. You can crush me until I can't breathe, and you're sure I'm dead, and then do you know what?"

Flynn looks at me, his mouth a compressed line. "What?" he finally asks.

"I will get up, and I will fight some more."

Flynn's eyes flick to Jocasta before boring back into mine. "This is one of those decisions you'll have to live with." He looks at Griffin, too, the same somber message in his heavy dark-brown stare.

Jocasta glares at Flynn. "Why are you so sure I'm incompetent?"

"I don't think you're incompetent," Flynn answers harshly. "I don't think you're prepared for *this*!"

Carver tilts his head back against the closed door, his eyes at half-mast, one foot propped up against the wood. His relaxed stance doesn't fool me at all. "I think our opponents will see you're the weak link, and we'll spend all our energy defending you until we finally run out of muscle. Guess what happens then?" he asks, his tone both biting and soft.

Jocasta whips out a knife and throws, planting the blade in the aged plank not an inch from Carver's sword hand. I arch an eyebrow. Even if she's gained the skill, it takes balls to actually make a move like that, even with Selena here to clean up the potential mess.

Carver straightens off the door, scowling. He rips the knife from the wood and then hands it back to his sister. "I can't believe you did that."

"Then maybe you don't know me," Jocasta says. She turns to Griffin. "What do you think?" She's not asking for his sanction, just his opinion.

"I don't want you out there. You've always had the heart of a warrior, but you don't have the training for this."

Jocasta's chin stays perfectly level. She turns to me. "Cat?"

I don't want an opinion. I don't want an opinion. I don't

want an opinion. "You're not prepared, but who ever is for something like this? Everyone is here by choice. I won't order anyone to fight, and I won't turn you away. The Gods are with us. I put my faith in them."

Jocasta nods once. "Then I'm in."

Flynn pales. His mouth works for a moment, but he doesn't speak again.

Everyone is quiet until Selena says a single word. It's from the old language. I don't recognize it, but the magic blackens my vision and knocks me off my feet. Everyone else lurches, even Griffin, which means whatever she said was helpful, not harmful. Obviously.

Griffin helps me to my feet, and I lean on him more than I probably should. I can't catch my breath. My heart is racing, and my last meal feels like it's ready to come back up.

I swallow once, twice. *Ugh.* "What was that?"

Selena's smile is enigmatic at best. "Let's get some rest." She moves fluidly into the other room and then douses the torch.

Typical. I swallow again, trying not to pant.

Kato covers Cassandra with a blanket, pulling it over her bloodless face. Guilt and anxiety churn in my stomach, and I lose the battle not to be sick. I lurch toward the privy and then vomit, overwhelmed by the sheer awfulness of the last half hour and the weight bearing steadily down on my shoulders. I start shaking and can't stop.

Kneeling down next to me on the floor, Griffin keeps my braid out of the way and rubs my back. When I finally sink back onto my heels and wipe a shaking hand across my mouth, he hands me a cool cloth. I refresh myself with it and then drink the water he offers.

The sharp bite of magic still gnaws at my skin. "Whatever Selena just did hit me hard," I say roughly.

Griffin looks at me oddly. Worry creases his brow, and the lines stand out starkly. I should have told Jocasta no. We should have found a plan B.

"You can still stop her," I say in a low voice for just the two of us. "Stop all of this." I almost hope he will.

Griffin grips the back of my head and kisses my forehead. Against my skin, he says, "I could. But I'm letting you out there, aren't I?"

"It's not the same. I'm made to fight. And survive. A week ago, you wouldn't even let Jocasta out of Sinta City."

Griffin takes my hands in his before meeting my eyes again. His are troubled. "I know it doesn't make sense, but something tells me this is the course we're meant to follow. I wish to the Gods Cassandra wasn't dead, and that Jocasta wasn't taking her place, but the gates are sealed now, and there's no replacing her with anyone else. Either Jocasta fights, or we'll be forced to withdraw." He squeezes my fingers. "We need to be out there on the sand tomorrow. I *feel* it."

Griffin's instincts are uncanny, and I think, deep down, I feel it, too. "It could go badly for her. For any of us."

Griffin rises, pulling me up with him. "She knows that, *agapi mou*. So do I."

I'd feel almost normal again after emptying my stomach, except that dread over what's ahead is like an ice-cold block of marble inside me. Everyone is still exactly where we left them in the main room, the tension in the air thick enough to suffocate the lot of us.

It's Flynn who moves first. He takes a downy white feather from the pouch at his belt, holds it between two fingers, and then drops it at Jocasta's feet.

Her face drains of color. My heart lurches when I recognize the feather he took from her hair that day in my room.

Flynn turns his back. For a second, I'm afraid he'll leave, but then his footsteps veer away from Carver and the door, and he stalks into the deep shadows of the suite among the farthest beds and the extra gear. He lies down on a cot and throws his arm over his eyes.

I watch him, but he doesn't move again. I don't know what he'll do tomorrow.

Maybe Flynn doesn't, either.

CHAPTER 29

THE IMPATIENT YELLING AND THE POUNDING OF THE audience's feet is nothing like the excited, festive rhythm I'm used to from the circus. This is violence and anticipation, brutality and expectation mixed into a thundering roar for blood.

Deep-seated aggression swells inside me. Adrenaline surges until my pulse beats like a drum in my ears. The heavy, loud thumping nearly drowns out the noise of the crowd.

"Cat's not interested in putting on a show, and neither am I," Griffin says. "No unnecessary risks."

"Nonfatal wounds when possible. Quick and clean," I remind everyone. "Let's get out of here fast and intact."

I glance at Jocasta. She has her own knives as well as Cassandra's leather upper-body armor and lightweight sword. Her wide, blue eyes are glued to a big splatter of blood in the center of the arena. There's a severed limb.

Her terrified gaze rises to find Flynn. "What if you were right?" she asks so quietly I barely hear her.

"Right or wrong doesn't matter anymore." He looks at her hard. "I'll protect you. You *know* that."

She nods, but then her eyes swing back to the bloody stump.

The gate across the arena from us rattles. They let us out first, which I think means the Gameskeepers consider us the weaker team. It's more fun to see us sweat.

The name we gave our team flows like an undercurrent around the arena, spoken by many beneath the rowdy cries.

Elpis. The personification and spirit of Hope. There are enough people here that know the old language and legends to dig up the truth behind Elpis, and they're probably confused, given the setting, but to us, it makes perfect sense.

Elpis. The word seems to swell in the air until it's all I can hear, even though the shouts for blood are infinitely louder.

Pandora opened her box and filled all worlds with plagues and misery and the potential for evil. But one thing remained—steadfast, unshakable, not flying from the box.

Elpis.

Thalyria has suffered. We will all suffer before we win these Games, but no team here will break us. For what is Hope if not unbreakable? And what is Hope if not the natural extension of suffering, that which eventually overcomes?

Gears grind, metal clanks, and the far gate begins to rise. I tense, ready to spring into action.

"This is just another fight," I say. Albeit carefully orchestrated for the most potential blood loss and carried out in front of a sanguinary, paying audience.

"And we've seen plenty of those." Kato grips his mace, showing no fear.

I quickly take in the rest of my team. Flynn with his ax, a short sword in his other hand, his wild auburn hair pulled back with a leather tie, and his eyes still on Jocasta. Jocasta looking back up at Flynn, her lips white and her face gray. Carver, long, lanky, and ready, his sword just another part of his arm, his sharp eyes focused on the jangling gate.

And then there's Griffin. No man ever wore weapons better—or looked more ready to use them.

Griffin's eyes meet mine. He pins me with his granite stare. "Don't take any hits to the middle."

Frowning, I say, "Uh, okay. You either."

His beautiful mouth flattens. "Or anywhere else, for that matter."

Nodding, I turn back to the front. Six competitors are fanning out on the far side of the arena, already moving toward us. All men. Four are burly and wearing a lot of blades. Number five is in a long, voluminous cloak, and the sixth one carries only a sword. No creatures.

The gong sounds, signaling the start of our round. The imminence of battle slams into me like a Centaur's kick, and my fingers tighten around my knives. I straighten to my full height, which isn't much, and take a deep, steadying breath. Here goes nothing. Or possibly everything.

"Did I ever tell you that I kicked a Giant's ass with only a throwing knife?" I ask loudly enough for the competition to hear.

Griffin shakes his head.

"I was eleven. I was eye-level with its shins."

The six men stop twenty feet from us, taking our measure. Two look like Tarvans, not quite as sun-browned as Sintans and not quite as olive-toned as Fisans. They're marked with the swooping, archaic symbols of ward lines, drawn across their foreheads. I recognize a broad-spectrum block, geared mainly toward Elemental Magic. If I gain any magic during this fight, I can't use it on them. It's too dangerous, knowing how wards corrupt my power.

My eyes flick over the rest of the team. Fisan, or at least I think so. Two of the men are of slightly smaller build and probably Magoi. The one completely covered in a dark cloak is carrying a wooden staff. I hate staffs. They're either pretentious and purely for show, or else they carry a wallop I don't even want to think about.

The cloaked man steps forward and pushes his hood back,

revealing lank brown hair and mud-green eyes. Definitely Magoi. Moderately powerful. The staff is for show.

His swampy gaze widens when he gets a good look at the clear bright-green of my eyes, the only part of my face not hidden by cosmetics and kohl. I bare my teeth in a mockery of a smile. *That's right. I'm going to walk all over you.*

But he smiles back, which I don't like at all.

He looks right at me. "I've got something up my sleeve." Chuckling, he opens his cloak.

I gasp, revolted. He's crawling with spiders, completely covered from neck to toes in a moving, scuttling blanket of little black beasts. They're furry in places and the size of full, ripe olives. They crawl all over each other, pushing and sliding and bumping, because there are *layers*.

A collective groan of disgust sweeps the arena. Then the whooping, cheering, and hollering begin again.

The Magoi throws me a vicious sneer. He raises his hands, and the spiders split into two racing currents that disappear into his billowing sleeves. An instant later, they fly from his outstretched arms, shooting straight toward me on a strong, unnatural wind. The second Magoi raises his head for the first time—bright-green eyes. The Elemental Mage's wind slams into me along with a horde of prickly spiders.

They hit me everywhere at once and then converge on my neck and head. Hopping like a maniac, I drop my knives and start ripping them off me, but a tight, sturdy web forms in seconds, circling my throat. I start to panic, mainly due to a life-long loathing of anything creepy-crawly or slithery. They're in my eyes. Pinching my ears. Scraping my scalp. Up my nose. In my mouth. *Oh my Gods!*

Other hands start tearing the spiders off me, but there are too many, and they just keep coming back.

Before I can't breathe anymore—or they start biting me—or something equally awful—I force myself to calm down and stop howling. This is compulsion, and this Magoi is only powerful enough to drive nearly mindless spiders. About a million nearly mindless spiders, but I won't think about that. I'm stronger than he is. I can make his spiders eat each other—or him.

Griffin shouts my name. His hands are all over my neck and face, flinging spiders off me. They're so thick I doubt he even knows about the noose. I keep my eyes closed, but even so, it's like the middle of a pitch-black night. They cut out all light.

The web suddenly jerks on my neck. The spiders drop, and daylight hits my face in a blinding flash. The army of arachnids yanks me off my feet, racing as one toward the Magoi. I grab the noose, struggling to get my fingers under it as I bump over the rough sand, gasping for air.

"Cat!" Griffin lunges for me, missing me by mere inches.

The brute force of the opposing team chooses that moment to spring into action and leap over me, cutting me off from the others. Griffin ducks a ferocious swing and then comes up in an explosion of muscle and steel. Metal clangs, men grunt, and utter mayhem breaks out.

Scraped raw by the sand, I tumble to a stop at the Magoi's feet, only a trickle of air still making its way down my throat. His knife flashes above me, but I wrap my free arm around his ankles and jerk hard. I don't have the leverage I need to pull him over. He stumbles, though, and I pivot on my hip, getting my feet between us and kicking out. Grunting, he reels back. Spiders start crawling on top of me again. On my left, blades meet and shriek and slide off each other in a grinding cacophony of savagery and sound. There's the thud of leather and flesh. The first spray of red arcs through the air, and there's a moment of silent, breathless glee before the bloodthirsty crowd goes insane.

The spider-controlling Magoi raises his long, curved knife again, an ugly smirk curling his upper lip. I make a rude hand gesture, smirk back, and then disappear.

Shock registers on his face. The audience gasps. The Magoi still jabs downward, but his moment of hesitation gives me the time I need to roll away, crushing spiders underneath me.

With one hand still dragging at the noose, I scramble to my feet and put some distance between us, bringing a slew of now invisible spiders along with me. They dangle from the web, cling to my arms and clothing, and make my skin twitch and itch. I squash some underfoot, cringing at the revolting, crunching pop.

Taking a knife from my belt, I stop breathing while I carefully work the blade between my neck and the web. Blood drips down my throat from the shallow cut I can't avoid making. I push out, slicing the sticky fibers, and then gulp down air, accidentally sucking a spider into my mouth along with it. Gagging, I spit the awful thing back out.

Both Magoi turn sharply, and I fling the blood-stained noose away from me along with the spiders still attached to it. While the Fisans focus on the severed web, I silently circle the other way, getting behind them to assess the situation.

Griffin is fighting the two Tarvans at once. One is nursing a bruised or broken rib and a very bloody, mostly useless arm. The other is still dangerously intact. Kato and Carver have a Fisan each. Every strike is fierce and ear-splitting, bone-jarring blows coming from both sides in a brutal dance of strength, speed, and skill.

Flynn is hanging back to guard Jocasta when he should

be taking an opponent from Griffin. He can't leave her now, though, because with me out of sight and the spiders scuttling back to their master, the two Magoi focus on Flynn and Jocasta with malicious intent.

Mud-Eyes flicks his hand, and his terrible black army scuttles into motion. A wind picks up, propelling the spiders along.

Still invisible, I fumble to latch on to their tiny minds and turn them around. *Why did I never practice this!* The spiders are four feet from Flynn. Three. Two... *Time's up.*

I spring forward and slam the blunt end of my knife down on the Magoi's head. He crumples without a sound. The Elemental Mage gapes at his fallen teammate. Then his head jerks around, and his bright-green eyes search the empty space for me. I stop moving, not stirring a single grain of sand.

He lifts his hands, conjuring a fierce, circular wind. My still solid form alters the flow of swirling grit. He finds me almost instantly and jabs with his sword. I spin out of the way, drop, roll, and come up in the calm space around his body.

He turns in place, searching for a disturbance in the cyclone. I'm too close to him, and he brushes my arm. He lashes out. I swerve to avoid his blade and then plant my dagger in his sword arm, hitting close to the elbow joint. He can't lift his weapon anymore. I pop back into sight, pulling my knife out with a twist.

His eyes blaze with pain. Then burn with rage. The Elemental's mouth opens on the start of a snarled chant, and I punch him in the arm wound, cutting the spell short. He gasps. I grab his hair and drag his face down as my knee flies up. His nose cracks, and he staggers back, doubling over. The wind dies, and sand thuds to the ground. I shift my balance, spin, and kick him in the head. He crashes like a marble statue, blood spraying from his nose.

A quick check reveals the other Magoi still down and unconscious. I run toward Jocasta while shouting, "Go!" to Flynn. I'll protect her, and he can help Griffin better than I can.

Exchanging places with me, Flynn races into the fray. The injured Tarvan disengages from Griffin and deflects the first mighty blow from Flynn's ax. The force of it makes the man stumble. Flynn follows up with a brutal strike from his short sword, and his opponent drops and rolls away. Flynn stalks after him, his weapons raised.

Jocasta clutches my arm from behind. "Can't we do something?"

"Stay out of the way." I learned that lesson the hard way, thanks to the Hydra.

"Something else!" she cries.

I shake my head. "They're moving fast and turning a lot. It's risky to throw a knife. We're trying not to kill anyone, especially our own."

"But they're trying to kill us!"

I glance over my shoulder. Jocasta looks less terrorized than before. She's agitated and bouncing on the balls of her feet.

A slight bite creeps into my voice. "You get into one fight and start thirsting for blood?"

Her eyes widen. "No! I just want it over."

"Our men are better," I assure her. "If they were fighting to kill, it would already be done. But we're making a statement. Strength with mercy. The new beginning and all that."

Jocasta scowls. "Humph."

My thoughts exactly. Mostly.

The audience starts yelling, but it's nothing like the usual raucous cheers and jeers. I look toward the loudest of the noise. Left to their own devices, thousands of spiders are now climbing the divider between the sandy arena and the coliseum seating. They spill over the top in a seemingly endless, scuttling black wave. Screaming spectators jump up and scramble for higher ground. It's the beginning of a stampede.

My eyes return to the pit floor in time to see Carver sink his long blade into his opponent's abdomen. The thrust is clean, going all the way through without hitting ribs or spine. Carver slides his sword back out. White-faced, the Fisan holds his belly and keeps swinging through the pain. Carver parries, looking bored.

A kid screams, high-pitched and terrified. Turning again, I search the crowd. *Who would bring a child to the Agon Games?* I see him then. A boy. His small, dark head disappears, pushed down as bigger, stronger people race up the steps. I yell, pointing, which is completely useless, but then I see a sharp-faced man stop and haul the boy up before propelling him forward.

Suddenly seething—*kids at the Agon Games!*—I march toward the swarm of spiders. Jocasta follows, trying to drag me back.

"What are you doing?" she asks.

"Getting the spiders."

"What!" She digs in her heels. "Don't touch them!"

"I'm not planning to." I'm really, really not.

Jocasta leaps back, kicking out when a hairy straggler crawls over her boot.

"Stay behind me," I order. "Tell me if anyone's coming."

She turns without question, and I concentrate on one thought—urging the spiders back down into the pit. I don't feel anything at first, but then a tiny light starts to glow inside my head. Another flashes, then another, and another, and then so many so fast I can't keep track. They flood me in a bright, barely sentient rush, and I corral each minute spark of each minuscule brain. In a heartbeat, they turn into a cohesive, pulsating mass, ready to obey.

Come.

An undulating sea of black washes back over the wall. It rolls toward me, and then thousands of spiders are suddenly swarming up my body.

Screeching, I hop and dance like a deranged puppet, flinging them away. "Not to me! Off! Off! Off!" I give the glowing orb of spider consciousnesses inside my head a mental push, and they jump, evacuating like I'm on fire.

Jocasta shrieks, high-stepping back.

Spinning in circles, I slap at my body. They're all off me now, but I can still feel them. I shudder. *Everywhere.*

In a circle all around me, countless hairy legs spin and strain. Spiders twist, trying to right themselves while others crawl all over them in a mad rush for space and air. I inevitably crush some underfoot. They burst and ooze, and I wince, my stomach turning over violently. *Hate spiders! Ack! Ack!*

Still wiggling like an idiot and using completely irrelevant hand gestures, I mentally direct the spiders toward our opponents. They reach Flynn first and start climbing his legs. I flap my hands, yelling, "No! No! Not him!"

They drop and swarm the Tarvan instead. Distracted, the Tarvan leaves himself open. Flynn cocks back his big fist and knocks the man out with one punch.

The crowd roars in approval. The spectators closest to Jocasta and me have come back down and are swarming the barrier, just like the spiders, only without crawling over the top. They shout and point toward Griffin's fight.

That's where I was going anyway. I move the spiders toward Griffin's opponent. They're halfway there when pain bursts behind my eyes. I hiss and clutch my head. The spiders stop, and I feel their confusion like a slow blink in my mind.

There's a sharp pinch and then a yank that throws me off balance. The Fisan with compulsion is sitting up—and giving me an epic evil eye. He wants his spiders back.

Regaining his feet, the Magoi sends out a mental call that dims the light inside my head. One by one, the sparks extinguish, and the spiders flit from my grasp. The ones I lose start racing back toward me—and not in a friendly way.

I have a choice to make, and not much time to decide. Catch the spiders again. Or catch *him*. That's a line I've never crossed before, not on purpose, anyway. I was too young to put words to it at the time, but I remember the thick, oily dread, the polluted feeling, and how I shook when I understood what I could do. That I could control humans. That I was a rare and terrible breed. That I was just like Mother.

My sister Ianthe was a screaming baby. I was a terrified six-year-old who wanted her to be quiet before Mother stormed the nursery in a rage. I inadvertently commanded Ianthe to shut her mouth. A compulsion is different than just wanting or thinking something. There's a specific, conscious desire that you have to isolate, nourish into intensity, and then send out with a target in mind, but I didn't know that then. All I knew was that she had to be quiet, or we'd all pay—Eleni, me, and the little ones. Ianthe didn't eat or drink for three days and almost died before Thanos and I figured out what I'd done.

Six years old and already almost a killer. We grew up fast in Castle Fisa.

I look at the Magoi, still snipping and snapping at my mind like a little dog, ripping his spiders back one by one with an effort that makes him shake. I inherently know I could make him dance a jig and then run himself through with his own knife, but he's not worth corrupting one of the few parts of myself I've managed to keep pure.

As spiders swarm my legs, I envision a yank, like I felt from the other Magoi. I imagine plucking the glowing spider minds right from his brain and bringing them back to mine.

The Fisan screams. He starts convulsing. His eyes roll back, and he drops, blood dribbling from his ears and nose.

The crowd gasps, and my lips part in shock. I blink. I held back. I really did.

The spiders make for the barrier again, and people start to panic. I rein them in, easily this time, and then separate them into two swarming masses. Carver has his adversary on the ground, his sword at his throat, so I send the spiders further on. They hit Kato's and Griffin's opponents at the same time. Just a thought has the spiders encasing both adversaries in mountains of sticky webs. Immobilized, the men topple over—spiders *mostly* on top—and then about a gazillion beady, black eyes turn to me.

I grimace. *Good spiders. Gross, but good.*

They chitter happily, and my skin crawls.

Kato and Griffin cut air holes over the downed men's mouths, and a hushed silence falls over the arena. The crowd watches with bated breath. A dull murmuring begins. It turns into a clamoring that escalates with every passing second of inaction. Flushed faces, fevered eyes, pumping fists—the spectators are hungry for blood, and we're not giving it to them.

I look around, disgusted. They can starve.

Another full minute goes by—clearly, the Gameskeepers are wondering what in the Gods' names we're doing, too—before the gong finally sounds, barely audible over the frenetic chant of "Death! Death!"

I look at Griffin, and his sober expression reflects my thoughts. There'll be plenty of time for killing. We won't have another round like this, and we'll do whatever it takes to defend ourselves.

The gong sounds a second time, a long, low, metallic rumble. The third hit finally resonates, and until the eerie vibration stops, we can either finish off our adversaries permanently, our opponents can stay down, or they can get up again and keep fighting. If even one person on an opposing team is standing when the sound dies, the round goes on.

The man Carver ran through twitches, and Carver gives him a close enough look at the tip of his sword that the man goes cross-eyed. "Next time, the blade goes into your head. Healers have a harder time with that." Carver's tone is utterly amiable.

The man stops moving and keeps his hand pressed to his belly. The gong fades into silence. People grumble. Jeer. It gets louder. We deprived them of a slaughter, which is exactly what we meant to do. Not a single person is dead—I think.

Ignoring the energetic heckling, I run to Griffin. He lifts me high into the air and spins me around, his gray eyes shining.

I grip his shoulders, grinning. "I told you we'd walk through the first round."

He lowers me and then kisses me hard on the lips. "And you were right."

"Aren't I always?"

Chuckling, Griffin bends me over his arm and ravishes

my mouth so thoroughly I get dizzy and can't tell which way is up.

Wild cheering suddenly drowns out the lingering boos. Some of the spectators start to shout "El-pis! El-pis!" and I doubt they have any idea what they're really saying, but it catches on and sticks until our name is thundering around the arena.

Sure, now they like us. Violence. Sex. Satisfied.

Ugh.

"*You* are putting on a show," I say when Griffin eventually releases my mouth. I sound breathless.

He smiles. It's a devastating flash of teeth under a delectably hawkish nose. One of his eyes is blackening, making him look even more dangerous and piratical. "I am a crowd-pleaser."

Heat whips through me, singeing me all the way to my toes. "And a merciless teaser."

He lifts dark eyebrows. "So you *can* rhyme."

My mouth drops open. Griffin takes advantage by invading it all over again.

"What are you doing?" I squeak, feeling my face flame kalaberry-red. "There are thousands of people watching."

"Showing the world we're the Alpha couple. We work together. We don't indiscriminately kill." He sets me back upright, and I hold on to him for balance, light-headed from the way my heart is bouncing against my ribs. "And I also had a burning desire to kiss my amazing wife."

My flush spreads. "You're right, I am amazing. And terrifying. And smart. And fierce. And—"

"Extremely modest, as usual."

I grin. "I know! That *is* one of my better qualities."

Griffin laughs, his face lighting up.

A dozen Gameskeepers jog out and begin gathering our

opponents, going to the more seriously injured first. The other team's healer lays his hands on the man Carver ran through as soon as he's off the sand. I hear the swordsman's pained grunt as they disappear into the tunnels below the arena.

The Fisan whose brain I accidentally squashed moans, causing us both to look over. *Oh, good. Not dead.*

"What happened there?" Griffin asks, tilting his head toward the Magoi being lifted up and carried away.

"I gave him a mental flick when he tried to get his spiders back."

"A flick?"

I nod.

"Good thing it wasn't a shove."

"True. I need practice."

He grips my hips, drawing me in close. "How does one practice that kind of thing?"

Uncaring that our team is gathering behind us, I fit myself against him, curves to planes, muscle to muscle. "Preferably without exploding anyone's brain."

Griffin laughs again, and I decide it's my favorite sound in the world. I could listen to it all day.

"I'm glad I'm immune," he says.

"I wouldn't practice on *you*," I huff, curling my hands around his neck. "Weren't you worried about me?"

"I'm always worried about you. But you have more tricks up your sleeve than the Kobaloi, and you're far too stubborn to let anyone knock you down and keep you there." He squeezes my waist. "Even with spiders."

I grin. "Look at that. You've finally learned how to sweet-talk me," I tease.

One side of Griffin's mouth kicks up higher than the other, but his eyes spark with something hotter than humor.

His voice lowers, for my ears only. "I know you inside and out, *agapi mou*, and it's not sweet you want."

Muscles deep in my belly tighten, reacting to his words and to the hint of dark gravel in his voice.

Griffin and I break apart when the gates clang again, and more officials arrive to escort us to our quarters. I recognize the scribe who registered our team, and he doesn't look happy.

"I need a big crate," I tell him.

His mouth pinches into a frown. "Competitors don't make demands."

"Fine. I'll let the spiders loose, ruin ticket sales, and probably cause widespread panic throughout the city." I flash my teeth. "Sounds like fun."

The man snaps his fingers. "Get her a crate!" His expression sours further. "You didn't mention compulsion, which is the only path to creature driving."

I shrug. "You didn't ask."

"Compulsion is generally considered offensive magic."

"Compulsion is neither offensive nor defensive magic." I quote one of the many tutors of my youth. "It's the Magoi's disposition that determines its bent." I stare the Gameskeeper down even though he's about a foot taller than I am. "He threw the spiders at us. I simply threw them back."

"With brain-hemorrhaging power."

"So?"

"And you disappeared."

Again... "So?"

"What else can you do?" His eyes narrow. "Who *are* you?"

Luckily, a big wooden crate arrives—an old weapons chest—saving me from answering. Not that I would have anyway. I herd the spiders into the chest, sever my connection with them, and then address the two men latching down the top. "Take them to the Fisan Magoi. If he's unable to care for them, bring them back to me." I'll figure something out. Maybe a trip to the woods when this is all over.

Assuming we live.

We exit the arena to a decent amount of cheering considering we barely drew blood, and I even hear a few calls of thanks for keeping the spiders under control. Flowers and tokens rain over the barrier. I pick up a long-stemmed purple blossom and then use it to salute the crowd as we pass under the gate. The applause grows deafening.

"Now who's putting on a show?" Griffin whispers in my ear.

Grinning, I elbow him in the ribs.

Carver snags my flower and gives it a sniff. Grimacing, he hands it back. "Can't you use the spiders in the next fight?"

"Initiating an attack would mean using offensive magic," the official answers for me, eyeing me suspiciously. "Only return what comes at you first, or I'll have you eliminated."

I nod curtly, but I want to crow. In front of several Gameskeepers, he just sanctioned my use of other Magoi's creatures, and even their magic.

Selena precedes us back to our suite. She ushers us inside, closing the door on the curious Gameskeepers with an imperious command to bring food. They don't even think about arguing.

She takes in the scrapes and bruises she'll need to treat, coming to me first. Her gentle touch on my cheek and jaw sinks hot pinpricks of healing magic into my skin. "You bled where you scraped through the sand. And here." A long, smooth finger traces the cut on my neck where I sliced through the web.

I try not to wince as Selena's magic bites and stings,

healing me quickly. "For the first time in my life," I say, "I really don't care."

Arching perfect dark-blonde eyebrows, Selena moves to the sand-encrusted scrapes on my arms, washing them with water first. My elbows are a mess.

"She'll know where you are," she says.

"Mother will wonder what I'm doing here. It'll drive her crazy."

Selena smiles faintly, and I grit my teeth when she concentrates on a particularly raw spot. She's so powerful that the whole process is over quickly.

"Done." Straightening, Selena touches first my chest and then my forehead. The currents of magic in her fingertips offer sweet sensations now—home, shelter, peace— things I've only ever felt with her or with Griffin. Her scent washes over me, soft rain on new leaves, the freshness rejuvenating. Her bottomless gaze roams my painted face. "Shadows to light." Her expression is both wry and a little sad. "He might be good for you after all."

My heart beats faster. A sudden tightness grips my chest. *Has Selena decided to approve of Griffin after all?*

She turns to Griffin next. "Excellent idea with the kissing. The crowd needed a reason to get behind you. You were boring them to tears with the lack of brutality and bloodshed." She heals a shallow gash on his upper arm and then moves to the bruise darkening his left eye and cheekbone. The skin is split. "Unexpected mercy, romance, mystery… They appeal to even the most fickle and violent of hearts."

Selena slowly circles Griffin, satisfying herself there's nothing else. Griffin inclines his head in thanks. She nods back without any irony, which I assume means the Underworld has, in fact, frozen over.

Carver and Jocasta have no injuries at all. Selena moves on to Kato and then to Flynn, smoothing out bruises and cuts. These small fixes take almost nothing out of her, which is good, because next time will be worse.

I lean against Griffin while she works, settling my cheek on his solid chest. He took off his leather armor, and I can hear the low, steady thump of his heart. "I'm offended that you kissed me out of strategy."

His arms close around me, and ribbons of heat wind through my body.

"It was pure torture." His eyes glitter like the first stars at dusk as he lowers his head and presses his lips to mine.

CHAPTER 30

GRIFFIN SLAMS INTO ME, LOCKING HIS ARMS AROUND MY torso. The impact from the full force of his hard body jars the air from my lungs and propels me backward through the pelting rain. He twists, and his back slams into the sodden ground. His grunt hits the top of my head, and then he rolls, ending up like a lead weight on top of me.

Metallic feathers pepper the wet sand where I just stood, their serrated edges flashing in my peripheral vision. The harsh, tinny sound of more feathers sliding loose somewhere above us in the arena grates in my ears. The huge, relentless Stymphalian Bird is about to rain down more blades.

Griffin cages my head with his arms, leaving no part of me exposed. Metal sings, and blades splat into the muck around us. Griffin hisses air in through his teeth, and then something warm starts spreading over my hip.

My heart jumps up and punches me in the throat. "How bad?" I ask.

"Not bad," he grits out.

Men always say that. I free a hand from underneath him and then carefully run it over his side. His breathing changes when I hit the long, lethal feather. It's low on his waist and goes straight through the side of his leather armor to plant its sharp tip in the sand. Most of the blade missed. If I were any wider, it would have sliced me, too.

"Bone?" I ask. It's close to his lowest ribs.

He shakes his head.

I grip the feather between my thumb and forefinger, holding it awkwardly to avoid the razor-edged sides. "I've got it. Shift left."

Griffin slides sideways off the edge of the blade. I leave it in the sand. There's nowhere I can hold the creature's metal feather that won't slice my hand to bits.

Griffin twists his head to search the dull sky. Rain runs in rivers off his face and onto mine. "It's circling for another pass."

He pumps up off me, grabs my hand, and we rise together. The dark stain on his side makes my stomach clench, but Griffin looks like he doesn't even feel it. We run hand in hand, and the crowd, dry under their festive, multicolored, oiled awnings, erupts into wild cheering.

The sight and sound sicken me. The mix of pageantry and violence, so like the daily punishment of life in Mother's court, turns my stomach in a way little else can. In both places, murder is a sport, and the trophy is prestige, gold, and the fear you put in other people's eyes.

The audience seems to love us, though, which I suppose I should feel some satisfaction about. Griffin and I became the darlings of the arena overnight—lovers in the Games, northern Magoi and southern Hoi Polloi, Fisan and Sintan, flouting convention left and right. Their unexpected, enthusiastic support, overriding even their initial thirst for blood, proves what Griffin has been saying all along. Thalyria *is* ripe for a change, and Thalyrians are hungering for a new reality, whether they realize it or not. While old prejudices run deep, especially among the Magoi minority, it took one relatively boring combat for many of the people gathered in Kitros for the Agon Games to conceive of something different and then throw themselves behind it—behind *us*.

Of course, it would be more gratifying if I weren't

certain they'd love to see us suffer horribly before we ultimately triumph.

I look away from the cheering spectators before I do something rash and rude and search for the Stymphalian Bird against the clouds. The creature is the same color as the knife-metal sky, as fast as thunder, and has been easily keeping Griffin and me separated from the rest of our team. We've spent this entire round so far diving out of the path of deadly feathers and sprinting in the opposite direction of where we need to be.

As I sweep the arena for signs of the bird, my eyes snag on the royal box. The Tarvan royal family is in attendance this time, having come the handful of miles from Castle Tarva to neighboring Kitros. No one is smiling in the luxurious, sheltered seats. Unsurprisingly, the royals look downright hostile, and they're watching Griffin and me with blatant antipathy.

The heavy rain obscures my vision, but something pulls at my gut and makes me look more closely at a woman in the back. She's young, maybe eighteen. She stares at me, her hair snapping on the damp wind and tangling into a mess. She doesn't move. She doesn't care.

Familiarity slams into me like a tidal wave, drowning me in sudden shock. Her hair is the darkest of browns. Long, wild waves fly out from under a circlet woven with what I know must be fat Fisan pearls. Her nose is straight and long, her back stiff, her frame small yet generous. Details I haven't laid eyes on in over eight years surge out at me, or maybe my mind supplies them automatically, because even from a distance, I know she looks just like me. Thick-lashed, elongated eyes that are a shade brighter than spring leaves. Dark, slashing brows. A firm chin that juts out in almost perpetual defiance. Shoulders that curl inward when she's scared. And lips that lift naturally at the corners, giving her an expression of secret, closely guarded humor when nothing about her life is funny.

A violent mix of emotions propels something savage through my breast. Looking at that young woman, I suddenly feel capable of the kind of destruction that can tear a world apart. I burn to start with this arena. I physically ache to stop what's sure to become a bloodbath and to take the look of permanent dread out of one Fisan girl's eyes. Mostly, I want to rip into myself. I failed her. Utterly.

"Cat!" Griffin shouts.

He's right next to me, but he sounds far away. I breathe shallowly, in a rapidly narrowing void. My vision tunnels, shadowy around the edges, my little sister imprinted like a pinprick of pain in the blinding middle. Six years my junior, always hiding in Eleni's room because she was scared of the boys. They were horrid to her. They were horrid to everyone.

"I left her." Light-headed, I reach for Griffin's arm. "Eleni would never have left me behind."

Griffin frowns. Then he whips around. He pushes me behind him and then wields his sword in a deadly arc, hitting the huge Stymphalian Bird with a jarring, metallic clang.

My whole body jerks in shock. My hearing sharpens, and my eyes focus again. I turn and see the lethal creature spinning off to one side. It recovers before it hits the sand and then swoops back up with a piercing cry.

"What happened?" Griffin growls. "Where did you go?"

He just saved my life. Again. His hair is soaked through and curling around his face and neck. Rain drips from the ends, streams from his nose and chin.

Swallowing, I blink water from my eyes. "Ianthe is here."

Griffin's eyebrows slam down. "She won't recognize you."

My cosmetics are layered on, and the kohl around my eyes is an exotic, sweeping disguise that flares outward toward my temples like a swirling tattoo. It won't wash off in the rain. It doesn't matter. The woman in the royal box is still looking at me, her fists clamped against her middle, her face stark-white, and her mouth half open. She looks on the verge of a scream.

"She knows. She could betray me at any time." To the Tarvan royals. To the world.

Griffin's eyes turn a steely gray that matches the storm-dark sky. He grips my elbow and starts moving. "One problem at a time," he says, rushing us toward our team.

Thunder rumbles, dulling the thuds and grunts coming from the opposite side of the arena. I squint through the curtain of rain. Jocasta has her knives out, but I haven't seen her take a shot. Her back is to the wall. Carver, Kato, and Flynn are in front of her, but they're outnumbered and struggling without Griffin and me. They're facing Fisans and Fire Magic, and if it weren't for the soaking wet conditions, they'd probably be dead.

We're halfway to our teammates when dully glinting wings, a strident call, and the blade-sharp ring of feathers sliding loose force us off course again.

I swat rain from my eyes, frustration and fear driving a foul curse from my mouth. "I don't know how to kill it!" I've lost all but one knife in the bloody swamp that is now the arena, and Griffin has hit the creature a dozen times all over its armored body. We haven't found a single chink.

"Then get control of the bird!" Griffin shouts over the downpour.

"I'm trying!" So far, my efforts at compulsion have slid right off, doing the sum total of giving me a pounding headache. I can't latch on to the bird, and I haven't had any success in wresting it away from the Magoi driving it, either. She's too strong. And I can't concentrate when we're constantly under attack.

Like Griffin's shadow, I stick close to him as he keeps the creature at bay. Feathers slam down, and we dart left, then right. He knocks a serrated blade away with his sword, sending it flashing end over end. A few steps later, Griffin yanks me into him. My braid follows a split second later, and another feather slices off the end, taking the leather tie and about five inches of hair. I gasp, a shot of pure adrenaline jolting my pulse into overdrive.

My hand gripped fast in his, Griffin takes off again as my braid starts to unravel. "Too close, Cat!" he snaps over his shoulder, fear for me sharpening his tone.

I race after him, breathing hard. "Not everyone has wings on their feet! Just Hermes—and apparently *you*!"

He scowls, still holding on to me. We stop and track the bird as it spirals back around, preparing for another pass.

"Catch the bird like you did the spiders," he barks over the rain.

"Spiders are stupid!" I bark back. "And their driver was unconscious when I latched on to them. This is a magical creature and a team member in its own right. It's not the same!"

Griffin makes a series of quick, preemptive strikes, driving the bird back up into the storm before it can unleash more feathers. "Then we take out the Magoi controlling it." His eyes flash briefly to mine, hard as rocks. "By any means."

I nod, more easily resigned to the thought of killing than I should be. Maybe because I've had so much practice.

We sprint across the arena again. Rain pelts the top of my head. My sopping hair bounces against my back and tangles with my arms. The reddish-brown muck drags at my boots, slowing me down. My foot catches on something left over from a previous fight, and I pitch forward, landing on my hands and knees. I sink up to my wrists in a revolting puddle, my loose hair swinging down into the gruesome sand. My stomach turns over hard. I wrench my hands free and scramble to my feet.

Ahead of me, Griffin stops and turns around. "Faster!" His voice whips past me on the driving wind. A cloud bursts overhead, and rain shatters down.

"Where's the bird?" I yell over the sudden, violent downpour. I can't see our team anymore. Our enemies. Anything!

A metallic nightmare materializes just above me from out of the storm. I throw my arms over my head an instant before the Stymphalian Bird's bronze beak jabs down with bone-jarring force.

Mother of Zeus! Fire races across my right hand. I snatch it down, cradling it against my stomach as the monstrous bird swoops back up, disappearing into the rain again.

Griffin races back to me, lifts my hand, and inspects the wound. He curses violently. There's a two-inch gash. It's deep. In some places, I see bone. Rain washes the blood away as quickly as it appears, adding to the stains around us.

I press my lips together and breathe roughly through my nose, the short bursts not giving me enough air. I try to make a fist. Only my thumb moves, and throbbing heat explodes toward my elbow, making me gasp.

I look at Griffin, my eyes wide. "I can't hold a knife." Or a sword. Or even hit—my left hook isn't worth thinking about.

His mouth thinning, Griffin scans the clouds for the Stymphalian Bird. Not seeing it, he takes the time to rip a strip from the bottom of his tunic and then wrap it around my hand, tying it tightly.

"You can throw with your left," he says, letting go of my injured hand.

"I'm not as accurate."

"You'll still be better than everyone else."

Tingling, burning warmth climbs steadily toward my shoulder, and a new seed of fear sprouts in my belly. *Poison?* My whole arm feels heavy.

Jocasta cries out. We both turn toward the sound and start running just as the rain eases back to a steady but not so blinding downpour. I hold my bandaged hand hard against my chest, trying not to jar it. White-hot pain pulses from the wound. Air whistles between my clenched teeth.

The Stymphalian Bird doesn't intercept us this time, and we get a better look at what's happening with the others. Carver is locked in a fierce battle with another swordsman, their blades so fast and fluid my eyes can't keep up. It's the first time I've seen Carver truly challenged in a one-on-one fight, and the whining, sliding, and striking of metal is constant and deafening, even over the pounding rain.

Flynn is farther away, beating back a second warrior wielding a variety of blades. His ax sings a funeral dirge with every ferocious swing, his short sword filling in the gaps. His opponent takes a step back, then another. The man stumbles, his knees buckling under the brutal assault. Fury mottles Flynn's hard-set face. His eyes are murderous, and the same violent urge rises in me when I see why.

A long knife sticks out of Jocasta's thigh. There's another one in her left shoulder. They match the set still on the warrior's belt. I can see Jocasta shaking from here. Her teeth clatter from shock. Blood turns the sand at her feet the color of wet clay.

Snarling a curse, Griffin starts to outpace me again.

"Trial by fire!" I shout after him. "Look at her. At the knives. She's okay." Relatively speaking, anyway.

It's Kato who worries me right now. He's surrounded by two men and a woman, all Magoi, and he's a bloody, blistered mess. The woman is hanging back. She's the one driving the bird. There's a circle of fire around her, burning hot and high in spite of the rain. That won't stop me from getting to her. It won't stop Griffin, either.

The other two Magoi are wielding different types of fire. One is throwing balls of it from his hands. The other is able to turn his whole body into a weapon. Flame coats his skin and, by extension, his sword.

Fire is the most common type of magic. What makes the difference is how hot it burns, and how long a Magoi can keep it going. Some Magoi have only a few minutes of power in them before they have to retreat and recharge. Others can go on and on. These men are somewhere in the middle, but they're taking turns attacking, so they never let up.

I head straight for the fire wielders before the bird can drive us back again. I'm going to take their magic, which means getting burned.

My whole body tenses. *Once burned. Twice. Three times. Four...*

The taller Magoi, a man with long blond hair so pale it's almost white, throws a flaming ball at Kato's head. Worn down and slow to move, Kato only twists enough to avoid getting hit in the face. The fireball explodes where his shoulder meets his neck, leaving a ragged circle of blistered flesh. Kato groans and staggers sideways before falling to his knees.

The pain in my hand and arm fades in the face of sudden

panic. I start to sprint. Griffin keeps moving toward his sister until a sharp call and a metallic clank ring out behind us. He whirls but shouts for me to keep going, so I don't stop running as the Stymphalian Bird dives at us again. Behind me, wings beat the air with a tinny sound I'm pretty sure is going to replace my usual recurring nightmare. Then there's a battle cry I know well, a piercing shriek, and a sickening crunch.

I skid to a stop, turning at the same time. My gut clenches in fear. Griffin is on his back with the Stymphalian Bird squawking above him. *He impaled it!* But the bird's lethal wings pound all around him, slicing his skin to shreds. Its tail feathers lacerate his legs, and the bronze beak, sharp and hooked, snaps dangerously close to his face and neck.

Oh Gods! I can't let it bite him. It's poisonous. I know because I can barely feel my right arm.

Griffin holds the enormous bird above him. His arms strain. The hilt of his sword presses into his chest, all those sharp, churning feathers not even a full sword's-length away. Their frantic beating doesn't give Griffin a chance to shield himself, or even to get a foot up to kick the creature away.

I start back toward him with no idea what to do about a metallic bird that's as big as I am and a whirlwind of blades. Then Kato calls out for me, a ragged sound that tears my eyes from Griffin. I turn. The flaming Magoi steps in and strikes with his blazing sword. Kato deflects the first blow from his knees, but the second one sinks deep into his abdomen. My heart lurches. Kato's face drains of what little color it had left as the Magoi shifts his balance and kicks. His burning boot crashes into Kato's hip and throws him off the blade. Kato hits the sand on his back, and the Magoi raises his sword.

My blood ices over. I have one knife, a left hand, two men, and no time.

I'll be useless against the bird, so I slide my last blade from its loop and throw, letting instinct take over the motion. The Kobaloi knife hits the Magoi in the neck, just below his ear, sinking straight to the hilt. My aim felt off, but the knife struck true. The man falls, his flames extinguishing.

Kato's head lolls to the side. His eyes meet mine, glazed with pain, and he says my name. I can't hear it over the crowd and the rain, but I read it on his bloodless lips.

"Hold on!" I yell back.

Kato keeps looking at me. His throat works, like he's swallowing the idea of death.

I glance toward Griffin. He's a mess, but still holding his own.

The fireball-throwing Magoi turns on me. I head straight for him and take a direct hit to the chest. The top of my leather breastplate burns away. Sparks shower my neck, chin, and shoulders, and I hiss. He hits me again, and my exposed flesh blisters as breath-stealing pain sears me in a flash of hot red and angry black.

The need to end this round and get us all out of the arena alive overrides the pain as my body absorbs the magic, learns it, and then begins to heal. Fire ignites in my left hand. The Magoi's eyes widen in disbelief. *That's right. A magic thief.* Not something you see every day. Or ever.

I throw, and he ducks. *Damn it! I missed.*

I throw again, and again, wasting the magic I've gained because he's fast and I'm lumbering toward Kato with an increasingly useless right side. My foot drags through the boggy sand. My arm hangs limp at my side. I don't even feel the hole in my hand anymore. Finally, when I'm standing protectively over Kato, I throw the last fireball I have in me and then squat to swipe a knife from Kato's belt.

Rising, I dart another look at Griffin. Blood runs in rivers down his lacerated arms. Razor-sharp wings crash into the sand, his arms, his sides. Griffin tries to bring his legs up to push the bird back with his feet, but the creature curves its tail feathers under and loosens a triumvirate of blades into his upper thighs. Griffin throws his head back and howls.

My emotions flatten into deadly calm. This ends *now*.

I take aim at the fire thrower as he turns on Flynn, who just planted his ax in his previous opponent's chest. Leaving his preferred weapon behind rather than take the time to dislodge it, Flynn rushes the Magoi, speeding up as he tosses his short sword from his left hand to his right.

A fireball flies from the Magoi's hand. Flynn dives, rolls, and rises without ever slowing down. He charges like a Centaur, his big shoulders bunched, his auburn head lowered, his strong feet kicking up sand.

Backpedaling, the Magoi gathers another blaze in his palm. Flynn bears down on him with death in his eyes.

I draw my left arm back, cursing the lead weight of my right side. My balance feels off, and my sense of where my body is and how it should be moving has been annihilated. Cold sweat dots my brow. I send out a hurried prayer to Poseidon as I stiffen my wrist, my blade reflecting the lightning streaking across the sky.

A knife lands in the Magoi's chest, but it's not mine. I didn't let fly. He stumbles, and his fireball implodes before he can launch it at Flynn.

Jocasta throws a second knife. Her aim is bad. Her feet aren't right because she's favoring her injured leg, and she lets go too soon. The knife still sinks into the Magoi's chest next to her other one.

Kobaloi. Tricky little creatures. Suddenly, I really do believe the sinew wrapping the hilts of our knives retained some of the Kobaloi's innate magic. I missed when I was aiming at Titos and then hit the flaming Magoi when I thought I wouldn't. Another Kobaloi knife just corrected Jocasta's faulty throw. They were shockingly expensive, but not such a worthless purchase after all.

The fire thrower drops to his knees, dragging in a breath that will never fill his lungs or satisfy his craving for life. I limp past him as he hits the wet sand face-first. No hope of air there.

The rain tapers off, then stops altogether. The crowd is going wild. Carver swings his sword one final time, the tight arc severing his opponent's head. Before the man even hits the ground, Carver is running toward Griffin at a speed no human should be capable of.

Griffin has help, so I turn to our final adversary apart from the bird. Eliminating her may be the only way to stop the creature. The knife in my hand has only one target now, and she's behind a thick, burning wall so high I can't see her to take aim.

Hardening my resolve, I move toward the flames and then limp straight through them, taking a breath of fire. Silence descends on the arena, making the roar of the blaze in my ears and my inevitable scream that much louder. My clothes are too waterlogged to go up in flames, but they heat and sizzle and steam, burning me anyway. My skin reddens, blackens, blisters. My hair crackles and glows. My eyes feel like glue. The rest of me is an inferno.

Bathed in agony, I draw magic deep inside. It burns through me until it becomes mine. My body shifts—readjusting, healing, overcoming—and when I emerge from the flames, I'm upright, I'm breathing, and I can see.

With the influx of new power comes knowledge. This is Phoibos's Fire. Rare. Uniquely Fisan as far as I know. Named after the Magoi who helped an ancestor of mine annex a chunk of Tarva during a Power Bid. They pushed the Tarvan border back enough to steal three great cities. Sykouri resisted. My ancestor let his army plunder the metropolis and then ordered it burned to the ground with most of its population trapped inside. Phoibos's Fire is one of the hottest, fastest burning fires known to man and Gods alike, outdone only by Dragon's Breath and matched only by the flaming exhales of certain deadly Drakons.

My boots crunch over sand heated into glass. Old fears make my heart pound. I just announced to the world that I can steal magic. That I can walk through an Elemental Mage's fire and live. I am an anomaly. I am stupefying. Terrifying.

The crowd is still hushed. Too much attention. Too many eyes. Too much expectation. My life now—mine and Griffin's.

"You have one chance," I tell the Fisan Magoi. "Call off the bird." My voice rolls from me with a low, thundering pitch. It carries, louder than it should be with power I don't understand. Movement in the arena haunts my peripheral vision, thousands of people cringing at once. Their fear doesn't make me happy, but it somehow feels right. It's *my* right.

The female Magoi stares at me with a mixture of horror and fascination. She draws a sword. It's about the same length as mine, which I leave on my back. She takes a careful step away from me, wary of her own fire. Her straight brown hair wafts on currents of heat.

"Who are you?" she asks.

A seductive, dark part of me wants to push into her mind. To order her. Punish her. Make her bleed like Griffin is bleeding. I haven't been able to wrench the bird from her. Maybe I'll just wrench her.

My thoughts are steeped in bitterness. Wouldn't that make Mother happy? The Agon Games ripping my conscience to shreds.

"I am mercy, but I am also death. Call off the bird."

She doesn't move, but her flames suddenly slam into my back, engulfing me.

I feel no pain, just more magic, and my lips twist in a feral smile. Power is a whirl of color and heat. Fire rides my skin. I inhale it deep into my lungs. This magic is mine now. It can't hurt me, and yet I could turn it back on her and melt her down to bone.

The look on her face tells me she knows it. Her flames crawl higher, burn hotter. I step out of the blaze before my clothing disintegrates. I won't let Griffin suffer a moment longer.

Floating on a magic charge helps me forget the lead weight of my body. My fingers tighten around Kato's knife. The metal is hot, but the grip is wrapped, allowing me to hold on to it. Even with my left hand, my aim is good. Perfect even. Right in the eye—soft, easy to penetrate. Ending. The woman falls backward, carried over by the knife's momentum. An instant later, her flames snuff out, leaving me suddenly cold.

I turn and nearly run into Flynn and Jocasta. *Were they trying to reach me? Through a wall of fire?*

Seeing them and the anxiety in their eyes snaps some of the threads holding me together and saps my courage. I want to fall into Flynn's arms. I want him to carry me because I'm so heavy and tired, and my feet don't work like they should.

Instead, I drag myself toward Griffin as fast as I can. Carver is banging away at the bird, but his blade slips off the armored feathers. The only chink seems to be in its underbelly, and the huge metallic bird is still thrashing over Griffin. The hilt of Griffin's sword pounds into his chest with each powerful beat of the creature's wings. His arms shake, and there's a terrifying amount of blood.

My feet tangle up in each other, and I nearly fall. Flynn catches my elbow, but I shake him off, not willing to lean on him, not even looking at him. Believing I need help is the beginning of the end.

"I have a plan." I stumble forward, counting on will-power and sheer insanity to get me through.

"What plan?" Flynn sounds distraught. He sounds sick with worry.

I don't answer. He might try to stop me.

When I reach Griffin, my husband roars at me to get back. His cheeks and jaw are sliced to ribbons, like his arms, sides, and legs. Shredded clothing. Split muscle. Bone. But he's still fighting. He caught the bird so I could eliminate the Magoi. His strength amazes me. Honors me. I'm not sickened by his state. I'm impressed. The man I love endures. He is me, and I am him. We are forged of the same passion and violence, and we have hearts of iron.

"I know what to do." Magic leaps inside me. The ice shard around my neck throbs once, sending a shock of cold through my chest. It gives me strength. Griffin gives me courage.

"Get back!" he bellows. His grip slips on the blood-slicked hilt of his sword, and his face reddens as the ball at the base grinds viciously into his chest. His great, bloody arms tremble. "You swore to me!"

I swore to take only calculated risks. I calculated.

A final step puts me right behind Griffin's head. My left arm flies out as the Stymphalian Bird's head jerks up. Its black eyes meet mine, and I clamp my hand around its beak in the split second before its wings sweep forward and stab my arm.

Blades pierce both sides. Pain is sharp. Then hot. Then consuming. I grit my teeth and don't let go. *I can do this.* I force my focus away from my throbbing arm and search for the spark of consciousness I need to take inside me and overpower.

The bird wrestles its head down, pulling my hand down with it. It unleashes the metallic feathers from its crest, and three short blades slam into my abdomen.

The sound that explodes from my mouth is inhuman. Griffin cries out with me. Shadows pulse around the edges of my vision—a blackness that threatens us all.

Terrified of the growing dark, I look down. Griffin looks back at me, and I have light. But my light looks like his heart just broke.

I grip his eyes with mine like I grip the Stymphalian Bird's beak, simply refusing to let go. The heavy numbness on my right side spreads across my chest to my left shoulder. The blades in my left arm burn like the fires of the Underworld, and my upper abdomen is on fire. Not sobbing in agony defies human nature. But Griffin's eyes hold mine back, grounding me and enthralling me like every day since the moment we met.

"You are Catalia Fisa." In his words, I read a fuller meaning. He believes in me. He believes I can do anything I set my mind to.

I breathe again. Once. Twice. Selena is just beyond the gate. Our bodies will hold out because I'll give them no other choice. Survival is a mind-set. I will live. Griffin will live.

The spark I'd been searching for ignites in my head. The bird's consciousness merges with mine, and a concentrated point of magic bursts behind my eyes, blinding, then uncomfortable, then simply there.

"Retreat!" The command is louder in my mind than in my mouth. We don't know how to kill the Stymphalian Bird. A hole straight through it doesn't even make it bleed. The best I can do is force it to leave, eliminating our final opponent in the arena.

The creature stops thrashing. I draw more power like a breath, pulling it from my own body. Currents of magic move like lightning under my skin and thunder through my veins. My hair lifts on a strong wind, and the ground beneath my feet shakes as a thunderbolt cracks overhead. Flashes and rumbles follow even though it's not raining anymore. This is another storm.

People scream, and I smile. There's blood in my mouth. It coats my teeth. It tastes like victory.

I own the bird now, for as long as I choose. "Retreat."

Metallic feathers slide from my arm, pulling on muscle and grating through bone. I release the beak with a gasp. Griffin moans at the same time. Not for his own wounds. It's my pain that's too much to bear. My storm crashes to the pit floor with enough force to shake the venue. I stagger, falling into Jocasta. She catches me under my arms, but I hardly feel her. The venom from the bird's bite is dulling everything and turning my limbs to rocks.

"Go to Kato," I say. "Don't leave him alone."

Jocasta steadies me and then goes, limping and slowed by her own injuries.

Using their swords, Flynn and Carver push the bird off

Griffin's blade. The creature lands in the sand and then rights itself, bringing its lethal wings docilely against its sides. The hole in its body closes over. Metallic feathers regenerate. It cocks its head and looks to me for direction because my will is its entire world.

I stare back, suddenly seeing a kindred spirit in this unbreakable creature. It didn't choose to be here. It was caught and used. I can intimately relate.

"Go," I command. "Go to the Ice Plains and there, be free."

The Stymphalian Bird takes flight, its terrible wings slicing a whistling knife-song through the wind.

Griffin throws his sword aside and then rises partway. He pushes up on one elbow, but then his arm gives out, and he splashes back into a lake of his own blood.

I sink down next to him. His chest is one of the few places that isn't shredded, so I lay my head on it, my ear above his heart. The beat doesn't sound like usual. It's irregular, pounding. His large hand comes up to grip the back of my head.

I exhale magic and strength, unable to keep from losing both. My bones are anchors, my blood thick, my muscles like stones. I'm down now, and I'm not getting up. My vision dulls. Pain goes distant, which is never a good sign. I try to keep it alive in my mind, as if that will somehow keep the darkness away.

The first gong sounds. Two more, and then the Gameskeepers will come. Selena is close. I don't know what state Kato is in. Jocasta is injured. Griffin has lost a small person's worth of blood, and I...

I swallow with difficulty. "Did it bite you?"

"No." Griffin's voice rumbles beneath me. I want to be closer. I want to fall inside him and sleep.

"Why?" He sounds wary. And tired. And far away.

"Poison."

He grips me tighter. He doesn't know his own strength at times, but I don't care. His fingertips press into my scalp and tether me to him. To the world.

"You're stronger than poison. You're stronger than anything."

His faith in me is humbling. It's sometimes delusional, but not today. Today, I will live, because I am Catalia Fisa, and I do not break.

CHAPTER 31

GROANING, I STRETCH AND THEN FORCE MY EYES OPEN. OUR second combat was three days ago, and there's not a single part of me that doesn't still ache. Poison is the pits. Getting burned and stabbed isn't much fun, either.

I turn into Griffin's big, warm body. His cuts are healed, his split muscles knitted back together, his blood replaced by food and rest. His heart beats steadily under my ear.

It took some work to fix Griffin up, and the healing had to go painfully fast so he could stop bleeding. Selena easily closed Jocasta's stab wounds, which hadn't hit anything too terrible. Flynn and Carver were more or less fine. It's Kato who worries me. Even healed—and Selena only just got to him in time and treated him first—like me, he's still at half strength.

Testing myself for what must be the hundredth time in the last two days, I probe my body for Phoibos's Fire. I must have burned through my magic reserves with the compulsion, the storm, and then healing from my injuries, because there's nothing left. It's just me, and even my invisibility is dormant, walled up until I more fully recover.

Stifling a yawn, I keep my touch light as I smooth my hand over the hard ridges of Griffin's abdomen. I couldn't use Phoibos's Fire in the final round today anyway. The Gameskeepers would eliminate us for initiating offensive magic since I didn't declare any upfront. Still, it would have been nice to have something like that in reserve. Better to be kicked out of the Games than killed.

I close my eyes again, but thoughts of this afternoon keep me awake. Winning the final round wins us entry into Castle Tarva. It wins us access to the Tarvan royals without spilling any blood outside the arena. It's a good plan. A crazy, wonderful, terrifying plan. But even if we win the Agon Games, the fight won't end today in Kitros. The Tarvan royals won't go down easily, which is something we've all sort of ignored thinking about.

I take a deep breath. *One battle at a time.*

The sound of Griffin's steady breathing relaxes me enough to fall back toward sleep. Healing comes with extreme fatigue, for both the injured and the healer. Even Selena has hardly risen for two days.

Just when I'm drifting in a comfortable place, Mother's voice snaps me fully, harshly awake. *"The Agon Games? Really, Talia, that's something we watch, not something we involve ourselves in."*

Adrenaline floods my veins in a painful, heart-pounding rush. I search the room. She's not here, of course. She's in my head, and with the blood I've lost, my weakened state, and being geographically closer to Castle Fisa, it's a wonder I didn't hear from her before.

"I'm in it for the pot of gold." I shouldn't engage her in conversation. I should shut her out before she gets into my head in far worse ways than just the obvious.

Mother makes a tsking sound. *"You have gold here."*

There's a pinch and then a tug in my mind. I recognize it now, having done it myself to the spiders and the bird. This isn't just communication. She's trying to latch on. *"Hoping to buy me, Mother?"*

"Can you be bought?"

"If you must know, it's the prestige I'm after." Shockingly, that's part truth. A win gets us an audience

with the Tarvan royals. A spectacular win assures we'll be talked about and even revered. What better way to begin our campaign than to capture the hearts and imaginations of people across the realms?

"My spies in Kitros reported a young Fisan woman of great magic, strength, and courage. Fearless, they say. I would have known it was you even before I tracked your blood."

I hate the way her words affect me, that leap of pride in my stupid heart when all she's ever tried to do is destroy me little by little.

"What do you want, Mother?"

"You, of course."

A spasm entirely wrought of irrational emotions rips across my chest. How can she still do this to me? Am I really that weak? That needy? *"You can't sway me, buy me, punish me, or beat me into submission. You've already tried."*

"I can teach you to be a queen, powerful and feared. I'll make you what you're meant to be."

What I'm meant to be doesn't appear to be up for debate anymore, and it's not what Mother thinks. *"I'm already powerful, and I don't crave anyone's fear."*

"Come home, Talia." Her command drags heavily through my mind, pulling at places I need to preserve. I push back, protecting them.

"Do you honestly think your compulsion will work on me?" Despite the scathing tone I sink into my question, I know it could—if she were closer. But even then, I would put up a colossal fight.

She pulls harder, and pain blossoms behind my eyes. I resist, and the sharpness of her invasion lessens until she redoubles her efforts. Slicing heat arcs under my skull, but I don't make a sound. She'd hear it.

"You are Beta Fisa. You are the Kingmaker. You'll be a queen. I'll set you up in Tarva, and we'll be allies. Come home where you can play your part. Don't throw your life away on a Sintan dog, a usurper king only using you for your magic."

And there's the Mother I know and hate. *"I am the Kingmaker, but the king made himself. And I'm not just a queen, Mother. I'm the Queen."*

A moment passes, a long, heavily charged beat of silence. The pain in my head lessens, probably as a result of her shock. I just declared myself her rival and hinted at our intentions.

Finally, she says, *"You're nothing as long as you dance to the tune of that mangy hound."*

I snort softly. *That mangy hound* is the only reason I'm doing *anything.* *"What do you imagine would happen if I came home?"* I ask bluntly. *"That I'd dance to* your *tune? That I'd still let you abuse me and others, and that you'd eventually die peacefully in your own bed before I ever wore your crown? I knew you were insane. I didn't think you were stupid."*

Her voice ices over. *"You can't rival me. Trying would be your undoing. With you in Tarva, we'll both benefit."*

"We'll both benefit from your getting out of my head before I squash your brain."

Her laugh raises goose bumps on my arms. *"That would take more power than you'll ever have."*

I start pushing in earnest. *"I've seen the Plain of Asphodel. It's beyond dismal. I have a feeling you're going to have a nice, long vacation there."*

Mother forces a cyclone of power through our connection, and my vision momentarily goes dark. I feel a trickle of blood slide from my nose as my body starts to twitch under conflicting information. A very convincing part of my brain is telling me to leave the arena, get on my horse, and race to Castle Fisa.

I curl my hand around Griffin's arm. There's no way in Hades I'm leaving him, and she can't make me.

"I named my sword, Mother. I thought of you, and I named it." I throw a veritable tidal wave of power back.

This time, her laugh sounds strained. *"Is this where I'm supposed to ask what you named your paltry little sword, Talia?"*

Yes. *"I named it Thanatos."* Death.

I shove with all my might. There's a hiss of pain on the other side of our connection as I hurl my mother from my mind.

CHAPTER 32

I GLIMPSE IANTHE OUT OF THE CORNER OF MY EYE. Nervous as a sailor in siren-infested waters doesn't even begin to describe my little sister. Her eyes are wide and round, her hands clenched tightly in her lap. She's as stiff and straight as a cypress, and I have to wonder: Is she scared *for* me, or *of* me?

I want to race up the stone steps and drag her from the Tarvan royal box. Why is she even with them? Gods forbid she's betrothed to Alpha Tarva. As the only Fisan princess left, or so most people think, it's entirely possible. Galen is more than twice her age. He's a widower and a sneaky bastard who probably likes to poison people, including—if the rumors are true—his former wife.

But that's not my only problem. At the moment, it's not even my worst. There's a Cyclops on the other side of the sand. *A bloody Cyclops!* Why did anyone agree to this? No one should listen to *me*!

No wonder there's been so much blood in the arena. So many body parts all over the place. The creature is a house-sized colossus that tears people limb from limb. I'd be petrified even at full strength and with combat magic. All I have today are my knives, collected by the Gameskeepers after our last round, my sword, and about a hundred and ten pounds to put behind swinging it.

That and compulsion. Maybe. The episode with Mother this morning drained me, but after inhaling food like air, I might be strong enough again to manage creature driving.

Cyclops driving, I very much doubt. And I don't want to take that road anyway. It's a slippery moral slope.

Griffin forms a plan while I'm still standing there with my mouth wide open. "Most people use knives like swords, to slice and jab in close combat. They won't expect us to attack from a distance. Throw the second the gong sounds. Keep them back and keep them down, even if it means the kill. Then we take on the Cyclops."

I already have a knife in each hand. "I've got the two on the right." Instinct tells me they're powerful Magoi.

Griffin claims the burly one in the middle.

Carver shakes his head. "No good with a knife."

"Not from this distance." Kato grimaces. "I don't have the arm for it today."

Flynn's mouth turns down in a hard frown. He doesn't look confident, but he switches his ax to his left hand and then draws a knife with his right. "Far left. Then whoever can gets the last woman."

"The woman," Jocasta practically snarls, staking her claim.

Flynn's eyes flick to her. "No one's asking you to become a murderer, Jo."

"I already am," she says tightly. "And no one asked for your opinion."

"You'll get it anyway," he grates out.

Jocasta snorts. "That would require your talking to me instead of just glowering all the time."

He glares. She glares back.

"And on that happy note," I mutter under my breath, "we all might die."

Griffin slants me a pointed look. "Not today, Catalia Eileithyia."

He's confident and calm, even in the face of terrible odds.

Griffin doesn't add Fisa to my name this time. Apparently, I'm universal now.

I take a deep breath. It straightens my spine. "Not today." Because we all know saying it out loud makes it true.

The gong sounds. My pulse leaps, and my heart kicks me in the ribs. Instinct takes over, shoving aside nerves and leaving only the will to protect and survive. I let fly my first blade before our opponents even take a step. The woman I aimed for goes down, a knife in her throat. My second target is looking right at me, and in the time it takes me to cock back my hand and throw, he dives out of the way. Now, I'll have to get him on the run.

Griffin hits his mark. The stout man falls, Griffin's knife in his heart. Flynn misses his moving target and curses as he draws a second knife. Jocasta has yet to throw, and her target is charging, a wooden shield now blocking most of her torso.

The Cyclops hasn't moved. It doesn't have to. It's terrifying everyone just by being there.

I lock on to the way my man is moving. Quick steps, agile. Every three to four paces, he moves right while Jocasta's woman fans left. Are they trying to get around us? Herd us toward their monster?

One, two, three—throw! My knife sticks in my target's well-muscled shoulder. He wheels around to face me, more enraged than damaged, and I immediately throw again.

The small, round shield strapped to his left arm stops my knife at his eye-level. He rips my blade from the wood and then throws it back so fast he nearly catches me off guard. I twist, and the blade lands tip-first in the sand behind me.

A pained, feminine gasp makes my stomach take an anxious plunge. I spin, my eyes landing first on Jocasta and then on the woman she struck. They both look stunned, like neither of them quite believes what happened. Jocasta's knife is in the woman's pelvis, just beside her hip bone.

I wince. *What a place.*

"Got him!" Flynn shouts.

I whirl. An upper torso wound. Not fatal, although it might make breathing hard.

Griffin scoops up the Kobaloi knife near my feet and then throws it from down low. It hits Flynn's target under his chin, driving up into his head. The man drops, on his way to an abrupt heart-to-heart with Hades.

Three down.

Two humans left, both wounded.

One Cyclops.

Raising his battle-ax, Flynn closes in on Jocasta's woman. She's Tarvan, tattooed but not in the southern style, and a Magoi. Her eyes spark with magic an instant before Flynn's ax flies from his hand and lands at her feet, splashing sand up her legs.

A Metal Mage. *Son of a Cyclops!* She can take our weapons.

Surprised, but still moving toward her, Flynn draws his short sword before I can warn him to keep it sheathed. The Metal Mage makes a grasping move, wrenches it from his grip, and then sweeps her hand out with a quick, violent snap. The sword flies straight for Jocasta.

"Jo!" Flynn's cry is nearly lost in the deafening gasp of the crowd.

Jocasta dives to the sand and then pops back up with a shallow slice and a splash of blood on her arm. She doesn't look terribly injured. She looks livid. She draws a knife, and it immediately starts vibrating in her hand. Looking at the blade like it might bite her, she shoves it back into the loop on her belt, securing it.

Griffin and Carver both step in front of their sister. Flynn backs up until all three of them are between Jocasta and the Tarvan woman.

"Cat!"

I turn at Kato's frantic call, realizing I'd lost track of him.

My eyes widen, and I leap back, swallowing a scream. A massive snake looms over me. I draw my sword, and it rattles in my hand. I tighten my grip. I am *not* losing Thanatos with a gargantuan snake on top of me.

Its fangs elongate, curving into lethally sharp points. A bead of venom drips off one side, smoking when it hits the sand. I wheel back, finally getting a look at where it's coming from. The serpent sprang from the male Magoi's chest. I failed to kill him, and he hatched a snake out of his breast!

There's a pop and a rip. I cringe at the sound of splitting flesh. A second snake forms, growing fast in scaly fractals. The thick, muscled body hits the ground, taking its weight from the Magoi's chest while its already huge head lunges for me, quick as a whip.

I dive right, cartwheel with my sword in my hand, and then come up swinging.

Both snake heads rear back, hissing at me. The long necks twist, winding around each other, and then drop as one. I barely sidestep the reptilian bomb and then take a two-handed swing, hitting a fang and slicing it off half-way down.

Venom splashes my hands. *Mighty Gods on Olympus! That burns!* My skin smokes, turning an angry, cratered red.

Kato slams into the snake heads from the side, jarring them away from me. They lift and untwist. One strikes at him and the other at me. I swing my sword again, but the venom weakened my grip, and Thanatos flies from my hands before it can connect, collected by the Metal Mage.

I snarl a curse and scoot out of the snake's path, rolling along the scaly side of its head. As I turn, I whip out a knife and backhand it into the snake's eye. Both the man and the serpent jerk in pain.

Kato leaves his mace in its harness, not risking losing it. Shouting, he draws the second serpent farther away from me. It lunges and eats air. It attacks again, its giant jaws slamming shut just inches from Kato's leg. He scrambles from side to side, and it follows.

The pit floor suddenly shudders, and I risk a glance over my shoulder. The Cyclops just decided to get involved.

Griffin, Carver, Flynn, and Jocasta scatter, their weapons either gone or locked down. The Cyclops swings its massive club for the first time, missing Griffin by inches. Griffin races across the sand, forced in the opposite direction from me.

Swallowing the knot of fear in my throat, I turn back around an instant too late. The half-blind snake rams its head into me with a hiss of sulfurous breath. I flail, grasping at anything, and my fingers hit my knife. I grab it and rip the blade from the snake's eye before landing hard on my back under its neck. With the air still momentarily punched from my lungs, I jab upward and then slice along the yellowish scales.

Useless. They're like armor.

I roll away and regain my feet, trying to find my breath again. I have to get the Magoi.

The snake swings back on me, and I jump, launching myself onto the back of its head and surprising us both. It rears up, nearly unseating me, but I grip hard with my thighs and hold on to the bony ridges above its eyes.

"You are mine," I tell it forcefully, throwing all my mental energy behind the compulsion in one fierce, all-out grab. I dive straight for the spark I need—no hesitation. "You will obey me."

The snake goes still. A rush of consciousness floods my mind, cold, slithery, and dark. Goose bumps shiver down my arms. There's hunger. There's hate. There's obedience warring with a bitter longing to be free. I latch on to that last emotion because it's familiar to me, and the connection solidifies, burning brightly behind my eyes.

The Magoi starts muttering. A half-dozen words into his frantic chant, I recognize a blocking spell, but it's too late. This serpent is mine.

I glance at Kato, who is still keeping the second serpent distracted, and swallow hard. Now I have to make this snake kill its brother before its brother kills mine.

Kato is breathing hard, slowing down. He's still keeping the creature away from me, but he's not as strong or as fast as he needs to be—or usually is. With a lightning-fast strike, the second serpent seizes Kato's arm. The venomous fangs just miss piercing his flesh, searing two bright-red, burning lines down the back of his biceps instead.

Dread explodes in my chest as the reptile lifts its huge head high into the air, its prize clamped brutally between its jaws. Kato's legs dangle eight feet above the ground, all his considerable weight on his compressed arm. His face washes of blood and turns the color of pain.

Thump! Thump! Smack!

I whip my head around and see Griffin dive. The Cyclops's club beats the sand where he just stood, spraying coarse, reddish grains into the air. Griffin somersaults to his feet, never slowing down as the monster swings its huge weapon again. On Griffin's right, Flynn rattles the arena with his bellow, and the Cyclops changes target, rotating its huge body toward the noise. On the other side of the pit, my teammates run, weaponless and small.

I look on, horrified. I don't know who to help first. Or if I can save anyone at all.

The Metal Mage limps toward Kato and me, leaving the Cyclops on its own. An arsenal of weapons hovers all around her, sharp ends pointing our way. Her lower half is soaked in her own blood.

I have to free Kato before she reaches us. "Bite the other snake's neck," I command.

My snake turns and clamps vice-like jaws down on its counterpart's neck. The second snake drops Kato and starts writhing, fighting to break free.

Kato lands awkwardly in the sand. For a moment, he doesn't move, and fear freezes me inside and out. Then he rocks onto his side, pushes up with his good arm, and limps away. His right arm is not only blistered and mangled, it's completely crushed.

As the Metal Mage bears down on us, I take a deep breath and icily order, "Bite down." Ruthlessness fills me, and I nurture it. It makes me hard. It makes me win. "Crush the bone."

There's a loud crunch. The second snake's neck collapses, and its head hits the sand. The Magoi roars in pain. Then he coldly cuts the dead weight from his chest, slicing the serpent off like it wasn't just a part of his own body. The moment it's severed from him, the snake disintegrates into dust.

I focus on the Metal Mage next. All's fair in war and war. "Eat her," I order.

My snake lunges, dragging its Magoi creator behind it. The Magoi starts hacking at the scales, muscle, and sinew attaching the serpent to his chest. I pull a dagger from my belt and throw it at him, not aiming for the kill because I don't want to end my snake just yet. The dagger stops a foot from his chest, flips in the air, and then races back toward me.

I duck, plastering myself to the top of my snake's head and sucking in a sharp breath when my own knife grazes my left shoulder blade, leaving a stinging line of heat. The knife lands at the Metal Mage's feet.

Rage wells up in me. She's got quite a collection. Time to take it back.

Thump! Thump! Whoosh!

I look toward the battering sound and see the Cyclops swing its giant club at Jocasta. She darts out of the way, but it keeps coming, forcing her toward the wall. The Cyclops feints, she jumps the wrong way, and it nearly crushes her against the barrier. She stumbles. Behind the enormous creature, Griffin and Flynn bellow like madmen, trying to attract its attention. Carver is closest to her, and he races toward Jocasta.

I cry out just as Carver throws Jocasta aside. The Cyclops's club arcs down with monstrous force, catching Carver in the chest. He flies back and then crashes into the stone wall. He crumples to the sand, unmoving, and my heart comes to a complete standstill. There's no way he could take a hit like that without severe damage. Or worse.

Screaming, Jocasta flaps her arms and runs, drawing the Cyclops away from Carver while Griffin and Flynn swerve between its legs, hacking at tendons with weapons they drew the moment the Metal Mage turned her back.

Knowing he's of no use to me in his current state, Kato lopes over to Carver with a limping stride. With his mace in his left hand, he stands guard over his friend, his eyes never leaving the hulking creature shaking the arena with its every step.

My snake and I are practically on top of the Metal Mage now, close enough to see the sweat on her brow and the fear in her eyes. With a swipe of her hand, she sends the weapons she gathered flying at us with enough force to penetrate hard scales. The serpent hisses. Its whole body jerks, but I don't let it stop. My will is its will, and until it's dead, the snake will obey me, no matter what.

The Metal Mage calls her weapons back, but we slither forward with a burst of speed. My snake throws its head back, nearly dumping me on the ground, and then strikes. The next thing I know, the Magoi woman's legs are sticking out of its mouth, the whole upper half of her body stuffed down its gullet. The snake's throat muscles pulse beneath my thighs, working her down. She disappears little by little, her struggles and muffled screams vibrating underneath me until she gives one final kick and then goes still.

My stomach contracts on a wave of nausea. "Good snake. I'll never forget you." *That's for damn sure.*

I'm about to set the poisonous serpent on the Cyclops when the tubular body underneath me turns to dust. The snake's life spark snuffs from my mind in a breath-stealing, brain-jarring, ripping second that leaves me reeling from the savage disconnection.

I fall six feet to the ground and land next to a dead woman. Sharp, blinding sparks burst behind my eyes. Pain thumps between my ears, expanding to encompass my entire head and then my body. Groaning, I try to crawl back from the venom-drenched Metal Mage, but I'm disoriented and can barely move. A shadow creeps over me, and then the Magoi kicks my side with cracking force, sending me spinning into the female's disintegrating skin. I gasp, pain pounding along my ribs. The exposed skin down the side of my arm burns against the Metal Mage's body.

Black boots enter my blurred vision. Seeing a dull glint, I grope for one of the blades the Metal Mage hurled at the snake, but the Magoi kicks the dagger out of reach.

I squint up at him, grimacing in pain. The two raw spots on his wide, bare chest are already healing over. One look at his expression tells me he hopes he can kill me slowly.

"When I first saw you, I thought you'd put up a decent fight. But not breaking the connection before I killed my snake..." He shakes his head. "That's an amateur's mistake. If you're that stupid, I don't know how you even latched on."

My head won't stop spinning. Air only partially fills my lungs. My ribs ache with every shallow breath as I grate out, "Raw power. More than you'll ever have."

"Not much good if you don't know how to use it."

Tell me about it. "Is there a point to your yammering? I've had more interesting conversations with a goat."

He smirks down at me, his lips in a cruel twist. "Here's a hint before I end you." He drives his boot into my ribs again, and I groan. "There's no glory on the other side. No Styx. No Underworld. No Elysium. There's *nothing.*"

Something hard digs into my hip as an image of the Shadowlands fills my mind. I close my hand around the hilt of the Kobaloi knife Jocasta threw into the Metal Mage, my palm burning with snake venom as I rip the blade from the dead woman and then drive it into the Magoi's calf.

"Maybe not for you." I twist the blade, feeling a satisfying scrape of bone.

He howls, spittle flying from his mouth as he curses me from here to the Underworld. Then he winds up, and his great big fist comes hammering toward my head.

I cringe, but his hand never connects. Griffin appears from out of nowhere and grabs the man's arm from the side. He spins him around to deliver a jaw-crushing punch. The Magoi staggers back, spitting blood. A snake starts growing from his back, but the serpent is slow to form and much smaller this time. The Magoi is likely out of juice, and he knows it. He swings at Griffin with the knife in his hand.

Griffin ducks. Then his arm shoots out in a blur. He snatches the Magoi's thick wrist, crushing until the other man drops his blade. Griffin gives a savage jerk, and the bone snaps. The Magoi gasps.

The knife is bright, shiny, lethal, and not too far away. I crawl toward the dagger, pick it up, and then lurch to standing. The whole arena seems to tilt beneath my feet.

Griffin yanks on the man's broken wrist, pulling him in close to lop the small snake from his back. The creature disintegrates before it even hits the ground, and the Magoi hisses in pain.

Griffin sinks his fist into the man's abdomen and then shoves him back hard, leaving the Magoi doubled over and struggling for breath.

"Do you know what happens to anyone who tries to hurt *my wife*?" Griffin's voice is both iron and thunder as he flips his sword around and then delivers a punishing backhanded blow with the base of the hilt to the man's ribs. He hits the same place where the Magoi kicked me. "Either she kills that person"—Griffin flips his sword back around—"or I do."

He runs the Magoi through and then brutally lifts his blade, cutting a foot-long gash straight to the man's chin before drawing his sword back out.

I blink. Mercy is off the table. Clearly.

Gingerly, I touch my aching side. "He called me stupid."

Griffin's eyes blaze anew. "Then it's a bloody shame I can't kill him twice."

Feeling steadier now, I find Thanatos among the blades on the ground. I pick up my sword and then sheathe as many knives as I can. Griffin gathers weapons as well.

Thump! Thump! Thump!

Our teammates yell warnings to us as the Cyclops pounds our way.

"Go!" Griffin shouts. He runs one way, and I run the other. The club slams down between us, flinging up sand.

Griffin races toward Flynn, tossing him his ax, while Jocasta flaps around, trying to keep the monstrous creature's attention from landing on Kato and Carver who are up against the wall. Kato has his mace but doesn't look all that capable of using it. Carver is terrifyingly inert.

I crane my neck, looking at our final opponent. There's only one sure way to kill a Cyclops, and it means going up. I dart back under the coppery smelling club to get behind the creature. The Cyclops's gigantic boots are back-laced and knee-high. Securing Thanatos on my back, I sprint alongside the monster, jump, and then grab a thick rawhide strap, holding on while the Cyclops stomps forward. I swing and bang against the hard leather boot until I finally get a secure hold. Breathing through the pain in my side, I start to climb.

The boot bindings chafe my venom-damaged hands, weakening my grip, and the creature's thudding steps threaten to shake me loose. Still, I could make this climb without too much difficulty if it weren't for my bruised ribs. Until I reach the Cyclops's enormous naked back, that is. I'm not sure what to do then.

The Cyclops swerves. I lose my footholds, and my

legs swing out over the pit. My shoulders wrench in their sockets, and pain darts across my side. My hoarse cry is drowned out by the loud, collective gasp that sweeps the arena.

Sheer determination gets my feet back under me and somehow propels me to the top of the gigantic boot. I pull myself up to standing with the help of the rough linen of the Cyclops's brown pants and then let my shoulders sag for a few thundering heartbeats. I don't bother looking up. I already know there's a long way to go.

The Cyclops seems to forget about me once I'm not on the sand. With the rest of its team gone, it's only imperative is to kill us before we kill it. I don't think it even feels me start to climb the back of its tree trunk of a leg, using its pants to haul myself up, arm over arm. It definitely can't hear my groans over the noise of the crowd, which is going berserk. I can barely hear myself—my pounding blood, my rasping breath, my aching muscles—but I feel them all under my skin, violently loud.

Throbbing hand over throbbing hand. Reach. Grab. Pull. My shoulders burn. My arms lose strength, and my fingers start to cramp. None of that compares to the pain in my side. I almost weep with relief when I reach the Cyclops's belt and somehow loop my trembling arms around the leather strap.

My breath sawing in and out, I look down. Griffin, Flynn, and Jocasta are running around like mad rabbits in order to keep the creature occupied while I climb. The Cyclops's club smashes down terrifyingly close to Griffin and then nearly bowls Flynn over on the backswing. Griffin snags its attention again while Flynn races in from behind and swings his ax with all his mighty force, sinking the blade deep into the back of the creature's boot. The ax head comes away bloody, probably with essence of heel tendon on it.

The Cyclops bellows and whirls. I keep my arms wrapped tightly around the belt, but my legs fly out, my body stretches flat, and I lock everything down, tensing from head to toe. I slam back into the monster's hard buttock with a groan.

Below, Jocasta darts in with her sword, swings with her whole body behind it, and plants the blade in the same exact indent Flynn already made. She slices hard as she pulls the sword back out. The Cyclops kicks and nearly hits her, but she bounces out of the way and then takes off running.

Griffin shouts and throws a knife. The blade sticks in the monster's shoulder, tiny and ineffectual, but enough to distract the Cyclops away from Jocasta. Seeing that Jocasta is safe, at least for now, Flynn changes course and charges back in for another hit to the same spot.

The Cyclops limps its next step and then staggers. They're trying to bring the creature down. They're trying to save me the other half of going up. But the Cyclops is so huge, its skin so tough. They'll need time. They'll need a saw. And even on its knees, no one on the ground will even come close to reaching its one sure vulnerability.

The team scatters again, pulling the Cyclops's attention in different directions and always away from our injured. With his good arm, Kato begins carefully moving Carver toward our exit, getting him that much closer to Selena. Carver's chest seems too flat, and he leaves a trail of blood in the sand. Even from high up and far away, his face looks chillingly blank.

I turn away, fear for him twisting my insides into a tight, hard knot. Gathering my strength, I swing my legs up and onto the thick ridge of the Cyclops's belt. Sideways and not hanging on by much, I grab a knife from my belt, throw my arm up, and plant the dagger in the base of the Cyclops's back.

The skin twitches, sending vibrations down my arm. I drag myself up using the handhold I created and then crouch on the edge of the belt. Balancing against the Cyclops's beefy back, I stand and drive a second knife into the muscle above my head. I grip the sinew-wrapped hilt with both hands, put my foot on the hilt of the first dagger, and then push off the belt.

My weight shifts the blades. The Cyclops swats at the annoyance, ramming me hard into its back and stunning my lungs. I somehow hold on, although it takes a moment to breathe again. My ribs and arms ache so much I have to convince myself to start the whole process over again. Stubbornness wins out over pain and exhaustion, and I plant another knife near my hip, creating an attainable foothold. I step up onto it. Using one hand on the upper knife to pull myself up and keep my balance, I then drive another blade higher up into the Cyclops's back for climbing.

Foothold. Handhold. Repeat. I can do this. I am Titan. I am Olympian. I do not break.

I do, however, run out of knives.

Letting loose a string of growled curses that would make a Fisan pirate fall off his boat and drown, I rest my forehead against the Cyclops's meaty back, my harsh breathing pounding the space between us. Balanced between the knife at my feet and the final knife between my raw hands, I inhale disbelief and exhale denial. I can't go up, and I'm not entirely certain I can go down.

Great plan, Cat. Way to think ahead.

The Cyclops's skin twitches violently, and I look up.

There's a Kobaloi knife just where I need it, the throw perfect and precise despite the moving target.

I glance over my shoulder and see Jocasta prepping for another throw, her eyes narrowed and her right arm cocked back. The Cyclops is facing away from her, thrashing the sand with its club and roaring in frustration. Griffin and Flynn dash back and forth, slashing at its legs and then racing out of the way. I've never been more grateful for their agility and speed in my life.

Looking back up, I steel myself for more pain, reach for Jocasta's knife, and then climb.

Jocasta throws again. The creature jerks, but I hold on. Foot up. Hand up. Again. Her blades land just where I need them, and then I have it, the thick cord around the Cyclops's neck. I latch on to the strip of leather and don't let go. Now there's just the question of how to reach its eye.

It's all or nothing at this point, and I don't have a better plan, so I stand on the Cyclops's shoulder, draw my sword, and wave it around. "Hey! Hey, mutton brain!" Maybe it'll turn toward me enough that I can jab Thanatos into its eye.

No such luck. Reaching across its body, the Cyclops closes its huge hand around me, squeezing from under my armpits to my ankles. It rips me from its shoulder so fast I'm scared my neck will snap. The creature brings me in front of its monstrous face, giving me far too close a view of its overgrown, coarse features and bulbous nose. One enormous milky-blue eye blinks. The dark pupil dilates, framed by thin, crusty eyelashes. Knobbly fingers squash me until I can barely breathe, and my injured ribs grind with every shallow breath.

"I'm going to kill you, you son of a Cyclops!" *Gods! That's not even an insult!*

The Cyclops offers a small, brutish smile, showing me its brown and broken teeth. Its voice is guttural, its speech halting. "Did the human think Myopies didn't know she was there?"

Myopies? No wonder the Cyclops hasn't pulverized anyone on the ground since hitting Carver. If the etymology of its name is any indication, it can't see properly past its own nose.

"Steps, steps, steps, up Myopies's back, climbing like a little bug."

I get an unfortunate image of myself popped like an insect. The Cyclops kicks out, grimaces, and then limps a step before stopping again.

I weigh my limited options. If I throw my sword at its eye, even if I use Thanatos like a spear, I'm afraid I'll miss. The target is big, but my mobility is bad, and sword throwing isn't exactly my specialty. My only hope may be to get the Cyclops to impale itself.

A Cyclops is enough like a human, albeit gigantic, that I didn't want to resort to compulsion, but integrity doesn't mean much when you're dead and the people you love are killed along with you. Griffin was right when he said that people like us don't always have the luxury of a moral high ground. If this works, I'm about to fall off that cliff.

I block out the din of the crowd, the pain of my compressed body, the hammering of my heart, and the beat of fear in my ears, and concentrate, searching for that spark I have to ignite between us.

I can't find it. It eludes me entirely, and I recoil from the thick, sludgy darkness of the Cyclops's mind. I try again, pushing harder, but the results are no better. The strength of my magic has always been linked to the strength of my body, and there's not much left of either right now.

It knows what I'm trying to do, and the Cyclops squeezes me in its giant fist. My mouth pops open. I gasp.

"Puny human girl."

Before it's too late to do anything, or at least try, I throw Thanatos like a lance. The tip of my sword hits the hard ridge of the Cyclops's upper nose, under the eye, barely breaking the skin before dropping to the ground.

Bollocks! Why did I think that would work?

Thick fingers tighten around me, and an instinctual call for aid thunders inside me, racing toward Olympus. It's both silent and mind-numbingly loud.

Not even a heartbeat later, a lightning bolt splits the air directly behind me, heating the back of my neck. Currents prickle my skin, and all the small hairs on my body stand on end. The thunderclap rattles my eardrums. I don't know if the dead quiet afterward is me going momentarily deaf, or if the world around me is stunned into silence. The dry, singed smell of charred sand rises from under the Cyclops's churning boots, and the ground the creature treads on suddenly crunches like glass.

The Cyclops shakes its head, blinking rapidly. Its pupil shrinks to almost nothing, leaving a huge expanse of cloudy-blue. An eerie howling begins, and the creature freezes. The ghastly sound opens a pit of despair in my chest, and all I can see are the dreary, hopeless souls on the Plain of Asphodel, coinless and cursed to wander with the wicked who are waiting out their punishments in the endless, swirling mists.

The Cyclops cringes. Its head drops, and its massive shoulders lift toward its misshapen ears, trying to block the awful sound. I know, like the Cyclops must, that this is its fate. Not Tartarus, reserved for punishing those who defy the Gods, but Asphodel and lifetimes of *nothing*.

An icy wave of seawater splashes over me, shocking a yell from me. Briny water stings my eyes and leaves the taste of salt and rocks between my lips. My whole arm jerks under the weight of the golden trident that suddenly appears in my right hand. The sleek shaft is as long as my own body, and so thick I can't fully wrap my fingers around it. It's incredibly heavy but balanced to perfection.

I stare in rapt awe, blinking my spiked eyelashes and forgetting to breathe. Zeus, Hades, and Poseidon all answered my plea. My grandfather and my uncles. Lightning to blind, a future to terrify, and a weapon to kill.

This time, I don't even feel my squashed ribs as I haul back my arm and launch the weapon of a God into the Cyclops's eye.

CHAPTER 33

THE CYCLOPS'S ENORMOUS HAND GOES LIMP. THE creature goes over backward, and I drop straight down. My stomach flies into my mouth. I might scream a little. Or a lot. I definitely make some noise.

"Ooof!" Strong arms catch me, and the breath leaves my body with a hard jolt. Griffin grunts and staggers.

I gasp for air. "Griffin! Oh my Gods! You caught me."

"Of course I caught you." He sounds offended.

I throw my aching arms around his neck. He lowers his head, and his lips cover mine. I kiss him back, ecstatic to be alive. Ecstatic he's alive. Ecstatic the Games are over.

We break apart, and Griffin sets me down. Wobbling a little, I look around. The amphitheater is as still as death and utterly silent.

The Cyclops's slack face sags toward the ground. Its huge, punctured eye is wide open, its broad, thick-lipped mouth slightly ajar. The trident glows white-hot and melts what's left of the eye before disappearing with a sizzling pop, leaving a gaping hole in the Cyclops's craggy forehead.

The quiet starts to buzz. Murmurs fill the air.

"It's only a matter of seconds before the stories start." Griffin glances around the venue. "Who saw what. How it happened. They'll mushroom and spread." He squeezes my hand, as if to ask if I'm ready for that.

"I guess that's a good thing at this point." I try to sound convinced.

"By nightfall, only half of it will be true."

A lot of people are already talking and gesticulating with enthusiasm. Even more are pointing at me.

I chew on my bottom lip. "In that case, I hope they embellish my size."

Griffin doesn't answer. His eyes are on his brother now, his expression grim. We start toward the gate before the first gong even sounds, gathering Flynn and Jocasta behind us. Griffin drops my hand and moves on without me as the second gong rings out, low and loud.

I follow as fast as I can. The noise around us swells like an unchecked wave, turning deafening. By the time the last gong signals the end of the Agon Games, the audience is going wild, calling out our name.

"El-pis! El-pis!" they scream, chanting for Hope, whether they realize it or not.

My gaze sweeps the arena, taking in the excited expressions, the favor. We just proved ourselves in the face of almost impossible odds. Once they understand our goal, how many more people will stand behind us now that they don't just hope we can win, they *believe*?

Griffin lifts Carver into his arms as the gate begins to rise. Carver's dark head lolls against Griffin's shoulder. His long limbs dangle, frighteningly loose. I can't tell if he's breathing, but I think so. His skin is still too flushed and pliant for death. There's a ghostly tinge to his lips, though, that sends a shock of fear straight to my heart.

The moment he can fit under the gate, Griffin ducks beneath the pointed spikes. Selena pounces, unbuckling Carver's leather armor and then ripping his tunic to get her hands on his bare skin. She starts chanting, something she almost never does out loud.

I knew it was bad, but her frantic muttering confirms it.

My lungs squeeze tight. We can't lose him. I promised I wouldn't lose anyone. He's our family, and Griffin would never recover.

I hardly feel my own aches and pains as we fly through the underbelly of the arena, leaving the fevered roar of the crowd above and behind us. In our quarters, Flynn and Jocasta set about frantically lighting torches and oil lamps. Kato bellows for hot water, not looking at all well himself. Sweat rolls down the sides of his pallid, grit-streaked face. He cradles the weight of his crushed arm against his middle.

Griffin lays Carver on a cot. His muscles tense as he tries to be gentle, but Carver doesn't feel anything at this point. His upper body isn't just injured, it's destroyed. A large pocket of blood swells on his side, distending already tight skin.

Selena doesn't let up for a second. Her beautiful face shows the terrible strain, and her hands shake from the sheer amount of magic pouring from them. Her lips move so fast I can't keep up with her chant. She sometimes throws in powerful words from the old language, many of which I don't recognize, but which send magic exploding through the room. It ricochets off the stone walls, both biting and energizing when it hits my skin.

Long, horrible minutes pass with no visible change in Carver. Selena's voice grows hoarse as her healing power drains from her, and she pales until her blue eyes stand out like twin eruptions of luminosity in her face.

"Cat!" she snaps.

I race to her side.

"Hold on to me."

I clamp my hands around her shoulders and immediately feel an ungodly pull. Magic, life, energy—everything races from me and into her. She rips my insides out with one rough yank, and I scream. Selena screams. Carver wakes up with a yell.

I let go and stagger back, curling in on myself to guard what's left after the sudden, intense drain. Dizziness crashes over me, and I reach out, grabbing the nearest person—Flynn—for balance.

Across Carver's still shattered body, Griffin looks crazed. His eyes are big and dark, stark with panic. He looks back and forth between his brother and me, and I can practically see him ripping in two.

"I'm all right," I assure him. Or I will be. *I think.*

Griffin circles the cot and replaces me next to Selena, taking hold of her shoulders. Her hands never leave Carver's chest. She inhales, bows her head, and then pulls from Griffin like she pulled from me.

Griffin jerks. His eyes close, and his face takes on a grayish hue. A shudder runs through him.

"Stop." I don't like this. Taking from Griffin shouldn't even be possible.

No one listens. Carver groans, falling in and out of consciousness. Jocasta starts to cry.

"Stop!" I say more sharply, dragging on Griffin's arm.

He hunches his shoulders, ignoring me. A muscle ticks harshly in his jaw. His head drops forward, and his face twists under the shadow of his hair. He angles himself away from me, but he can't hide his agony. I pull harder when he starts to shake. His grip on Selena tightens. He won't let go. He'll leave bruises, but she doesn't seem aware.

"Help me!" I cry. Griffin is huge, and Selena left me weak.

Flynn bands his thick arms around Griffin's middle and then picks him up with a grunt, hauling him back. Griffin snarls. He stays latched on to Selena, and the two men end up pulling her back, too, breaking her contact with Carver.

Selena straightens and looks around as if coming out of a trance. Her eyes focus again, and I've never seen them so radiant or so eerily blue. All pallor gone now, her skin glows, illuminated by some magic from deep within. She sinks into a chair. Her hands tremble in her lap, but I don't think she's shaking with fatigue; I think she's jittery with power—and Griffin's life force.

Griffin slumps in Flynn's hold, his breathing shallow and irregular. His face is ashen. I've seen it that color once before, and it scares the living magic out of me. He collapses, and his weight drags both him and Flynn to the floor.

Fear exploding in my chest, I drop down next to him and take his face in my hands. "Griffin?"

He blinks. That's it. My great, strong, indomitable husband can't even move.

I spin on my knees, terrified and furious. "What happened?" I demand of Selena.

She holds my livid gaze, her expression inscrutable. Not sorry. Not belligerent. Almost cold. "I lost track," she says.

"You lost track? You nearly killed my husband because you *lost track*!" I fling my hand toward Griffin. "Look at him! Look what you've done!"

Her perfect features remain disturbingly smooth, but Selena reaches down and puts her hand on Griffin's chest. Griffin's back arches off the floor. The breath he drags in seems to last a lifetime, and then his big body settles.

I lean over him, almost afraid to breathe. "Griffin?"

His gray eyes meet mine, and his hand rises to cup my cheek. In a voice as rough as a rockslide, he asks, "Did we do it?"

Relief pushes tears to my eyes. But he wants to know if we saved Carver, and my heart breaks because... "I don't know."

I turn back to Selena. She's not luminous anymore. She looks awful, so pale I can almost see right through her. For the first time since I've known her, she looks like she's aged. She gave Griffin his considerable life force back—at the expense of her own.

I reach for her hands. "That's not what I wanted."

She squeezes my hands back with the strength of a butterfly. "Of course it is."

"But you—"

"Will be fine," she interrupts. "I just need to rest." She looks at Kato and then frowns.

"I can wait," he says stoically, reading the hesitation on her face.

I'm not sure he can. There's a feverish gleam in his cobalt eyes. I could help, but the only healing magic I'm capable of involves running water, and we don't have any here.

Selena beckons limply. "We'll just start. Then we'll both rest."

My heart does a terrible flip. I think she might actually care about him—about all of them—and not just for my sake.

Carver groans, drawing us to his bedside while Selena starts on Kato's arm. Jocasta brushes Carver's dark hair away from his forehead, her tear-streaked face bleak and marked by shock. Lying there, Carver looks like a younger version of Griffin, and parts of me I was only just holding together start falling apart at the seams.

Events overtake me in a rush, and my pulse starts pounding too fast. Sweat prickles different places around my body, and saliva floods my mouth. I swallow, battling queasiness and trying not to picture Griffin in Carver's place. I see it anyway. I can't seem to stop.

I reach for Griffin's hand and squeeze, assuring myself he's warm and alive. I understand how he feels now, about me and my recklessness. I've driven a sword through his heart so many times.

Griffin leans over his brother. "Carver?"

Carver slowly opens his eyes. Gray irises glint in the torchlight, their granite color another visceral reminder of what I could lose.

"No. *No!*" Carver's hands ball into fists at his sides. His face crumples, and he lets out a broken sound. "Send me back."

Griffin shakes his head, frowning. "It's all right. You're going to be all right."

With surprising force, Carver pushes Griffin away. "I saw her." His voice breaks, and he clears his throat. "Konstantina."

Griffin pales. Jocasta's eyes blur with tears again.

"She wouldn't let me cross the river." Carver swallows hard, but his voice comes out even rougher. "She still didn't want—" He stops talking, fighting something raw and awful inside of him. His eyes close, and tears slip from their edges. "She turned her back."

I can only guess at what's happening here, but sorrow climbs from my feet to the top of my head until my hair tingles at the roots, and a chill ripples over me. I can picture the scene all too easily for having been there and seen someone I wanted very badly wave me away from the other side of the Styx.

The pain inside Carver erupts on a heart-wrenching sob. An answering sob rises in my breast, and I fight it with a sharp breath.

Carver. The constant flirt. The easy smile. It's all a lie, an elaborate act, because he's been dying inside, and it doesn't take a genius to see he wishes he'd died on the outside, too.

"You should have let me go!" His barely healed body trembles with furious emotion. Bitter tears slide from his eyes. He's in pain, inside and out, and my heart hurts just looking at him. I feel so helpless. I want to do something, but I know I can't. What can anyone do?

"No!" Griffin slams his fist down on the wooden table next to the cot, startling us all. "That's not what she would have wanted. That's not what you want, either."

Carver abruptly stops crying. I think he stops breathing. Then, low and angry, "Don't tell me what I want. Not when you have everything you've ever dreamed of!"

Griffin flinches. I've never seen a moment of jealousy between them. Griffin gets possessive and overprotective about me, but this is something entirely different. Jocasta lets out a shocked gasp, turning as white as humanly possible. Flynn doesn't move, becoming a big, stiff, auburn-haired statue by her side. I'm starting to think emotion terrifies him. I can utterly relate.

"If she pushed you away, it's because she wants you to live." Griffin's voice is even, soothingly level. If I were Carver, I'd want to punch him in the face for trying to calm me down, but all the fight drains from Carver instead, leaving me even more uncomfortable than the tears and anger did.

Carver stares at the ceiling. "She *is* my life."

"She *was* your life," Griffin says. "Not anymore. And not for a long time."

Carver snorts, turning his head toward his brother. "What would you do if Cat died and I told you that?"

Griffin's mouth flattens. He looks down.

"That's what I thought," Carver says, but there's not much heat behind his words.

"It's been four years," Griffin says quietly, meeting his brother's eyes again. "Doesn't the pain lessen with time?"

Carver shrugs, then winces, seeming to regret the movement. "Sometimes. But then..." He swallows, and his throat bobs violently. "I saw her, and I didn't want to let her go."

"She let *you* go," Jocasta says fiercely. There's sympathy in her eyes, but iron in her tone. "She didn't choose you when she had the chance. She chose someone else. You don't have to choose her now. *Again*. Not in this life, or in the next."

Carver's mouth twists. It's not a smile. It's too sad and bitter by far. He doesn't respond and stares at the ceiling again.

On their knees on either side of his cot, Griffin and Jocasta hold Carver's hands. Flynn stands next to Jocasta, a motionless, masculine mountain of silence—and pent-up feelings, if I had to guess.

My heart heavy, I turn to find Kato and Selena asleep in their chairs. They don't need me, so I stay next to Griffin, side by side.

He loops his free arm over my shoulders, and I lean in to him, my aches and pains announcing themselves again with exhausting insistence. Fatigue rolls over me like a heavy fog, gradually obliterating my surroundings until I finally close my eyes.

I breathe in. Slowly. Cautiously. We did it. We won the Agon Games. We'll be invited to Castle Tarva. I didn't let Jocasta get hurt, not seriously at least. Carver and Kato are definitely the worse for wear, but we all lived.

Something lurches in my chest as I remember Cassandra and her eagerness to help, her belief in Griffin and me. She's gone, buried along with the other casualties of these bloody and brutal Games.

I open my eyes and don't try to find sleep again. I made choices. Now I have to live with them.

CHAPTER 34

WE'RE "INVITED" TO CASTLE TARVA NOT A HANDFUL OF
hours later by a contingent of armed guards.

Tradition obliges the Tarvan royals to see us. Tradition
also usually leaves the combatants nearly a week to recover
before arriving at the castle in full battle regalia amid glory
and fanfare. Being herded on foot and weaponless through
the silent, predawn streets of Kitros and Tarva City and
then being left to bake in the autumn sun without food or
water in a secured courtyard wasn't part of the plan.

My head throbs behind my eyes. There isn't a pocket
of shade now that the sun is high overhead and beating
straight down. Not permitted to come, Selena is waiting
for us back at the arena. Both she and Kato slept during
the hours before the royal guards pounded on our door,
which means Kato's arm is only partially healed. Carver
can barely keep himself upright, and my injuries never got
tended at all.

This isn't how we expected to face the Tarvan royals.
They aren't stupid—unfortunately. Galen Tarva might not
be known as the brightest bolt in the lightning storm, but he
got this right. Galen and his sneaky sister Acantha watched
us fight. So did Galen's two sons and his other sisters,
Appoline, Bellanca, and Lystra. Now the whole family has
"*danger!*" flashing through their brains on repeat.

I'm almost surprised they're going through with this
meeting at all, if they think they have to do it not even a day
after our hard-won victory and after leaving us to starve

and wilt in the sun. Not only that, but the royal guards led us straight through the blackened neighborhood in northern Kitros that Galen destroyed after becoming Alpha. No one's touched the rubble or vermin-picked bones since the day of the massacre, and I felt the sight of so much senseless death and destruction like the hard kick in the gut it was meant to be.

Galen's nearly inexplicable, vicious attack on his own people was either a one-time phenomenon he hasn't been able to repeat, or he keeps his magic on a very tight leash. Most people agree it's the former. That day, though, he didn't stop shaking the earth until every man, woman, and child he could see or hear was dead and silenced. All in return for a few shouted protests. Maybe a raised fist.

He murdered his father only to rule just like him— with a greedy heart and iron fists. People like Galen don't deserve to live, let alone rule. Griffin is right. Griffin is always right.

I'll have to tell him one of these days.

A scrape of keys and the tumble of a heavy lock drive home that we're being treated like prisoners instead of celebrated guests. The gate swings open, and I lick my parched lips.

Softly, and only to me, Griffin says, "Trust in the Gods, Cat. This is it, the beginning of the end."

Nodding, I try to swallow, but there's only dust in my mouth as the guards surround us.

They lead us through a series of gardens before we enter the castle itself and then make our way to a lavish throne room. I should focus on Alpha and Delta Tarva, but Ianthe is all I can see. She's seated on a small, cushioned chair on the far side of Lystra, Galen's youngest sister. Ianthe's eyes are wide, her anxious gaze glued to my heavily painted face. Her fingers curl around the arms of her chair, making her look ready to spring up at any moment and fly off the dais.

What is she thinking? Why is she here? Has she betrayed me?

Everyone already knows to spare Ianthe unless she attacks. We'll spare anyone who doesn't attack.

My fingers itch for knives I don't have. Despite the change in circumstance, not one of us suggested aborting our plan. We worked too hard to get here. But without weapons, we don't really even have a plan, and as my eyes finally land on Galen Tarva, I have to wonder what in the name of Olympus we think we're doing here. The idea of strolling into Castle Tarva and taking over the realm was dangerous to begin with. Now, it seems positively fatal— something no sane person should even consider.

There must be a sane person around here somewhere.

I glance at my teammates. No furtive looks. No subtly shaking heads. Nothing. Not a sane person among us, I guess.

I return my focus to Alpha Tarva. He's tall and thick, but not with muscle. His lips appear to be shaped in a permanent sneer. Cold, hard eyes betray nothing of his thoughts, but he must be on edge. Why else would we be here so soon? And why else would he have ordered his guards to march us straight through his deadly work from a decade and a half ago and then to cage us in that courtyard for hours?

"Congratulations, *Elpis*." Galen's obvious scorn turns the name into an insult. "Your unexpected victory will no doubt inspire verse and song."

Well, I certainly hope so.

Instinct takes over—the instinct to antagonize and defy anyone on a throne. "That's preferable to laments and dirges, which is the usual result of flattening a peaceful neighborhood. How many killed? Over four thousand? I'm sure those kids didn't want to grow up anyway."

Galen gapes blankly at me for a moment before his stunned expression ices back over, freezing into cold condescension. "You dare much."

I shrug. "You'd be surprised at what I dare." Which includes blatant bluffing because, right now, I have very little to back up my bravado.

Alpha Tarva's eyes narrow into slits. "Bow before me, or I'll have all your heads on spikes."

"Now that's just not nice," I say.

Everyone on the dais gasps. It's so in sync that it's almost harmonious. Galen shoots his family a black look, but the glare he turns back on me is positively murderous.

"There's been a change of plans," Griffin says coolly.

Alpha Tarva's reddish eyebrows slam together. His hair veers toward orange, but it's lackluster and graying in places. It's nothing like the blazing fireball all around his sister Bellanca's head. With hair like that, I'd bet my knife collection her magic is of the flaming sort.

The marble statues lining the walls start to rattle. Galen's temper shakes the ground, and unease unfurls in my middle. No one has heard of him using his Elemental Magic in years. That's why everyone assumes...

The stones under our feet rumble and quake, and I widen my stance to keep my balance as a crack streaks up the wall behind Galen's throne.

My unease turns into ice-cold dread. *Son of a Cyclops! I should know better than to assume!*

"A change?" Disbelief colors Galen's furious tone even darker.

My heart starts to race. I can't believe we're going

through with this. We're weak, weaponless. This is madness. But it's such an opportunity.

Trust in the Gods, Cat. Griffin's words come back to me with startling force. The Gods have always, *always*, been there for me. When the swimming really gets rough, Poseidon throws me a hand. Or gills. Or his trident!

I send a quick but fervent prayer to Olympus and then give Galen my sharpest, most chilling smile. "We've decided you should bow before *us*. And just so we're all clear, it's either that, or die."

Everyone on the dais stares at me, clearly shocked to their bones. If I had a knife, I'd use the moment of surprise to prove we're serious. I'm sure Galen doesn't need his kneecap. Or that extra roll around his middle.

Acantha is the first to react. Swiveling her head with the quick, sliding grace of a snake, she turns to look first at her brother and then back at me. The Drakon charmer hisses when she speaks. "The Cyclops slayer. Courageous, but stupid."

I put the weight of a thousand terrible moments fought and lived through into my heavy stare. "The last person to call me stupid didn't live long."

Unfortunately, she doesn't seem cowed. A small snake appears from somewhere behind her head and slithers down her arm. Its sinewy body hits the marble floor with a slap and then grows as it advances. The serpent keeps getting bigger. It looks mean. And fast.

I swallow. There's no way that's not venomous.

Next to me, there's a pop, a flash of light, and then a growl. Something shaggy and huge materializes at my side.

My eyes widen. "Cerberus!" *Hades must have sent him to us!*

The Hound of the Underworld leaps forward and snaps

up the snake. His three fang-filled mouths tear it apart. Within seconds, there's nothing left.

I grin like I'm not shocked out of my mind. "And here you thought you took all our weapons." I take a chance and, for the first time ever, reach up and lay my hand on Cerberus's back. His coarse fur twitches under my fingers, and I can't believe my hand doesn't melt—or fall off—or spontaneously combust.

"My boy's hungry," I tell Acantha. "Got any more?"

Acantha goes from blank-faced surprise to full-on rage. Her hair morphs into a headful of snakes, which is truly disturbing. They detach, leaving her bald, which is pretty disturbing as well, and then every last serpent slithers straight for me, growing exponentially as they converge.

Cerberus's lethal claws scrabble on the marble floor as he bays. The terrible sound of primal, excited violence scrapes down my spine and makes me want to cringe in mortal fear. Poisonous canine saliva hisses against rock and scales, and then the hound pounces, devouring the snakes as they come.

Galen's face turns ruddy with fury. His chin jerks up, and he flicks his hand. The armed guards that took us from the arena march down the long throne room.

Everyone here knows we killed a Cyclops and won the Agon Games. I wonder what they think they can do. Then again, we have no blades, no offensive magic, and some of us are severely injured. Everyone here knows *that*, too.

Ianthe leaps off the dais, fearlessly skirting snakes and Cerberus to get behind us. She places herself in front of the oncoming guards, and I turn to her, my heart hitting a wild, panicked beat.

"What are you—" My protest dies on my lips when the air suddenly turns so dry it hurts my eyes. Ianthe sweeps her hands in front of her, and a violent surge of water pours from her palms. The torrent washes the guards from the room in a tumbling, head-over-legs mess. The brutal spray keeps them back while Flynn and Kato race down the sides of the room. The moment our men are behind the high, double doors, Ianthe cuts off the magic so they can shoulder the heavy panels closed.

Kato slumps against the wall, clearly spent after the sprint, while Flynn drops the heavy crosspiece into the iron cradles, locking the guards out. Locking us in.

I gape at Ianthe. *My little sister is a Water Mage!* "That's unheard of in the Fisan line."

She cocks a dark eyebrow at me, smirking a little, and *my Gods*, it's like looking in a mirror. "Well, we all know Mother slept around."

"No." Galen exhales the word in disbelief. There goes my hidden identity.

Ianthe whirls on him. "You will *not* touch my sister, you *filthy* bastard!"

The explosive fury in her low, trembling voice carves a hole deep in my chest. I know in that instant that Galen has treated her horribly, possibly abused her in ways I can't bring myself to even think about. I also know I have another true ally, and my racing heart jerks painfully inside me. I don't deserve her loyalty. If only I'd defended her half as well.

Ianthe puts herself between Jocasta and me, looking downright savage, and I feel her staking her claim to her rightful place at my side. Our eyes meet in a flare of bright green, and for a moment, everything else stops.

"Ianthe!" Lystra yells.

My sister doesn't look away from me. "The three youngest Tarvan royals are like us."

Us. The word knots in my stomach. *What does she think I am? What if I'm not?*

"Enough!" Galen snaps. Magic gathers around him. Significant power. I feel it pulling on the air. On me.

He rips Ianthe from my side with a powerful, pinpointed gust of wind. She cries out, and I lunge for her, grabbing air. Tossed like a leaf in a winter gale, she twists and spins until she hits the marble wall on our right with a horrible thud. She falls to the floor, silent.

No.

I blink. *No!*

Lightning spirals down my right arm and coils around my fingertips. Heartbreak and rage erupt on a scream as I point my hand at Galen and let the bolt roll off me with a thundering crack.

He dives out of the path of my fury and then slams his hand down on the ground where he lands. A fissure splits the floor and races toward my feet, widening fast. There's no time to move, and I drop into the gaping hole, hitting uneven ground and jarring my injured ribs.

"Cat!" Griffin shouts.

I look up. The crack runs the length of the room and is twice my height. Griffin's clothing flaps under the force of Galen's wind, but the Elemental Magic has no effect on his body. Galen must be trying to drive Griffin into the hole with me, but not even a hair stirs on Griffin's head. He's utterly immune.

Griffin gets down low and reaches for me. I'm too far away, and he curses.

Galen starts chanting, and the jagged walls begin to close. Fear kicks me into action, and I start grappling for a hold. Dirt and rock dust crumble under my hands, sliding down the sides of the hole. I turn in a frantic circle. There's nothing to grab on to. Not a root or a stone!

Griffin vaults over the side of the crack and lands next to me.

"What are you doing?" I cry.

Without a word, he squats, grabs my ankles, and then heaves me out of the hole.

I land on the edge with a grunt and then throw my legs over the top. Cerberus is still eating snakes, his three-headed, canine body too massive to be moved by the gale. Acantha is behind Galen, along with Galen's two sons. The three youngest Tarvan sisters are huddled around Ianthe against the wall.

I glance over my shoulder. Flynn, Carver, Kato, and Jocasta have all been blown across the room, and Galen's wind is pinning them to the double doors. It starts blowing me away, too, and I spin on my belly to grab the edge of the crack.

"Griffin!"

He looks up from searching for a way out. The walls are still closing in. Griffin spreads his arms and pushes. His muscles bulge. His arms shudder, and then his elbows bend.

Panic whips through me. I have to take out Galen. I have to stop his chant.

I push up onto my knees, automatically reaching for my knives as the wind slides me across the floor. *Weaponless!*

I need another lightning bolt. I pull with my heart, reach out with my hands. *Fail!*

"Griffin!" Keeping low, I claw my way back toward the fissure. The hole is only a few feet across now, and relentlessly narrowing.

Cerberus raises his heads. A limp serpent dangles from one mouth. The hound swats a tangle of snakes aside with a giant paw and then bounds over to the pit and drops in a head. The head reappears an instant later with Griffin's entire upper body stuffed between its jaws.

I gasp, terrified.

Galen's wind cuts off abruptly, and the sudden silence is resounding.

Cerberus rears back just as the deep crack bangs shut with a cloud of stone dust and billowing grit. The room stops shaking. Cerberus opens his mouth and tosses Griffin at me. Griffin slides on his hip across the wet, debris-littered floor, twisting to a stop next to me. Gasping for air, he shakes damp, plastered-down hair out of his face. The leather and clothing from his shoulders to his waist are half eaten away by poisonous dog slobber, but Griffin himself appears to be fine. *He's even immune to that!*

Cerberus starts pouncing on snakes again, and we scramble to our feet, Griffin inevitably putting himself in front of me.

Galen blasts his wind again, and I huddle behind Griffin's back. I look behind and see the violent swell of air stop Flynn's advance and send the big warrior crashing back against the throne room doors again with the others.

To the right of the dais, Bellanca and Lystra stay crouched over Ianthe's unmoving form. From the way they're carefully touching her, I think she might be alive, and I send out a fervent prayer to the Gods that I haven't lost her just when I found her again.

A sudden, deep boom resonates throughout the room. The double doors shudder, and our friends struggle to move over to the side. The guards have brought a battering ram.

Galen cuts off his wind again, stopping the monumental force barreling down the throne room and driving into the heavy doors. The battering ram's next hit cracks the crosspiece holding the doors closed. The hit after that sends the panels crashing open. Eight soaking-wet guards rush into the room. A dozen others are sprawled in the hallway beyond, still knocked out by Ianthe's wave.

Flynn throws Jocasta at Carver, Kato plants himself in front of the two of them, and then Flynn charges with a roar.

"Go." I push Griffin toward the others. "I have Cerberus."

He looks at me, clearly torn, but then takes off running. Cerberus is no joke.

I turn back to face Galen and Acantha. My eyes widen. *What in the Gods' names is Appoline doing in the middle of things?* Her expression oddly vacant, she wanders in front of the royal dais, looking lost.

I dart a glance over my shoulder again, keeping Cerberus as a buffer between the Tarvan royals and me. Flynn has fallen back to protect our weaker elements while Griffin rams into the guards single-handedly. He takes a hit, and blood washes down his arm. Anxiety tears through my chest, but Griffin got in close enough to grab the guard and take away his sword. He throws the blade to Flynn, leaving himself weaponless again. My stomach does a nauseating somersault as Griffin powers forward once more, using the guard as a body shield.

I turn back around. I know Griffin. He'll do whatever it takes to get a sword, and then he'll be unstoppable.

Galen looks on, his expression tense and furious. Fuming as well, Acantha keeps sending out snakes, which, along with her conniving intelligence, is apparently all she's got. Cerberus snaps them up as fast as they come, sometimes shaking them like giant rope toys before throwing their mangled carcasses back at Acantha's feet.

A marble statue on my left shudders and then cracks in half. The bust hurtles toward me on a driving wind, and I dive out of the way. Galen throws the bottom half at me before I'm even on my feet again and then breaks another statue in two with his stone-shattering power.

I leap left, then right, dodging, but my feet slip on the damp floor and catch in rubble. Panting and clutching my aching ribs, I try to take shelter behind Cerberus again, but he's chasing snakes and moving too much to really cover me. Since I don't feel even a hint of my lightning inside me, I grit my teeth and reach out for Galen's magic instead. If I can crack stone and drive wind, maybe I can toss some of this wreckage back at him.

Within seconds, I know it's a useless effort. I'm too weak to access my own magic, let alone steal his.

I underestimated Galen, and he was smart all these years to not call attention to himself apart from his initial outburst. He's probably the most powerful Elemental Mage of our time. Air. Rock. Ground. Astounding control over it all. No wonder Acantha was sneaking her way toward the Sintan throne. She knew better than to take on her older brother. All this time, we were following her moves when we should have been watching *him*.

With just the power of a thought, Galen's marble throne comes spiraling toward me on a surge of wind. I dive, but there's no getting fully out of the way. The heavy chair clips my legs, sending me spinning across the floor. Loose stones scrape my arms and jaw as I skid, sprawled out, thrown even farther from Cerberus. The impact jolts me all over, but something searing and harsher burns through my legs. Gasping, I try to stand and collapse back down, my feet sliding out from under me.

"Cat!"

I turn, my breath hissing between my teeth. Frantic gray eyes meet mine. I don't move—I *can't*—and Griffin turns into a raging animal, a sword in each hand, his entire body a weapon. He's coming, but he's outnumbered. And nowhere near me.

"Cerberus!" I yell. The hound keeps jumping on snakes. They're wriggly and crunchy, and he's having the time of his life.

Galen saunters over, unhindered by man or beast, and pulls a dagger from his belt. Fear trips through me at the look of self-satisfied calculation in his eyes. I remember that look from when his family visited mine. I remember his cruel laughter, the flash of rubies and gold on soft fingers that never saw a day of labor, and the way he callously boasted whenever his father wasn't around that he would soon become Alpha. I remember Galen, a young man at the time, disappearing into a bedchamber with my mother when I was hiding in a little-used hallway, and then Thanos explaining to me why.

The dagger flashes, catching the ray of sunlight spreading through the new floor-to-ceiling crack in the wall. My nails scrape over marble as I use my arms to drag myself away. My legs slowly start to regain feeling, and I dig in my heels, scooting back another foot. Nerve endings up and down my legs catch fire, and I clamp down on a cry.

My feeble attempt to flee puts a malicious smile on Galen's face. He actually grins at me, revealing a healthy set of teeth.

"The Lost Princess." His ruthless gaze sweeps over me with chilling interest. "Your mother had such high hopes. We made a deal, years ago. She was going to give me the Kingmaker once you were more grown up. The deal stood because neither of us ever believed you were dead. When the time came, I would have conquered the world."

My jaw goes slack. *Is that why Mother wants me to go home so badly? Because she bargained me away to Alpha Tarva?*

I stare at him, horrified. "The leveled neighborhood in Kitros. You showed her what you can do. What you're willing to do in your own backyard."

Galen's blue-green eyes gleam, like he's pleased I have a quick mind.

There's nothing but acid in my stomach, and even that curdles. Everything is suddenly so clear. He promised to leave Andromeda alone until a reasonable old age, and she promised to turn me over, willing or not. He threatened her, and she offered up the Kingmaker to secure her own safety. Galen couldn't resist. With me under his control, he'd never be duped. He'd always know who was trying to cross him.

Truths slap me as if I were hearing them out loud, or through lies. Mother isn't all-powerful. She can be bullied, cornered, and even scared. This also explains her infuriation over Griffin, and her obsessive need for me to return home, even though it would mean having a rival in her nest. Although not for long, I guess. My Kingmaker Magic never detected any lies in her words because she *does* want me back in Castle Fisa, and she's always wanted to "teach" me to be a queen just like her, but she was going to ship me off to Galen Tarva before I lost myself entirely and turned against her in cold blood.

I swallow a sense of bone-deep betrayal, infuriated to even feel it. It's not as though I thought Mother could turn over a new leaf—or ever would.

Oh Gods. Did she send Ianthe here as insurance that I'd eventually comply?

As much as I despise her, I'm not above using Mother to get us out of this. "Alpha Fisa wants me alive."

Galen chuckles. It's a dark sound. "Even Alpha Fisa doesn't always get what she wants."

And with me dead, all pacts—or binding promises—involving me are off.

"Here you finally are, in my castle, and I've decided I don't need you after all." Galen smirks. "A Power Bid came early, thanks to Beta Sinta, and I won't wait any longer. My time has come."

He doesn't even know Beta—*Alpha*—Sinta is in the room. "And you'll do what? Level everything?"

"That would be counterproductive to comfortable living." Galen shrugs. "Fisa City and Sinta City should suffice."

I gasp. That could mean hundreds of thousands dead. Even Mother never mass-murdered.

I stare at Galen, aware of Griffin clashing violently with the guards somewhere behind me and of his frantic shouting for me to get up. I wish I could. I swear to the Gods, I'd listen to him for once. But my legs just won't work after getting hit with the throne, although they are twitching more. I was so sure something would come up, like it always does, and that somehow we'd win the day. Cerberus came, but the hound could have destroyed our enemies by now, and he hasn't. I never imagined Galen's strength, or the physical and magical cost of my own exhaustion.

Galen lowers his voice until there are hints of a growl. "I'm going to end you with a knife."

A hot rush of feeling sweeps down my legs. I turn my grimace into bared teeth. "Short and lethal. My favorite."

He chuckles again, his mirth grating and harsh, and yet disturbingly genuine. "Little Talia, how you've grown."

"Yeah? You're still old."

His mouth turns down. "It was Eleni I wanted. Beautiful. Much more biddable. But you had…special talents."

"Eleni would have eaten you alive."

He steps closer, eyeing his sister Appoline with impatience. She's hovering off to one side. *Humming?*

Bone crunches not far behind me. There's a masculine howl. It's not Griffin's.

A true megalomaniac, Galen keeps talking like he has all the time in the world. "In the neck, right? Isn't that how you do it?"

A vision of Thaddeus punches me behind the eyes. My knife in his throat. His blood on my hands.

Of course Galen knows about that. All the royal families keep tabs on each other.

Galen pounces like the predator he is, and no last-minute magic erupts to save my life. I throw my upper body to the side. Griffin's horrified yell rings in my ears. There's the sickening thud of steel sinking into flesh, and I cringe—but feel nothing at all.

I twist back around in time to see Galen pull his blade from Appoline's chest. He glares at her, shock and anger in his eyes.

Appoline staggers and then falls on top of me. My arms come around her slim body, and I somehow sit us both up to face her brother. She's shaking, and I try to work her behind me. Appoline is slight, smaller than I am, but whatever strength she has left makes it impossible for me to move her.

"What are you doing?" I try to shield her. She feels so fragile, like a child in my arms.

Her heart thumps hard under my wrist. "Protect you."

I don't understand. "Why?"

His eyes as cold and hard as chips of ice, Galen raises his bloody knife again. Griffin rams into him from the side, sending both men flying. Over by the wall, Bellanca lets out an enraged shout and runs toward them. Sparks snap like wildfire between her fingertips. Flames lick over her hands and up her arms.

Still locked together and grappling fiercely, the men rise to their feet. I shout a warning to Griffin, but Bellanca slams into her brother's back, not Griffin's. She wraps her now furiously burning hands around Galen's thick neck.

Galen roars in pain and tries to wrench out of Bellanca's hold. A mighty twist pulls him free of Griffin's hands and hauls Bellanca right off her feet. She squeezes with all her might. There's no way she's letting go. She looks out of control. Demented. Impressive.

I cradle Appoline against my chest, wondering where this family came from, and if they're the ones I should have been terrified of all along.

"You don't have to do this," Griffin calls to Bellanca over the snap and snarl of her raging fire. "I can do it for you."

My heart catapults up my throat. He made that offer to a woman he doesn't even know because of me, because of how killing Thaddeus left a black mark on my soul and nightmares in my life. But this is different. This is like with Otis. This is revenge, not self-preservation.

Bellanca looks at Griffin, seeming to hear what he said, but then grips her brother even harder. She screams, sounding unbalanced in a familiar way. Her magic races over her shoulders and then surges higher to frame her face. Her long, thick mass of red hair swirls and mixes with the flames. Blue-green eyes glint like jewels in the heart of a volcano, and then the firestorm leaps from her and engulfs Galen.

His shouts grow deafening and then stop abruptly. He falls, his substantial weight finally dragging him from Bellanca's fiery grip. At her feet, Galen Tarva burns until there's nothing but smoldering bone on the shattered marble.

Bellanca slowly closes her fists. Her hands shake as the

fire still coiling around her head and arms disappears back into her body.

"That's one way to do it," Carver murmurs next to me, a hint of wary admiration in his voice.

I nod, then glance to my sides. Everyone is here, and apart from Flynn and Griffin, who look like they've just gone three rounds with a Centaur, I see no damage they didn't already have when we arrived.

Movement against the wall draws my attention. Lystra helps an unsteady but conscious Ianthe stand, and my heart sings with joy as the two girls stumble over.

Apparently done playing with snakes, Cerberus finally decides to be helpful again and turns on a cornered Acantha. It only takes two mouths to rip her in half while his third head bays in gory triumph.

Cowering on the dais, Galen's two sons don't say a word. They look catatonic with fear. Auntie Bella just showed them a thing or two; their father has ceased to exist; and the three-headed guardian hound of the Underworld is chewing on Aunt Acantha's bones. *What a day.*

Ignoring everything and everyone else, Bellanca drops to her knees next to Appoline. Her red hair still sparks, and she smells faintly of wood smoke and burning leaves. With quick flicks, Bellanca's sharp gaze takes in the way I'm holding her sister. Then her eyes turn glassy and fill with tears. "Appie?"

Appoline's chest shudders under my hand.

"Someone get a healer," I say. "It's not too late."

Bellanca leaps up, but Griffin catches her around the middle, stopping her.

"I'm sorry," he says gravely, "but I can't let you leave this room."

Fire crackles all over Bellanca again as she struggles

against Griffin's hold. Fueled by fear and fury, she burns holes in his bloodstained clothing and then howls in frustration when her magic doesn't work on him.

"Lystra!" she yells. "Run!"

Lystra abandons a still-swaying Ianthe and sprints for the double doors, only to run into the stone wall that is Flynn. He's so covered in the guards' blood that she hits him with a wet smack and then squeals in disgust. Flynn shackles her wrist, and she immediately starts beating on his chest with her other hand until he grabs that one, too, and forces it down.

Not a spark of magic nips the air around her. *Poor girl.*

"Don't hurt her!" Bellanca screams, her whole body raging with fire again. She kicks back at Griffin's legs and then slams her head toward his jaw. His shins take a beating, but he angles his face away just in time.

"It's...all right, Bella." Appoline looks up at me with the weirdest smile. "I knew it would be like this."

"No!" Bellanca looks even wilder now, truly terrified.

"Griffin!" I cry. "There's still time. We can heal her!"

Appoline keeps smiling at me. She's older than I am, but I feel oddly maternal and protective of her as she leans on me and grips my hands. Harsh prickles stab at my eyes. I plead with Griffin again, my voice raw and rough, but he shakes his head. My heart hollows at his denial, and I feel like the epicenter of an earthquake, not sure if I've wrought ruin on the innocent, or leveled a terrible construct.

"But she saved me!" Appoline sacrificed herself for me, just like Eleni, and I don't even know why.

"If I let one of these women out of the room and she doesn't come back, she will always be a threat to us. All of this will be for *nothing*," he says fiercely.

"No." I shake my head. "She'll come back for her sister."

His expression remains firm, grim as well, and his eyes tell me two things. Maybe I'm right, or maybe I'm transferring onto other people my own guilt and regret for not going back for Ianthe. Either way, he won't budge, and I realize something about Griffin; he'll make decisions I never could.

I swallow. "Ianthe, then." I turn to my sister. "She'll bring the healer here."

Griffin hesitates, considering. I'll never know if he would have agreed because Appoline stops us all.

"I have my coin." Appoline pats my hand. Her increasingly unfocused gaze slides over me from below. "I saw this was my time."

I blink in shock. "You're a seer?" *How did I not know that?* No wonder she looks so lost. Her eyes are turned to the inside!

"I sent our healer to the hunting lodge this morning. She's across the grounds." Her voice comes out wheezing and wet, but Appoline still sounds like she thinks that was a fantastic idea.

Bellanca goes limp, the fight and the fire draining from her. Her eyes fill with tears again. "But why?"

"So you'd know you couldn't reach her in time. So you wouldn't get hurt trying." Appoline smiles again. "So you wouldn't blame the Alpha and the Origin for my death."

I gasp, and my stomach does something truly acrobatic that leaves me short of breath. My eyes fly to Griffin's. He looks just as stunned.

Bellanca shakes her head, quietly crying. Lystra sobs loudly, and Ianthe goes to her.

"Let them go!" I order sharply.

I'm almost surprised when Griffin and Flynn comply. They look more than ready to grab them again, but the two Tarvan women don't try to run.

"Listen to me," the seer tells her sisters, something steely veining her fading voice. "I believe in the Alpha and the Origin. No harm must come to Princess Eleni. You must protect her with your lives."

The blood drains from my face so fast I see spots. When it comes roaring back, it thunders like a storm in my ears. Just for a moment—a crazy, irrational moment—I thought maybe it wasn't real. That I was wrong. Otis. The knife. My sister's blood. But I know better. She *is* gone. It *was* real. I saw her in the Underworld.

"You can't save her." I can barely push the words past the burning thickness of unshed tears in my throat. I try to blink the sting from my eyes but end up seeing her long blonde hair spread out like a sunset, gold streaked with red. "Eleni's dead."

Appoline looks so peaceful, but the blood on her lips turns the saliva in my mouth to ash. "Eleni is dark like the night." She lets go of my hands, and her fingers brush the end of my sable braid. My heart starts beating too fast. I know whose hair is darker than mine. "And bright like the day." Appoline's small hand stops over my heart. "She joins *everything*." Her hand doesn't move again, but she's still smiling, like she accomplished some great feat, or this day ended exactly how she meant it to. Her eyes, blessed—and cursed—with the sight, don't close. They stay open and haunting.

She joins everything. Night. Day. North. South. Magoi. Hoi Polloi.

Me. Griffin.

An anguished sound leaks from me that mixes with Bellanca's and Lystra's broken sobs. The spark of life low in my belly is suddenly so obvious I can feel it pulsing with every thump of blood through my veins. My heart hammers. I can hardly breathe. Only panic jumps up and down my throat. I fought the living dead, braved the Ice Plains, nearly drowned, got mauled by the Hydra, competed in the Agon Games, and confronted the Tarvan royals…all with *a baby* inside me?

I slowly turn my head, and my wide eyes collide with Griffin's steady gray gaze. He looks appallingly unsurprised.

I can't believe him! All those times he ordered me to be careful, to not take a hit to the middle, his paying closer attention than usual to what I eat. That must be how they grow such big men in southern Sinta. Stuff pregnant women with meat.

I see joy in his eyes. And worry. *Over my reaction?* He *should* be worried. "You knew, and you didn't tell me!"

Griffin looks taken aback. "No. But I thought maybe… I hoped…"

"I've risked my life over and over!" I explode.

He crouches next to me, the line between his eyebrows deepening into a harsh groove. "And over and over, I asked you to stop taking unnecessary risks."

I snort loudly. "What I consider an unnecessary risk completely changed about thirty seconds ago!"

He takes a deep breath and then swipes his hand through his hair, shoving it back. "I didn't want you worrying about one more thing when I could have been wrong. There are plenty of reasons for you to be tired and emotional."

"Tired and emotional!" *Oh Gods, I have been tired and emotional.* "So this was another 'wait and see'? How is that *ever* a good idea?"

"If I'd put ideas into your head, ideas that might not even have been true, you would have fought differently, overthought things. You don't change technique in the middle of a battle, Cat. That's how you lose your sword."

I get what he's saying. I'm not sure I agree. And he doesn't know that powerful Magoi, *if* they're paying attention, can feel the new life force inside them almost immediately. "Well, I might have hesitated once in a while!"

"Exactly. Hesitating is what gets a person like you killed."

"A person like me?" My voice turns strident.

Griffin doesn't say anything. Wisely.

I'm angry, but some part of me knows I'm not being fair. He was just guessing, probably based on some fairly obvious clues, when I should have *known*. I should have felt her. I should have wondered why fatigue and tears were coming so easily. I should have realized my stomach wasn't acting up because I was overwrought, and I definitely should have realized I hadn't had my monthly courses in ages, but there's been so much going on.

While I'm still too bowled over to move, Flynn lifts Appoline from my lap and carries her to an undestroyed part of the throne room. Bellanca and Lystra follow, still holding their dead sister's hands. Watching them, sympathy overwhelms me. I know what they're feeling. I know they'll feel it for years.

Jocasta suddenly takes off running, making me look left. Galen's two children are heading for the crack in the wall—and freedom. Like the rest of her family, Jocasta is remarkably fast, and the pudgy boys don't stand a chance. She erupts between them and twists their ears, sending them crashing to their knees with howls.

At the same time, a number of drenched guards start edging into the throne room, looking uncertain about what to do. I have yet to stand, but Ianthe turns to face them, and you'd never know she'd just been knocked unconscious. Her green eyes glint. Her smile is awful, her spine straight, her chin set at a hard angle. A small, immovable force, Ianthe looks more than ready to take on the lot of them. Again.

"Bow to your new sovereigns," she commands, "or I'll wash you clear out of the city."

There's a scant moment of hesitation, and then the guards bend their knees. Their heads lower in deference to Griffin and me.

"Now I know what you looked like five years ago." Griffin shakes his head. "Actually, that's what you look like now."

I cock my head. Ianthe looks like a warrior. Is that what Griffin sees?

"Help me up," I say under my breath.

Griffin grips my elbow and lifts. My legs feel…all right.

"Rise," I tell the guards. Sure that someone went to raise the alarm, to the two closest I say, "Go to the barracks and call off whatever attack is being mounted. Don't risk your lives to give Galen's boys a chance at ruling just like their father. Appoline sacrificed herself for me. Her sisters are with us, and we expect the same loyalty from you."

There's another slight hesitation while their uncertain gazes slide over us. Over Cerberus, the hound carefully surveying the scene with six watchful eyes. Over Bellanca and Lystra, who aren't paying any attention to us at all.

"Yes, Alpha Tarva," the one who seems to be their leader answers.

"Queen Catalia," I correct, only choking on the title a little. I lay my hand on Griffin's arm, mostly for balance, but no one needs to know that. "This is King Griffin. We're both Alpha. Together." There's no point in mentioning my being the Origin. They won't understand what I barely understand myself.

"Send riders to fetch your healer from the hunting lodge

and ours from the arena," I add before they go. "Quickly. These soldiers need tending." While a mess, I don't see anyone who looks irretrievable. Yet.

Looking somewhat confused—either by the novel idea of an Alpha couple, or by the equally novel idea of anyone in power caring what happens to simple soldiers—the guards nod. The two closest to us rush to do my bidding.

I point to two more men. "You and you, go to the agoras of Tarva City and Kitros and announce that Elpis, the victors of the Agon Games, have seized control of Tarva. Since your new royals also rule Sinta, the two realms are now and forevermore joined as one."

Slow blinks and tentative nods greet my bold pronouncement. This will take some getting used to—for everyone.

"You." I point to another two. "Find me whoever is in charge of city planning. I want the destroyed neighborhood in Kitros cleaned up and replaced by an olive grove. Bury all the bones beneath the new trees. Our winnings from the Agon Games should more than finance the project."

The nods are quicker this time, almost eager. Expressions relax. Eyes brighten. Men straighten.

Elpis.

Hope moves like a shimmering current through the air, almost tangible, an unspoken whisper, a promise I didn't even realize I was making until it was already done. Intention anchors itself deep in my bones. Goose bumps rise on my arms. Excitement. Fear.

"You." Another waterlogged guard snaps to attention. "Find me the castle scribe. We have news to spread. Sinta and Tarva are now one, and the Lost Princess of Fisa is coming for the rest of her kingdom."

Eyes widen, and pretty much everyone in the room sucks in an audible breath.

The beginning of the end.

All but two of the remaining intact guards depart.

Turning to me, Griffin lifts his brows. "That'll stir things up."

I nod. *The new beginning.* My heart pounds like a herd of Centaurs. Our baby's tiny life beat flutters along in response. "At the very least, Mother will know the deal is off."

"Deal?" Griffin asks.

"She was going to turn me over to Galen Tarva once she got her hands on me, giving him the Kingmaker in exchange for leaving her alone."

Griffin visibly shudders. "He must have threatened her with earthquakes and windstorms."

My lips thin. "I underestimated his magic. Dangerously so."

Griffin takes my hand and squeezes lightly. "You've had three minutes of practice, and you're already a formidable queen."

It's my turn to shudder. "What did you mean, a person like me?"

He smiles a little wryly, his gray eyes glittering with that silver lining that's become my future and my hope. "The same as always. Impetuous. Reckless." His thumb brushes my knuckles. "Terrifyingly selfless."

This time, none of that sounds like a criticism. I'm too relieved to hold on to any anger, anyway. "Don't forget exceedingly clever and very good at rhyming."

Griffin grins, and my heart flips over so hard it hurts. Then he cups my face with both hands, his eyes meeting mine. "My chest is bursting with pride."

At his quiet words, mine just about explodes.

"Queen Catalia." The look on Griffin's face nearly

melts me into a warm, gooey puddle. "The woman I love is carrying my child. I'm going to be a father."

I smile, a tickle of featherlight wings skimming the insides of my ribs. He'll be a wonderful father. He's definitely the one getting up at night.

"What made you suspect?" I ask.

Griffin's mouth lifts. His eyes glimmer, crinkling at the corners. "I first wondered outside the Chaos Wizard's house. You went from starving to lustier than a horde of Nymphs to weepy in the space of one conversation. Not like you at all."

I scowl. "What do you know about a horde of Nymphs?"

"Only what I saw of Lycheron's pack. Pretty. Eager." He wiggles his eyebrows. "Flexible."

I mash my lips together, my eyes narrowing. "There once was an Alpha named Griffin." I stop, at a loss. "Son of a Cyclops! Nothing rhymes with Griffin."

He chuckles. "You'd have more luck with 'An Origin named Cat.'"

"Easy. She's as crazy as a bat, and kind of a brat."

Smiling, Griffin drops his hands to my waist and pulls me in close. His lips trace a scorching path across my cheek to my ear. "And I love her just like that."

His gruff whisper sends a shiver down my spine.

"Why did you collect that hellipses grass outside the wizard's house?" I ask, suspecting I already know.

"I was thinking about making a rattle, or a doll." He shrugs. "It was good grass. I wanted to save some, just in case."

"It was good grass," I agree. "Good enough for a Goddess."

He winks. "Or a princess."

Grinning like an idiot, I hug him close, inhaling citrus and sun—and the coppery scent of blood along with a faint essence of dog breath.

Excitement floods me. *A baby!* My mother will *never* get her hands on my child.

I sober instantly. "How can I fight a war with a baby?"

Griffin sobers, too. "We'll need to move fast."

"But you said not to change technique in the middle of the battle, and this changes everything."

"This battle is over, *kardia mou*. New round, new rules."

I frown. "What does that mean?"

"It means it's time to figure out your magic and face your mother. And you'll do it, because you won't let anyone harm our baby."

A great, burning fist seems to seize hold of my heart and squeeze. Little Eleni could have already perished in so many ways. Thinking back, I know Titos saved us both.

Lifting my head, I take a deep, steadying breath. My eyes light on Galen's two sons and then on Bellanca, Lystra, and Ianthe. The latter three aren't our enemies. Ianthe chose me the second she saw me, and by protecting me at the cost of her own life, Appoline gifted her sisters' loyalty to me. To Eleni.

Galen's boys are a different matter, but I'll permanently hobble them in the least violent way I can. Jocasta still has them hobbled in her own surprisingly effective way.

Ear twisting. Who knew? I'll have to remember that.

I move toward them with Griffin by my side. "I'm about to extract the longest, most comprehensive binding vow these little Magoi boys will ever say in their lives—which will be short, if they don't agree to it."

Overhearing me, the boys' eyes widen in horror. As one, they glance toward Cerberus, and their round, freckled faces pale.

I smile a little evilly. It's hard to resist. "And before you even think about breaking a binding vow, let me tell you that it's horrifically painful. Your skin will burn, your eyes will melt, your blood will turn to liquid fire, and that's before the Furies even show up to tear you limb from limb."

The boys recoil in terror, and I feel a pinch of guilt. I might need to work on how I communicate with children. Good thing I have time. About seven months, I'd say. Plus, babies don't talk or really do anything for ages, right?

"And then we'll go home," I add to Griffin. *Because, Gods, I want to lie down and not get up for a week.*

"Sinta?" Griffin asks. "Or Fisa?"

I stop walking and raise my fingers to the familiar, hard lines of his face, taking comfort in them. *Rest or battle? Peace or Mother?* "Sinta first. To show your family we're okay."

"We can't leave just yet," he says, glancing around. "We have to settle things here first."

I nod. "We will. And we'll also come back. This is a good location for us. Central. Closer to Fisa."

Griffin lifts my hand and kisses my palm. Then he lays it flat against his chest, a ridiculous grin spreading across his face. "I go where the Origin goes. Because she's my wife."

I snort. "You've been wanting to say that for a long time, haven't you?"

He winks. "All my life, *agapi mou*. All my life."

Hand in hand with Griffin, I survey our second castle. Right here, it's mostly rubble, but I think the damage is localized. "Our kingdom just doubled in size without a war. Maybe we can get Lycheron to guard the border with Fisa if we throw a bevy of Nymphs at him."

Griffin chuckles. "We can try."

I smile, too, but then a chill steals over me despite today's almost inconceivable success and my husband's strong, warm hand around mine. Griffin may not have had the benefit of a prophecy, but the Fates wove his future just as painstakingly as my own when they threaded our lives together. Having a destiny is both a blessing and a burden when the outcome remains uncertain, and Griffin's unyielding vision for us is getting under my skin, invading my soul, and learning the path to my heart.

No more hiding. No more head in the sand. No going back.

My free hand curves around my belly, protecting the tiny, delicate gift inside of me. I look up at the man I love, marveling at what we've created together and knowing that with Fisa in our sights, and the most inhuman person I know between us and reuniting the realms, life is precious—and more fragile than ever before.

HERE'S A SPECIAL SNEAK PEEK AT BOOK THREE IN AMANDA BOUCHET'S KINGMAKER CHRONICLES TRILOGY

❧ *HEART ON FIRE* ☙

"LET CAT GO," GRIFFIN DEMANDS IN A LOW, FURIOUS VOICE. He stalks forward, his face terrible with rage.

His brother Piers drags me back again. One step. Two. My lungs feel crushed. I can hardly breathe.

"Why are you chanting?" Griffin keeps advancing on us but holds out a hand to keep his young sister Kaia back. "What's going on?"

Fear twists my heart. *Why doesn't anyone listen to me! When I say run, I mean it!*

The indecision washes from Griffin's face, replaced by hard resolve. He starts to close the final steps between us, and even though he doesn't understand what's happening yet, I know from his stony expression that he'll fight his own brother down to blood and bone in order to set me free.

As a last, desperate resort, I twist furiously in Piers's arms and scream like a lunatic. It stops Griffin in his tracks and seems to startle Piers into loosening his grip. Feeling the change in pressure around my ribs, I stop thrashing and drop. My dead weight breaks his hold. I land in a crouch and take off, yelling for Griffin and Kaia to go before me.

Thank the Gods, they spin and run without question, knowing I'm not far behind. I'm fast, but Griffin and Kaia outdistance me quickly. Griffin looks back, hesitating, and

I gesture frantically for him to keep going. I don't slow down even though my lower belly tightens, and the muscles there feel like they're turning to stone. If he's chasing me, I'm guessing Piers is as swift as the rest of his family, and I run faster than I ever have in my life, my legs flying and my lungs burning.

I'm halfway to the road when Piers hits my back. Everything tilts, I go weightless for a sickening second, and then we both hit the ground with a bone-jarring crash. I just barely keep my head up, and my bare arms scrape painfully from my palms to my elbows as we skid across the dirt. Piers is flat-out across my back, and I wheeze a frightened sound, terrified of knocking little Eleni loose even though I know she's been through worse.

Griffin shouts my name again, and every protective instinct in me rebels. *Don't come back!*

Footsteps thunder in my direction. Piers is as heavy and solid as a Centaur. He's somehow still chanting as he pushes me into the hard-packed earth. I try to breathe, but fear chokes what little air I have left in my lungs. He's almost done, and I can't let this happen. Griffin and Kaia are too close.

I free an elbow and swing wildly back, hitting somewhere that makes Piers grunt the last word of the final repetition, sealing our fates forever. *Ares.*

He just summoned the God of War.

Piers springs off me, spitting a curse as he backs away. I flip over and surge to my feet. Air flows more freely into my lungs again, but it still feels like I can't breathe.

"What in the name of the Gods is going on?" Griffin bellows, charging the last few steps to me. He came back. He'll always come for me, and Kaia's right behind.

I throw out my hands. "No, Griffin! Stop!"

A deafening roar sets off a series of explosions in my head, painful, like magic punches to the brain. Then the ground shakes as a man—no, *Ares*—drops from the sky like a lightning bolt. The terrain's no longer that dry, but dust billows up from somewhere deep as the earth cracks all around him, fissures branching out like an enormous, tangled web.

We all stagger, trying to keep our feet under us as the ground rattles with the force of an Olympian God. Griffin grabs my arm, trying to steady me. He latches on to Kaia, too. I gasp, my head still reeling. This is no ethereal, regal entrance like Artemis made on the Ice Plains. The stealthy and light-footed Goddess of the Hunt wove through our senses like moonbeams on a melody. This is the God of War landing like a thunderclap in our midst.

His gray eyes widening and turning frantic with growing comprehension, Griffin shoves us both behind him with a hard thrust. Kaia and I hit like two hands clapping and grunt, and then Griffin quickly backpedals, forcing us to move with him.

I twist enough to peer around my husband's arm. Piers is on the other side of Ares, facing him in awe and apparent satisfaction. The God is looking at him, too, the person who did the summoning, and all we see is the broad and muscled back of the most colossal male I've ever seen. He's bare from the waist up and wearing a wide, bronze, studded belt loaded with weapons of all shapes and sizes that brush his thick, leather-clad legs.

"No one has summoned me in an age." Ares's voice is rich and deep. So is the chuckle that washes over me like a warm wave, the kind of inviting yet dangerous swell with an unpredictable undertow. It'll drag you under and dash you against the rocks if you don't know how to swim the waters. "This promises to be interesting."

Or heartbreaking.

I tap Griffin's arm, and he angles his head enough that our eyes catch for a split second while I hold a finger to my lips. If we're silent and still, maybe Ares won't notice us?

Before Griffin turns back around, I see the same haunted fear I'm feeling building in his eyes. He knows what his brother did.

Call a God, lose a soul. One of us isn't leaving here with the others.

Ares dips his head, and hair the color of polished olive wood glints in the sun. It brushes his massive shoulders, the locks a tawny blond streaked with darker tones. "I see. This is about the woman you call a warmonger."

An explosive jolt of adrenaline sends my heart slamming against my ribs. My pulse leaps to accommodate the accelerated beat, and I try to control the sudden panting rhythm of my breath. My lower belly tightens again and feels like lead. The Gods aren't joking when they say they know everything.

Piers nods and jerks his head at me, the ratter. So much for staying quiet and hidden. "She's violent and a brute. She'll fit right in with you."

Violent and a brute? Fit right in with you? Did he just insult an enormous God? He certainly offended me.

The muscles across Ares's back stiffen. "That's your only request? To take her away?"

Terror closes in on me like a club swinging down with brutal force. I can't leave Griffin. There's Eleni!

But if it's not me, it's Griffin or Kaia. That simply can't happen. I won't let it.

Griffin's fingers dig painfully into my arm. He's gone impossibly rigid and pale. I feel more than hear his breath hitch, and know the sickening whoosh of betrayal is sweeping through his body like an ax cleaving him in two.

"Only request?" The slightly baffled look on Piers's face makes me think he translated the old parchments wrong. You don't call a God just to get rid of someone. There are weapons for that, sometimes bare hands, and if you're a sneak and a cheat, there's always poison. You don't call a God to do that kind of dirty work. You call a God to request something epic, something you can't possibly accomplish on your own. Losing a soul close to you is the consequence, a payment of sorts—one people finally caught on to. That's why they eventually hid the scrolls, burying them deep in the archives of the knowledge temples.

Not deep enough, obviously.

"Believe me, she's enough," Piers finally says with enough acidity to practically slap me in the face.

I stare, starting to shake and horrified on so many levels. He's unbelievable. And criminally shortsighted. Piers has done the unthinkable, so he might as well at least help out the brother whose heart he's tearing out. I can hardly believe it, it's so unconscionable. He doesn't even want Ares's assistance—the God of *War*—to help Griffin conquer Fisa?

Ares folds his arms over his chest, making his monstrous biceps bulge. Something in the Olympian's expression must make Piers think Ares needs some convincing.

COMING JANUARY 2018

ACKNOWLEDGMENTS

My first thanks and immense gratitude are for my husband and children, who have seen less of me over the last year than any of us ever imagined they would. Their patience and understanding every time I shut myself away to write and then said, "just two more minutes"—which inevitably turned into an hour—make them the best kind of super-heroes in my mind. My parents and sister have also been there for me every step of the way. Your encouragement, help, and enthusiasm mean the world to me. I'm so lucky to have such a wonderful and generous family, and I love you all!

My heartfelt thanks also go to my dynamite editor, Cat Clyne, for all her efforts and time spent helping to make this book shine. I love what we did with it together! I'm incredibly grateful to the whole Sourcebooks team for their excitement, support, and hard work. I'd especially like to thank Amelia Narigon for being such an extraordinary publicist and Rachel Gilmer for her eagle eye. My sincere thanks also to Dawn Adams and Gene Mollica for creating the most amazing book cover I've ever seen.

I'd also like to express my appreciation and admiration for my agent, Jill Marsal, who knows just how to encour-age and reassure, and who never leaves me hanging with a question, despite the nine-hour time difference between us. You're the best!

I'm also incredibly grateful and excited to have had the support and encouragement of Darynda Jones, Nalini Singh,

Damon Suede, C.L. Wilson, and Thea Harrison. The kindness these wonderful authors have shown me has been beyond amazing!

Also, to the bloggers, book enthusiasts, and reviewers who have gone out of their ways to help this series get noticed, I can never thank you enough! And to the readers who have connected with me personally over the last months, please believe me when I say you make my days.

Finally, thank you to the friends I've made on this writing journey. Rusty, Adriana, and Heather—you ladies help keep me sane, whether we're crying, talking about books or Alpha heroes, worrying over deadlines, or just trying to figure this whole thing out. And Callie—I'm so grateful that I can always count on you for an email that makes me laugh or helps me feel better about something, a much-needed break, a last-minute proofread, or simply being on my side. You're the most amazing friend a person could ever have. You're my anchor and my kite.

Do you love fiction with a supernatural twist?

Want the chance to hear news about your favourite authors (and the chance to win free books)?

Keri Arthur
Kristen Callihan
P.C. Cast
Christine Feehan
Jacquelyn Frank
Larissa Ione
Darynda Jones
Sherrilyn Kenyon
Jayne Ann Krentz and Jayne Castle
Lucy March
Martin Millar
Tim O'Rourke
Lindsey Piper
Christopher Rice
J.R. Ward
Laura Wright

Then visit the Piatkus website and blog
www.piatkus.co.uk | www.piatkusbooks.net

And follow us on Facebook and Twitter
www.facebook.com/piatkusfiction | www.twitter.com/piatkusbooks

piatkus